DERBY
DAY

Fiction
Great Eastern Land
Real Life
English Settlement
After Bathing at Baxter's: Stories
Trespass
The Comedy Man
Kept: A Victorian Mystery
Ask Alice
At the Chime of a City Clock

Non-fiction
A Vain Conceit: British Fiction in the 1980s
Other People: Portraits from the '90s (with Marcus Berkmann)
After the War: The Novel and England Since 1945
Thackeray
Orwell: The Life
On the Corinthian Spirit: The Decline of Amateurism in Sport
Bright Young People: The Rise and Fall of a Generation 1918–1940

DERBY DAY

D. J. TAYLOR

PEGASUS BOOKS
NEW YORK

DERBY DAY

Pegasus Books LLC
80 Broad Street, 5th Floor
New York, NY 10004

First Pegasus Books cloth edition 2012
First Pegasus Books Trade Paperback edition June 2013

Library of Congress Cataloging-in-Publication Data is available.

ISBN: 978-1-60598-444-5

10 9 8 7 6 5 4 3 2 1

Printed in the United States of America
Distributed by W. W. Norton & Company, Inc.
www.pegasusbooks.us

Felix's

... I felt sure that if I could find a theme capable of affording me the opportunity of showing an appreciation of the infinite variety of everyday life, I had confidence enough in my power of dealing with it successfully; but the subject – then, as now and ever, the chief difficulty – where was I to find a scene of such interest and importance as to warrant my spending months, perhaps a year or two, in representing it? Until the year of which I write – 1854 – I had never seen any of the great horse races for which England is so famous, and my first experience of the modern Olympian games was at Hampton; when the idea occurred to me that if some of the salient points of the great gathering could be grouped together, an effective picture might be the result ...

W. P. Frith, 'The Derby Day'
My Autobiography and Reminiscences (1887)

Part One

Part One

I

The Conversation in Clipstone Court

A foreign gentleman, who had run horses with great success on the plains of Bremen, once enquired of me: 'Where is it that the sporting men of England may generally be found?' 'My dear sir,' I told him, 'this is a universal passion, its devotees are everywhere, and of all sorts and conditions. A gentlemen's club in Mayfair; the humblest inn in a Whitechapel rookery; the most somnolent village in Barsetshire, but that it has a meadow and a rail for jumping; anywhere and everywhere – these are the places where the sporting men of England are generally to be found.
The Modern Sportsman: His Dress, Habits and Recreations (1865)

Sky the colour of a fish's underside; grey smoke diffusing over a thousand house-fronts; a wind moving in from the east: London.

Clipstone Court lies on the western approach to Tottenham Court Road, slightly beyond Goodge Street, and is not much visited. There is a cab rank at which no cab was ever seen standing, and a murky tobacconist's over whose lintel no customer in search of enlightenment from the copies of *The Raff's Journal* and *The Larky Swell* that hang in the window was ever known to tread. An occasional costermonger, thinking to forge a path into Cleveland Street – only the way is barred – drags his barrow through the dusty entry, notes the silence and desolation of the place, and gladly retires. There is also a pump, which nobody ever uses – the quality of the water being horribly suspect – the Clipstone Arms, Jas Fisher, prop., out of whose aquarium-like lower windows a face can occasionally be seen dimly staring, and a kind of rubbish heap made up of ancient packing cases and vegetable stalks which a furious old man who lives up six flights of stairs in a tenement

3

building hard by is always defiantly rearranging in the expectation that it will be taken away, only it never is. All of which gives the place a rather dismal and moral air, as if great truths about human nature could be extracted from it if only you knew where to look.

It was generally agreed that three o'clock in the afternoon – the lunch hour long gone, the evening an eternity away – represented Clipstone Court's lowest ebb, and that if anyone was going to hang himself there, this would be the time to do it: the cab stand vacant, the tobacconist's shop murkier than ever, and a breeze coming in over the rooftops to send the packing-case frames and the vegetable stalks flying over the greystone surround like so much flotsam and jetsam on the seashore. All this the two men in the downstairs bar of the Clipstone Arms saw and no doubt appreciated, but for some reason they did not seem cast down by it. They were sitting at a table in the window, very comfortably ensconced behind a strew of empty pewter pots, and not seeming to care that it was November, so that even now the light was beginning to fade across the court and one or two flakes of snow were drifting in to mingle with the soot on the peeling window sills. A visitor to the bar – and it was otherwise empty – might have thought that there was some mystery about these men, and that the mystery lay not in their outward appearance – they were identically dressed in shabby suits, dirty collars and billycock hats – but in the way they regarded each other: that one of them, taller and perhaps older, imagined himself to be a figure of consequence, and that the other, smaller and perhaps younger, was happy to support him in this belief.

'But you ain't told me yet,' the taller man was saying, looking into the pewter pots one by one to see if they contained any liquor, 'just how you're placed right now.'

'That's so, Mr Mulligan,' the smaller man replied, tapping the underside of his pipe on the table with an extraordinarily dirty hand. 'Well – the fact is, I does run – well – errands for Mr Whalen that keeps the Bird in Hand in Wardour Street, and he lets me – well – make up a book sometimes.' ·

Mr Mulligan was grimly pouring the dregs from four of the pewter pots into the fifth.

'It ain't a genteel house, the Bird in Hand,' he pronounced.

'No it ain't.' The look on the smaller man's face was quite wonderful to see. 'Dreadful lot of riff-raff they has in there. Irish, too. Never more than a shilling a time. But beggars can't be choosers.'

'You're a poor fish, McIvor, that's what you are' said Mr Mulligan. 'You'd have been better placed a-sticking to Mr Cheeseman that I put you in the way of.'

'You wouldn't say that if you knew about it, Mr Mulligan. Why, if that Cheeseman is worth a ten-pound note nowadays, that's all he is worth.'

Mr Mulligan put the pewter pot down upon the table and examined his fingers, as if they were a row of saveloy sausages he might very soon begin to eat.

'You aren't telling me, McIvor, that Cheeseman is light on the tin? A man as had his own carriage in the ring at Epsom only this May past.'

'It was the St Leger that did for him, Mr Mulligan. Took seven hundred pounds on Duke's Delight at threes, laid most of it off on Antimacassar – Lord Purefoy's horse, you know – and the animal, which everyone knew was a certainty, never came out of the ditch at the thirteenth.'

'Seven hundred pounds at threes!' Mr Mulligan shook his head, stuck his thumb into his mouth and bit off a piece of skin near the nail. 'Couldn't he have placed no more side-bets?'

'Antimacassar was so mortal 'igh among the fancy, Mr Mulligan. He'd had Lord Purefoy's man sending him intelligence from the stables, and you can't say fairer than that.'

Mr Mulligan inspected his fingers again, but he knew that the beauty had gone out of them. The snowflakes had stopped falling and the wind was whirling a little pile of dirt around the nearside corner of the court like a dervish.

'These are bad times, McIvor,' he remarked. 'Confounded bad. 'Ow a gentleman is to make an honest penny out of the game I hardly know. Why, there's some publicans'll split if they so much as sees a slip passing hands. And that McTurk has such a down on us.' Seeing a look of enquiry in his companion's eye, he went on: 'The p'liceman. Regular down he has. Why, there was half a dozen peelers went into the Jolly Butcher in the Kennington Road the other night, and bless me if the landlord ain't been summonsed. Lose his licence, most probably, poor feller.'

'They're terrible hard, them magistrates,' Mr McIvor said, who may have had some dealings of his own with the bench. 'But tell me, Mr Mulligan' – this was said with an extreme deference – 'what is it that you've been engaged upon since you last did me the honour of tendering some advice?'

'What have I been engaged upon? That's cheek, McIvor, and you know it. But seeing that you're a respectful young feller – yes, I will 'ave another go of this porter if you'll be so kind – I'll tell you. Fact is, I've been working for Mr Newcome that has the Three Bells in Shoreditch.'

'I've had dealings with Newcome,' said McIvor, with perhaps the very faintest note of asperity, 'and he never said anything about it.'

'No more he would. You don't think a man as employs a private detective to spot his wife in the crim. con. goes and advertises the fact, do you? No, I never come into the Three Bells. Leastways, not when there's anyone there. Just this last month now, I've been up in Leicestershire.'

'No meetings anywhere there this month, surely?' McIvor countered.

'No more there aren't. But it's where Mr Mahoney's place is – he that ran Tarantella in the Oaks – and that's where I've been.'

'And what did you do there?'

'I ain't proud' – in fact the expression on Mr Mulligan's face suggested that he was as proud as Lucifer. 'I can shift a load of muck with the best of them. No, I've been working in the stables.'

'What – and picking up gen?'

'That's about the strength of it.' Two fresh pots of porter, signed up to Mr McIvor's account, had now appeared on the table. 'Your very good health.'

'Why aren't you there now?' McIvor wondered.

'If we was brothers, I'd tell you. Seeing as we're not, I shan't. Besides,' Mr Mulligan added grandly, 'there's nothing to do in Leicestershire save chase foxes. You wouldn't catch me living there if I was made a present of forty acres. But see here' – and he leant across the table, speaking in a more confidential tone – 'this ain't buttering any bread. I take it you think I'm tolerably downy, McIvor?'

'I should think you ought to know what o'clock it was, if anyone should,' said Mr McIvor admiringly, who had been very impressed by the excursion to Leicestershire.

'Well then, here's a dodge that might serve us. Seventy–thirty split, mind. And you'd have to do the work.'

'It ain't taking a shop for some auctioneer's leavings?'

'No indeed. Just opening letters. And sending 'em too. A child could do it. But the trick is pulling 'em in. Once you've got them you're safe. And no one any the wiser. Now, you've a tip or two in your head, I suppose?'

'Everyone has tips.'

'Maybe they do. And there are fools out there willing to pay for them. But it's hartistry as counts. *Widder with three orphan children in her care has sporting intelligence to communicate* – that kind of thing. And colours. Always mention the colours. There's folk sets great store by them. Now, let us have pen and paper and set to work.'

These articles having been procured from the landlord, together with two more pots of porter, for which McIvor again paid, or rather said that he would do so, Mr Mulligan bent his head over the table top. Outside the shadows were crawling yet higher up the walls of Clipstone Court and the furious old man had rushed down his staircase and was angrily gathering up the packing-case fragments.

'Shy kind of place, ain't it?' Mr Mulligan said. Plainly the act of composition did not come easily to him. First he scratched negligently with his pen at the foolscap sheet before him, only to obliterate what he had just written. Then he took heart again, dashed off a sentence, looked at it sadly and then drew his nib carefully through at least half the words. McIvor stared out into the court and amused himself by looking at an engraving of the Battle of Waterloo that hung above a poster saying that Jack Dobbs the Rottingdean Fibber's benefit was coming off at John Dawdsey's shop, the Horseferry Road, and all sporting gentlemen were respectfully entreated to attend. In ten minutes, and with several rendings of the foolscap sheet, the business was done and Mr Mulligan held up the surviving fragment of paper proudly to the light.

'Here we are then. *A widowed lady, relict of a gentleman long esteemed in some of the highest sporting establishments in the land, is in possession of information pertaining to this year's Derby race, which she will gladly divulge in exchange for the sum of one half-crown, to be remitted to Mrs Faraday, Post Office, Drury Lane, London W.* Reads well, don't it?'

'I should say it does,' said Mr McIvor, who had been very impressed by the word 'pertaining'. 'But what do we do when folks start sending their money in?'

'What do we do? Why, we send them the name of an 'oss. Mind you, it's to be a good one, for if it succeeds, why, we can try the dodge again. That's the beauty of it.'

'What about Broomstick, Lord Mountfichet's bay, that was of Tanglewood by Saracen?'

'Gammon! They'll be turning him into dog-meat come next Michaelmas, if what I hear's true.'

'Mariner, then, that did so well at Doncaster.'

'Ah, but he's no staying power, has he? And they say that Mr Ticklerton don't care for the sport since his wife died. No, I say we go for that horse in Lincolnshire.'

Seeing from the look on McIvor's face that he had never heard of any horse in Lincolnshire, he went on:

'Tiberius. Mr Davenant's horse. The one that ran five furlongs in a minute and five on Newmarket Heath last spring, and that Joey Bailey would have rode in the Ascot New Stakes if he hadn't broke 'is collar-bone the week before. Was a feller talking of him no end in *Post and Paddock* the other month. I remarked it at the time. Mr Newcome is already offering tens on him, and nobody knowing whether he's to run or no.'

McIvor said he was sure that Mr Mulligan was right; the piece of paper was folded up and secured in the back pocket of Mr Mulligan's shabby suit, later to be conveyed in a dirty envelope to the offices of the *Holborn & St Pancras Journal* in Gower Street, two more pots of porter were called for, a few more flakes of snow drifted down over the sooty window-fronts, the gloomy doorways were gathered up in blackness, and evening came to Clipstone Court.

II

Belgrave Square

TIBERIUS from Paduasoy, by Architrave, whose grandsire was Cotillion. *Own.*
Mr Davenant, of Scroop, Lincolnshire. Captain Coker rode him very prettily in
the Lincoln Trial Stakes. A dainty horse, of no size (15h) but strong in the
field.

Fancyman's Guide to the Turf (1868)

Mr Gresham, the old lawyer who lived on the corner of Belgrave
Square where it runs into Chapel Street, had but one disappointment
in his life, and that was his daughter. He had married at fifty, and his
wife had died very soon after, and the daughter had been intended to
console him for his loss. Somehow this had not happened, and Mr
Gresham had been made miserable by it. And then, afterwards, his
misery had been increased by the fact that he could not quite understand why his daughter – Rebecca – fell short of the expectations that
he had of her. She was a slim, sandy-haired girl of twenty-two or twenty-
three, with features that, however placidly she composed them, hinted
at inward calculation, and one or two people said that she reminded
them of that other Rebecca in Mr Thackeray's novel.

Mr Gresham had heard something of this, and been wounded by it.
He was a hale, thin, unutterably respectable old man of seventy-five,
who had worked in the Equity Courts for fifty years, so old that he
remembered the Prince Regent in his carriage racketing along Cornhill.

He was anxious to stand well with the world, anxious for his daughter's happiness, if what could make her happy could ever be found, but aware, however obscurely, that in the course of his dealings with her something had gone wrong. Watching her at a tea table, on the staircase at some Pont Street party, or even stepping into the brougham that carried her around the park, he was conscious that there was a – slyness was perhaps too harsh a word – deeper motivation that he could not quite fathom. Mr Gresham liked spontaneity in women, he liked smiling countenances, soft looks and meek attention, and he did not find them in Miss Rebecca. He supposed – and it was a subject that he brooded on – that she had been spoiled, and that he had done the spoiling.

Old lawyers, even those who have worked in the Equity Courts for fifty years and are as rich as Croesus, seldom come to rest in Belgravia, but Mr Gresham had married a marquis's daughter and the house at the corner of Chapel Street had been part of the bargain. So, perhaps, had the daily carriage ride in the park. There were times when Mr Gresham regretted both the house and the carriage, and wished that he lived quietly in Manchester Square with a housekeeper and a couple of maidservants to cosset him, but the choice had been made and there was no going back from it. And so the pair of them went on in the big, draughty house, with the carriages rushing in the square beyond, irritating each other as only two people who are united by blood and detached by temperament can do. Sometimes Mr Gresham held out olive branches, and those olive branches were refused. Sometimes, thinking to appease him, his daughter revealed some part of her calculation to paternal gaze and he was disgusted by it. That was all.

All this had been going on for five years – certainly since that time when Miss Gresham had emerged from the schoolroom, been given her own maid and the keys to the pantry, and generally been charged with the upkeep of Mr Gresham's household – and it seemed to Mr Gresham, when he thought about it, that the situation needed some bold stroke on his part. He was thinking about it now – it was about nine o'clock on a cold morning in November – over the breakfast table, with his letters before him on a salver and *The Times* newspaper opened on his knee, but he could not for the life of him imagine what that bold stroke might be. Naturally there was a chance that she might marry, but this, too, was fraught with peril, for she might ally herself with someone Mr Gresham disliked, or someone manifestly unsuitable, and neither of these prospects Mr Gresham thought he could bear. And so he buttered his bread, drank his tea, watched the carriages in the square and was thoroughly miserable. As he did this he thought of his wife, who had sat in this same room with him a quarter of a century ago and who was now lying in Kensal Green Cemetery, and whose grave he did not visit perhaps as often as he ought. He was privately resolving to himself that he would make that journey on the coming Sunday when the door to the breakfast parlour was jerked sharply open, there was a swirl of silks, and Miss Gresham came rapidly into the room.

'Do you know, I never knew such a one for slamming doors as you, Rebecca?'

'Did I? Well, I am very sorry, Papa' said Miss Gresham, not, however, sounding sorry in the least.

Mr Gresham and his daughter fell into that category of people whose want of sympathy is made yet more flagrant by their inability to disguise it. They were not at ease with each other, and the civilities of the breakfast table only fuelled their displeasure. And so Mr Gresham read what *The Times* had to say about Mr Gladstone's disposition of his Cabinet, and Miss Gresham spread marmalade on a fragment of toast and snapped at it crossly as if she thought it might get away from her, and neither of them, in the matter of temperamental unbending, would give an inch. All this made Mr Gresham unhappy. He was still thinking of his dead wife and the visit to her grave. There was a miniature of her on the mahogany sideboard, done however many years ago, which he peered at surreptitiously from behind his newspaper – thinking that he had failed her, and that a better man would have been able to conciliate the daughter she had left behind. At the same time, he had something very serious he wanted to say to Miss Gresham – something that touched on both their destinies – and he did not in the least know how to say it. And so the father passed miserably from Mr Gladstone's

Secretaries of State to some choice speculations about the income tax, while the daughter crunched up her toast like some white-armed siren feasting on the bones of drowned mariners, and the clock ticked on towards the half-hour.

Finally, when Miss Gresham showed signs of being ready to quit the room, Mr Gresham laid down his newspaper.

'I take it you enjoyed yourself last night at Lady Susannah's?'

'It went off very well, though I could not imagine what they had put in the negus' – Miss Gresham was a connoisseur of evening parties and liked criticising their arrangement. 'They say Mr Hunt' – Mr Hunt had lately ceased to be Chancellor of the Exchequer – 'was there, but I can't pretend to have seen him.'

'Hunt never goes to evening parties.'

'Well, you may say that, Papa, but he was certainly supposed to be at this one.'

All this Mr Gresham found that he liked – up to a point. He approved of his daughter attending parties where the Chancellor of the Exchequer might or might not be present. He had never in his life hobnobbed with Cabinet ministers, but he had no objection to his daughter doing so. But he knew that he was no closer to that very serious thing.

'Was Mr Happerton there?'

Miss Gresham had jumped up out of her chair now, and was standing behind it. The portrait of her mother looked down upon her sandy hair.

'I declare, Papa, that if you are so interested in Mr Happerton's whereabouts, you should ask him to supply you with a schedule.'

Mr Gresham thought this was hard. He had an idea that this was not how girls spoke to their fathers – even in jest – and he knew that Miss Gresham had not spoken in jest. He knew, too, that he ought to rebuke her, but he had no idea how the rebuking might be accomplished. Looking up, he saw that she had left her chair-back far behind and was now a yard from the door.

'You'll oblige me, Rebecca, by sitting down and hearing what I have to say. You mayn't like it, but – there it is. Sit down now.' Seeing that she still stood a yard from the door, he motioned her back to her place at the table with his hand. It was a hand that, flung out theatrically in the Equity Court, had cowed many a junior barrister, but it did not have much effect on Miss Rebecca. 'The fact is that Mr Happerton has been to see me. I don't say that I care for the man, but at any rate he has done the proper thing.'

'What is the proper thing that Mr Happerton has done, Papa?'

'Well, he has asked – the deuce, Rebecca, you know very well what he has asked.'

Mr Gresham looked his daughter full in the face as he said this and thought that her air of demureness was exaggerated, that she was – there was no other word for it – sly.

'What did you say to him, Papa?'

There was a pause, artificially prolonged by the butler's coming in to clear away the sideboard and to present Mr Gresham with a telegram relating to a Chancery case on which he was engaged. Mr Gresham frowned at it. Then he frowned at his daughter who was not, as he had instructed her, seated in her chair but standing behind it with her hands clasping its back. People said that Miss Gresham had very pretty hands.

'I told him it was out of the question.'

Miss Gresham continued to stand with her hands clasping the chair-back.

'Why did you tell him it was out of the question, Papa?'

'He is a man that nobody knows anything of.'

'That is nonsense, Papa.' Miss Gresham shifted the position of her hands on the chair-back. 'Everybody knows all about him. He has an office in Lothbury and goes everywhere. Why, he has been to dinner at Aunt Muriel's.'

'That is not what I meant.' Mr Gresham was not exactly sure what he did mean. 'I meant that he is a man who scarcely knows who his own grandfather was.'

Mr Gresham's grandfather had sold hay at Smithfield Market, and his father had made his first money discounting bills for an attorney's clerk in Hatton Garden, but he had the memory of the marquis's daughter to appease. At the same time he was conscious that, while thoroughly disliking Mr Happerton, he was not being fair to his daughter. Catching something of this uncertainty, Miss Gresham began at once to play upon it.

'Gracious, Papa. That kind of thing is going out. Why, Lord Parmenter, whom you make so much of, always says that his grandfather was a crossing-sweeper.'

'That may very well be. People can't help their ancestors. But it is not Lord Parmenter that wants to marry you.'

'If it were, and Lady Parmenter had dropped down dead at Richmond Fair, I daresay you would not be so ill-natured. It is just that you have such a down on Mr Happerton.'

All this was very bad, and Mr Gresham was thoroughly disgusted with himself – not because he had failed to carry his point, but because he knew that he had a duty to his daughter – however vexatious she might be – which he was altogether failing to fulfil.

'Certainly I don't like Mr Happerton. I don't like his manner. I don't like the men he associates with and I don't like the way he makes his income. It's all very well, Rebecca, to talk about things going out and Lord Parmenter's grandfather – I'm sure he was a very respectable man – but you don't suppose that a father could be happy knowing his daughter was living on money got from race-meetings?'

'Well, Papa, he had better not let her marry the Duke of Devonshire then.'

Those Belgravia breakfast rooms are very bleak once the things have been taken off the sideboard and the tea has gone cold. It was by now nearly ten o'clock and Mr Gresham knew that he was needed at his chambers, where Serjeant Havergal proposed to wait upon him about the Tenway Croft case. Outside mist was rising slowly off the plane trees to fog the window. All this affected Mr Gresham with a profound feeling of melancholy. He told himself that the fault was his daughter's, but he suspected the fault was his. As he watched her – still standing with her hands clasped to the chair-back, with one little slippered foot straying out onto the carpet – he remembered certain incidents from her early life that had seemed to bring home to him his separateness from her. 'Why do you bully Mary so?' he had asked her once when she had sent a maidservant flying tearfully from the room. 'It is not her fault, surely, that she cannot find things you have mislaid?' 'Because she is stupid, Papa, and clucks around me like a goose,' Miss Gresham had replied.

Another time he had watched, fascinated, as she took a pair of scissors and with what seemed to him an extraordinary ferocity slashed at a picture of a young lady, lately affianced to some ducal heir or other, that had appeared in one of the illustrated magazines. 'My dear,' he had said, nervous even in his reproof, 'why is it that you need to tear at that paper?' 'It is that Lady Augusta Chinnery, Papa,' his daughter had replied – and the look in her eye had not been pleasant to see – 'do you not think she is the ugliest woman in the world?' All this Mr Gresham recollected. There was one obvious question he had not asked and so, hesitating dreadfully over the words, he asked it.

'Do you' – he could not bring himself to use the word that is generally used in such cases – 'have any regard for this Mr Happerton?'

'Certainly I have a regard for him, Papa. He talks, and is very amusing. Most men have nothing to say for themselves at all.'

'And what would you say if – if he were to ask you to marry him?'

'I can hardly say. Not even to you I cannot. But I think I should like to be asked.'

Mr Gresham heard this with genuine puzzlement. He could not decide if his daughter seriously wished to marry Mr Happerton but had chosen to throw him off the scent, or genuinely did not know her own mind.

'At any rate it is quite impossible.'

'But why is it impossible, Papa?'

'You have heard what I have to say.' Mr Gresham knew, as he said this, that he was being overbearing, but he had disliked Mr Happerton, when that gentleman had come to call upon him, so very much. 'There may be men ready to marry their daughters to racecourse touts, but I am not one of them.'

'I don't think Mr Happerton is a racecourse tout, papa.'

'You know nothing about it, Rebecca.' Mr Gresham was dreadfully unhappy. He would have liked to have reached out and gathered his daughter in his arms, assured her that he wanted only what was best for her, that the imperfections he saw in her were as nothing compared to the ties that bound her to him, but somehow he knew that it was impossible for him to do this. Instead he temporised.

'Gracious, but it is ten past ten. This is a serious business, Rebecca. I'm not saying I entirely forbid it, but it must be gone into. You'll grant at any rate that I have a right to advise you, and you to take that advice. But in the meantime, you ain't to see him. That I couldn't allow.'

'What if I were to tell you that you are breaking my heart?'

'Heavens, Rebecca, you say the oddest things. People don't break their hearts in my experience. Girls didn't when I was a young man, and they don't do it now. At any event you don't look as if yours was broken.'

'And yet it may well be for all that.' The knuckles of Miss Gresham's hands, as she said this, were quite white upon the chair-back. 'What if I find myself in his company – in the ordinary course of events, I mean?'

'That's easy. You should go nowhere where he might be found. Do you understand me? You were always a good girl,' Mr Gresham said, without very much conviction.

'I think I understand.'

'What shall you do today?'

'I thought of going to Harriet's.' Harriet was Miss Gresham's cousin, who lived a mile away in Eccleston Square.

And so the father said goodbye to his daughter, the one thinking regretfully that he had been hard done by but overreached himself in his complaints, and the other feeling that she had played her cards very well, and that Mr Gresham was a poor fish whom a few more tugs of the line would soon fetch up bright and gasping on the river bank.

*

Miss Gresham, once her father had left her, did not have the appearance of a girl whose heart is broken. A letter had come for her from a friend living in the west of England, and she browsed through it for a moment or two thinking that Eliza Sparkes was the stupidest young woman she knew and deserved the curate who wanted to marry her, and that Exeter sounded the dreariest place on earth. There was a French novel on the sideboard by Paul de Kock, which her father would certainly not have wanted her to read, and this, too, she pondered while the tea in her cup grew colder still and the mist climbed further up the windows like a great yellow cat rubbing its back upon the panes. She had read a number of French novels, and was not much shocked by them. A servant came in to clear away the rest of the breakfast things, and still she sat there with her hands resting on Eliza Sparkes's letter and the French novel, but seeing neither of them. She had a habit of unpinning a strand of hair – this she generally wore bound up behind her head – and sucking it through her teeth, which was very disagreeable to see, and this she did now, with her eyes staring into the embers of the fire and her foot tapping restlessly on the Turkey carpet. A second, a third and then a fourth strand of hair went the same way until, hearing the clock strike the hour, she went up to her room, looked in a mirror, put a shawl over her shoulders, found her hat and set off for her cousin Harriet's in Eccleston Square.

There was a general feeling in the Belgravia house – never openly stated but certainly assumed by Mr Gresham – that if Miss Gresham left the house she should do so under the protection of her maid. But as she descended the grey stone steps into Belgrave Square and wrinkled her nose against the fog, she told herself that she had not quite liked the sound of the girl's cough and that she would be better off indoors. Besides, what was there for her maid to do in Pimlico? And so she walked briskly around the eastern side of Belgrave Square, gave a sharp look at a gentleman who raised his hat to her and set off southwards in the direction of Victoria Station, the Pimlico squares that are such a godsend to respectable middle-class people on modest incomes, and her cousin Harriet. When Mr Gresham thought of his niece, which he did not often do, he conceived of her not exactly as a duenna, which no girl of five-and-twenty can be expected to be, but at any rate as a sobering influence. In this he was wrong. Both Harriet's parents were dead, and she lived with an aunt, and the aunt, though certainly respectable, was preoccupied and vague, all of which allowed Mr Gresham's duenna a degree of licence which would probably rather have alarmed him, had he known about it. It goes without saying that Miss Kimble was quite harmless – she liked rich people and West End gossip and guardsmen who saluted her in the park – but still, Mr Gresham would have been doubtful.

The house in Eccleston Square was no doubt highly convenient, but it was rather small, and shamed by its association with a Catholic missioner's office which lay next door. The two girls met in the hall.

'Heavens, Becca,' Miss Kimble said. She was rather a languid girl. 'Walking all this way in the fog. I shouldn't have cared to myself.'

'I don't think a little fog ever hurt anyone. Where is Aunt Muriel?'

'Oh, I think she is with Cook. But listen! Where do you think we have been asked for luncheon?'

'I'm sure I don't know. Lord John's? Mr Disraeli's?'

'It is very wrong of you to quiz me, Becca . . . To Mrs Venables'.'

This intelligence Miss Gresham received with a respectful nod of her head, for in the circles which she and Miss Kimble frequented, Mrs Venables was very close to being a lion. Having once – nobody quite knew when – been an actress, she was now married to Mr Venables, who sat in the Commons for the Chelsea Districts and when not engaged upon his parliamentary duties occupied a big house in Redcliffe Gardens. However, there was a difficulty in Mrs Venables' society, and it consisted in her having the reputation of being 'fast'. No one minds bohemianism, of course – it is the spice of life – but some of the gentlemen entertained in Mrs Venables' drawing-room, beneath the portrait of her by Etty, were known to have mislaid their wives, and some of the ladies were known to be estranged from their husbands. Mr Swinburne had once read some of his poems there, to general consternation. All this gave Mrs Venables' establishment a delightful air of naughtiness that was, in truth, quite factitious. The luncheons were the same as one gets anywhere in London, and the conversation just as dreary. But then, not everyone has been painted by Mr Etty or thought to have existed in some semi-intimate relation to a prince of the blood. All this passed through Miss Gresham's mind as her cousin conveyed the invitation, and there came to her face a look of annoyance, which Miss Kimble noted.

'Come, Becca. You ain't afraid of going to Mrs Venables', surely? Why, Mr Townend will be there, and Captain Powell that always speaks so pleasant to me in the park.'

'It's not that, Harriet.' And here Miss Gresham's features looked very keen. 'Of all things I should like to have luncheon with Mrs Venables.'

And so it was settled and they set off through the fog to Redcliffe Gardens.

*

If anyone had told Mr Gresham that his daughter was lunching with Mrs Venables (whose husband, in addition, was a firebrand radical) he would have been profoundly shocked. If, on the other hand, he had lunched with Mrs Venables himself he would have been profoundly bored. It was one of those absurd, pretentious meals – 'West End dinners' they are called, only that they are not quite given in the West End and are not quite dinners – where the talk is all green-room gossip and the food is brought in hot, or tepid as the case may be, from a caterer's wagon. Miss Gresham, sitting beneath the Etty portrait, which could not have been painted less than twenty years ago, recognised the absurdity and pretension of the occasion but was not insensible to its amenities. The people amused her and she found them witty. There was talk, too, of books and pictures – third-rate talk which the authors of the books and the painters of the pictures would have groaned to hear – but talk nonetheless. All in all Miss Gresham liked it, and for a moment her face lost that look of calculation it had worn over breakfast in Belgrave Square.

Needless to say, Mr Happerton's arrival at the luncheon was the greatest accident – he had not thought he would be able to get away, he had remembered only at the last moment, &c. – but there he was, standing on Mrs Venables' Axminster, whose supplier continued to send in his bill, giving his hat to the butler and looking around him with an expression of the keenest interest.

'Well then, Becky,' he said, when he saw her, shaking her hand with more than usual politeness. 'How are things with you?'

'Really, you must not call me by that name, Mr Happerton,' Miss Gresham told him, but not looking as if she were particularly outraged.

'Shouldn't I? Well – perhaps not. How is Papa?'

'He is very cross.'

'Old gentlemen are generally pretty cross, ain't they?'

'I know only one old gentleman, and that is Papa.'

And here Mr Happerton stopped in the lighting of his cigar – all the gentlemen smoked at Mrs Venables', and one or two of the ladies as well – and gave his companion a look of enquiry. It was not quite the reception he had expected, and he wondered at it. He suspected, just as old Mr Gresham had suspected, that some game was being played with him, without quite knowing how it was being played.

'Here,' he said, reaching into a canvas bag that had accompanied him into Mrs Venables' drawing room. 'Tell me what you think of this.'

It was a watercolour picture, perhaps eighteen inches square and framed behind glass, of a lithe black horse cropping the grass of what might have been Newmarket Heath.

'What is it?'

'That is Tiberius.' For the first time in their conversation, Mr Happerton became thoroughly animated. 'Won the Biennial Stakes at Bath only the other day. It was in all the newspapers. Though not the kind of newspapers *you* read I daresay, Bec—— Miss Gresham.'

'I never saw a copy of *Bell's Life*, Mr Happerton.'

'Eh? No, I don't suppose you did. Well, you may take it from me, Miss Gresham, that Tiberius is the coming thing. There are men who would pay five thousand to have him running under their name.'

'And are you one of them, Mr Happerton?'

'That would be telling too much, Miss Gresham, indeed it would.'

Still Mr Happerton could not make her out. He had an idea that he was being made fun of, but at the same time the humour was very agreeable to him. The part of the room in which they stood was inconveniently crowded, and he had been raising his voice to make it heard, but now he dropped it into what was little more than a whisper.

'Did your father say that I had seen him, Miss Gresham?'

'He said that – certainly.'

'And how did he seem to take it?'

'You have heard me say – he was very cross.'

Mr Happerton wondered at her. He liked strong-minded women who, as he put it, could say 'bo to a goose' but, in truth, he was a little scared of Miss Gresham with her green eyes and her sandy hair.

'But he could be brought round, Miss Gresham?'

The bell was ringing for luncheon, the men from the pastrycook's could be seen in the hall carrying in the first of the made dishes and there was a general press of Mrs Venables' guests to the dining room. 'No, you cannot be put next to Miss Gresham,' that lady had told him. 'I have promised her to Captain Powell.' Mr Happerton knew that if he had anything else to say, he had better say it now.

'But he could be brought round, Miss Gresham?' he asked again. The watercolour was still in his hand, preparatory to being put back in the bag. 'I tell you what,' he said, with renewed enthusiasm, 'if a certain event comes off, Miss G., then I'll see to it that he wears your colours, indeed I shall.'

Miss Gresham smiled and said something in an undertone, so that Mrs Venables, coming back into the room to chivvy her remaining guests, wondered what it was that that milksop girl with her sandy hair – Mrs Venables had no great opinion of Miss Rebecca – had said to make Mr Happerton laugh so heartily.

*

Such was Mr Happerton's enthusiasm for his picture, which he confessed to having paid twenty guineas for that morning at a dealer's in Bond

22

Street, that during the luncheon it was taken out and exhibited to the guests, handed round among them with the same finesse that the pastrycook's men handed round the dessert and eventually propped up against the epergne so that none of Mrs Venables' friends could have avoided it even had they wanted to.

Mrs Venables said that she knew nothing of horses, although her husband, had he been present, would certainly have given an opinion, but that it looked a nice sort of animal.

Captain Powell said that, demmy, he had seen him run at Northampton – long odds, but then they knew nothing of horses in Northamptonshire – and, demmy, he was the sweetest little horse you ever saw.

Mr Chaff, the member for Risborough, and a parliamentary crony of Mr Venables, said that there was some mystery about the horse, that it had been found in a field, surrendered up as part of a debt or some such, and the whole thing was deuced queer.

Captain Powell said that someone should enter him for the Derby, demmy, and if they did, he would back him by Jove.

Mrs Venables, thinking the company was growing tired of horse racing, assumed her sweetest smile and said that no doubt Mr Happerton's purchase of the watercolour was only a preliminary to purchase of the animal itself.

Miss Gresham, showing a greater animation of spirit than anyone in the room had previously thought her capable of, said that it was a beautiful horse and she hoped Mr Happerton could soon call it his own.

And Mr Happerton, seeing her framed between the looming figure of the pastrycook's man as he took away the dessert plates and Captain Powell's titanic jaw as he bent forward to make some further remark about horse racing in Northamptonshire, thought that if there were one finer thing than to watch Tiberius flying around Tattenham Corner, with the ragtag of the Derby in his wake, it would be Miss Rebecca's soft arm in his as he stepped across the Epsom paddock.

*

'I declare I never enjoyed myself quite so much,' Harriet said, as they made their way back to Eccleston Square.

'Mrs Venables seems to know a very queer set of people. I am sure that Captain Powell is the most odious man I ever met. I don't believe he ever went anywhere near that Maharani of Cawnpore in the Mutiny that he is always talking about. But of course he smiles at you in the park, so I had better be silent.'

'I suppose you are cross because you were not sat next to Mr Happerton,' Harriet suggested.

'There are things to make me cross beyond sitting next to Mr Happerton. You are a goose, Harriet, to say such things.'

And Harriet, like Mr Happerton half an hour since, thought that she could not make her cousin out.

III

An Addition to the Family

The gentleman who brings an acknowledgment of his preference to a young lady's father must not be surprised if he is received with no great cordiality. Inadequate birth, dress, demeanour, income – all these things may prejudice the opinion of a paterfamilias, vigilant upon his hearth-rug, in a way that would be very disquieting should the precise dimensions of the gentleman's falling short ever be publicly conveyed. What is needed on these occasions is good nature, persistence and pertinacity, and the constant recollection that faint heart ne'er won fair lady . . .

A New Etiquette: Mrs Carmody's Book of Genteel Behaviour (1861)

A week had passed since Mrs Venables' luncheon and Mr Happerton sat in an upper room of the Blue Riband Club smoking a cigar. The chamber in which he found himself was known as the library, and did in fact contain two or three newspapers laid out on a brass salver and two or three dozen books piled up anyhow on a single shelf of a gaping bookcase. It also contained Captain Raff, Mr Happerton's particular friend, who just at this moment was making a practice stroke into thin air with a billiard cue he had carried up from one of the downstairs rooms, and a couple of coffee cups on a little occasional table with which the two men had been recruiting themselves. There was no one else in the room, which in truth was not much used by members of the Blue Riband Club, and something in Mr Happerton's expression suggested that he was not very troubled by their absence.

The Blue Riband was an altogether new thing in the way of clubs. To begin with it was not situated in the West End, but in a dingy little square around the back of Thavies Inn, which its founders had

25

reckoned handy for the law courts and the City. Then again, its members were perhaps a shade more heterodox than is generally the case in St James's or Pall Mall. They tended to be sporting men – the walls of the club were covered with pictures of Mr Gully and the Tutbury Pet – commission agents and persons for whom the provision of stamped paper is an absolute necessity; there was no blackballing at the Blue Riband. People generally said, when they wanted to praise it, that it was not quite disreputable, and perhaps the same thing could have been said of Mr Happerton, who sat now in its library looking rather as if he owned it and wrinkling his face over the last of the grounds from his coffee cup. He was a tallish, rather florid-looking man of thirty-one or thirty-two, well dressed in a showy way, taking his place among the sporting gentlemen by virtue of a pair of top-boots and various pins and ornaments distributed about his clothing in the shape of horses, indolent-seeming but at the same time vaguely restless, and making little assaults on the coffee cups, the copy of the *New Sporting Magazine* that lay to hand on the brass salver, and Captain Raff, who continued, in a somewhat mournful way, to make his practice shots with the billiard cue.

He was quite a well-off man, people said – the members of the Blue Riband Club certainly said so – yet there was some mystery about how his money was made, whether it came from discounted bills, or commercial speculations, or, as was commonly thought, from the turf. Probably not even Captain Raff could have produced a proper explanation. For all his sojourning in Thavies Inn, Mr Happerton was known in the West End, rode a neat horse in the park, gave bachelor dinners at Richmond, knew a great many ladies and gentlemen from all walks of fashionable and bohemian life and – something that served to deepen the shades of mystery – was a particular friend of Captain Raff's.

The contrast between the two men was very marked. Captain Raff was a small, dirty and rather ill-favoured former officer, perhaps a dozen years older than his protégé, of whose career and emoluments after he had sold out of the Rifles no one was very sure, except that he occasionally made very bitter remarks about the Bankruptcy Court. But the greater difference between them was this: that Mr Happerton, in his top-boots and his equine pins, was respectable, invited to parties and made much of in the circles in which he moved, and Captain Raff, in his shabby highlows and a scarlet stock that seemed to have hung round his neck since he brought it back from the Crimea, was not. People said that he was Mr Happerton's jackal – which is not a nice word – that some disreputable bargain bound them together, that Mr Happerton had tried to throw him over but had not dared to, and that Mr Faker the celebrated West End card-sharp knew all about it, but in truth their association was not so very mysterious. Just as a duchess in Hay Hill needs her secretary-companion, so the Mr Happertons of this world need their Captain Raffs. They need their little errands done and their little commissions transacted, their confederates at Tattersall's and their emissaries at the sporting clubs, and if there are secrets between them, then a Hay Hill duchess has her confidences too.

Just at that moment a servant came into the room and handed Captain Raff a grimy pink envelope. Ripping it open, he read the contents with an expression amounting to not much less than stark horror, while his friend looked humorously on.

'Who's your correspondent, Raff? Some demented milliner ruining herself on your account?'

'Fellows shouldn't make jokes on such subjects,' Captain Raff said, folding the envelope into the breast pocket of his coat and altogether failing to disguise that this was pretty much the truth. 'By heaven, I have behaved badly in the affair I know.' Captain Raff did not look as if he thought he had behaved badly.

'I should rather think you have. Here, Raff' – Mr Happerton threw his arm conspiratorially around his friend's shoulder – 'never mind Miss Baker – poor girl, I'll send her a sovereign, indeed I shall. There is something I particularly want to talk to you about.'

'Is there now? I suppose it's that girl you are going to marry.'

'Well – maybe. But it is not quite settled.'

'Not quite settled! Last time we talked of Miss What's-her-name – Miss Gresham – I thought you were going to spout reams of poetry over her. Shelley and that kind of thing.'

'I don't think she's quite the girl for sending verses to, Raff.'

'Ain't she though?' Captain Raff remembered the pink envelope in his breast pocket. 'Marriage is such a serious thing. You'd have to give up Miss Decamp, you know.'

'Hush about Miss Decamp. Miss Decamp never existed. No, the truth is, Raff, I can't quite get to the bottom of her.'

'What? As to whether she'll have you?'

'Well – I suppose that's the rub of it.' And Mr Happerton explained, in so far as was consistent with good taste, some of his recent dealings with Miss Gresham.

'Playing some game of her own, I suppose,' Captain Raff said sagely. 'Well, either she'll take you or she won't, you can be pretty sure of that. And how much will the old gentleman cut up for?'

'I don't know that he'll cut up for anything. Rich as Dives, but fond of it you know.'

Captain Raff looked doubtful. 'That horse won't buy itself.'

'Well – maybe not. But there are other ways of buying horses. Look at these.'

So speaking, Mr Happerton took a notecase from his pocket, drew out a couple of pieces of stamped paper, written over with a thick, sprawling hand, and waved them under his friend's nose.

'What's them then?' Captain Raff was short-sighted.

'Two bills of Davenant's. The man that owns Tiberius. One for two hundred at three months, the other for three at four.'

'The deuce! How much did you pay for them, eh?'

'Not much over half. They are very shy of Davenant's bills in the City just now. They think he is going to go smash.'

'And you're set to help him. Ain't that the case?'

Mr Happerton gave his companion a sidelong glance, acknowledging that he might in some manner be beholden to him but contriving to suggest, by the way in which he shifted in his chair and glanced out of the window, where the rain had begun to fall over Thavies Inn, that Captain Raff would be prudent not to push this advantage too far. He wondered if he was not a little tired of Captain Raff. The bills were back in his pocket now, snug against an Astley's ticket and a note from his saddle-maker's. Captain Raff, meanwhile, had returned to an earlier subject.

'This Miss Gresham. Uncommon good-looking girl ain't she?'

'Well – I don't know about that. Dresses well, you know. Always wearing the new thing. Devil of an allowance the old fellow must give her.'

'There's no one like those doting old men to spoil a girl,' Captain Raff admitted.

'And as for looks, well she'd make ten of that Miss Tanqueray that Jackson swore he'd carry off to Gretna only her father had the coach stopped at Turnham Green.'

'But there's something not quite right, you say?'

'I wouldn't go so far as that. But I tell you what it is, Raff' – here Mr Happerton flung his arm conspiratorially around his friend's shoulder once more. 'There are times when I can't get to the bottom of her. You can come upon her sometimes and think that butter wouldn't melt in her mouth. But there's a look on her face now and again that reminds me of – who was that queen who rode in the chariot with the knives sticking out?'

'Boudicea?' Captain Raff wondered.

'That's the one. Now I like a woman to be imperious, no one better. The world's full of simpering chits. But I draw the line at a girl who looks as if she's about to ask me to go and see if the carriage is back from the stables.'

'That would change, I should think,' said Captain Raff, who was a bachelor, 'when you were married.'

'Perhaps it would.'

'And you'll need more than a pair of Davenant's bills at three and four if you're going to bring it off. You'll have to decide, you know. Famous frontal development's all very well, but what if she turns out to be a shrew?'

'See here, Raff. I have asked this young lady to marry me. Do you think I want her spoken of in terms such as that?'

'Upon my word, I didn't mean to give offence,' said Captain Raff, quite alarmed now. 'It's just that I never like to see a man throw himself away, you know.'

A gleam of light from the fire shone off Mr Happerton's top-boot. Captain Raff's wretched highlows were gathered up in shadow. Mr Happerton thought that he was very tired of Captain Raff.

'Never mind Miss Gresham for a moment,' he said. 'What about that fellow we are to send to Boulogne?'

There was no one but the two of them in the room, but even so Captain Raff was careful to lower his voice while telling him about the man who was to be sent to Boulogne and what he might find there, while the fire burned low and the rain fell over the darkening streets beyond the window. In Thavies Inn the trees dripped miserably onto the gravel thoroughfares, and little melancholy whispers of wind ran in and out of the doorways and through the ancient wainscoting, and Mr Happerton, looking down on it from his eyrie in the Blue Riband Club, grew a little frightened, thought of all the demons that this visit to Boulogne might release from their box, and determined that, whatever he might do, and whoever he might marry, and whichever horse might bear his name at the Derby, he would, above all things, keep his head.

*

Mr Gresham's chambers were at the top of an immense echoing staircase in Stone Buildings and presided over by an old clerk in an ante-room whose especial task it was to repel unwanted visitors. He had very nearly repelled Mr Happerton, but the ornament of the Blue Riband Club had a way of dealing with underlings and doorkeepers. Whether it was that he excelled in deferential small-talk or merely hinted at sovereigns no one quite knew, but there he was, rather to Mr Gresham's horror, advancing over his carpet and holding out his hand to be shaken. The old lawyer took the hand, but the expression on his face showed what he thought of the man who offered it.

'Tremendous lot of stairs to climb up you have here,' Mr Happerton said. He had a way of casting his eye round a room, inspecting the shine of its curtains and the lustre of the invitation cards on its mantelpiece, that infuriated Mr Gresham. 'But here I am again.'

'Indeed, although I don't recall inviting you, Mr Happerton.'

'Well – perhaps not.' As he looked round the chamber, with its cases full of dull, legal books, the back-numbers of the *Law Gazette* piled neatly on a damask-covered chair and the old lawyer's stuff gown hanging from a hook by the door, Mr Happerton thought that he was not in the least frightened of Mr Gresham. 'You see, I am pretty persistent when I put my mind to it.'

Mr Gresham thought that he was a persistent man too. 'What can I do for you, Mr Happerton?'

Mr Happerton knew that Mr Gresham hated his insouciance, but somehow he could not prevent himself from falling into the blithe, easy tones that he used with Captain Raff and others of his acquaintance. 'Well, it is the same old story. Young hearts are not to be parted, you know, as the poet says. It may be that you doubt my constancy.'

Mr Gresham knew he doubted more than that, but could not quite bring himself to say so. He was profoundly annoyed. In coming to see him at his chambers, Mr Happerton had dressed himself with all the decorum a man needs in the presence of his prospective father-in-law, but still, looking at him as he stood on the carpet, Mr Gresham saw through him. Mr Happerton's sober coat could have been spangled motley for all the good it did him.

'I know nothing about your constancy, Mr Happerton,' he said, 'but it is quite out of the question.'

'May I sit down, sir?' Mr Gresham could hardly let a visitor to his chambers remain standing, and waved him into a chair. 'Why is it out of the question?'

'I don't think, Mr Happerton, that I am obliged by law to explain my decisions to you.'

'But why not, sir?' Mr Happerton's expression, as he said this, was one of ingratiating good humour. 'A man is in love with a young woman. He discovers that this affection is – well – reciprocated. And yet the door is slammed in his face and her father won't say a word. Surely that is a little hard?'

Mr Gresham, who had resumed his usual chair on the far side of his desk, told himself that it was hard. He had an idea that all manner of things – custom, etiquette, propriety – entitled a young man to take his chance with a woman, provided he had the means to support her. But custom and propriety had not said anything about such a one as Mr Happerton. He acknowledged to himself – for he was a fair-minded man – that his dislike of Mr Happerton was merely personal, that he disliked his horsey pins, his casual air and his probable origins, and the small part of him that remembered the grandfather who had sold hay at Smithfield Market was faintly ashamed of this. When he opened his mouth again, consequently, he was somewhat more gracious.

'You must forgive me for speaking plainly, Mr Happerton. These things throw a man out of kilter. But the fact is – I know nothing at all about you.'

'Well, then' – again, nothing could have been more frank and good-natured than Mr Happerton's expression – 'let me tell you some of the things you wish to know.'

'There could be no point in such an interrogation – as you will understand if you think about it.'

'And why not, sir? It is tantamount to saying that whichever way I jump there shall be a ditch waiting to receive me. You say that your objection to my marrying your daughter is that you know nothing about me. I offer to explain myself and you tell me that the interrogation would have no point. That is hardly fair to me, and it is hardly fair to Miss Gresham.'

'I would prefer that my daughter married a man whose family I knew and with whose profession I was thoroughly conversant.'

'As to that, I can tell you all that is to be said. My father managed an estate in the north of England – near Hexham, I believe – although he died just after I was born, and my mother was governess to a family in Lancashire.' This was actually very near the truth. 'For myself, I have lately been employed in the discounting line by Messrs Rivington.'

32

Mr Happerton had heard of Messrs Rivington, but this did not make him like Mr Happerton any the better.

'As a partner?'

'Well – it amounts to the same thing.'

'But you derive a part of your income from the turf?'

'You mustn't think me impertinent, sir, if I say that so do half the noblemen in England.'

'That is their affair. I don't propose to marry my daughter to one of them.'

'I believe, sir, that I once read in *Bell's Life* that you advised the Duke of Grafton on a bloodstock case involving one of His Grace's horses.'

Now Mr Gresham had made a small fortune in the case of Ariadne, the duke's prize mare, supposedly got by Prince Regent from Josephine, but whose ancestry was eventually proved to be not much superior to a carthorse's. He had been as proud to advise the duke in the affair as he was enraged to be reminded of it.

'I think, Mr Happerton, that how I conduct myself in professional affairs is no concern of yours.'

'But, if you will forgive me for saying so, my professional affairs are of the very greatest concern to yourself, and yet we are not to be judged by the same measure.'

Mr Happerton knew that he was playing a dangerous game. 'Of course her father is as stiff as an old clothes-horse,' he had said to Captain Raff, rather late on the previous evening. 'But they say he is scrupulous. Wouldn't have a fellow hanged if there was a doubt, and so forth.' Mr Happerton had set himself to mine that vein of scrupulousness and he thought that, despite Mr Gresham's annoyance, he was succeeding. For his own part, Mr Gresham was thoroughly upset. He disliked Mr Happerton and knew that he would always dislike him, but he also knew that he was behaving badly.

In the silence that followed, Mr Happerton got up from his chair and walked over to the mantelpiece. There were a number of invitation cards placed there – legal entertainments, mostly, of the driest and most forbidding sort – but he browsed through them with the greatest affability, while Mr Gresham goggled at him. There were judges, Attorney-Generals, even, who would not have cared to sit in his chambers and start quizzing his invitations.

'So you see, sir,' Mr Happerton said eventually – and no one could have said that his words lacked respect. 'It is quite straightforward. I am sincerely attached to the young lady. The young lady is, as I hope and trust, sincerely attached to me. I have an income on which to support us – there's an accountant in Red Lion Square who'll be happy to show you the books, sir, whenever you care to step round. No doubt it's a pity that my father managed an estate in Northumberland and my mother taught little girls their letters, but it can't be helped.'

Now Mr Gresham, still seated in his chair, knew that there was something in this. He still disliked Mr Happerton – dislike was hardly a strong enough word – but he feared that a man with an income and the regard of the lady he proposed to marry was perfectly entitled to make that request. But did Mr Happerton really possess his daughter's regard? Then again, he knew – and he was honest enough to admit this – that there might be certain advantages in seeing his daughter married and gone from his house. Her presence reminded him of his disappointment. If the person could be removed, then might not the disappointment follow? Seeing something of his perplexity, Mr Happerton went on:

'But we are neglecting what ought to be the main point of a conversation such as this. What has Miss Gresham to say about it?'

Mr Gresham thought this was intolerable. 'I don't think that is a question I have to answer.'

'Oh, but I think it is. That is, with the greatest respect, Mr Gresham, what has Miss Gresham said about me?'

And here Mr Gresham simply gasped. Anything in the world would have been preferable to him than the sight of Mr Happerton in his chambers, reading his legal invitations and eyeing up his curtains like a draper's assistant. Even the marrying of his daughter, he thought, would be preferable to this. But he did not know what to say. He could have Mr Happerton pitched out into the street, but that would not stop the man paying court to his daughter. And so he sat there, resolving that he would say something sharp and inflexible – something unyielding and adamantine – but somehow not saying it. Whereupon Mr Happerton said, almost casually:

'I think, Mr Gresham, that we won't get much further with this. We won't indeed. It may be that you entertain some personal dislike for me. If that's the case then I'm very sorry – truly. But if you doubt my – my ability to provide for your daughter, then I think you ought to consult someone who could tell you more about myself than you are prepared to hear from my own mouth.'

'Who is there?' Mr Gresham did not know why he said this.

'There is Mr Rivington, perhaps.'

And rather to his surprise Mr Gresham found himself agreeing to consult Mr Rivington about the *bona fides* of his daughter's suitor. The old clerk, sitting in the ante-room beyond with Mr Happerton's sovereign in his fist, wondered at the time that had gone by.

'You'll write, then?' Mr Happerton enquired.

'Well – perhaps I shall.'

'And you will give my compliments to Miss Gresham?'

To this Mr Gresham merely inclined his head. Whereupon the two men shook hands, Mr Happerton with great affability, the man whom he hoped to call his father-in-law with an expression of the gravest regret.

*

Mr Gresham, who had had some slight professional dealings with Mr Rivington, hastened to renew his acquaintance with that gentleman. Not much more than twenty-four hours later he could be found in Messrs Rivington & Co.'s offices in Gutter Lane – rather cramped, if truth be known, and next door to a tanner's yard – asking their principal: what did he think of Mr Happerton?

'Mr Happerton?' Mr Rivington was a cautious, hawk-like and rather austere man of sixty who looked as if he might have been the founding partner of a society got up to suppress light nonsense. 'You won't mind if I close that winder, Mr Gresham? It's uncommon strong this morning. Mr Happerton's a very useful man, I should say. At any rate we have found him so on a number of occasions.'

'He was a partner in the firm I think?'

'Well no – he did not find it convenient. And besides, I don't think his capital was always at his disposal.'

'Wasn't it?'

'There was talk of his dealing in foreign loans. My partner, Mr Scrimgeour, could certainly tell you.'

'No, no, I should not trouble Mr Scrimgeour for the world. The thing is, Mr Rivington ...' And with a certain amount of hesitation that might have been taken for shame, choosing his words with great care and not liking to catch Mr Rivington's eye, Mr Gresham told his tale. Mr Rivington, for his part, grew steadily less austere. Now that the subject was not financial expertise but the question of somebody's daughter, he became almost worldly in his attitudes.

'So that is how it is,' he pronounced. In fact, Mr Rivington knew exactly how it was, Mr Happerton having called upon him a couple of days before. 'Well, he is a wide-awake young fellow enough.'

'I thought him – clever.'

'Yes, he is that, certainly. I don't think he is what you might call – a gentleman.'

'I don't know that I care so very much about that,' Mr Gresham said, who on the contrary cared very much.

'Let me tell you how I see it, Mr Gresham. You must understand that we have not been so very intimate as that, but he has dined at my house and the women – that is to say, my wife – liked him.'

Mr Gresham nodded his head.

'He is one of those thrusting young men that we hear about. He mayn't make a very great fortune, but I don't suppose he'll lose one either. The money will always be there, and I don't believe you'll have them turn up on your doorstep with a pair of carriage trunks and a nursemaid, as happened to poor old Jones who married his daughter to Lord Plinlimmon's son.'

'But what about his' – again Mr Gresham did not quite know how to frame the words – 'personal conduct?'

'As to that, young men will be young men I take it. You won't care for those boots of his, I daresay. The people here thought him rather loud, but I don't think I ever heard anything disreputable of him.'

'The world has changed very much since you and I were young, Mr Rivington.'

'No doubt it has,' said Mr Rivington, who did not quite see why he should be bracketed with a man fifteen years his senior. 'No doubt it has. As I say, the money will be there and I don't suppose you'll have much to complain of.'

*

'Well, I have done my best,' Mr Rivington said, meeting Mr Happerton later that night at a West End club of which they were both members, 'although I don't know what good it will do you.'

'I'm awfully obliged to you. How did he seem to take it?'

'Heaven knows how he took it. I take it he don't approve of you.' Mr Rivington's glance, as he said this, declared a rather greater intimacy than he had proposed to Mr Gresham. 'Now, one good turn deserves another you know.'

'Ah well, if you mean Tiberius, I am working at that. But let us say the thing is conditional.'

'Conditional on what?' said Mr Rivington, who had a cigar in his mouth and the air of one who is enjoying the fruit of his labours, and whose slowness of uptake could in these circumstances perhaps be forgiven him.

*

Whatever Mr Gresham may have written to Mr Happerton, and however Mr Happerton may have received it, a further letter was sent by messenger two days later to Miss Gresham at the house in Belgrave Square.

Papa is a great deal less cross. I shall call in the morning. Your own G.H.

*

'So it is to come off then, is it?' Captain Raff said to his friend over luncheon. They were sitting once more in the library of the Blue Riband Club, which looked more forlorn and melancholy than ever, and where a stone, flung from the street below, had cracked up one of the window panes. 'And I suppose I'm to be best man?'

'Well – as a matter of fact you aren't,' Mr Happerton told him.

'Not to be groomsman?' Captain Raff's look as he said this was quite piteous. 'What, a fellow that has stood by you all this time? That has done – done all kinds of things, you know. Why, I never was so insulted.'

'That's all gammon, Raff, and you know it. The fact is, this is a respectable affair, and has to be done right. I ain't saying you would shame us –'

'I suppose you'll have one of those West End fellows that act as though they were at a public meeting?'

'That's about the ticket. It is horses for courses, you understand.'

'You must stick by me,' Captain Raff said, very seriously. 'You must stick by me, do you hear? I haven't come this far with you, Happerton, to see it all flung away from me.'

'Oh I'll stick by you all right,' Mr Happerton said, not seeing the look on Captain Raff's face. He was thinking of what Miss Gresham had said to him that morning, and what Mr Gresham had written to him in his letter. 'Only I'll not have you hanging on my arm on my wedding day. Now, when shall we send Lythgoe to Boulogne and what shall we tell him to say?'

And so Captain Raff advised him as to when they might send Lythgoe to Boulogne, and what he might say, and nothing else was said about the question of Mr Happerton's best man.

*

All this happened around the end of November. Mr Happerton's marriage to Miss Gresham took place in the early part of February. If it was not the most fashionable wedding party ever to have set off from Belgrave Square, then it was generally agreed to have done Mr Gresham and his daughter the greatest credit. There were half a dozen brides-maids – rather cold in their light dresses – a marquis's daughter to receive the bride's bouquet as she stood at the altar, and the Honourable Mr Caraway to act as groomsman. Captain Raff skulked at the back of the church. It was thought that the morning coat he was wearing had been bought for him by Mr Happerton.

It is very often said that a man who is to be married spends the time before his wedding day sloughing off some of the affiliations of his bachelor life, and certainly Mr Happerton had made one or two gestures in this direction. In particular, a day or so before the ceremony he had taken a cab to a notably obscure part of the City to the rear of Shoreditch railway station and spent a few minutes in a dingy little office squeezed in between a ship-chandler's and a defunct watchmaker's. The man he came to see was called Mr Pilkington and there was no clue at all as to what business the office transacted, whether it lent money or speculated in guano or bought up land in Putney and built villas on it, but Mr Pilkington, who despite his name was a foreign-looking gentleman, welcomed him onto his premises and poured him a glass of sherry.

'So,' he said, when Mr Happerton had settled himself in his chair, 'you're to be married, I hear? Is it that Miss Casket, the brewer's girl?'

'No it is not,' Mr Happerton said. He was very polite with Mr Pilkington. 'It is Miss Gresham.'

'Well I congratulate you,' Mr Pilkington said, in what might have been a sardonic tone. 'Fifty thousand there if there's a penny. And so it's goodbye to the old shop, is it?'

'The capital's paid up, I believe?' Mr Happerton said. 'There's nothing to complain of, is there?'

'Nothing. Nothing at all. I did hear that Lord Maulever had a bill for two thou he was desperate to accommodate. Would take seven for it, or even six.'

'That's all finished,' Mr Happerton said.

'Old Gresham don't want a bill-discounter for a son-in-law. Is that it?'

Mr Happerton gave a little shake of his head. He was not very talkative with Mr Pilkington.

'Ah well, you had better take yourself off to Belgrave Square,' Mr Pilkington said. 'And I'll see what can be done about Lord Maulever.' After which Mr Happerton drank another glass of sherry and the two men shook hands. 'And yet he may find he wants me again sooner than he thinks,' Mr Pilkington said to himself as Mr Happerton's top-boots went tapping off across the yard.

There were some errands that were too private even for Mr Happerton. And so Captain Raff found himself instructed to take a £10 note in an envelope to the little back bedroom of a dilapidated house near the back parts of the Drury Lane Theatre. Captain Raff was not much shocked by the task – he had executed one or two commisions of this kind for Mr Happerton before – but he thought, as he made his way to the dusty staircase and looked out of the smeary windows at the unkempt yards beyond, that his good nature was being abused. The woman who opened the door knew why he had come, stared furiously at him and would have declined the gift. 'You'll have to give it up, you know,' Captain Raff told her, standing in the doorway in what he imagined to be a masterful manner – the room was done up in the French style, but the paper was coming off the wall and there were a couple of cabbages on the dressing table next to the pots of rouge – 'that is – there is no way of proving it', and in the end the note was accepted, and the door shut and he went back down the staircase thinking that Mr Happerton could have managed the visit himself.

'A bad business,' Captain Raff said to himself as he came out into Drury Lane. It was not that he sympathised with the woman in the room, with her cabbages and her rouge pots and her theatrical costumes hung up on the dresser with the saucepans – Captain Raff knew better than that – merely that he thought the commission horribly symbolic of the relation in which he now stood to Mr Happerton. There had been a time two or three years ago when Mr Happerton had deferred to him, he thought, and sought his advice. Now he kept things secret from him and sent him with £10 notes to shabby-genteel back bedrooms in Drury Lane.

There was a short interval between the wedding breakfast and the departure of the bride and groom, and Mr Gresham thought that he ought to occupy the time by addressing at least some words to his daughter. The house at Belgrave Square was in chaos, with servants hastening along the corridors and luggage piled up in the hall – and at first he did not know where to look. In the end, though, he found her in her bedroom, changed out of her wedding finery into a travelling dress, very cool and composed and examining the set of her bonnet with the aid of a looking glass. Mr Gresham saw himself in the mirror as he came towards her and thought that he looked old and worn and dissatisfied. There had been speeches at the wedding breakfast. Mr Caraway had spoken, and been gracious in his compliments. Mr Happerton had spoken, and said that he had been made happy. Mr Gresham had been conscious that his heart was not in it. But he was a conscientious man, and the sight of the mirror and the memory of the speech did not deter him.

'So, my dear,' he said, with an attempt at a smile, 'you are a married woman now.'

'As to that, Papa, I'm sure a hundred girls in London were married this morning.'

'They say Rome' – this was the destination of the wedding tour – 'is very cold at this time of the year. I hope you won't find it so.'

'I daresay we shall find it very comfortable, Papa.'

Mr Gresham looked round the room, trying to find some hook on which to hang the words he had come to say, but found only a little case of books and a reproduction of Mr Frith's painting of the seaside. He was conscious that his daughter had not been all to him that she should have been, and that he had not been all that he might have been to her. Thinking that the fault was probably his own, he determined to make some reparation.

'My dear,' he said again.

'Yes, Papa.' He was struck again by her composure. He thought that another girl, about to depart on her wedding tour, might not be so matter-of-fact. He realised that he had often, in the past, thought of this very day, thought, even, of this very conversation, and he was aware of the gap between his imaginings and the reality of the moment. From below he could hear the sound of the hired men crashing among the tables. What he wanted to say was: *There is no warmth in you, and little in me. How are we to restore it? Or was it never there?* But he knew he could not say it. In another five minutes the carriage requisitioned to take the newly married couple to Charing Cross Station would be at the door.

'Marriage is a very serious thing, Rebecca. I hope you will be happy.' What he meant to say was that he hoped she would think of him, and that he would think of her, but somehow he could not. Something of his indecision showed in his face and she looked at him curiously.

'What is it, Papa?'

'It is just ... I hope you will be happy, Rebecca. And that in your new life, with your husband, you will remember your old life with me.'

'I am sure I shall, Papa. I believe that's the carriage at the door.'

Mr Gresham, as he put his arm round his daughter's shoulders and kissed her forehead, saw himself again in the mirror and thought that he looked very old and worn.

And so the carriage came and took Mr and Mrs Happerton away on the first stage of their journey to Rome. Two things were noticeable about these preliminaries. One was that Mr Happerton was very keen to supply Captain Raff with the means of communicating with him during his absence. The other was that he took with him the picture of Tiberius, had it placed in his travelling bag for the train and seemed far more anxious for its safety than a man setting off on his wedding tour with a newly married wife at his side ought to be.

IV

Scroop Hall

Towards noon we began to pass through some of the villages that lie on the road to Lincoln – sixteen miles as the crow flies, and the crow is welcome to it, seeing that the potholes are so bad. Scroop I liked particularly – a meek little cluster of old houses drawn up on an ancient green, with the wolds behind it and the sun hanging low over the meadows, and yet this is a bare country, where the wind sweeps in over insufficient hedgerows and the sheep stand shivering in the fields. Scroop Hall a quaint, tumbledown pile, with an army of rooks lodged about its chimneys, dimly visible through the trees . . .
W. M. Thackeray, 'A Little Tour Through Lincolnshire', 1859

It used to be wondered how Mr Samuel Davenant had come by his champion horse Tiberius, which won the Epsom Two Year's Old Plate, altogether ran away with the Trial Stakes at Abingdon and absolutely tied with the Duke of Grafton's Creditor for the Middle Park Plate. Some people said that Mr Davenant hardly knew himself. Owners of racehorses are always supposed to be wealthy sporting men, with strings of thoroughbreds to their name and broad acres to run them over, but Mr Davenant was a country squire who lived in a small way in Lincolnshire, owned no other horses but a pair of ancient hunters and an old cob, and whose name had previously been as absent from *Bell's Life* and *The Field* as Tennyson's or the Archbishop of Canterbury's. When knowledge of Tiberius reached the sporting intelligence, they turned fanciful and said that Mr Davenant had simply found the horse wandering in one of his meadows or bought him from a Gypsy at Louth Fair.

But this was a falsehood, for Mr Davenant had merely acquired him as one of a number of items ceded by a country neighbour who

43

owed him money. There might have been some mystery as to how the country neighbour had come by him – he was supposed by one school of sporting opinion to have been got by Mr Fortescue's Tantalus out of Lord Faringdon's brood mare Belladonna – but at any rate that was nothing to do with Mr Davenant. Even then the horse might have lived out its life in the obscurity of the Lincolnshire wolds, but if Mr Davenant was not a sporting man himself he had friends who were, and when they advised him that he ought not to keep in his tithe barn a horse whose true stamping ground was Newmarket Heath, he took the hint. So a sporting man was brought in to manage the business, and Tiberius was shown at a couple of race meetings at Stamford and Lincoln, with which he duly ran away, was talked of for the Two Thousand and the Derby and, rather to his surprise, Mr Davenant found that he was a figure of remark in a world of which he had hitherto taken scarcely any notice.

As to what Mr Davenant thought about this, nobody knew. But then hardly anyone knew anything about Mr Davenant. He was a man of about forty, who had lived in Lincolnshire all his life and whose father and grandfather had done the same, very proud of the hundred acres which he and his tenants farmed, but with no particular interest in how his yields might be improved or his rents better remitted. He was a widower, which people said had made him melancholy, and he had a backward daughter, a girl of about fourteen with white hair and a big moon face, which people said had made him more melancholy still. Lincolnshire is rather a shy place, but even so Mr Davenant was not conspicuous in it. He had never sat as a magistrate; he took no interest in politics; he was never likely to be Lord Lieutenant. He liked going to church on Sunday, sitting in the family pew and thinking of his ancestors who had sat there, and running his dogs over the wolds, and dining with the very few friends he had in the neighbourhood, and so people said he was odd, and reclusive, that he lived only for his house, and that the dead wife and the moon-faced child were a judgement. It had rained on the morning of Mrs Davenant's funeral, which took place on St Andrew's Day, and it was said that Mr Davenant, with his white face and his hair all askew, and the mud on his hands from bearing the coffin, looked as if he had but lately risen from the grave himself.

But there were other matters in which it seemed that the fates had conspired against Mr Davenant. Tiberius had certainly made his owner's reputation – the Marquis of Loudon had sent a letter in his own hand positively entreating that he be allowed to cover his mare Miranda – but he had very nearly ruined him too. Thinking that where one animal had gone others might follow he had bought more horses, and they had not served him so well. One had broken its foreleg and had to be destroyed. Another had disgraced itself so thoroughly in its debut that it had never been shown again. And then Mr Davenant had done a very rash thing. He had begun a lawsuit with a neighbouring squire who, he alleged, had dug up part of his land for a quarry, and the neighbouring squire had defended himself and won. And people said that although Tiberius remained in his stable, and was already being spoken of in connection with the Derby, Mr Davenant scarcely had the hay with which to feed him.

Mr Davenant lived at Scroop Hall, near the village of Carlton Scroop, about sixteen miles from Lincoln, and somehow this increased the air of melancholy that hung over him. It was a big, old, rambling house, stoutly built and with comfortable rooms, but one of the wings was shut up, with the furniture hidden under blankets and brown paper. One or two of the guidebook compilers had passed that way, and said civil things, but somehow the public had never followed them: the place was too grim and too remote, too *Gothick* people said, who had read Mrs Radcliffe's romances. There was a pretty garden leading onto a picturesque wood, but the wind off the wolds blew the trees and the shrubberies into fantastic shapes and the entrance to the wood was guarded by a gamekeeper's gibbet, and the ladies did not like it. It had once or twice been suggested to Mr Davenant that the guests who walked about his grounds would have benefited from a bank of fir trees as cover, and the absence of half a dozen stoats' hindquarters and a badger's brush staring at them from the gamekeeper's rail and a pool of blood beneath it, but Mr Davenant had shaken his head. He liked the great wild garden with the wind careening over the grass, and the stinking gibbet, just as he liked sitting in the family pew, and the wolds where he coursed his dogs, on the grounds that they had always been there, an immovable rock to set against the shifting sands on which so much of his life seemed to founder. This was the history of Mr Davenant, Scroop Hall and Tiberius.

*

If Mr Davenant was rated odd and melancholy, he was not without allies. He had a particular friend called Glenister – owner of some of the fields that backed onto his wood – who had stuck with him during the business of the lawsuit. Mr Glenister was a bachelor and wealthy enough to employ a bailiff, so his time was his own and much of it was spent at Scroop. Just now he and Mr Davenant were standing on a little point of raised land – the only point of raised land for several miles around – set to the north of the house and commanding the road into the village. It was a dull, wet day in the later part of February, with no sound except the noise of the hedgerows dripping water and the scrape of boots on the turf, and yet full of movement. A flock of black birds was in sharp flight eastward, sheering away over the ploughed fields and the ancestral turf. Beneath them, a small carriage moved rapidly into view along the road.

'Do you know who is in that gig?' Mr Davenant suddenly demanded.

'I can't say that I do.'

'Two attorneys from Sleaford. I had word of their coming. It is very possible there will be an execution in the house.'

'Gracious!' Mr Glenister whistled through his teeth and manoeuvred his boot at a clod of earth with sufficient force to send it rolling down the slope. 'I did not know things were so bad.'

'They are bad – very. There is a governess coming this afternoon – to see to Evie – my sister, Mrs Cantrip, advised it – and it's likely I shan't be able to pay her salary.'

'It is all on account of that horse, I suppose?'

Mr Davenant passed his hand over his face to remove some of the water that had dripped there from the brim of his hat. 'That horse. That law business. A dozen things,' he said bitterly. They had begun to walk down from the knoll to a pathway that led to the gravel drive which abutted the front of the house. 'As for the horse, there wasn't a man in the county wouldn't have counselled me to buy him. Curbishley' – Curbishley was the sporting gentleman Mr Davenant employed – 'said the same. And then he went at that fence as if he meant to eat it and destroyed himself. It is very hard.'

'It is very hard – certainly,' said Mr Glenister, who had two thousand a year from his estate and never spent the half of it.

'And then there was that lawsuit. I don't think a man was ever more infernally used. Everyone knew that Scratchby was taking the sand. Why, his counsel admitted as much himself. And here am I to pick up the bill.'

By this stage they had reached the front of the house where the gravel drive curved around a patch of grass in the midst of which a disreputable caryatid balanced above a stone fountain. Mr Glenister looked up at the eaves and the distant chimneys, black and smoking beneath the lowering sky, and felt that they oppressed him. He felt, too, that there was an almost piteous tone in his friend's voice that he had not heard before. In the distance they could hear the noise of the gig beginning to crunch up the gravel at the further end of the drive.

'They have made good time, I think.'

'It's that Macadamed road I subscribed twenty guineas to,' Mr Davenant said. 'I tell you what, Glenister, I should have kept my money – and the potholes, too – and let them break their necks in a ditch.'

'Very gratifying to you, no doubt, but it don't stop an execution. Well, here they are – you had better talk to them.'

'I suppose I better had ... Damnation! It is that fellow Silas.'

'He does not look so very terrible to me. What is the matter with him?'

What Mr Davenant said in reply was drowned out by the noise of the gig grinding up the stones of the driveway as it came to rest a yard

47

or so from where they stood. Certainly Mr Silas, the Sleaford attorney, did not look so very terrible as, taking care of his coat, trousers, bag and feet, he climbed out of his equipage. He was a small, neat, demure little man, whose hat sat very solemnly on his head and whose spectacles oddly diminished the size of the eyes behind them, so that they looked like pebbles lying very far away on the beach. There was a clerk with him to deal with the driver, who now rattled off in the direction of the stables, and certain other cases and account books that were unpacked from the gig, and it would have been apparent to the smallest child from the look that Mr Silas gave him that he loved the clerk for the deference he showed.

'Dear me,' Mr Silas said, almost to himself, as he held out a little white hand for Mr Davenant to shake, 'the impudence of those drivers. If it wasn't that we have to go back to Sleaford, I should have Jones here pay him off. But how are you, Squire, and how are you keeping? That's a nasty flood you have on your road out there where it meets the common land. I wonder you don't have it drained.'

And Mr Glenister saw immediately what was so terrible about Mr Silas.

'This is Mr Glenister,' Mr Davenant said, with what sounded very like anguish in his voice. 'I trust you have no objection to his joining us?'

'Not at all! The more the merrier is what I always say. Know of you, sir,' said Mr Silas, gravely shaking hands with his host's friend, 'and proud to make your acquaintance. Jones, you might just attend to that case, else the mud will be all over it. The study is it we're to sit in?' – this to Mr Davenant – 'A fine room, sir. Never look out of the window without thinking so. Come, Jones, let us not keep the gentlemen waiting.'

No prince could have swept into Scroop Hall more grandly than Mr Silas. He saw a little mark on the lintel as he swept inside and winked at it and rubbed it with his finger. A cat looked up from a chair in the hall as he passed and he stopped and patted it very affably. He looked at the pictures in their frames and the pike that Mr Davenant's father had pulled out of the Wash in the year of Trafalgar with equal sympathy. Mr Glenister wished that he was back in his library at Glenister Hall with a book in his lap watching the rain fall over the apple trees in his garden.

Mr Davenant's study was not much used. There was a big japanned desk and a bookcase or two and a map of the county which Mr Silas went and looked at very keenly while further chairs were being procured and a maid brought in four sherry glasses on a tray: the decanter was already out on Mr Davenant's desk. It was so dark that lamps were called for, and Mr Silas's shadow burned black and monstrous off the wall, mocking the quaint little body that sat beneath it. Just now he was looking at some pieces of paper held in a wafer of card, which the clerk had presented to him. Mr Davenant sat behind his desk looking as if he wished the earth to swallow him up.

'Now, sir,' Mr Silas began, when he had seated himself in his chair, drunk half a glass of sherry, eaten a biscuit and bullied his clerk a little more, 'you'll have received our letter in advance of this visit, and you'll know how things stand. Very bad they are.'

'I've no doubt they are as you say.'

'Oh, indeed they are. Jones, just give Mr Davenant that schedule, would you? Bills you see, sir' – this remark seemed to be addressed to Mr Glenister – 'are very well providing they are renewed. But what if they aren't, eh?'

Mr Glenister suggested that there were some bills not worth renewing.

'That's it, sir. That's precisely it. But there are some folk, sir, as will press for payment even when they know they are not going to get it. Just for the mischief of the thing. Now, Mr Davenant sir, will you take a look at these figures and tell me if they're correct?'

'I am sure that everything is as you say it is.'

'A trusting nature, sir, is a thing to be applauded,' Mr Silas remarked. The clerk, laying down more paper at his side, looked at him with admiring eyes. 'But it can be took too far, if you catch my meaning.'

'I'm not sure I do catch it,' said Mr Glenister. He was thoroughly annoyed, not merely by the thought that he would have been better off in his library, or by Mr Silas's familiarity, but by what he imagined to be his friend's quiescence. He told himself that Mr Davenant was being unreasonably timid, and that a bold stroke or two would see the attorney back in his gig. Seeing that his friend still sat quite silent in his chair, his eye barely moving over the schedule that Mr Silas had given him, he went on:

'May I be frank, Mr Silas?'

'As frank as you like, sir. Frankness is something we always prize in a profession like ours, isn't that right, Jones?' Mr Jones simpered horribly.

'If I am to give my friend the benefit of my advice, based on the information you have given him, then it is necessary that I should speak to him alone. Perhaps you would excuse us for a few moments?'

'As long as you wish, sir. Half an hour if it suits you. Mr Jones and I will do very well here, I daresay.'

There was a passage on the left-hand side of Mr Davenant's study door that led to a second, outer door and thence into the stable yard. Here Mr Glenister led his friend, almost laughing as he did so.

'What a dreadful man.'

'He is terrible. I believe he is an elder of the Dissenting chapel at Sleaford, and that it has gone to his head.' Mr Davenant shook his own head at the iniquities of a legal system that allowed a Methodist attorney to come and patronise him in his own study. There was an odd look on his face. 'You knew my wife, didn't you, Glenister?'

'Certainly I did.'

'This house was everything to her. When I think of her it is to remember her walking in the garden there. Can you conceive what she would have thought of Mr Silas coming here and poking his finger at the spines of the books and sitting in my grandfather's chair?'

'It is not so bad as that, I think.'

'You would think it so if you had a letter from Mr Silas.'

Looking at his friend as he pronounced these words, Mr Glenister thought that some graver trouble afflicted him, and that it was not merely Mr Silas and his schedule that had extinguished his spirits. He liked Mr Davenant – liked him perhaps better than anyone else in the world – remembered his wife and her walking in the garden, sympathised with him and thought him hard done by, but he knew that he did not quite grasp the extent of his afflictions.

'But you should not let it disturb you. A few hundred pounds would settle it, surely?'

'No doubt they would. But it is worse than that.'

'How so?'

'There are other bills owing. Quite apart from Mr Silas's. And' – it was clearly a torture to Mr Davenant to say these things – 'there are people confederate against me.'

'What kind of people?'

'People in London. I scarcely know their names. It is all to do with the horse.'

Mr Glenister looked around the stable yard and into the sky beyond it, where there were grey clouds blowing in off the wolds, heard the cries of the rooks assembled in the eaves and a little melancholy drip of water that pattered somewhere in the distance. His friend lived in a very desolate place.

'Look here,' he said. 'Wait you a minute and let me speak to Silas. You are prejudiced against the man – I am not blaming you, but it is so – and not prepared to hear him.'

'You should not take such trouble over me.'

'Nonsense,' said Mr Glenister, and went back along the passage to the study door. 'A nice enough fellow,' he heard Mr Silas say, as he stepped inside, 'but he ain't got distangey manners, not by a long chalk.'

'Well now, Mr Silas,' Mr Glenister said, resuming his chair – Mr Silas's clerk bent his head meekly over the papers on the desk – and taking up a copy of the schedule. He had an idea of how Mr Silas might be conciliated. 'You must excuse my friend's ill humour.'

'Nothing to excuse, sir,' Mr Silas said, quite delighted. 'Of course a gentleman is not going to take kindly to his debts being parcelled up and left on his doorstep, so to speak.'

'Certainly he is not. By the by,' said Mr Glenister easily, 'I think I heard of you from Lady Mary Desmond.'

'Did you, sir?' replied Mr Silas, who had never talked to Lady Mary in his life. 'Well, if Lady Mary has spoken of me, I take that as a great compliment.'

'As to Mr Davenant,' Mr Glenister went on, 'I think he feels that his creditors oppress him unduly. Why' – he picked up the schedule and studied it for a moment – 'there's not more than six hundred pounds owing here.'

'No more there isn't, sir. But you see, there's that account with Loveday the saddler in Lincoln that's been due for ever so many months. Not to mention what's owed to the lawyers still. Tradesmen – professional men too – do like to be paid, sir. It's only human nature.'

'I think Mr Davenant feels, too, that there is some kind of conspiracy set against him.'

Mr Silas and his clerk exchanged glances.

'That's it. That's it exactly, sir. But it's none of our doing, indeed it isn't. He's nothing to fear from us. Not at all. Four hundred pounds – well, four hundred and fifty, say – would settle this, and old Loveday bow him into his shop next week as if nothing had happened. Thin memories those shopkeepers have, you know. Even that lawyer might take a note of hand at three months if it was managed right. But there's a gentleman in London been buying up his paper, sir.'

'Which gentleman is this?'

'Mr Hipperton. Poppleton. Some such name.' Mr Jones looked as if he had something to say, but, seeing the look on his superior's face, meekly subsided.

'But why should he want Mr Davenant's paper? If what you say about his position is true, there would be no advantage in owning it.'

'Indeed there wouldn't – Jones, I'll thank you to stop fidgeting. No, you see, it's the horse he wants.'

'Davenant'll not give that up.'

'He may have to, sir, if this Mr Hipperton is on his track. You see, you may not know it – for all that friendship blossoms in life's stagnant garden, as the poet says – but Mr D. here's an embarrassed man. There's the money he borrowed to buy that horse that broke its leg, and the money he owes to the lawyer, and half a dozen other things besides. And what's he got in the way of assets?' Still the clerk was making agitated motions with his forefinger. 'Why, there's this house, in which we sits today, drinking this uncommon good sherry, which is mortgaged, sir, up to four-fifths of its value, and there's that horse sitting in its stable, which may win the Two Thousand or the Derby or then again may not. Why, if it wasn't for me not wishing to disturb a gentleman's comfort, the bailiffs would be in here tomorrow taking away the furniture. What is it, Jones? Anyone would think you were a jack-in-the-box, the way you jump up and down so.'

'His name is Happerton,' Mr Jones squeaked out.

'There you are, Happerton. Why didn't you say so?' Mr Silas turned solemnly to Mr Glenister. 'The man's name is Happerton. And he ain't buying up Mr Davenant's bills so he can discount them, that's for sure.'

Mr Glenister thought about the information that had been vouch-safed to him. He could do nothing about Mr Happerton and his schemes, but he thought he might arrange the present business.

'Four hundred and fifty, you say, would settle this morning's affair?'

'Well, four hundred and seventy. That Loveday, you know, is so very wearing. Let us say four hundred and seventy-five.'

'You would take my note of hand? To be drawn on Messrs Gurney in Lincoln?'

Mr Silas thought about this. Mr Glenister was a bachelor with a substantial estate, none of whose stamped paper or other evidence of his indebtedness had ever been seen anywhere inside the borders of Lincolnshire, and who was assumed to lead a thoroughly blameless life.

'I think we could see our way to accommodating you, sir,' he remarked. 'Jones, have a paper drawn up, would you? Here, let us mark it on the schedule. It would be in Lincoln you saw Lady Mary, I don't doubt, sir, for she goes there often I hear.'

And so the business was done. Mr Glenister signed his name on various documents produced by Mr Jones from out of his coat pocket

('No need for stamps,' Mr Silas graciously conceded. 'This ain't a bill in the regular way of things'), the clerk packed up his paper in various pocketbooks and ledgers that had come in from the gig, and the party debouched into the hall. Here Mr Silas became more affable still. He complimented the maid who held open the door on her complexion, remarked the deer's antlers that hung over the door-frame and shook his head over a crack in the window pane. Shaking Mr Glenister's hand on the doorstep, which he did with the air of one who had sealed an eternal friendship, he murmured:

'They do say the horse will be entered for the Derby.'

'Very probably he will be,' Mr Glenister said, thinking that the horse might very probably not be entered by Mr Davenant.

'Naturally in our line of worship we can't countenance such things, but it's well to know of them, I think. They do say that Septuagint — that's a blasphemous name for a horse — is coming on strong. You'll remember me to her ladyship I hope, sir?'

'Certainly I shall,' Mr Glenister said, handing him into the waiting gig and thinking that he would be damned if he did. The wheels rolled a little in the dirt, the clerk gave a sort of hiccup, and Mr Silas, sitting seraphically beside him, with quite as much dignity as if he had a mitre on his head, was borne away back to Sleaford with Mr Glenister's note for four hundred and seventy-five pounds in his pocket.

When he had gone Mr Glenister did not, as he had first intended, go back into the stable yard. Instead he roamed about the lower parts of the house with the air of a man who is searching for something he cannot quite put his finger on. He peered into the drawing room, where half a dozen old Davenants looked down at him from a wall whose paper had been quite the fashion in Mr Davenant's grandfather's day, put his head into the kitchen where the day's milking lay on the great oak table waiting to be scalded, stared at the maps and prints of old Lincolnshire that hung in the vestibule next to Mr Davenant's ulster and his collection of walking sticks, and by degrees walked back to the room he had left five minutes before. A maidservant came along the corridor carrying the half-empty bottle of sherry and the four glasses and he stood to one side to let her pass. Far away in the upper regions of the house there came a little rustling noise and the merest gust of what might have been laughter. Mr Glenister thought the house was very run down: two of the panes in the hall were cracked, the door swollen with damp and the fire that burned in the drawing room insufficient for the season. 'I suppose Davenant knows what he is about,' he said to himself. A copy of Mr Silas's schedule lay on the desk, underscored with marks from Mr Silas's pen, and he picked it up and put it in the pocket of his coat. The little rustling noise came again from somewhere high in the rafters of the house and he cocked his head to one side to listen to it.

'How many servants do you keep indoors now?' he asked, when he returned to his friend in the stable yard.

'There is Mrs Castell, the housekeeper, and a couple of maids. Why do you ask?'

'No particular reason. What became of Kennedy?' Kennedy was the Scroop Hall butler.

'Ah, Kennedy and I don't see eye to eye these days, I'm afraid . . . But what did that man have to say?'

Mr Glenister gave the version of his dealings with Mr Silas that he thought might be least objectionable to his friend's ears. Mr Davenant shook his head.

'I am very much obliged to you – but you shouldn't have paid the money.'

'It was nothing – nothing at all.'

'It was very much more than nothing. I am ashamed to be beholden to you, Glenister.' But something in Mr Davenant's eye said he was grateful too.

'Who is this Happerton fellow who is set on ruining you?'

'Ruin me?' Mr Davenant gave a savage laugh. 'He is a scoundrel, no doubt, but he does not want to ruin me. If he wished to do that he could have done it ages ago. No, he is after – Tiberius.'

'And you never heard of him before?'

'I think I did – just. One of those men who speculate in horses as you would in guano or shellac. Heaven knows what he may do. But come, Glenister, let us take a walk. I feel that if I went inside the walls would press in on me and seem set to crush me.'

Mr Glenister wondered at this turn of phrase, but consented to follow his friend along a path that led from the rear of the stable yard past the eastern side of the house and down towards the garden and the wood beyond it. As they neared the point at which the lawn began its slow decline into the trees there came a sudden blur of movement, and a pale, white figure – a girl in a print dress with her boots flying over the turf – came and buried her face in Mr Davenant's shirtfront.

'Evie.' Mr Glenister, watching the tremor of the girl's white head, was struck by his friend's solicitude. 'You should not be here. You should not, indeed. Where is Mrs Castell?'

Getting no answer, he made a little delicate movement with his hand and raised her face up to meet his own. 'What if you were to fall, and no one to see you?'

The girl murmured something that Mr Glenister could not catch. He thought, staring closely at the quivering head – it was not often that he met her on his visits to Scroop – that her skin had no pigmentation in it all. Then he saw that her eyes had perhaps the faintest tinge of grey.

There was a sound of hard breathing and urgent footsteps a few yards away, and a stout woman in an apron with her hair coming down her back came shambling into view around the side of the house.

The girl opened her mouth – she performed this act in the manner of a fish that lies stranded on a river bank – and looked as if she might shriek her displeasure, but then lowered her head and walked meekly back to the spot, about ten yards away, where Mrs Castell, very indignant and with her hands on her hips, stood waiting for her.

'She is no better, I suppose?' Mr Glenister wondered, as they carried on down the path.

'Evie? No, she is no better. She can read, you know, after a fashion. I won't say what fashion, but – well. She made a drawing of a pheasant the other day, that Raikes' – Raikes was the keeper – 'had shot in the

56

wood. But there are times when you would think she did not know me, when she flies into passions and Mrs Castell does not care to have her in the room.'

'Do the doctors say what is wrong?'

'Nothing. They say she should see other children, but there are none that would willingly see her.'

'Perhaps the new governess will be able to do something with her.'

'Ah yes, the new governess,' said Mr Davenant absently, and Mr Glenister knew that his mind had gone back to his other troubles.

They had reached the entrance to the wood, where the gibbet barred their way. Here the keeper had nailed up a stoat and a pair of martens, and a black shrike was tearing at the stoat's head with an odd, repetitive motion of its beak. There was blood on the grass and Mr Glenister, looking at the martens' sightless eyes and the stoat's ravaged skull, knew that if it had been left to him he would have taken down the gibbet.

There was not, in truth, a great deal to Mr Davenant's woods. Anyone who was not their owner could have walked through them in five minutes and thought that he had not missed anything. But they were Mr Davenant's pride and joy – more so now that his position as the owner of Scroop Hall was in jeopardy – and he took Mr Glenister through them with a kind of defiance.

'You'll see that tree there, Glenister? I was advised to have it down, as the man said that the wood was rotted. But I told him it should not be touched and, do you know, it has righted itself?'

'It is certainly a very fine tree,' Mr Glenister said, who had had this miracle of nature drawn to his attention half a dozen times before.

And so they pottered about in Mr Davenant's wood, as the clouds marched off towards the coast, and a very weak sun came out to supplant them, and an occasional pheasant scuttled out across the path, and all the time the shadow of Mr Happerton hung over the skyline together with the retreating rain. In the end Mr Davenant could find no more to say about his trees.

'Did you ever feel,' he asked, quite out of nowhere, 'that you had not made the best of your life? I don't mean in the manner of making yourself comfortable, but in taking the chances that were offered you?'

'I suppose we all of us feel that,' said Mr Glenister, who had never thought such a thing in his life.

'Do we? My brother – I don't think you ever met him – is a Fellow of Balliol. He could have had the living here, only the place bores him. He told me so. He wrote a book about – Greek particles. I looked into it once and could make neither head nor tail of it. And yet he has taken his chance. I never did that.'

'But you were not your brother,' Mr Glenister said, good-naturedly. 'As you say, he never wanted to live at Scroop, and yet you did.'

'And what have I done? I have had the house I loved, I have spent all my money on it and now there is this Mr Happerton, a man I never met or knew, come to take it all away. It is very hard, Glenister,' Mr Davenant went on. 'Do you know, when we were first married, my wife used to write verse for the keepsakes? She wrote a poem for Evie when she was born. I don't think I could bear to read it now. There is a scrapbook full of them in the house. I used to read them in the evenings, to keep me – to keep me sane. If that man ever comes here I shall burn it and throw the ashes in the yard.'

They had come back out of the wood now and were approaching the stable yard. Mr Glenister searched for a way to raise his friend's spirits.

'Let us see that horse of yours that Mr Happerton thinks so much of.'

'Well – if you wish it.'

The stable was empty except for a man shovelling up a collapsed straw bale, who touched his hat to Mr Davenant as he passed. The horse stood at the further end, in a little pen of Mr Davenant's own devising, with an oak rail and a metal gate, the light that illuminated it coming in from a little square window up in the eaves. Some months ago a sporting newspaper had printed a description of his attributes which Mr Glenister, who was amused by such things, had cut out and kept in a drawer of his desk. The man who had written it had no doubt been commended by his editor for his historical and literary knowledge, for every name that had ever been given to a horse had been ceremoniously invoked. There was talk of Pegasus and mention of Houyhnhnms. It was suggested that Richard Crookback, had he wanted to escape Bosworth Field, should have had him standing by. Looking at him through the murk of the stable, as his eye became habituated to the uncertain light, Mr Glenister thought that he was very lithe and slim, with perhaps a touch of the Arab that distinguishes the very greatest ornaments of the turf.

'He is a fine fellow.'

'Yes, isn't he? He was got by ...' And here Mr Davenant reeled off a list of genealogical detail, most of which was already known to Mr Glenister from the columns of *Bell's Life*.

'Where does he get his exercise?'

'Oh Curbishley gallops him on the wolds. Curbishley knows all about it. Hi! You there!' He gestured angrily with his fist, and Mr Glenister saw that a short, bearded man was staring into the space before the stable door and talking to the labourer engaged on the collapsed straw bale. When he saw Mr Davenant the expression on his face, which had formerly been one of high good humour, changed on the instant and he came forward, very timidly, knotting his hands together in submission. Rightly supposing that this was not a conversation that concerned him, Mr Glenister went back to his inspection of Tiberius's points. Looking up a moment or so later, he saw that the man had returned to the stable door, while Mr Davenant continued to gesticulate at his retreating back.

'Who was that, I wonder?'

'Wilkinson? You recollect him, perhaps?' Mr Glenister thought that he did not. 'He used to help with some of the outside work. I had to dismiss him, but now he is always coming back and hanging around the place.'

'Why should he do that if he is dimissed?'

'It is the horse,' Mr Davenant said. 'Why, I think Wilkinson would work for no wages if he could be near the horse. It is the same with

Curbishley. I found him practically mooning over him the other day, like a nursemaid looking at a dragoon in the park.'

As it was now about half past twelve – Mr Davenant suggesting to Mr Glenister that he might like to have lunch – they strolled once more round to the front of the house. Here the winter sun had got out above the drive and the disreputable caryatid, there was light sparkling over the window panes and Mr Glenister forgot about the melancholy walk, the shrike's darting head and the blood from the dead marten spilled over the wet grass. There was another vehicle – a little gig, albeit of a faintly agricultural kind – unloading baggage onto the gravel, and a tall, sad-looking girl bent over a trunk that had fallen haphazardly on its side. Mr Davenant, who had lapsed into silence on their walk from the stable, raised his head.

'That must be the governess.'

'What is the young lady's name?'

'Miss Effingham? No, that was the old admiral. Miss Ellington? Well, we shall find out in due course. Good morning, Jorkins.'

This was addressed to the owner of the cart, who first tapped his finger to his bald forehead and then reached into a canvas bag he wore around his waist and presented Mr Davenant with a newspaper and a buff-coloured envelope. Mr Davenant peered at the superscription, was about to put the letter in his pocket, but then thought better of it and tore it open.

'Not another of Mr Silas's bills I hope?' Mr Glenister said, a couple of paces away and preparing to help the governess with her trunk.

'It is from Happerton. For God's sake, Glenister, never mind Miss Ellington's things and come inside.'

And so the two men went indoors, Mr Jorkins took his fare and departed, Miss Ellington – if that was her name – who looked as if she was nearly in tears, rang upon the bell in the hope that someone would attend to her, but all that could be heard was the sound of the cart, growing ever more remote, grinding up the gravel of the drive.

V

Marriage à la Mode

*The married young lady who sets out upon her wedding tour may wonder
what recreations – save, of course, the constant society of her husband –
are available to her. And yet she will discover, if she only looks about her,
that there is a great deal to do, a great deal to see and a great deal on which
to inwardly reflect. Above all there is that delightful opportunity to engage in
conversation with the person to whom fate has joined her, and the delicious
intimacy that such talk habitually promotes . . .*

A New Etiquette: Mrs Carmody's Book of Genteel Behaviour (1861)

Six weeks had gone by since the wedding breakfast at Belgrave
Square, and the Happertons were still in Rome. In fact only a day or
two of their holiday remained to them, and preparations for their departure were well advanced: several valises, packed and unpacked, lay
across the floor of the apartments in which they were lodged, and the
portrait of Tiberius had been taken down and stowed in Mr Happerton's
travelling case. Just at this moment – it was about ten o'clock on a
Sunday morning, with the bells of countless clocks ringing the faithful
to Mass – the Happertons were at breakfast, Mrs Happerton in fragrant
déshabillé, Mr Happerton in one of the violently checked suits he thought
appropriate for foreign visiting. It is doubtful whether Mr Happerton
noticed the *déshabillé*, as his head was bent low over a three-day-old
copy of *The Times*, and he was thinking hard: not about anything the
newspaper had to say to him, but about the six weeks that had passed
and the infinity of weeks that were to come.

The Happertons had done all the correct things in Rome. They had visited the English church – once. They had observed the Forum and the Doria Palace. They had walked up to St Peter's and descended into the catacombs, and Mr Happerton thought that he had enjoyed himself. He had looked at the pictures, sneered at the superstition, eaten the dinners without serious digestive hurt, and, he imagined, done everything he could to make his wife comfortable. As to whether Mrs Happerton had enjoyed herself, Mr Happerton had not the faintest clue. She had looked at the pictures – she knew a little about pictures, he had discovered – sneered at the superstition and eaten the dinners, but none of her ideas about them had been communicated to her husband. Mr Happerton had an inkling that newly married persons, thrown upon their own society in a continental city, generally said more to each other than he and his wife had done, and these silences baffled him. He would ask a question of her simply for the satisfaction of hearing it answered, make some comment about scenery or locale merely to contrive a response. At other times, as now, covertly, behind his newspaper, he took to staring at his wife, and when he did so he discovered that she seemed to be brooding – not miserably, as he had sometimes seen ladies of his acquaintance brood, but with a fierceness that rather alarmed him. 'What are you thinking about?' he had several times asked her, and Mrs Happerton had said, very promptly, that she was wondering which dress to wear; if it would be fine for their drive; whether the post would bring a letter from home. But Mr Happerton, marching at her side through some picture gallery, gazing with brisk contempt at the statuary of some Roman church, or vigilant behind his newspaper, had not believed her.

'What a deuced racket those bells make,' he exclaimed now, putting down the newspaper and looking at his wife across the breakfast table.

'I suppose they have to call the people to church.'

'Horrible popish places. They would be better off staying at home.'

To this Mrs Happerton did not reply. Looking at her, as she reached forward to refill her coffee cup with a long white hand, Mr Happerton wondered what he thought about her. Even now, he discovered, after six weeks' intimacy, he could not make her out.

'I have had a letter from Captain Raff,' he began again. Captain Raff had sent several letters during the course of their stay.

'Oh indeed. What has Captain Raff to say?'

Captain Raff was rather a joke between them.

'Oh – nothing very much, you know.' In fact Captain Raff had had a great deal to say about the man who had been sent to Boulogne, and another man who might be coming back from Boulogne, and a third man who was already offering odds of a hundred to seven on Baldino for the Derby.

'Then I am surprised Captain Raff took the trouble to write.'

The bells had stopped ringing. The only sound Mr Happerton could hear was the squeak of his boots – he had a new pair of top-boots, bought specially for his wedding tour – as he shifted in his chair.

'Well,' he remarked, after another long pause. 'We have seen all there is to see of Rome, I suppose. I hope you have enjoyed yourself, my dear.'

'I have enjoyed myself very much,' Mrs Happerton said.

'And now we must go home again, eh? One can't sit around for ever, you know. Not when there is work to be done.'·

Mr Happerton knew, as he said this, that he was not making himself plain, that there were things he wanted to say to his wife – about their joint future interests, about one very particular thing that he wanted with regard to his own personal security – that he could not quite bring himself to utter. It was not exactly that she intimidated him, he told himself, merely that the look on her face awoke in him a kind of self-consciousness that he had not experienced before.

'Your father is rather an old man,' he began again.

'I suppose he would be thought – old.'

There was a coolness in the way she said this that almost made Mr Happerton quake in his top-boots. But he persevered.

'The halest man for his age I ever saw. He'll be with us for a good many years, I suppose, and a very good thing too.' Mr Happerton had never quite gauged the relationship between Mr Gresham and his daughter. 'Do you suppose that he has made a will?'

'He has never said anything about it.'

'Well, I suppose not. Only they say a lawyer is always the first to make a will – ha!' Mr Happerton knew as he made this joke that it was not a very good one. 'The first to change it, too, when circumstance demands.'

Mr Happerton could not tell why he was proceeding in hints and allusions rather than telling his wife what was really on his mind, but – there it was.

'I suppose', Mrs Happerton said, with the asperity of a governess rebuking a young lady of fourteen who has broken a pen nib, 'that you wish for some of Papa's money?'

'Eh?' Mr Happerton was astonished to hear her say this. He had known many women in his life, and was fond of saying that he could talk to a dairymaid as well as to a duchess, but he had never thought to hear a lawyer's daughter from Belgrave Square tell him that he wanted her father's money. For a moment he wondered whether he had made a dreadful mistake. He did not know, such was the sphinx-like stare that Mrs Happerton had turned on him, whether he was being asked for information, rebuked, or connived with, and the confusion flustered him and sent him back to the hints and allusions in which he had previously dealt.

'I tell you what it is, my girl,' he said, with a husbandly affability he did not altogether feel. 'I am thinking of buying – a horse.'

'A horse?'

'Well yes. Tiberius, that has been hanging on the wall above us these past six weeks. The owner is embarrassed and will very probably sell if he is dealt with in the right way. Such things don't come cheap, indeed they don't. Now, if your father could advance me a little money – merely in the form of a loan – it would help me a great deal in this undertaking.'

'Where is Tiberius?'

He could see that the story interested her, that there were things he might have said he wanted to buy that were a great deal worse.

'Just at the moment he is in Lincolnshire. If I bought him I should probably want to keep him there.'

64

'Papa has always been very down on horse racing.'

'People used to be very down on slaving, but that never stopped them running blackbirds along the Cape,' Mr Happerton said bravely. 'He'll understand that it is really an investment.'

'Do you wish me to ask Papa for money?'

Again, he was astonished by her matter-of-factness. If he had produced a corpse and she had suggested that they might bury it together he could not have been more surprised. Only this time he found that her frankness encouraged him. There was something in her tone that suggested she might be his ally, that she was not averse to her father's money being spent – the idea of its being lent was a polite fiction – on a horse. A horse that might, moreover, do all manner of wonderful things and repay the investment a dozenfold.

'Well now,' he said, a shade more confidentially. 'I don't think perhaps that it ought to be said outright. But you could talk to him about it in general terms, you know. Give him a hint about the kind of thing I'm engaged upon and so forth. That would be the way to begin, I should say. Old gentlemen don't like to be flustered, I've always heard.'

Mrs Happerton gave him a nod, which might have meant that she knew old gentlemen didn't like to be flustered, or that the pen nib had better have stayed unbroken, or half a dozen other things, and went away to her room to dress. And Mr Happerton sat amidst the litter of their breakfast, with his top-boots stretched out before him, and the last letter from Captain Raff in his breast pocket, and his eye upon a little statuette of the Madonna that winked at him from a recess in the wall, half triumphant, but half puzzled, thinking that he still could not make her out.

*

Coming back to Belgrave Square in the first week of April, the Happertons found that a great deal had happened in their absence. To begin with, old Mr Happerton had been ill – not so ill as to have been confined to his bed for many days, but ill enough to seriously disturb his professional engagements. In the account given to his daughter and son-in-law of this illness there had been some deception. The old servants at Belgrave Square had represented him as being merely inconvenienced, but calling at the chambers in Stone Building, Mr Happerton discovered the truth. 'No, sir, he hasn't been here in a month,' the old clerk told him, not approving of Mr Happerton, but mindful of the sovereign that had passed between them. 'Sir Timothy Grogram' – Sir Timothy was adjutant to the Lord Chancellor – 'has sent half a dozen messages. And what am I do with the papers in the Tenway Croft case?'

Mr Happerton had no idea what should be done about the papers in the Tenway Croft case. He inspected Mr Gresham's chambers, which were rather mournful and dusty, took away such letters as he thought material and returned to Belgrave Square shaking his head. On the following morning Mr Gresham did make some attempt to resume his daily routine, put on his black suit and appeared at breakfast, but it was clear that his heart was not in it, and that his hand shook as he laid it on the banister preparatory to his exit. 'I think, perhaps, that your father had better not go to chambers this morning,' said Mr Happerton. Mr Gresham was put to bed and the doctor called.

All this necessarily affected Mr and Mrs Happerton's schemes for the commencement of their married life. There had originally been an idea that they should take rooms while they looked for a house in one of those Kensington squares that are so genteel and so ideally placed for the West End. But Mr Gresham's illness threw this plan into confusion. 'I think we had better stay here for the moment, had we not?' Mr Happerton said to his wife on the day after Mr Gresham's hand shook on the banister, to which Mrs Happerton replied: 'Certainly, if you wish it.' Mr Happerton did wish it. He liked walking up the big grey steps and rapping on the great black door with his stick. He liked the butler's deference and the housekeeper's bob. A room was got ready for them and, though nothing was ever said to Mr Gresham about this, Mr Happerton took charge of the key to the plate chest. It must not be thought, however, that this assumption of responsibility in any way lessened his respect for Mr Gresham. The old gentleman had a habit of spending the morning in his room and then coming down to occupy the remaining hours of the day in front of the drawing-room fire. Here, invariably, he would find Mr Happerton, whose solicitousness for his father-in-law's health was quite charming to see, and whose dexterity with sofa cushions and fire-tongs trumped that of the most attentive domestic.

'Why, Mr Gresham,' he began on one of these occasions. 'You are looking decidedly better, if I may say so, sir.'

'Am I? Well, I suppose I am. I was never very ill, you know.'

The fiction that Mr Gresham was only very slightly unwell had been kept up a week now.

'Well – perhaps not. Will you sit in this armchair, sir, or on the sofa?'

Invalids like to be cosseted, and Mr Gresham was no exception. He was, in point of fact, distinctly unwell – not suffering from any organic disease, perhaps, but enfeebled in a way that rather scared him – and it suited him to be told that he looked better and to have the sofa cushions plumped up on his behalf. Mr Happerton noticed this and played upon it.

'We enjoyed ourselves very much in Rome,' he remarked, after his father-in-law had shown some faint interest in the wedding tour. 'You never went there, I think, sir?'

'No, I never did.'

'It is a very good place if you wish to look at pictures or see sights, or smell queer smoke coming out of churches, but I don't think anyone ever did much work there.'

All this accorded exactly with what Mr Gresham thought of Rome, and he began to think that in certain respects he might have misjudged his son-in-law.

'You'll be returning to your business soon, I take it?' Mr Gresham asked, at about this time.

'Certainly I shall. Sofa cushions are all very well, but they get in the way of a man's earning his bread.'

This statement, too, Mr Gresham silently approved, and if he did

67

not actively look forward to his afternoons before the drawing room fire with a glass of sherry on the tray before him, and Mr Happerton stationed attentively on the sofa beside him, they were at any rate not the most unhappy portions of his life.

It was the same with the evenings. Mr Happerton could not possibly dine out, he announced, when his father-in-law was ill. Consequently, the three of them dined at eight before returning to the drawing room, where Mr Gresham yawned over the fire while his daughter read novels and Mr Happerton made bright conversation. Never having been ill before in his life, Mr Gresham took a great interest in his infirmities. He thought he should be given hot milk with arrowroot, of an evening – it was what his mother had given him when he was a child. Mr Happerton agreed. 'The sovereignest thing, milk and arrowroot,' he said. 'But you should never let a servant mix it.' Accordingly, at about ten o'clock each evening Mr Happerton went to the kitchen, brought up the milk and mixed in the arrowroot himself. The servants – the butler, the housekeeper and the tall footman – saw this and approved it. 'He mayn't do for Devonshire House,' the footman said to the house-keeper, 'him with his pins, but he is a good feller.'

At the same time, Mr Happerton did not neglect that part of his life which took place beyond the drawing room at Belgrave Square. He was seen with his wife at Astley's and at the theatre. He gave a gentlemen's dinner down the river at Greenwich at which ever so many bottles of Sauternes were drunk. Miss Decamp of the corps de ballet, Drury Lane, having written him several piteous entreaties, retired into the country for her *accouchement* with her letters unanswered. And there was time, too, for several conversations in the library of the Blue Riband Club with Captain Raff.

'Now,' Captain Raff said, on one of these occasions, 'that fellow is back from Boulogne. Pardew, or whatever his name is.'

It was about the third week in April and the flowers were out in the gardens of Thavies Inn. Someone had taken it upon himself to open the library window to admit a scent that was about a third horse dung, a third curing smoke and a third genuine spring air.

'Whatever his name is, it is not Pardew,' Mr Happerton said, rather brusquely. 'Arbuthnot, or Scatterby. Anything you wish, but not that.'

'Of course it shall be as you like,' Captain Raff said, very much intrigued by the phantom Mr Pardew, but affecting to conceal it. 'There was some story about him, was there not?'

'No story I ever heard,' said Mr Happerton, more brusquely than ever. 'You'll oblige me, Raff, by not referring to it. Now, perhaps you can oblige me even more by ringing for the servant and seeing if he'll bring us some curaçao.'

'Oh certainly,' Captain Raff replied, thinking that perhaps he knew what the story was. And the curaçao was brought up and drunk, for all that it was only three o'clock in the afternoon, after which the two men felt better.

'As to that other affair,' Captain Raff said. 'I think it should take a couple of thousand.'

'Don't forget,' Mr Happerton said, somewhat mysteriously, 'that we have Mr Arbuthnot to consider too.'

'I ain't forgetting that. But it is all deuced uncertain.' Captain Raff looked rather anxiously around the room, at the open door, at the shabby curtains that billowed in the breeze and at the picture of Tarantella winning the Oaks that hung from the adjoining wall, but found nothing to alarm him. 'You're sure you want to go on with it? We shall have enough to settle with, surely, as it is.'

At this Mr Happerton murmured something about 'having great hopes of the old gentleman, but not so great as that'. Presently he took his leave – Captain Raff went off to play billiards, which he did with a facility that was rather alarming to watch – and walked in a leisurely way to Holborn Circus and then northwards to a little street that led away from the further end of Hatton Garden. Moving easily between the costers' barrows and the dry-goods shops, and keeping his boots well clear of the steaming gutter that ran through the middle, he turned eventually into a tiny court, not much bigger than five yards square, and struck his hand on a dirty wooden door whose paint had perhaps been last renewed at the time of the Coronation.

'Well, Solomons,' Mr Happerton said, when the door was opened and he was standing in the quaint and almost furnitureless room that lay beyond it, 'what have you got for me today?'

Mr Solomons was a Jewish-looking gentleman of about sixty, with a hooky nose and very bright eyes, who clearly did not leave his premises very often, unless it was that he was accustomed to go walking off down Hatton Garden in his dressing gown and slippers. Seeing Mr Happerton, whom he recognised and winked at, he went over to a battered desk in the corner of the room and did a great deal of riffling about, during which he was careful to interpose his body between the contents of the drawer and Mr Happerton's view of them, and came back with a couple of dirty brown envelopes clasped between the thumb and finger of his right hand.

'There's these. I had a deal of trouble finding them, as you'd expect, and they ain't cheap.'

Mr Happerton inspected the first of the papers, a bill in which Samuel Davenant Esq., of Scroop Hall in the County of Lincolnshire, promised to pay Messrs Barstead, saddle-makers, of Sleaford, the sum of £300 on the 30th of June 186–. He knew, as soon as he saw it, that it was a document he burned to possess, but he was anxious not to betray this enthusiasm to Mr Solomons.

'Well yes,' he said, casually, looking at the cracked plaster of Mr Solomons' ceiling and his smeary windows. 'This is certainly one of Davenant's. How much do you ask for it?'

Mr Solomons hesitated. He, too, had his schemes. 'Ah well,' he began, in what might have been intended as a humorous tone, yet sounded anything but. 'You're a sly one, Mr Happerton, indeed you are. If I didn't know you better, I'd be wondering what you wanted this bill *for*. There's no chance of getting it renewed, or selling it on, no indeed. Mr Davenant's a ruined man, as everybody knows, and there's not everybody wants his paper.'

'In that case you can't have paid so very much for it,' said Mr Happerton, who thought that he detested Mr Solomons and would never walk up Hatton Garden again.

'And yet there's some people that does want it – very badly, it seems. There's you, and there's that Mr Christopherson. Perhaps it's that hoss of his you wants. I'm sure I don't know,' Mr Solomons said, failing to disguise a suspicion that he did know very well.

'I'll give you a hundred and twenty,' Mr Happerton said.

'It can't be done, sir. Can't be done. Not with Mr Christopherson being so very pressing. And there's this, too, sir.'

Mr Happerton picked up the second bill, which was lying in the palm of Mr Solomons' outstretched hand, and stared at it.

'Great heavens, man! The signatures don't even tally. Look how the "a" slopes down over the page. Not that it mightn't be useful. A hundred and fifty for the two.'

'It can't be done, sir.'

There was some further discussion, during the course of which Mr Happerton twice put his hands in his pockets and glanced at the door, whereupon Mr Solomons conceded that it might possibly be done after all. Mr Happerton offered his own bill at three months by way of payment, was stoutly repulsed, and eventually produced fifteen ten-pound notes from the breast pocket of his coat. 'Cash, sir. Cash is how I likes to deal,' Mr Solomons said sententiously as he stowed the money away in the folds of his dressing gown. By the time he looked up, Mr Happerton was gone.

That evening, after Mr Gresham had drunk the milk-and-arrow-root that his son-in-law had brought him and been escorted up to bed, the Happertons held a conference before the drawing-room fire. It is always said that young women are changed by their marriage, that certain qualities in them are brought out, while certain other qualities recede into shadow, but Mrs Happerton was not at all changed – except that perhaps her hair seemed a little sandier and her eyes a little greener, and that she was a little quieter and a little more reflective. She had read many novels, she had been taken to Astley's and the theatre, she had watched the preparation of the milk-and-arrowroot and made one or two sharp little remarks. But still there was a way in which she had become intimate with her husband – not perhaps in any open displays of affection, but in the conversations Mr Happerton initiated about the progress of his business affairs. Hearing him talk with old Mr Gresham over the drawing-room fire, watching him as he administered the hot-milk-and-arrowroot – he made a joke, sometimes, of the patient's duty to finish it all up – she would sometimes cast him a look of sudden interest. Mr Happerton noticed the looks and was comforted by them. He thought he and his wife were getting on.

'Your father seems very tired,' Mr Happerton began comfortably. 'He will go to sleep at the table one of these days. What does Mr Morris say?' Mr Morris was the Greshams' doctor.

'I don't know Mr Morris says anything other than that he should not exert himself.'

'Well, he is certainly following his instructions then,' Mr Happerton said, a little less comfortably. 'Has he said anything about returning to chambers?'

'No, he has said nothing.'

'Nor of . . . of that business affair I asked you to mention to him.'

'He said, when I asked him, that he was not disposed to give you any money. He said' – Mrs Happerton's expression as she said this was quite horribly demure – 'that gentlemen who wanted a thing should find the means of paying for it.'

Mr Happerton stared into the fire. He was not cast down by this information, for he fancied that his position with regard to Mr Gresham was growing stronger by the day.

'There would be nothing quite so advantageous,' he began again, 'as two thousand pounds in my account at Overend & Gurney. Of course, if the money is not forthcoming then the plan will have to be given up. You might tell your father that.'

'Certainly I shall tell him.'

'And now – well, you could come and sit beside me here if you liked, you know.'

Mrs Happerton went and sat beside him, to the slight disarrangement of her dress. The tall footman, coming into the room for the tea things, saw them from the doorway and went away again. What she said to her father next morning, is uncertain, but two days later a cheque for £2,000 drawn in favour of George Happerton, Esq., and signed by Mr Gresham was presented to one of Messrs Overend & Gurney's tellers in Lothbury.

Not long after this, one of the sporting newspapers carried a paragraph that assured gentlemen of the racing fraternity that they would be delighted to learn that TIBERIUS, the champion horse formerly owned by Mr Davenant, had been purchased by that well-known sporting gentleman Mr Happerton, known to all patrons of the turf as one of its most doughty supporters, etc.

'So he has brought it off,' Captain Raff said to himself, reading the paragraph at the Blue Riband. 'See here,' he said to the young man with whom he was playing billiards. 'There is my friend Happerton coming out for that fellow Davenant's Tiberius. Let us hope he has the bargain he thought, eh?'

Part Two

VI

A Situation in the Country

*It may sometimes happen that a young woman, though of good education
and an amiable temper, garlanded with every golden opinion that long exposure to the best families can procure, may find herself not so conveniently
situated as she might wish. In these circumstances she will apprehend that
her accomplishments, her disposition and her good humour are of little
moment, and that only fortitude will see her through.*

The Young Lady's Infallible Guide and Companion (1867)

And so it was settled, and she was to go to Lincolnshire, and be
governess to Mr Davenant's daughter, and live in a great windy house
that looked out over the wolds where there were more rooks than
Christian folk: that was what Eliza said when Miss Ellington told her,
although naturally she meant only to be kind. And when the letter
came for her, although she had long expected it, Miss Ellington went
out into the garden and was so very sad, thinking that she should never
see the dear friends she had made there again, until Mrs Macfarlane
seized her hand, and told her not to be a goose, as there was nothing
here for her to do. Seeing the sense in this – for Eliza was to be married,
and Jane to go to Miss Brotherton's at Warwick and the schoolroom
all emptied – and remembering what her mama had always told her,
that she should be brave, Miss Ellington went inside and busied herself,
played at ombre and read to old Mrs Macfarlane out of the newspaper,
and Mr Macfarlane, coming in from his business, told her that she was
a *dear good girl* and that they *never should get along without her*, and

77

that a bedroom should be kept ready against her return, so that she altogether broke down, in spite of her best resolves, and shed tears all over the *County Chronicle* as she read.

'You will be a country girl now, you'll see,' Eliza said, 'with nothing to stir you but sheep and mangel-wurzels,' and Miss Ellington said she could not see the difference, as they were very quiet and genteel here, and saw almost no one. 'In any case it is not for a fortnight,' Jane said, thinking to cheer her, 'and we can be very jolly in that time.' Yet Miss Ellington had to allow that the two weeks hung heavy on her hands, and though countless small recreations were proposed for her – a visit to Kenilworth, an excursion in Mr Murray's carriage, he that was to marry Eliza – and though she professed to enjoy them, her heart was not in the business. She supposed it was always so, and that the soldier who is to be posted to India gets no pleasure from his furlough. She knew she got no pleasure from hers.

'You are a sad girl, Annie, for all that you profess to be gay,' Eliza had once told her, and Miss Ellington supposed that she was right. Certainly there was a moment as she sat in her room assembling her things when she was almost overcome with melancholy, for each had some pleasant association: the *Christian Year* that Mr Atherton had given her when she made her first Communion, and Macaulay's essays that had been her father's, a comforter that Jane worked for her one December and everyone thought was for Mrs Macfarlane. But then, having stowed these articles away, and reflected on her circumstances, she felt suddenly more bold and thought that there were other places in the world than Warwickshire and other folk than the Macfarlanes, for all their kindness, and that it would be a relief to get away from that odious Mr Murray, who had once taken her hand and tried to kiss her. She determined that she should make a list of her accomplishments, which her papa always said was the sovereignest way of inspiring confidence in a young woman.

Of my appearance I perhaps ought not to speak, other than to say that I am twenty-three years old, five feet four inches in height ('a maypole'

Mama used to say in jest, who was only four feet ten) and with hair that ill-natured people would call red but I should style chestnut.

Of my capacities, I might say that I have a sound knowledge of English grammar, and its peculiarities, an undoubted proficiency in the languages of France and Italy, and a little, a very little, Latin.

That I have studied English history from the date of the Saxon invasions to the Restoration of his Majesty in 1660.

That I have travelled in mathematics to the pons asinorum *and beyond it.*

That I am generally considered to have a fair contralto voice, can sing rounds and glees, accompany at the pianoforte, play at ombre, *preference and other games.*

That I lived fifteen of my years in Thirsk, where Papa had his practice, two in Leicester at Miss Engledow's establishment, and the rest in Warwickshire.

That I have read a good number of Mr Dickens's novels, and Mr Tennyson's poems, Mrs Chapone's letters and Mr Chambers's Cyclopedia.

That a gentleman once proposed for me, but that, seeing the connection could not possibly be advantageous to me, and would be even less so to him, I declined his offer.

There! Miss Ellington wrote, with the ink spilling out of the pen onto her fingers, *I think I have said enough.*

*

Miss Ellington bade farewell to the Macfarlanes as they clustered around their veranda, with the station fly waiting at the gate, and old Mrs Macfarlane, who could not leave her chair, waving from the parlour window and Eliza saying that she *never would forget her*, and Mr Macfarlane smiling, and even Harrison the gardener, whom she had never loved, looking up from the far lawn to bob his head. The carriage rattled along the newly Macadamed road and into Warwick, and the figures whom she tried her hardest to keep in view faded away to nothing, and for all her semblance of good spirits she felt what she oh so often felt, that she was all alone in the world with only God to guide her.

*

Lincoln, where Miss Ellington's train took her, was a very clerical town. She thought she had never seen a place so full of clergymen: the station forecourt was quite black with them, and Mr Alloway said it was hardly possible to throw a stone without hitting a minor canon on his way to early service. Mr Alloway was a friend of Mr Macfarlane's, commissioned to give her luncheon, and this passed off very pleasantly in a great high dining room looking out over a languid river, where Miss Ellington ate oysters, which she never did in her life before. Mr Alloway, whom she thought a very civil man, was greatly interested to hear that she was to work for Mr Davenant, and remarked that she should want for her wages, as that gentleman was sorely pressed. 'And what of his daughter,' she asked, 'whom I am to teach?' But Mr Alloway only shook his head and said that she should see what there was to see when she saw it.

There was a gig to take her to Scroop – it was but fifteen miles – and as Mr Alloway handed her into it she looked up to see the spire of the cathedral with grey clouds massed behind it and the birds whirling through the pale sky – a melancholy sight, it seemed to her, to which all the clergymen who hopped and croaked about like human versions of the rooks were welcome. And so she sat in the gig, with her feet above the trunks, and took stock of her surroundings. Such a country as this she *never saw*, and as unlike their dear Warwickshire as it was possible to conceive. Nothing to be seen but low, flat plains, with the wolds rising away in the distance, the waters out over the bright green grass and a breeze blowing in from the east across the tops of the brown hedgerows, so that it would not have been strange to peep between the fence posts and see Lady Dedlock out a-wandering. Nothing to be heard but the cries of the birds and the sough of the wind, the rattle of the transom and the horse's breath. Something of her feelings must have communicated themselves to the driver of the gig – a very picturesque gentleman in a moleskin jacket and gaiters – for there came a moment when he grinned and said he hoped she was not tiring of the view. 'No indeed, sir,' she said, 'for I have seen nothing like it.' And so they went on, past mouldering piles of beet and turnip racked up at the roadside, and mournful little turnings into nowhere, and shy farmhouses huddled under grim fir hedges, meeting no one save a farm cart or a squire on his cob, while the wind blew and rain began to fall, and she unfurled the umbrella that Mrs Macfarlane had given her and was thankful for its shelter.

Presently the gig jangled along a little cindery path, past an inn nearly suffocated by the weight of thatch that lay upon it, and the driver announced with great solemnity that 'Here be Scroop' as if they were approaching the Haymarket rather than a dozen little cottages, a tumbledown old church with the stone falling into the road, and a dismal green that seemed more in the river than out of it. She could see the roofs and turrets of the hall in the distance, beyond a patch of woodland, and here the gig bounced and tumbled first along a terrible dirt track and then a long gravel drive that led up to a great grey house, with the water dripping from its eaves and the rooks raging in the elm trees yonder. Here on the steps two gentlemen stood talking, to one of whom the driver, who doubled as postman, handed a letter and a newspaper, before depositing her trunk on the ground, and she supposed that one or other of them would assist her, only neither of them did, but hurried away in a very emphatic manner into the house, leaving her with her baggage upon the stones. And all this – the grinding motion of the gig, the melancholy of the surround, the unyielding flatness of the land, the incivility of her hosts – made her wish most fervently that she had not been fetched there, and that she was safe in Warwickshire with her dear girls, or reading to old Mrs Macfarlane out of the newspaper, or even talking to that odious Mr Murray, such was her desire to see a familiar face and not the dismal hedge-tops of Lincolnshire waving in the wind and the rooks taking flight into the great wide sky.

*

It was a bad time to come to Scroop, Mrs Castell observed, for the master – she pronounced the word 'maister' in the drollest way – had lost his money and the house would very likely be sold up. This was said at tea, which seemed to Miss Ellington a very curious meal and not at all like the genteel refections of Warwickshire, where the bread and butter rarely came in inch-thick slabs placed threefold upon your plate, or the bohea brewed up so strong that it required equal amounts of milk to make it palatable. Still, she allowed that they were very comfortable in the kitchen, with the fire glowing beside them and a candle or two spilling light onto the great oak table at which Mrs Castell presided; and in the conversation that followed, although the Lincolnshire dialect was unintelligible to her, she learned much about the circumstances of her arrival. The gentleman who had driven her from Lincoln was Mr Jorkins. ('That Jorkins,' said Mrs Castell, with an infinite contempt. 'Wife dead and two babbies to raise,' Hester added, who perhaps had her hopes.) Mr Jorkins had brought a letter, its author unknown, by which Mr Davenant had been much put out, and which had closeted him in his study with his confidential friend, Mr Glenister ('All on account of that horse', Dora suggested, and was immediately shushed by Mrs Castell). Who was Mr Glenister, Miss Ellington asked, and received the answer that he was 'a gentleman who lived near by' (Dora), 'Mr Davenant's friend as is heeded by him in all things' (Hester). Dora and Hester had each of them great white faces and hair done up in sausage curls, which was not a fashion that they knew on the streets of Kenilworth.

They had not been long at tea when Mr Davenant himself arrived in their midst, carrying a piece of paper which he instantly threw into the kitchen fire. He was, Miss Ellington decided, a rather short, grave-voiced man, perhaps forty years of age, with a singular manner. When

82

he saw her he at once commanded her to stay in her chair, from which she was on the point of rising, and apologised for the bad grace with which, as he acknowledged, he had greeted her arrival. Had she had a pleasant trip from Lincoln? He hoped that she had not been incommoded by that Jorkins, who was a shocking bad driver of a gig, as everybody knew. He said he was hungry, took one of Mrs Castell's mighty slabs of bread and butter, but left it crumbled on his plate. He accepted a cup of tea, on which he complimented Hester, who had brought it, but left half of it untouched, and Miss Ellington wondered what he had to vex him and why he looked at the tea things, and the fire, and Mrs Castell's Madonna front (which altogether failed to conceal the grey curls behind it) as if they were the most mournful prospect in the world.

When the tea was finished, and Hester had cleared away the leavings, and Mrs Castell stoked up the fire, which she did in a furious way, as if she smelt unseen enemies hidden behind the coals, Mr Davenant proposed that she might like to see his daughter, and so, behaving in a very polite way, opening and closing doors with an extreme punctiliousness, which courtesy quite won her over after his previous ill manners, he led her into the hall of the house and thence along a winding corridor on which hung the portraits of some very dismal old ladies and gentlemen whom Miss Ellington supposed to be his forebears. 'You will find that my daughter is not quite all that she might be,' he said as they approached the corridor's end, with what she took to be a little catch in his voice, and she remarked that she liked all children and wanted only to serve them, whereupon he gave her a sad look and said that he would be very grateful indeed if she could find a way to serve this one.

Miss Ellington had barely time to remark the singularity of these words when, opening the door with a little silver key he produced from a chain that hung around his neck, he led her into a small, gloomy chamber, the window of which looked out onto a wild, windy garden, all quite gathered up in the long shadows flung by the house. Here, in a chair, quite silent, with her hands folded in her lap, sat a girl of perhaps fourteen, with an odd, twisted face, very pale eyes and the whitest hair Miss Ellington ever saw. There was a scattering of toys on the carpet before her, and a jigsaw that looked as if its pieces had never been disturbed. 'This is Evie,' Mr Davenant said, and the girl, who had taken no notice of their coming into the room, now started up at the mention of her name, gaped at the sight of her father standing in the doorway and plunged towards him, so that he caught her hand and secured it in the crook of his arm.

'Here is Miss Ellington, Evie,' he said, in a voice too loud for the room, and the girl looked at her, wildly and without comprehension, like Caliban, she thought, first glimpsing the visitors to Prospero's island. 'I am pleased to meet you, Evie,' she said, imitating Mr Davenant's stentorian tone and putting out her hand, and the girl took it very shyly between her fingers and indeed would have kept hold of it had Mr Davenant not told her to give it up. The sight of her was a horror to Miss Ellington, but she enquired, as brightly as she could, 'Is this where Evie spends her time?' and Mr Davenant said that hitherto she had been accustomed to sit in the kitchen, under Mrs Castell's eye, but that there was an old schoolroom, at the top of the house which he had had put in order. All this time the girl was regarding them with bold, unyielding eyes, darting out of a skin so white that it was all one could do to determine where flesh ended and hair began. And then the wind rushed under the door to set the candle a-flicker, a footfall sounded in a passage far away, and Miss Ellington thought that she should not like to be Evie Davenant, here in this great lonely house in Lincolnshire, with the waters out across the meadows and a strange lady come halfway across England to quench her spirit.

That night they dined in a great shabby dining room under a dusty chandelier. The child sat with them, but took no interest in the food on her plate. She had a toy – a rag doll, very miserably stitched up – that she twisted about her face and neck in a disagreeable manner. Mr Davenant talked very freely before her, at the same time keeping up a pretence that she understood what was said. 'My daughter has been looking forward above all to your coming,' he said at one point. 'Is that not so, Evie?' And Evie, thus appealed to, ran the rag doll along her cheek and looked at it very eagerly. 'And I have been looking forward to it very much too,' Miss Ellington replied, 'for I am sure Evie is a good girl who will repay her teaching.' 'She is a very good girl,' Mr Davenant said again, and Evie, hearing him speak, balanced the doll on her shoulder in a way that was half comic and half terrible. Outside the wind was raging against the window and the trees lashed at the panes like so many wooden fingers.

After dinner Mrs Castell took Evie away to bed – she treated her very tenderly, Miss Ellington noticed – and she and Mr Davenant sat alone at the great table built for a dozen. 'You will perhaps have gained some idea of my daughter's accomplishments,' he said, and she bowed her head, not thinking there was anything she could decently say. 'She must of all things be kept quiet,' he went on. 'Have her wants and fancies attended to. I am sure I do not need to explain. Mrs Castell knows her better than I.' 'I am sure,' Miss Ellington said, feeling that she could not stay silent, 'that she is very loving.' 'Loving?' He repeated the word. 'Eh? Oh yes, I have no doubt she is, in her way,' he said, and the look on his face was very poignant to behold. 'And now, Miss Ellington, we had better see if they have provided for you, etcetera.' After which Mrs Castell marched her away to an attic room under the eaves, to which her boxes had already been carried, informed her that candles were expensive and scarce, and, it being about nine o'clock, and the rural habit to retire early, left her to her own devices. And so she lay awake, listening to the rain beat upon the window, and the mice scuttle in the roof, and some sharp, insistent noise which terrified her until she discovered that it was her own breath rising in the night air, and wished very much that she were back in Warwickshire with a silent lawn beyond the window rather than a great wild garden, and a grandfather clock ticking comfortably behind the door.

*

As to their establishment there in Lincolnshire, Miss Ellington discovered it to be a very modest one. Three indoor servants, two men to work the stable yard and Mr Curbishley to oversee them was the limit of Mr Davenant's staff. Once, Mrs Castell said, there was a butler and a kitchenmaid and a regiment of gardeners, but all that was gone along with Mr Davenant's money, and now Mrs Castell wound the clock herself, the master poured his own wine, the grass grew a foot high and there was no one to cut it. Nobody came unless it were the baker's van, or Mr Glenister, or a travelling pedlar unpacking his wares on the kitchen table so that Hester could buy a penn'orth of pins or two farthings' worth of silk thread. Mrs Castell went to bed at nine, the front door was locked half an hour later and the house was asleep by ten. And yet post there was a-plenty, all brought up by Mr Jorkins, laid out on a silver tray and taken off straightaway to the master's study for him to ponder.

But if they were modest and quiet, did not tend their garden, and spent their money on penny pin-packets, they were not, Miss Ellington discovered, without their resources. On the contrary, they had a consuming interest that lay beyond any human association or social prospect, for all that it resided in a stable, slept on straw, lived on hay and had its water from a bucket. What did they talk about there in Lincolnshire? Why Tiberius. Nothing but Tiberius. Dora said when the Derby was confirmed – which everyone supposed it should be – she would wager the money she had in the National Savings Bank upon him. Hester had a little keepsake book full of pictures of him cut out of *Bell's Life* and *The Sportsman's Magazine*.

There came a day when, such was the volume of chatter about this Lincolnshire Pegasus, that Miss Ellington determined to see him for herself, borrowed a pair of pattens that lay on the block by the kitchen door and set off across the stone yard to the stables. She did not quite know what she expected to see there, being unable to tell a thoroughbred from a carthorse, but Tiberius, she thought, was decid-edly slim: a lithe black horse that stood all alone in the corner of the stables, would not be petted and stamped his feet very violently if anyone came near. She remarked to Jem Claypole, the stable boy who stood nearby, that he seemed a very nervous animal, and this Jem

86

confirmed: 'It's twice he have run away wi' the maister, for all a whip were taken to him.' And then just as she was about to return to the house, finding the smell of the beasts, and other things, not to her taste, a curious thing happened. A small, dark-faced man stuck his head in at the door and, seeing them there, hastily withdrew it, but not before the boy made an angry gesture at his retreating figure and indeed seized up a pitchfork that stood against the rail and would, she thought, have actually assaulted the man had he come nearer. 'Who is that, that you should wish to take a pitchfork to him?' she enquired, whereupon he said that it was John Wilkinson, who had been dismissed by the master but would keep a-coming back and a-spying on the house, and maister had given instructions for him to be druv away.

All of which confirmed Miss Ellington's opinion that Scroop was a remarkable place, and its inhabitants yet more remarkable still. She asked Mrs Castell once – remembering the pleasant recreations of Warwickshire – if the servants ever went anywhere, and the house-keeper said that once a year, on the May holiday, Mr Curbishley hired a wagonette and drove them to Lincoln for the fair. In the dark evenings Dora and Hester played spillikins together, while Mrs Castell read at *Foxe's Book of Martyrs* with a very dreadful expression. There was talk of ghosts and spectres, of a path in the woods where not even Mr Davenant would go in broad daylight and a parlourmaid that drowned herself for love and stalks the lower field, beseeching the Gypsy who betrayed her; talk, too, of the master and how he was a broken man and would not bear the shame of being sold up, and of there no longer being Davenants in a place where Davenants had always been.

Patchwork of ivy and scrollwork of fern!

And so the days passed, with such an undifferentiated regularity that the smallest trifle took on a momentous significance, a letter to Hester from her cousin in Leicestershire became a great event and a walk in the woods or the fields beyond a grand excursion. As for Evie, the poor child was very backward in her little intellects, stared blindly at the words printed on the page before her and was quite deficient in sensibility. Thinking to amuse her on their first day in the schoolroom Miss Ellington took down an almanac which she had found on the library shelf showing ladies and gentlemen in costumes of olden time – a knight tilting at the quintain, Queen Elizabeth and her courtiers at Tilbury Dock – but from this she shrank, saying that they frightened her. Miss Ellington asked her what there was that did not frighten her, and that she liked, and she said the cat, and a ride in a carriage, and her papa. And yet she was an affectionate thing, would smile and chatter if you did not tax her, and gave great longing looks out of the window into lands that none could see save she herself. Miss Ellington had her story from Mrs Castell, which was that she was born early, being then so inconsiderable a scrap that she must be kept in cotton wool in her father's cigar box and fed milk through a straw.

And this, Miss Ellington found, was the limit of their life there in Lincolnshire. Mr Davenant sat in his study or took his dogs out a-coursing; Tiberius stamped in his stable; Dora and Hester went whispering by on the stairs; the wind murmured in the reed-beds; the cut logs mouldered by the barn.

*

Mr Glenister's visits were as regular as the rain. Mr Glenister who, with his bailiff and his estate and his £2,000, was, as Mrs Castell put it, 'as neat a catch as ever a young woman put out a hook for'. The difficulty, alas, was that there was not a single spinster lady in the parish, excepting the rector's sister, Miss Trafford, who could not be less than sixty-five years of age, and Miss Trimmington of Scroop Parva, who never left her bed on account of some deformity of the spine. For herself, Miss Ellington thought Mr Glenister, who was certainly tall and nice-looking, somewhat supercilious, for when they first met he made an allusion to one of Mr Browning's poems and seemed surprised that she recognised it, and said that she was no doubt a great bluestocking.

There was another singular thing about Mr Glenister, Miss Ellington discovered, and that was his affection for Evie. The interest was reciprocated, for she ran towards him whenever she saw him, and altogether delighted in the things he told her, though Miss Ellington doubted that she understood the half. They were sitting in the schoolroom one morning, with the cat between them and a slate on which Evie had scratched a few hieroglyphics of her own devising cast aside on the carpet, when, having come into the room and let fall a few pleasantries, he looked very fondly at Evie, who had now turned her attention to the cat, and said:

'She is a dear good girl, is she not?'

Miss Ellington said what she truthfully believed, that she thought she had a most affectionate nature, whereupon he smiled very courteously and continued: 'And yet it seems to me, Miss Ellington, that there are times when you are sharp with her. I make no criticism of you, you understand, for I know the poor girl would try a saint's patience, but it pains me to see it.'

This was so nearly the truth that Miss Ellington did not like to dispute it, but said merely that she should do her best not to be vexed, &c., her cheeks crimson all the while, whereupon he smiled and said that she should have to find someone else to bluestocking, for it could not be poor Evie.

'Who is this Mr Happerton of whom everyone talks?' she asked, the next time that she saw him.

'Mr Happerton?' he said – they were sitting in the schoolroom again, with the cat prowling between them and Evie teasing it with a ball of darning wool. 'Who has been talking of Mr Happerton?'

'Not I, for one,' she said, thinking that he was vexed by the question. 'But Dora and Hester have spoken of him, and Mrs Castell supposes that he will be coming soon.'

'There never was a secret to be kept in a country house,' Mr Glenister said, more amused now than irked. 'Mr Happerton is a gentleman with whom you will very shortly have some acquaintance. Indeed, it would not surprise me if he were here within the week.'

'But who is he?' Miss Ellington wondered. 'And why should he come to Scroop? Has Mr Davenant sold his estate?'

'Not that,' Mr Glenister said. 'Rather, he has sold Tiberius.'

'Tiberius!' she exclaimed.

'The very same,' Mr Glenister went on. 'Mr Happerton has bought him, but he has no property of his own and, so far as I understand, wishes to have the horse kept here until some better prospect offers itself.'

'Will that not be . . .' – she hesitated to find the correct word – 'inconvenient for Mr Davenant?'

'It will be more than inconvenient,' Mr Glenister said, who had a trick of smiling in a very quizzical way. 'I should say that it will eat into his soul. It is not that he cares so very much about horses, simply that to lose it would be like having his wood grubbed up. But Evie' – raising his voice – 'you must not persecute that cat. It has done you no harm, and its ears are its own, surely?'

And so it became known in the house that Mr Davenant had sold Tiberius, his pride and joy, and that Mr Happerton, whom nobody knew anything of, and as Dora said could not in the nature of things be a gentleman, would be coming to claim him.

*

Scroop possessed a cat, to which Evie was violently attached. Indeed it was sometimes thought that she preferred Pusskin – this was the animal's name – to any of the human company she saw around her. But this is by the by. It was a clear April morning, not much more than a day or so after Miss Ellington's conversation with Mr Glenister, and they had not been long at the breakfast table, when it was discovered that Pusskin was not in the house. Generally this would not have excited any remark, for Pusskin came and went, was devious in his ways and promiscuous in his associations, but by the luncheon hour, when he had still not returned, a search was instituted, the barns looked into, the dairy investigated to see if he had not been locked in among the cream-pots, &c. Still there was no sign, and Evie, who had been assured that all would be well, grew quite disconsolate and would have blundered through every room in the house had she not been prevented. So the afternoon progressed and, being for a short while at liberty, Miss Ellington decided to take a walk in the gardens, not absolutely in search of their absent friend, but with the thought that she might, as she went, look out for him, call his name and so forth.

It was a bright, sunny afternoon – the first such, Miss Ellington thought, since she came there – and having reached the limit of the garden, it was a small matter to press on into the wood. Here, she knew, Mr Davenant kept his gibbet, with all the vermin of the estate hung up by their forelegs, but such was the promise of the day that she thought: I could bear even this. Imagine her horror, then, when, approaching the block, she found strung up on it nothing less than the body of Pusskin, stone dead, with a great nail driven through his neck into the wood beneath. So startled was Miss Ellington by the sight that she gave a cry of terror and ran back into the kitchen and, such was the pitch of her sobbing, could tell no one what had happened until Mrs Castell made her plunge her face into a tub of water and drink a glass of cherry brandy.

Subsequently – the whole house by now being in uproar – an investigation was made. Mr Davenant himself went down to the gibbet and retrieved the body of Pusskin, whom he interred beneath the hawthorn tree, but as to how he had come there and who had played this cruel trick, there was no clue. The keeper knew nothing, said that he had left the rail almost bare the previous night with nothing on it but a pair of polecats, and Mr Davenant swore that any man in his employ who could be proved to have done it would be instantly dismissed, which could not be, as the stable lads valued Pusskin as a mouser, and Mr Curbishley said that he liked nothing more than a sight of a fine, proud cat. And so they had another puzzle to add to the mystery of Mr Happerton, and how he had come by Tiberius, and who could tell which should be the more readily solved?

*

'And who lives here, I wonder,' Mr Happerton remarked as the carriage swung along the road from Scroop at great peril to its springs. 'Bluebeard and his wives?'

'Don't seem much of a shop,' Captain Raff observed – he was sulking because Mr Happerton had declined to stop at Lincoln for lunch. 'Doosid lot of timber all over the place.'

'All gone to seed, too,' Mr Happerton observed. 'Five years since it was cut down, I'll be bound. And see how that field next to the fence posts is taking the water. A man who took an interest in the place would have the thing drained.' The carriage was in sight of the disreputable caryatid and a cloud of rooks went swarming up into the dull grey sky. 'Now, who is there to open the door?' Mr Happerton mused. 'No butler these days, I daresay. Well, we shall have to make do with Mrs Castell.'

'Mrs Who?' Captain Raff wondered, as that lady appeared on the step with a white-faced maid behind her.

'Housekeeper,' Mr Happerton remarked, who seemed remarkably well informed about Scroop and its retainers. 'Been here since the old king died. Thirty pounds a year and that kind of thing. How do, Mrs Castell? No, I didn't come in Jorkins' cart. Don't know Jorkins. Found a carriage from the livery stable more convenient. Tell the boy – if there's a boy – to put it up somewhere, would you, and I'll just step down. Mr Davenant here? No? Well, tell him I look forward to waiting upon him, would you?'

And with Captain Raff to support him, and Mrs Castell casting anxious glances at the carriage – which was not quite a barouche but something very similar to it, the like of which had not been seen in that part of Lincolnshire for half a dozen years – and the rooks soaring into the leaden sky, Mr Happerton jumped down and took his first steps – very confident steps they were too – into Scroop Hall.

*

It was generally agreed that Mr Happerton came to Scroop as if he meant business. As well as Captain Raff he brought with him a carpet bag, apparently cut from the same cloth, as both were left to kick their heels in the hall while Mr Happerton went on a tour of the premises. Mr Davenant saw him come from the study window, where he sat with the bills on his desk, heard the loud voice in which he addressed Mrs Castell and ground his teeth in shame. He heard Mrs Castell ask 'Would the gentlemun take a glass of wine?' and Mr Happerton remark that no, dammy, a cup of tea would do for him, and somehow the shame was redoubled and the bills stared up at Mr Davenant from the desk like little white lozenge-stones in a graveyard.

It was also generally agreed that no one at Scroop had met anyone like Mr Happerton before. He was what is known as a fashionable sporting gentleman, which is to say that he wore a pair of top-boots, and a cutaway coat, and a white stock, and was decorated with more pins and brooches, all of them in some way describing the shape of a horse, or a bridle, or a pair of spurs, than would generally ornament a pincushion. Certainly, they never had anything like him in Warwickshire. He was a tall, broad-shouldered, thrusting kind of man, rather red in the face, lately married – there was apparently a Mrs Happerton left behind at her father's house in Belgravia – and very inquisitive. Jem, who accompanied him on his tour, said that he looked into everything, peered into the bins where the bran was stored, inspected the whips and the curry-combs, asked Mr Curbishley what he thought about a dozen things, all in the space of five minutes, while Captain Raff walked about in the yard, asked where the dairy was and was later observed to put his thumb in the cream.

Curiously enough, when they convened later that evening in the servants' hall, with the door shut and the gentlemen drinking port in the dining room, they agreed that, of the two, it was Captain Raff that they did not like – 'a nasty, sneaking kind of a body' Mrs Castell said, and Hester wondered that he could not find somebody to brush his coat for him. As for Mr Happerton, although they were startled by his dress and his demeanour – for he was somewhat loud as well as talking incessantly of horses – they thought that he meant no harm. He had heard something of Evie, too, talked to her and asked her how she did, and this, too, was noted and approved of.

And yet Miss Ellington acknowledged that it was Mr Davenant that she wondered at most, who roamed about the place like a ghost, who sat very miserably at dinner while Mr Happerton made his little jokes and Captain Raff cracked filberts into a saucer, and who closeted himself very comfortlessly in his study to hear whatever it was that Mr Happerton had to say to him. There was a particular morning when Mr Happerton saddled up Tiberius, and with Captain Raff following on an old cob, cantered off across the wolds to 'put the horse through his paces', as he said, and the look on Mr Davenant's face as this little cavalcade set off along the drive was one of simple torture.

And so Mr Happerton's stay continued, to the satisfaction of nearly everyone. He went to church on Sunday morning and sang the hymns and the responses very loudly. He won great approbation by stopping an old woman in the lane, as she laboured back from the village bake-house with her dinner in a pail, taking the dinner home for her and presenting her with a shilling into the bargain. He looked at all the tenants' cottages, admired their design and admitted the cheapness of their rents. Captain Raff meanwhile lounged in the shrubbery smoking cigars and looked as if he were very bored.

'Mr Happerton seems a very agreeable man,' Miss Ellington remarked to Mr Glenister as they sat one afternoon in the schoolroom, where he had come to see Evie.

'Agreeable? Eh – oh yes. Very agreeable, I don't doubt,' Mr Glenister said, with a rather peculiar look on his face, as if he thought her impertinent for saying as much.

'Captain Raff, I think, is perhaps less so.'

'Captain Raff!' Mr Glenister laughed, as if she had said something amusing. 'Do you know, I have asked Captain Raff half a dozen times what regiment it was that he sold out of and never got an answer? Here Evie, let us untangle this wool and see if it cannot be put to good use.'

'It is very hard for Mr Davenant,' Miss Ellington said.

'Very hard. Here, miss – you will never unwind that knot by pulling it so. But there is some mystery about Mr Happerton, I think.'

'A mystery? What kind of a mystery?'

But Mr Glenister would not say any more, continued to unwind the ball of wool with Evie, whose absorption in her work was very droll to see, and presently rode away to his dinner.

There was one more incident from Mr Happerton's stay at Scroop which Miss Ellington noted, for it seemed to her almost as curious as Mr Glenister's conversation in the schoolroom. There came an evening – perhaps it was on the day before Mr Happerton's departure – when Evie disappeared. This was a not uncommon event, and by no means alarming, as she did not leave the house and was generally found hiding in the dairy or beneath one of the beds. On this occasion – it was about seven o'clock and growing dark – she was in neither of these places, and, growing vexed, Miss Ellington stepped into each of the lower rooms of the house in turn, calling her name, sweeping up curtains and peering behind doors.

There was no sign of her, and Miss Ellington was about to return to the kitchen, when she heard from Mr Davenant's study what she imagined to be the noise of wood upon stone, and, remembering that she sometimes crept in there to sit in her father's chair, the governess determined to roust her out. 'Evie,' she began, advancing into the room, 'you are a bad girl to run off so, when everyone is looking for you.' Only it was not Evie sitting in Mr Davenant's oak-backed chair with a sheet of paper before him on the desk and the lamp burning at his side but Mr Happerton. Greatly embarrassed, Miss Ellington made her apologies and was about to retire, when Mr Happerton called her back.

'A very natural mistake to make, Miss Ellington. You saw a light and assumed it was Miss Davenant. I suppose she has a habit of absenting herself in this way?'

'I think she likes the upset it brings, though she is always very contrite when we find her.'

'Is she? Well, who is to tell what goes on in her head, I wonder?'

He looked as if he might be about to say something else, when all

of a sudden there was a tap on the door and one of the stable lads –
whose presence in the house confirmed the urgency of the request –
declared that Captain Raff wished to see him particular in the yard. At
this Mr Happerton instantly quitted the room, leaving Miss Ellington
in solitary possession. The sheet of paper at which he had been working
still lay on the desk, and she could not disallow the curiosity she felt
to see what he had been writing. Imagine her surprise, then, to discover
that it was not a letter or a schedule of some kind but Mr Davenant's
signature – Samuel R. Davenant – in facsimile ten or twenty times
down the page. And then, just as Miss Ellington stood with the paper
in her hand – she had taken it up the better to inspect it – there came
a cry from the kitchen, announcing that Evie was found, and she hurried
away to comfort her, so that the question of why Mr Happerton should
want to sit in his host's study with his host's lamp at his side contriving
versions of his host's signature vanished altogether from her mind.

VII

Boulogne-sur-mer

No true Englishman goes abroad after the summer. Those that do are an obscure and extravagant breed. They can be seen slinking through the streets of Munich, Pau, Ostend and half-a-dozen other places. No respectable inn will take them; no gentleman wants them at his table. Their particularity is this: that each, singly and severally, has something to hide.
John Bull: A Study in National Temperament (1866)

Boulogne out of season is not much of a place. The wind tears in off the sea and sends the masts of the fishing smacks drawn up in the harbour all a-clatter, and, blowing in against the sails hung up for repair in the chandlers' yards, makes the most melancholy sound ever known. The nursemaids and their charges who were here in summer have packed their boxes and gone home, and the sleek papas come for a month's recreation from their counting houses or their offices on 'Change have all gone with them. There are no more fashionable preachers to delight the congregation of the English church, and the little circulating library with its three hundred English novels and its guinea subscription is in dusty hibernation. In fact the place is altogether deserted except for half-pay officers, a lady or two who is perhaps no better than she should be, and one or two strange, dilapidated men with devil-may-care moustaches and defiant attitudes in whose whereabouts the sheriff's officers may possibly take an interest, but about whom nobody else cares a jot. Curiously the disappearance of the English

– the English papas with their newspapers and their tall hats, the English children shrieking down to the beach at low tide, the English mamas taking the air on the promenade – has had a lowering effect on the indigenous population. Certain of the shopkeepers in the Haute Ville have closed up their shutters for the winter and gone. The fruit-sellers, whom half a dozen painters have so charmingly taken off, have no fruit to sell. The cobbles look as if they had not been swept for a month. It is all dreadfully dull.

To little Mr Lythgoe, making his way gingerly up the path from the harbour – it had been a heavy crossing from Dover and his feet had a habit of walking off in directions where he did not want them to lead him – it seemed even less of a place. It was a bright, cold morning towards the end of January, with gulls screeching over the tops of the fishing boats, and Mr Lythgoe thought that he had never seen such a spectacle. The Haute Ville and its dirty cobbles had no charms for him. The famous ramparts he dismissed with a glance. He passed the cathedral, whose spire aggrandises over the town, and as a follower of Mr Wesley, was disgusted by it. The column which a great emperor had erected to honour his army disgusted him even more. He had a piece of paper in the breast pocket of his coat to which he kept referring, and this, together with frequent solicitation of passers-by – he would hail them with a *pardonnez monsieur* and thrust the piece of paper under their noses – impeded his progress, but he laboured on, shielding his face every so often against the wind, at one point losing his grip on the paper and having to chase it into a disreputable courtyard where an old woman feeding sardines to a cat looked at him enquiringly, and made his way past the cathedral and Napoleon's column to reach the southernmost quarter of the town.

As Mr Lythgoe continued along an esplanade on which marram grass grew over the sand hills and bathing huts with rusting wheels lay waiting for someone to repair them, the houses of the town began to thin out, became no more than a series of tumbledown cottages, made out of wood and plasterboard, with gaps showing in their frontages and stovepipe chimneys tilting at crazy angles to their roofs. The air was decidedly nautical – there were nets hanging out to dry over upturned barrels, with the ends secured by stones from the beach, and rowing boats in need of caulking propped up on wooden stands – and Mr Lythgoe, consulting his piece of paper, thought that he had mistaken the way. 'An odd sort of place, anyhow,' he pronounced, looking at the fishing nets and the upturned rowing boats, and a pile of fish-heads – the eyes of which, to his horror, seemed to follow him as he passed – and other nautical leavings over which a couple of cats and a dog were squabbling. But then another habitation, set a little apart from the line of cottages, with smoke drifting from its tin chimney-stack and rank grass rising almost to its door, caught his eye and he moved hesitantly on.

The door of the cottage was half-open and there was a figure standing on the wooden steps, half in and half out under the lintel, so that the front half of his body was exposed to view but his face gathered up in shadow. Mr Lythgoe, squinting up through the wind, saw a tall man, who might perhaps have passed his fiftieth year, hatless, with iron-coloured hair, a protuberant jaw and very hard grey eyes. Mr Lythgoe thought that he did not like those eyes. The eyes and the hair gave way to an equally grey waistcoat, with a watch chain and some seals hanging out of it, a white shirt and a pair of black trousers. All this convinced Mr Lythgoe that the apparition was very probably a gentleman and almost certainly the person he sought.

Seeing Mr Lythgoe, the man gazed down curiously from the steps, and Mr Lythgoe told himself that he did not like that look. But then he remembered that he had been commissioned merely to deliver a message, that the manner in which this message might be received was nothing to him, and that whatever happened, the man could not eat him. Accordingly he put down the case he had been carrying and asked, with an air of genuine enquiry, but in the manner of one who wants an opinion confirmed:

'Mightn't your name be Pardew?'

The man moved out of the doorway so that the whole of him could be seen in the frame of light that glowed from the room behind.

'No one of that name here,' he said, shortly. 'Arbuthnot or Harrison might serve, but not that other.'

A yard or two distant now from the grey eyes and the prognathous jaw, Mr Lythgoe could see that there were several buttons missing from the waistcoat and that one of the shirtsleeves inclined to raggedness. He had an idea, too, that the tobacco packed in the bowl of the pipe the man had in the corner of his mouth was of the very cheapest kind, that stevedores and sailors smoked. All this served to lessen his respect.

'Gammon,' he said. 'Your name's Pardew or I'm Lord John. Why, I've a letter in my pocket from the gentleman who sent me, taking you off to a "T".'

'Well, you and that gentleman are mistaken,' said the man who did not wish to be called Pardew. 'You ain't a policeman, are you? Nor a sheriff's officer?'

'No, I'm not. And you know I'm not. Policemen and sheriffs' officers don't come all polite, or asking a person's name.'

'Well – perhaps they don't. And what might your name be, Mr——?'

'Lythgoe,' said Mr Lythgoe, who was growing rather tired of this conversation.

'And who might be the gentleman that sent you?'

'Fair's fair. You didn't want to tell me your name. I suppose I don't have to tell you his?'

'No more you don't,' said the man who was not Pardew. 'But then, if I was that way inclined, I could shut the door in your face. But I'm not that kind of man, you see.'

'Ain't you, though?'

'Perhaps you'd better step inside, Mr Lythgoe. Jemima!' he called over his shoulder, although every word of his previous conversation would have been clearly audible to any occupant of the room behind him. 'Here. There is a visitor come.'

Climbing nimbly up the steps, with his case under his arm, and the last of the wind tugging at his legs as if it meant to overcome and subdue him even yet, Mr Lythgoe found himself in a small, untidily furnished chamber, very much cluttered with old boxes and upturned crates, into which the light came haltingly through a single, dusty window. There was a fire burning in the grate – not a coal fire, but one made of odds and ends of wood – and before it, on a wooden chair, sat a young, but not so very young, woman in a print dress with her eye bent upon the flames.

'My wife,' the man who did not wish to be called Pardew said, rather brazenly, as if one or two people had previously questioned this relationship. 'My dear, this is Mr Lythgoe.'

Mr Lythgoe, who thought she was very good-looking, and wondered how she liked living in a hut, took off his hat.

'Very pleased to make your acquaintance, Mrs——'

Mr Pardew laughed. 'Ha! We'll have no more of that. But the secret's yours and mine, do you hear? My dear' – he addressed himself again to the woman in the chair, while Mr Lythgoe looked at an envelope on the mantelpiece plainly sent to *R. Pardew, Esq.* and thought that if this was a secret it was not very well kept – 'Mr Lythgoe and I have business to discuss. Perhaps you would oblige.'

'If you wish it,' the woman said, and Mr Lythgoe thought that if Mr Pardew might narrowly be described as a gentleman, his wife, if that was what she was, though certainly very good-looking, was probably not a lady. There was a wooden staircase at the back of the room leading to an upper chamber and to this she somewhat hesitantly repaired, giving her master a look – half-meek and half-defiant – that Mr Lythgoe thought very curious. Mr Pardew watched her go.

'Snug little place you have here,' Mr Lythgoe said, who could feel the draught rising under his feet. 'You ain't in any danger when the tide comes in, I hope?'

'None I know of,' said Mr Pardew, who looked at that moment as if he were capable of flinging the sea back personally with his bare hands. 'Now, who is the gentleman who sent you to me, and what does he say?'

Mr Lythgoe hesitated. 'On no account give him my name, d'you hear?' Captain Raff had insisted, but Mr Lythgoe did not think that he was beholden to Captain Raff. 'Well now,' he said nervously, 'I don't know that I can tell you that.'

'Can't you? Well, I don't think there is anything I can tell you then. What will the gentleman in London – for I take it you've come from London, Mr Lythgoe – say when he hears that?'

'It is – Captain Raff,' Mr Lythgoe said, feeling a little queasy from the ship and wishing that he could sit down and be given a glass of water.

'Captain Raff? I don't think I ever heard Captain Raff's name,' Mr Pardew said, rather failing to disguise a suspicion that he and the captain might have had some slight knowledge of each other. 'What does Captain Raff have to say to me?'

Mr Lythgoe hesitated again, and remembered the conversation he had had with Captain Raff in the library of the Blue Riband Club, whose association with horse racing, being a Wesleyan, Mr Lythgoe very much deprecated. 'You can just sound him out,' Captain Raff had said, without explaining what this sounding-out might consist of. 'Give him a hint, and so forth, you know.' In the matter of Captain Raff, Mr Lythgoe knew his conscience to be clear. He thought that Captain Raff was a thoroughly bad man, but even thoroughly bad men may have messages taken for them, and he was mindful of Mrs Lythgoe and his children, who were currently living in two rented rooms in Hoxton. In the matter of Mr Pardew, on the other hand, his conscience was deeply uneasy. The only light reading that Mr Lythgoe allowed himself was the *Methodist Recorder* and one or two of Mr Gilfillan's celebrated literary portraits, but even he, somewhere in the remote chambers of his mind, had heard dim rumours of Mr Pardew. He could not quite recall what it was that Mr Pardew was supposed to have done – whether he had forged a caseful of cheques or robbed a train, or whether he had somehow forged the cheques and robbed the train together – but he suspected that in dealing with Mr Pardew he was touching pitch. And Mr Pardew, looking at him as he stood nervously on the threadbare carpet, knew that his visitor both feared and despised him.

'What does Captain Raff have to say to me?' he repeated. And Mr Lythgoe, who felt that if he did not sit down he would probably faint, cast his mind back again to the conversation in the library of the Blue Riband Club. 'You'll have to entice him,' Captain Raff had said. 'Flatter him a little, you know. Even money says he's up to these dodges, but, well, men like it.' And Captain Raff had impressed on Mr Lythgoe the desirability of persuading Mr Pardew to return to London, which had apparently not had the pleasure of his company these past two years, without at this delicate juncture telling him precisely what it was that he was wanted in London for. 'You see,' Captain Raff had said mysteriously, 'we can't have him knowing our business and then taking his hook, you know?' Mr Lythgoe had not known, but he had remembered the two rented rooms in Hoxton and said that he would do his best.

'I am ... That is ...' He stopped, reaching out a hand to steady himself on the mantelpiece. 'If you'd only give me a glass of water.'

'A glass of water? Certainly. You look as if you would be better off with brandy.'

'No, not brandy,' Mr Lythgoe insisted. He drank off the water slowly, one hand clasped to his forehead. 'The captain is anxious for you to come to London,' he said finally.

'On what errand, I wonder? You see, I'm very comfortable here.' Mr Pardew waved his fingers airily around the cluttered room, with its upturned cases, its dusty window and its little eddies of draughty air, and Mr Lythgoe could not work out whether he was joking or not. 'We have been away for nearly two years, Jemima and I. Why should we want to come back? Did Captain Raff have anything to say about that?' Seeing that the answer was altogether beyond Mr Lythgoe, he went on: 'No, I don't suppose he did. He should have come himself instead of sending some d——d proxy. I mean no offence, Mr Lythgoe. I suppose he has your paper?'

Mr Lythgoe gave the barest perceptible nod. 'There is this,' he said. 'I was told to give you this.'

Mr Pardew took the square envelope, which was bound about with twine and fixed up with a red wax seal, placed it on top of one of the packing cases, but did not appear to want to open it.

'Well, you may thank Captain Raff from me for that – I shall look him up in the Army List and find out all about him – and tell him that I'll consult it at my leisure. And now, if I were you I should take myself off. There's a boat sails at three, I believe. And I should take a glass of brandy. It settles the stomach. And the nerves,' he added, as Mr Lythgoe stepped out of the door.

When his guest had gone, Mr Pardew stood for a long time in the doorway watching the retreating figure pick its way along the marram grass and past the rowing boats that awaited their caulking and eventually gain the esplanade. Then, shutting the door behind him, he went inside. There was more wind blowing in from the sea, and the last thing he saw as the door slammed to was Mr Lythgoe's hat part company with his head and go careening off over the dunes. It was barely two o'clock in the afternoon, but already the light inside the cottage had the greyness of an aquarium, so that Mr Pardew with his jutting chin and his sharp eye might have been some curious fish gliding through the murk of the ocean floor. He lit a lamp, sat himself down on the chair that Jemima had occupied before the fire, tore open the envelope and spilled the contents out over his lap. 'Probably some deuced prospectus,' he said to himself as he did so, but a moment or two's inspection revealed that the first of the pieces of paper on his lap – there were three of them – was a page torn from a newspaper or magazine.

Looking at it closely, Mr Pardew deduced that it was a trade journal of some kind, probably intended for locksmiths, for it described a safe that had lately been installed in the strongroom of Messrs Gallentin & Co., the Leadenhall Street jeweller, a safe made of solid cast iron, to a depth of two inches, and with a lock, devised by Mr Chubb himself, of such ingenuity that a former safe-breaker, let out of prison for the purpose, had spent a morning trying to negotiate it and declared himself baffled. No such safe, the writer declared, had ever been seen before in London, and Messrs Gallentin reposed every confidence in it. A man had been invited to take a sledgehammer to its springs and done nothing, and even

Captain McTurk of the Metropolitan Police Force had signified his approval.

All this Mr Pardew read with great interest. He traced with his finger a little pencilled mark that someone had made beneath Mr Gallentin's encomium to the safe. He smiled very much over the difficulties of the safe-breaker, and when he came to the mention of Captain McTurk he gave a little start, as if he knew the name but did not wish to be reminded of it. Then, putting the article to one side, he picked up the other slips of paper that had fallen out of the envelope. One of these, he instantly saw, was a ferry ticket from Boulogne to Dover. The other was a letter, bound up in a neat little blue envelope, not very lengthy, as it consisted of no more than a couple of pages of foolscap, with no address or date above it and no signature beneath it, but containing one or two suggestions and pieces of advice that Mr Pardew looked at very keenly. He was a thorough man, and the reading of the article and the letter took him a good quarter of an hour. Then he put article, letter and steamer ticket back into the larger envelope, placed it in the drawer of a little lacquered desk – about the only thing of value in the room – and sat down in the armchair. Grey rain was coming in from the sea – the first drops were already scudding against the window – and he watched it as it fell, and listened to the wind whistling through the ships' masts in the harbour.

Presently there came the noise of footsteps descending the stair and Jemima appeared in the room beside him.

'Your friend has gone?'

'He is not my friend, but he has gone. I daresay he will be on the boat by now. Heaving his stomach over the side, I shouldn't wonder.'

'He looked rather a timid little man.'

'Timid? I daresay he is. No doubt when he gets home to his wife and children he is as bold as a lion. It is always the same. Did I ever tell you of the time I met the Earl of Littlehampton?'

'I don't think you did,' said Jemima, the look on whose face suggested that she loved stories of this kind.

'A man who makes a great noise in the world, of course. But put him in a public room, or with fellows who don't know him, and he's as docile as a lamb. They say he eats the countess for his breakfast, though. By the by,' he went on, the tone of his voice changing as he did so, 'how much is owing just now?'

'I think it is about a hundred francs,' Jemima said, with a readiness that suggested she was quite as interested in domestic economy as the Earl of Littlehampton. 'And there is that money to the baker.'

Mr Pardew thought – or perhaps did not think – about the money owing to the baker, staring into the embers of the fire. He shot another little glance at the lacquered desk, and then rose to his feet and began to put on a coat that he retrieved from a hook behind the door.

'You are not going out, surely?'

'It is only a little rain. There is something I need to do.'

Jemima accepted this with her customary meekness. 'Shall you be long?'

'An hour, perhaps. Is there anything in the house?'

'There is not.'

'Then I had better get something,' Mr Pardew said, with his great hand on the door-knob.

Beyond the row of cottages and the marram grass there was a track that followed the line of the sea for a hundred yards or so before rising to the distant cliffs. This Mr Pardew began to follow. He had taken a stick in his hand as he left the house and as he walked he slashed at the bushes that lined his path. The rain fell in torrents around him, driving into his face as he marched, but it could not be said that he noticed it. As he walked, certain incidents in his past life rose unbidden into his head and he found himself thinking about them: a little house he had once rented in St John's Wood with a princely drawing room ornamented by Mr Etty's cupids; a meeting in a room in Carter Lane with policemen's whistles sounding in the street outside; a man who had been Mr Pardew's business partner, and who had unaccountably died, and whom people said that Mr Pardew had murdered. Mr Pardew remembered them all, and as each bygone face and domicile rose into his consciousness he made another slash with his stick.

For all his pride and his savagery, Mr Pardew was a clever man, and he knew, as he stalked along the clifftop with a flock of seabirds whirling above him quite as if he were their chieftain and they meant to follow him to the ends of the earth, that the sealed room in which he fancied that he lived his life had now been opened to admit a chink of light. He had been gone from England two years, and his wanderings in that time would have astonished even one of Mr Cook's dragomen. He had spent some months in Italy by the lakes; he had gone to Geneva; he had been seen as far afield as Leipzig. But somehow the schemes he had designed to sustain him on his travels had come to nothing. It would take a history to explain the journeyings that Mr Pardew had made in Old Europe those past two years, the odd places he went to and the queer company he kept. Perhaps Mr Pardew was part of that queer company himself, yet he looked at the shabby French counts he saw taking the cure at Baden, or the knowing gentlemen he played *écarté* with at Munich, with a thoroughgoing contempt. He was a tourist, passing through, and they were a picturesque spectacle got up for his entertainment.

It was the same when he met English people – the half-pay majors solemnly eating their dinners in the Dresden hotels; the jaunty foreign correspondents sending back their six-line despatches to the newspapers at home; Miss Jetsam, who was such a hit at the Drury Lane theatre thirty years ago but now finds it convenient to live abroad. Mr Pardew knew what they were worth, and his valuation was never very high. But this knowledge did not make him happy. He fancied that here, on the shores of Lake Como, in the Munich beershops, at the faro tables in Dresden, he was losing a vital part of himself, and the suspicion pained him. And meanwhile, gnawing at him all the time, there had been the question of how to live. Mr Pardew had brought a sizeable sum of money with him from London two years before – how the money was got it is not necessary to go into – and the money had been intended as the foundation stone of a towering fortune.

The things Mr Pardew had meant to do with that money! It was going to buy German mining stocks. It was going to sit in a great vault at Leipzig and bring him 7 per cent. It was going to underwrite a new process for distilling sherry wine in Cordova. Somehow it had done none of these things. There had been a commercial venture or two with certain of the English people met upon the way, but for some reason these had not prospered. Mr Pardew had distrusted the people with whom he had gone into partnership and they had returned the compliment. So Mr Pardew had shaken his head and decided that this was not the Europe of his salad days, and that people were too cautious and hidebound. And now the money was gone and there was a hundred francs owing to the tradesmen of Boulogne.

By this time Mr Pardew had nearly reached the summit of the cliff. He stood for a moment on the sodden grass, a yard or so from the edge, with the birds whirling above his head, looking out at the mutinous sea. To return to England would, he knew, be fraught with peril. Certain hounds who had been straining for a scent of him these past two years would be on his tail as soon as he landed. There would be places he could not safely go and friends to whom he could not safely speak. But Mr Pardew knew that in his heart he wished to see England again, that Paris, Munich and Dresden were nothing to Oxford Street. Even Captain McTurk, he thought, could not deny him England if he went about it in the right way. But he should have to be careful and he should have to ensure that the persons who employed him were careful too. Care, in fact, should be his watchword.

When he came back to the cottage half an hour later, having made one or two purchases in the town and carrying a brown-paper parcel under his arm, he found Jemima sitting half-asleep in front of the fire. He thought, as he watched her, that she was very loyal and that another woman might not have stood the fisherman's hut and the hundred francs owing.

'How should you like to go back to London?' he asked, not meaning to speak so boldly but finding that the words came out in a rush almost without his having wished them.

'I should like it above all things.' Jemima did not love the French, who hung songbirds up for sale in their shop windows and slaughtered poor horses on their butchers' blocks.

'Well, there is a chance that we shall go.' He saw her enthusiasm and was more cautious. 'In a week, perhaps. Or maybe two.' He watched her as he said this, knowing that she would be recalling certain other things he had said in the past two years.

'I thought you said it was an impossibility?'

'Did I? Well, perhaps I did. But this Mr Lythgoe has brought me a letter.' It was a weakness in him, but he could not suppress his delight in conveying to Jemima any interest that the world took in him. 'There are some gentlemen in London who think that I may be able to help them.'

'And we could live there?'

'It would have to be very quietly done,' Mr Pardew said, and Jemima, who was by no means as ignorant of his position in life as she some-times appeared, nodded her head. After that nothing further was said about London, or the gentlemen that he might be able to help, and they ate their supper very companionably together over the fire.

*

And over the next fortnight the business was done. A second letter arrived with a London frank on it, which may well have contained a bank note, as Mr Pardew was known to have spent money renewing his credit in the town. The contents of the fisherman's cottage were packed into a couple of trunks – very little there was of it when all assembled – and taken off to the ferry office, and a second ticket bought for Jemima. There cannot have been very much remaining from the banknote, as a donkey-cart came to carry the trunks away to the harbour and the human cargo walked. And a couple of hours later the pair of them might have been sitting with sundry other passengers – a clergyman in a collar and a soft hat, a bag-man with a sample-case under his arm, four little giggling girls being hushed by their governess – on the front deck of the Dover packet. But it might have been noticed, by anyone who knew Mr Pardew of old, that he had allowed a beard to grow over his jutting jaw and that his hair possessed a tint of blackness that had not previously been there. As for Jemima, she was in raptures, having been promised a carriage-ride in the park and a house at Richmond.

VIII

What *The Sportman's Magazine* thought about it

Stable-yard jottings from 'The Lounger at the Rail'

To be sure it is that season of the year in which the equine world is in meek hibernation. Towcester track is, we hear, under three feet of water, and the only thing seen on it is a flotilla of ducks. But if no horse in England has put its nose outside a stall since Christmas, the most interesting intelligence continues to reach us about the Derby, which we are pleased to set before our readers. Mr Burnett's MUTINEER will not figure, having been over-run in the autumn. Mr Burnett always over-runs his animals, which would be better left to the sweet otiums of their paddock. BOSKY BOY: still Mr Hamilton persists with this benighted quadruped, which would be better off put to drag a mail cart. WARWICK LAD (Mr Coveney) – our correspondent saw him at a gallop at Lambourn and remarked his want of style. The same, alas, may be said of his owner ... There is talk of CHAUNTICLEER coming forward, in which case a vet had better be got to examine his teeth, for all Mr Tackaberry will insist that he is three years old ...

PENDRAGON: a nice horse, a nice owner, a picturesque study, certainly, for the manufacturers of sporting prints, but what has he ever done? Is Mr Duchesne's TELEMACHUS still living? We have heard no report of him: he may be cat's-meat by now for all we know. TIBERIUS: in this animal (lately purchased by Mr G. Happerton) we repose the highest hopes. There are good reports of SEPTUAGINT, although it has been suggested that Lord Trumpington, that prudent and resourceful orna-ment of the Upper House, is playing a waiting game. Will HIBERNIAN be fetched over from Wicklow? It seems scarcely worth his owner's trouble. FELIX; EMPEROR'S FRIEND; AVOIRDUPOIS – there is simply no point in the gentlemen responsible entering these animals, and we implore them to desist. BALDINO: no word yet on the foreleg that he damaged at Lingfield. SKYLARK, PERICLES, THE COALMAN: all thought certain to run . . .

IX

Mr Happerton's Haunts and Homes

The newly married young lady, fresh from her wedding tour, will generally find that the first few months in her new home are not a time of unalloyed pleasure. A wife will very properly devote her full attention to her husband, but a man will, necessarily, have a dozen extraneous interests: his business; his profession; his club; his stable; his acquaintance. Prudent is the wife who can accommodate herself to these schemes and happy the young woman who can survey them with a fond and conciliating eye . . .

A New Etiquette: Mrs Carmody's Book of Genteel Behaviour (1861)

How does a man possessed of a moderate income, a comfortable house – albeit a house belonging to someone else – and no very definite occupation spend his time in London? And how does he spend it if that man is Mr George Happerton, late of Cursitor Chambers, Berwick Street, W., now (for the time being) of Belgrave Square? Let us follow Mr Happerton through the first half-dozen hours of his day.

It was about nine o'clock in the morning and Mr Happerton was at breakfast – not with the wife of his bosom in Belgrave Square but in the downstairs parlour of Mr Finucane's establishment in Wellington Street, Strand. Quite how long he had been there only Mr Happerton and the meek waitress knew, but there were two empty coffee cups by the edge of his plate, not to mention the remains of some devilled ham and half a dish of kidneys. He was alone – or rather not quite alone, for there was an old Irishman with red eyes and a furze of grey hair escaping from under the brim of his hat who stood a little way off to whom Mr Happerton occasionally made *sotto voce* remarks. The

Irishman muttered in return, the steam rose from the great urns that Mr Finucane kept in his window to beguile the passers-by, and whatever was said disappeared into a cacophony of rattled cutlery and scraped-back chairs.

Anyone who saw Mr Happerton in Mr Finucane's parlour would have guessed his familiarity with it. He knew the name of the meek waitress, and her associate who presided over the hot plates and the chafing dishes, and the damson-faced gentleman who guards the coats and hats in the vestibule. He nodded at Mr Finucane and sundry other persons taking their breakfast in other parts of the room. He knew where the little bowl of toothpicks was, and the spittoon, and was sufficiently regarded by Mr Finucane as not to have to settle his bill – over which there was almost a struggle between the attendants as to who should have the pleasure of bringing it to him – on the spot, but to have it taken away behind the counter for future reckoning. Having ordered that this should be done, drunk off his coffee, presented the meek waitress with a florin and told her with a grin that she looked younger than ever and would she do him the favour of marrying him next Thursday week, he took his hat and walked out into the street. The old Irishman sat down at the empty table and began to eat the remaining kidneys.

Outside in Wellington Street it was a bright April morning, with carts and wagonettes passing back and forth and a very lugubrious tumbler trying to get up a collection on the pavement's edge. Mr Happerton headed north. Covent Garden market was in full swing and he browsed among the barrows with the greatest interest, examined a pineapple and nearly bought it, paused to remove some mud that had attached itself to his shiny top-boots, and by degrees took himself to the cab rank that stands on the corner of Langley Street and had himself taken off in the direction of the City. Descending onto the kerb at Lothbury, he made his way to a small, black-bricked building with a profusion of brass plates on the door advertising the presence of attorneys, black-lead companies, insurance agents and the like, took out a key, admitted himself and, making a great noise with his boots, walked up to the topmost floor.

Here there was a tiny landing, a portrait of the Queen in her Coronation robes on an otherwise bare wall and a tiny office, not more than eight feet square, in which sat Mr Happerton's clerk. 'Well, how are we, Sikes?' Mr Happerton wondered, and Mr Sikes said that he was very well. He was a thin, stooped man with a tremor on one side of his face and looked anything but. 'And has anything come in?' Mr Happerton enquired, his eye turning to the equally tiny window where the dome of St Paul's tyrannised the skyline, and Mr Sikes murmured that something *had* come in. There was only one chair, so Mr Happerton sat on it while Mr Sikes fussed over him, brought out some loose papers that were hidden in an old brown envelope and some others crushed into conformity by the paperweight on his desk. 'So it is all right, is it?' Mr Happerton asked at one point, and Mr Sikes said, with a very mirthless laugh, that it was quite all right. 'There are bills, I suppose, from Lincolnshire,' Mr Happerton continued, and Mr Sikes agreed that there were bills from Lincolnshire, and Mr Happerton, having looked at them, took out his pen and scratched at them once or twice. He had a cigar in his mouth, and even now he could not stop caressing his top-boots as they rested before him on the desk, but he did not look like the man who had eaten his breakfast in Mr Finucane's parlour three-quarters of an hour before. A splash of ink fell on the cambric of his shirt-front and he dabbed at with his forefinger, so that a black stain like a bullet-hole lay next to his heart. 'Raff's account here?' he enquired a moment later, and Mr Sikes gave him a little pile of paper fragments, which he inspected very closely, at one or two of which he laughed, and two or three of which he tore up and flung into the waste-paper basket.

A church clock began striking the hour and Mr Happerton stood with his head on one side listening to the chimes. There was a shuffling noise from beyond the door, and an old woman who had got into the building on the pretext of selling commercial directories was discovered on the staircase and routed out by Mr Sikes. Mr Happerton smiled and said he didn't suppose that Mr Sikes had many visitors, and Mr Sikes said that he didn't, and they listened to the old woman bumping her way down the stairs. 'How much do you suppose then?' Mr

Happerton wondered, and Mr Sikes wrote down some figures on a slip of paper, added them up, murmured something under his breath, struck them out and tried again. 'Don't come out quite, do they?' Mr Happerton sympathised. He put the slip of paper in his notecase, rocked back and forth on the heels of his boots, so that the boards cracked beneath them, and took his leave.

In Lothbury there were clerks wandering to and fro and bank messengers going importantly about their business, and a ducal carriage setting down its occupant on the pavement, but Mr Happerton took no notice of any of them. He was thinking of Scroop Hall, and its great wild garden and Tiberius in his stable, and the wind tearing in off the wolds. He took another cab in the direction of the West End, had himself set down at the foot of Shaftesbury Avenue and went off along the southern side of Piccadilly. Clearly Mr Happerton was not in any hurry. He looked in the window of Mr Manton's gunshop. He walked into Mr Anstruther's the tailors and had himself measured for a suit of black-cloth. He marched up to the counter of the florist hard by and gave an address to which all manner of blooms were straightaway to be sent. Then he turned into St James's Street and went into a little club called the Stoneleigh. He could see Captain Raff in the window as he strode up, and found that gentleman in the hallway as he made his entrance.

'What's the hurry, Raff?' Mr Happerton said, as he handed his hat to the servant. 'Anyone would think you were anxious to see us.'

'Anxious?' said Captain Raff. 'I ain't anxious, but – well.'

'Well what?'

'A fellow can't talk here. You had better step up to the billiard room.'

The billiard room at the Stoneleigh looked out onto a grim little court where white duck trousers were hung out on a line to dry. Captain Raff made a listless attempt at play, struck a couple of balls desultorily, watched them tumble into the pockets and made a phantom stroke with his cue.

'Well,' he said. 'I have seen him.'

Mr Happerton was looking down into the grim court. 'I daresay you have,' he replied. 'I'll not see him myself. You must tell him that.'

'Oh, I shall tell him ... I say, Happerton,' Captain Raff went on, 'you couldn't lend me ten guineas, could you?'

'What on earth for?'

'Well – the fact is, my subscription here is owing. And it's so deuced awkward, you know, having the secretary come up to one when there are fellows standing about.'

Mr Happerton thought that he really was very tired of Captain Raff. Nonetheless, he furnished the ten guineas. Then, lowering his voice, he said: 'So when is the affair to come off?'

The promise of the ten guineas had not raised Captain Raff from the pit of absolute gloom in which he appeared to be sunk. 'A week. A fortnight. I say, Happerton' – Captain Raff's face as he said this was quite piteous – 'ain't you taking no end of a risk?'

'I don't see that I am. Who is to know about it, eh? Why, it is you that has been visiting him, not I.'

'But if – if he was to get caught.'

'He won't get caught.'

'And then you have the horse already, you know. In that stable in Lincolnshire. And don't tell me you haven't got ready money, not with old Gresham eating out of your hand.'

Mr Happerton hesitated. He had a scheme in his head to which, he knew, Captain Raff would eventually have to be made party. But he also knew that the longer he could keep full details of the plan from Captain Raff's enquiring eye, the happier he would be. He thought that he might tell Captain Raff – not everything, but – something.

'Certainly I have the horse,' he said. 'But that isn't the end of the affair. To do what we wish to do will take a mint of money.'

'So you're going to back it, are you?' Captain Raff said knowledge-ably. 'I thought you would. There was a group of fellows the other night at the Blue Riband saying that you wouldn't, but I told them "If you knew Happerton as I do, you'd say different." But you'll not get much in the way of odds, you know, what with it being in the papers and so forth. But I'm sure you know your own business.'

'Well, maybe I do ... Raff, why did you sell out of the 25th, eh?'

Captain Raff nearly shrieked.

'That's a terrible question to ask a fellow, knowing how I was situated, and how the mess turned against me, and what Colonel Devonish said . . .'

'Precisely. There's some questions you don't care to be asked, and some I don't care to neither. That's why we are such good friends and fall on each other's necks so happily.' At this moment the only thing Mr Happerton looked ready to see fall on Captain Raff's neck was a noose. 'Now, just be a good fellow, do you hear, and when there's anything to know you'll be the first to know it.'

'You ain't angry with me?' Captain Raff asked.

'No I ain't. But don't go telling fellows you meet at the Blue Riband whether you think I'm likely to back a horse or not.'

'And . . . would you like a game of billiards, old fellow?' Captain Raff asked, almost tearfully.

'No I shouldn't. Go and find Wilkins the secretary. Perhaps he'll play with you now your subscription's paid.'

And Mr Happerton made his way back down the marble staircase, leaving Captain Raff to recall the various reasons why he had sold out of the 25th, and why the fellows in the mess had turned against him, and what Colonel Devonish had said.

Leaving St James's, Mr Happerton marched back to Piccadilly, proceeded a little further along it and then turned left into the Green Park, where it was very bright and blue and there were nursemaids out with their charges and old gentlemen rambling through the spring sunshine. Keeping to the left-hand side of the rail he strolled along at a brisk pace, came to the western gate and strode into Park Lane. It was the part of London that Mr Happerton liked best. He had walked down it when he was a boy and had no money, and he fully intended to be driven down in that bright, unclouded future when he was as rich as Croesus. Here there were great carriages sweeping by and gentlemen's cobs heading for the Row, and Mr Happerton bobbed admiringly along beside them before veering sharp right into Mount Street, where he arrived eventually before a little house with turned-down blinds and a door so freshly painted that it looked as if it had been furbished up by the letting agent only the other week. What Mr Happerton did on these premises was a mystery, but he was there an hour – the gentlemen's cobs were out in profusion now, and the carriages continued to roll along Park Lane – and when he left the prettiest little white hand could be glimpsed at the window waving him off.

Quite what Mr Happerton did during the remainder of the day, where he ate his luncheon, how he occupied his afternoon, what clubs, horse-dealers' and saddle-makers' shops he looked into, and how he got his tea, was his own affair, but at six o'clock he walked up to the house in Belgrave Square as fresh-complexioned and jaunty as on the moment he had quitted it, just as Mr Gresham's doctor was standing on the step with his black medical bag pulled up under his arm. It was only natural that Mr Happerton should wish to enquire after his father-in-law's health, and he did this with the greatest suavity.

'He is coming on, I take it?' he asked, while the doctor stood on the step buttoning his coat.

'Well – I rather think not. There's no organic disease, I should say ...'

'He seems very tired.'

'That is it exactly. You had better keep him comfortable.'

Mr Happerton said that he would keep him comfortable, shook the doctor's hand, nodded at the butler, who, hearing the conversation, had had his good opinion of Mr Happerton confirmed, and went into the drawing room. There was no one there but Mr Gresham, who was sitting in an armchair, and some powder, or assemblies of powder, which the doctor had left lying on a table nearby. He looked very old, and the newspaper he was holding shook in his hand.

'Well, sir,' said Mr Happerton in a booming voice, 'I gather you are coming on splendidly.'

'Is that what the doctor said?' Mr Gresham asked, with a rather pathetic eagerness.

'Well – these medical men are always very cautious, I fear. Should you like me to have anything fetched for you?'

'No, no. I shall do very well.'

'There is no business I can attend to on your behalf?'

'Perhaps you might send to my chambers for the Tenway Croft papers. It is a fortnight, you know, since I looked at them.'

'I shall have a message taken round,' Mr Happerton said, privately resolving that the Tenway Croft papers should come nowhere near Belgrave Square.

He found his wife in a little sitting room that she had appropriated for her own use on an upper floor of the house. There had been a time in the early weeks of their marriage when, entering a room after some absence, he had saluted his wife on the cheek in that expression of marital harmony which is so very pleasant to behold. Now he merely said:

'Did you go out at all today?'

'I took Father to the park. And cousin Harriet was here for luncheon. It was all very dull.' She did not ask him what he had been doing.

'You're a dear, good girl and I'm sure Papa is very pleased with you.'

She gave him a queer look, seemed as if she might be about to say something and then thought better of it. She was always giving him queer looks, he reflected. But she had come up trumps with that cheque. It was all very strange.

There was a guest at dinner that night. This was the Honourable Major Stebbings, the eldest son of the late Mrs Gresham's younger sister. His presence at Belgrave Square, where he had not been more than half a dozen times in his life, had come about in this manner. 'I never could forgive poor Julia for throwing herself away on that Mr Gresham,' his mother had said to him. 'But now they say he is ill, and your cousin Rebecca, whom I always thought a well-conducted girl of whom something could be made, has married a dreadful man that no one knows anything about. You had better go and dine there, Henry, and see what is going on.' And so the Honourable Major Stebbings, greatly regretting his lost dinner at the club, had gone. He was a tall, thin man of perhaps thirty-five, his hair already greying at the temples, very diligent in his professional duties and very dull, who, in addition, had been got at by serious religion. Hearing a little of Mr Happerton, and not liking what he had heard, he had come to Belgrave Square, if not determined to find fault, then anxious to resist any of the blandishments that might conceivably be thrown at him. 'I never was at a race meeting but twice in my life,' he replied to the first question asked of him, and Mr Happerton knew that he had best be careful.

It was a very dull dinner. To the old butler, who crept among them with a bottle of Marsala, the four figures seated at the dining table in the big old room with its bleary chandeliers must have looked like so many effigies in their tomb. In addition to his seriousness, the Honourable Major Stebbings was particular about what he ate, and sent back several dishes untasted, to the distress of the cook. As for the others, Mr Gresham nodded between the courses and Mrs Rebecca frankly sulked, and only Mr Happerton, who gobbled up his cutlets as if he had had no food since breakfast, seemed not to be cast down. Still, it was a family gathering, and such things are not generally allowed to pass without some small attempt at conversation.

'How is your mother, Henry?' Mr Gresham asked at one point, various pleasantries from Mr Happerton about the new overground railway and the extension of the franchise having failed to stir any response. 'I'm afraid we do not see her as much as we might.' Mr Gresham had last set eyes on his sister-in-law three years ago.

'She is very well, sir, for her age.' Lady Stebbings considered herself a juvenile lady of fifty-seven, and never missed a day in her carriage on the Row. 'But how are you? I understand you have not been well.'

'Not well? No, I suppose not. But then, old gentlemen are sometimes not very well, aren't they?'

'Indeed, sir, I don't doubt that you'll outlive us all,' said Mr Happerton good-humouredly. 'But you shall not sit up all night if we can prevent it. You see, sir,' he said, addressing himself to the Honourable Major Stebbings, 'my father-in-law is a fanatic about his responsibilities. He will not allow that there are men forty years his junior happy to relieve him of his burdens.'

'I shouldn't care to give up work I knew was mine to do,' the

Honourable Major Stebbings said. He was a slow man, but he did think, as he considered the matter, that Mr Happerton was good-natured and that he might have misjudged him.

And so the dinner went on. Mr Gresham all but went to sleep between the courses; Mrs Rebecca looked sulkier than ever; the Honourable Major Stebbings sent back a summer pudding on the grounds that it would wreak havoc with his digestion, but consented to talk about the subject dearest to his heart, which happened to be military finance.

'It is like this, sir,' he said to Mr Gresham, 'unless we get a more equitable system of provision we shall never do anything. The French and the Prussians will beat us at our own game, and then where shall we be?' And Mr Gresham, nodding his head over his wineglass, said that he supposed it was very bad.

After dinner they repaired to the drawing room, and it was perhaps a little livelier, for all that the Honourable Major Stebbings would not touch a playing card and Mrs Rebecca could not for the life of her be induced to sing. Here again the Major noted the way in which Mr Happerton plumped up his father-in-law's cushions, brought him his glass of hot-milk-and-arrowroot and was generally solicitous of him, and thought once more – he was a fair-minded man for all his stiffness – that he might have misjudged him.

'He is not very well, I am afraid,' he remarked to Mr Happerton as Mr Gresham, assisted by his daughter, had left the room to go to bed.

'Well – perhaps not. The important thing, I think, is that he should be kept content and not over-exert himself. There's port here if you would like it.'

'I never drink port wine in the evening,' said the Honourable Major Stebbings. But calling on his mother on the following afternoon, and seated in her drawing room, which was full of the gayest ornaments and decorations, out of which Lady Stebbings' worn old face peered incongruously, he conceded that he might have done Mr Happerton an injustice. 'I daresay he is not very gentlemanlike, and there are those dreadful pins he wears, and I gather he is making a fool of himself over some horse, but, really, I think my cousin could have done worse.'

'And how is my brother-in-law?' Lady Stebbings wondered.

'He is not very well, I daresay. But then, he is rather old.'

'Oh, horribly old,' said Lady Stebbings, who considered herself a blooming girl still. 'And how is my niece Rebecca? Does marriage suit her?'

'I thought her deuced cross,' the Honourable Major Stebbings said.

'I've no patience with those Greshams,' Lady Stebbings said, and went back to looking at her milliners' samples.

'Your cousin seems a very well-informed man,' said Mr Happerton to his wife, after the Honourable Major Stebbings had taken his leave and they sat together in the empty drawing room, with the candles burning low.

'Those military men always give themselves airs.'

Mr Happerton stared at his wife. She was sitting in an armchair, with her head set back against the antimacassar, as young ladies are advised to sit in etiquette books, eating grapes from a bowl on her lap, but with a decorum and in a silence that would have had the compilers of the etiquette books nodding in approval, and she looked sandier-haired and greener-eyed than ever. And again Mr Happerton wondered at her. He had tried respectful attentiveness, and this had failed. He had tried brusque jocularity, and thought that this had failed too. He did not quite know how to induce his wife to respond to him, but he knew that her glacial consumption of the grapes rather scared him. But Mr Happerton prided himself on his thick skin, so he told himself that for once he would be matter-of-fact, let the consequences be what they might. Waiting until all the grapes had been eaten up, he said:

'Now look here, Becca. There is something I want to tell you. You know that I have bought this horse, Tiberius.'

'Certainly I know it.' She was looking at him stealthily, with her great green eyes flashing.

'It will wear your colours when it runs.' Privately Mr Happerton wondered what these colours might look like – he had never seen a horse run in sea-green and sandy red. 'Is that not something?'

The look in her eye said that it was something. 'Where is the horse?'

'In Lincolnshire. The man I bought it from still has it. It may be convenient to keep it there. I don't just know the best thing to do at the moment.'

'Perhaps Captain Raff can advise you.'

'Captain Raff could not advise me where to eat my dinner,' Mr Happerton pronounced in his briskest manner. 'Let's not have any shilly-shallying about this. I am engaged on a little scheme that may make our fortunes.'

'If you want more money from Papa you had better say so, and I shall ask him.'

'Well then – ask.'

He was surprised at how easily the business was conducted. He reached out to draw her to him, and she snatched his hand away and grasped it between her fingers so violently that he whistled.

'Gracious, Beck, you'll break a fellow's wrist if you go on like that.'

'Shall I? I wonder.'

Later, as he lay in bed, a foot or two from the sea-green eyes, now closed, and the sandy hair, now done up under a nightcap, he thought about the other part of his scheme. It was, as Captain Raff had deposed, extremely risky. There was every chance that it would not work. But then, he thought, even if it did not work, he could not see how the trail should be traced back to him. And the capital it might realise would transform his modest resources into a cataract of money. It was about midnight now, and Mrs Rebecca slept soundly on, but Mr Happerton was not in the least tired, and so he lay awake, listening to the sound of her breathing, and musing on his opportunities, on Scroop Hall and its great wild garden, and the black horse in its stable, as the wind blew over the Belgravia rooftops and the sound of the policeman's tread echoed in the street below.

X

Shepherd's Inn and elsewhere

Bred up, like a bailiff or a shabby attorney, about the purlieus of the Inns of Court, Shepherd's Inn is always to be found in the close neighbourhood of Lincoln's Inn Fields, and the Temple. Somewhere among the black gables and smutty chimney-stacks of Wych Street, Holywell Street, Chancery Lane, the quadrangle lies, hidden from the outer world . . .

W. M. Thackeray, *The History of Pendennis* (1850)

Shepherd's Inn is generally owned to be rather an obscure locality. Chancery Lane is only two minutes distant, and the shops and the taverns of Oldcastle Street hard by, but somehow the Inn has detached itself from the bustle of their traffic and the old porter who sits in a chair before the lodge gate can sleep for hours at a time without anyone disturbing him. Fifty years ago the Inn was full of Chancery lawyers and black-coated attorneys' clerks, but the lawyers have all gone now and the place is given over to black-lead companies and commission agents and persons so enigmatic as not to advertise their existence, and the brass plates on the doors change hands at three-month intervals. Mr Crutwell, the celebrated divorce lawyer, has chambers here, only he never visits, and Mr Abrahams, who lends money to the nobility and whose wife has a 'drawing room' in Portland Street, keeps an office somewhere nearby. But the private residents are all rather retiring: middle-aged gentlemen in threadbare coats who stalk in and out of the arch as if they really had somewhere to go; young men in shirtsleeves who never seem to have any work but are always about the place smoking cigars and chaffing the porter. Very occasionally a carriage or a gig stops at the gate and a visitor walks over the gravel paths, past the statue of the shepherd's boy behind its iron palings, to search for someone who will most likely have moved out six months before, but this is still a great event in the life of the Inn, where the pattern of the days is altogether less conspicuous.

It was here in Shepherd's Inn, on the top floor of a house set at right angle to the lodge gate, that Mr Pardew and the lady who called herself his wife had come to rest. The inhabitants of these dwelling places do not generally take much notice of each other, but anyone who took an interest in Number 3 would have seen that its latest set of tenants seldom left their chamber, that the gentleman, in particular, only came out very late at night or very early in the morning, that the blinds in the windows were usually pulled down, and that scarcely anybody, least of all the postman, came to call. For his own part, Mr Pardew thought that he had a very comfortable lodging, where nobody cared who he was or what he was about and where he could probably have set up as a resurrection man, robbing corpses out of the graveyard at Lincoln's Inn Fields, without anyone taking the slightest notice.

It was about three o'clock on a spring afternoon – a raw afternoon with rain desultorily falling – and Mr Pardew, with a mackintosh drawn up to his chin and a scarf wound very tightly around the lower part of his face – was coming back through the archway. In one hand he held his stick, and in the other a provisions basket, and the porter who sat, not in his chair, but behind the smeary glass of the lodge-gate window, noticed that as he reached the arch he turned very deliberately on his heel and looked back the way he had come. A fat woman dressed in black with a put-upon expression on her face came waddling towards him over the stone flags and he stood aside to let her pass by before making his way to the open door of Number 3 and proceeding stealthily up to the third floor. There was a faint smell of meat roasting and a woman's voice softly singing, and Mr Pardew stood on the mat for a moment considering them before producing a latchkey, twisting it in the lock and stepping inside. Here the suspicion that had occurred to him during the walk from the lodge was confirmed by the sight of a tray containing a teapot, a milkjug and a second, incriminating cup.

'Why have you had that person here?' he demanded, very sharply, as Jemima came into the room to greet him.

'It is only my sister, Richard. I don't suppose you would wish me to turn her away.'

'I should have turned her away, and all the rest of that d——d family of hers, too.' Mr Pardew's expression as he said this was very striking. 'What does she want?'

'It is a pity a woman can't see her own flesh and blood after two years away from them.'

'A pity! It is a pity you ever wrote to her at all. I shan't have her here. She will –' Mr Pardew very nearly said 'betray us all' but stopped himself. In fact the possibility of someone betraying him was not one he thought at all likely. He had been here a fortnight now, living very inconspicuously, revisiting none of his old haunts, and he fancied that he was no danger. To be sure, there had been an occasional fright. He had been smoking a cigar once in a shilling divan when a man had addressed him by name, but he had kept his head, produced a card that said his name was Abernethy, received an apology and gone on with his cigar. Another time a policeman had looked very hard at him as he walked down Cursitor Street, but Mr Pardew had assured himself that policemen sometimes do look very hard at the most innocent passers-by and continued on his way. Apart from this, in his wanderings around London, he had gone unmolested.

'I shan't ask her again, if you wish it,' Jemima said, very meekly, and Mr Pardew looked at her fresh complexion and the neat little apron she had round her waist and was mollified. A top-floor set in Shepherd's Inn is not perhaps the easiest lodging to render cheerful, but somehow Jemima had made it so. There was a bright little screen in the far corner and a picture or two fixed to the walls along with the smell of the roasting meat.

'You will never guess,' he said, pulling off his gloves and talking in a more companionable manner, 'who I saw today?'

'Who was it?' Jemima wondered, half in and half out of the kitchen.

'Well – in point of fact I walked round to see Lord Fairhurst at his club.' In fact, Mr Pardew had gone nowhere near Lord Fairhurst or his club, but he was determined to make up for his bad temper.

'Gracious,' said Jemima, who, as Mr Pardew knew, loved talk of this kind. 'How was his lordship?'

'Well – I have seen him better. A touch of the gout, I should say.' No one who saw Mr Pardew's face could have doubted that he had sat in Lord Fairhurst's club and taken tea with him. 'They say that his uncle, who owns half of Hampshire, made him his heir on condition he gave up drinking port. But all that was a long time ago.'

'There was a gentleman called while you were out,' Jemima now said.

'What sort of a gentleman?'

'Well – he said that you would know him, and why he called.'

Mr Pardew set down the cup of tea that had just been brought to him – very fragrant tea it was, in the most delicate little cup – and walked over to the window, whose blind for once was raised. Down below in the courtyard a man in a shabby coat with his hands plunged deep into his pocket was walking nervously back and forth, casting sharp, uneasy glances at the archway and the porter's lodge.

'Is that the man?'

'Yes – that is him.'

Mr Pardew continued to stare for a moment or so, drank some more of his tea – it seemed less fragrant to him now – and then went yet more stealthily back down the staircase. Captain Raff met him just beyond the outer door.

'Why, Pardew, there you are. How I missed you coming back to your rooms I can't imagine.'

'And yet somehow you did,' Mr Pardew said. 'Here, you'd better come upstairs.'

The sitting room was empty on their arrival, a fact that Captain Raff seemed greatly to regret. Plucked from the courtyard, and safe behind a locked door, he seemed less ill at ease.

'Ain't your wife going to join us, Pardew? Deuced pretty woman, if you don't mind my saying so.'

Mr Pardew looked as if would have liked to kick Captain Raff back down the stairs whence he had come. Instead he picked up the stick, which he had put down when first returning, and weighed it in his hand.

'Perhaps I do mind your saying so.' Mr Pardew thoroughly despised Captain Raff. 'But never mind. I take it you've brought the twenty pounds.'

'Twenty! You've had fifty already.'

'Fifty. Seventy. A hundred. These things don't come cheap, Raff, as well you know.'

'I daresay they don't,' Captain Raff conceded. He had seen the stick now – it was an inch thick, at least, around the middle – and was becoming uneasy again. 'But, well – twenty pounds, you know.'

'You'll make fifty times that if it all comes off.'

'Ah, but that's the question, ain't it?' said Captain Raff, who seemed delightfully unaware of how much Mr Pardew disliked him. 'When will it come off, eh?'

'When will it come off? I'll put an advertisement in the *Gazette* if you like. Should that suit?'

'I never knew a fellow for flying off the handle so much,' said Captain Raff, almost piteously. Evidently he had come to Shepherd's Inn prepared to meet Mr Pardew's demands, for he took a notecase from his pocket, and with a kind of sigh, as if he could not hold himself responsible for any circumstances that might arise, began to count out four five-pound notes onto the table before him.

'I shall need assistance, you know,' Mr Pardew said as he gathered up the notes with what, Captain Raff could not help noticing, was a kind of disdain. 'Should you like to come with me?'

'Come with you!' Captain Raff gave a look of stark horror. 'No, I should not. That sort of thing ain't in my line at all, you know. Lythgoe will do it, I dare say.'

'Lythgoe?'

'The little chap as we sent to Boulogne in search of you. Mr — that is, we have his paper, you know.'

'Do you indeed?' Mr Pardew gave him a look that made Captain Raff glance at the door and measure his distance to it. 'Well, you had better let Lythgoe know that he's needed. But there is one thing you can tell me, Raff. Who's your principal, eh?'

Captain Raff looked yet more stricken. There was a wild look in his eye. 'You shall have your money,' he said. 'A promise is a promise, you know.'

'I don't doubt I shall have my money. But I want to know who's giving it to me. It ain't you, is it?'

'No, it isn't me,' Captain Raff said, very humbly, all the while measuring the distance to the door.

'Well then, who is it? To whom do I apply if, well, let us say, if things ain't to my liking? Why — let us be straight about this — should I have to deal with you, eh?'

'As to that,' said Captain Raff, recovering something of his dignity, 'I suppose I can carry a message as well as the next man?'

'I don't doubt you can, but what if the message ain't to my liking? Why, I might have to shoot the messenger, if you take my meaning.' But all this was lost on Captain Raff, who looked more terrified than ever. Mr Pardew grinned. 'No, don't alarm yourself, Raff. I'm not going to shoot you. Nor yet anyone else, I hope. You had better go back to your Mr ——, give him my compliments, and tell him the thing will come off. But there's to be no splitting, mind.'

'Certainly not,' Captain Raff said, so relieved that the interview was over that he walked down the stairs quite proudly with his head in the air, telling himself that he had brought the business off with a flourish, and that Mr Happerton would be pleased. 'No splitting eh?' he said to himself as he passed through the gate and went out into Oldcastle Street. 'Well, we shall see about that.'

Once Captain Raff had gone, Mr Pardew made as if to fling himself into a chair and resume his cup of tea. Then, setting down the tea cup, he went and stood by the window, where Captain Raff's receding figure could be seen approaching the lodge. Picking up his stick, and regretting the smell of roasting meat which continued to pervade the room from beyond the kitchen door, Mr Pardew walked down the staircase and by moving very rapidly across the courtyard contrived to emerge into Oldcastle Street just as Captain Raff could be seen turning into a side alley thirty yards away. Fortunately Oldcastle Street and its surrounding thoroughfares were full of people, and by keeping himself to a safe distance and trusting to the Captain's lack of observational powers Mr Pardew had no difficulty in holding him within his sights without himself being seen.

In this way, face well down under his coat collar, and with sundry excitable flourishes of his stick, he followed Captain Raff along the southern edge of Lincoln's Inn Fields, watched him saunter negligently across Chancery Lane, where he was abused by a crossing-sweeper and nearly knocked down by a hay-cart, and then shadowed him eastward along Cursitor Street and into Plough Place. Just as Mr Pardew was beginning to think that the game was not worth the candle and that Captain Raff might walk all the way to Whitechapel without stopping, his quarry paused, stood uncertainly on a street corner and darted into a building whose doorway was ornamented with a brass plate that read BLUE RIBAND CLUB. Mr Pardew retired to the other side of the street to a print-seller's displaying views of Old London, and amused himself by examining the passers-by while keeping an eye on the club's doorway.

Perhaps a quarter of an hour went by in this way when Captain Raff appeared in the doorway with a tall, stoutish man arrayed in a pair of top-boots who looked about for a cab, and then had himself and Captain Raff carried away in the direction of Fleet Street. For a moment Mr Pardew wondered about summoning a second cab – there was one moving up towards him from St Andrew Street – and renewing his pursuit, but then it occurred to him that the information he sought might be more readily to hand. Accordingly, tucking his stick up under his arm, he marched off across the road, stalked into the doorway of the Blue Riband Club and buttonholed the servant who kept guard over the vestibule.

'Dear me,' said Mr Pardew very mildly. 'Was that my friend Captain Raff just stepping out of the club? I fear I must have missed him.'

'Yes, sir. The capting's gone this instant. Him and Mr Happerton both together.'

'Ah, with Mr Happerton is it?' said Mr Pardew, almost to himself, and walked back into the street.

Mr Pardew was a resourceful and sometimes a studious man, and in the course of the next week he marshalled his resources and made a study of Mr Happerton. He enquired of the Blue Riband and found that it was a club for sporting men; he consulted an ostler or two, and turned up a saddler's shop which Mr Happerton was thought to patronise; he spent at least one morning in a library examining back-numbers of *The Times* newspaper; and before long he had assembled a little dossier about Mr Happerton that would have done credit to a police detective. He knew how Mr Happerton had made his money. He knew about his marriage and his trip to Rome. He knew a great deal about Tiberius. All this information Mr Pardew stowed away, not having any immediate use for it, but thinking that it might very well prove to his advantage in future days, when certain other schemes had come to fruition.

It might have been said of Mr Pardew in these days by anyone who knew him – and there was only Jemima to notice where he went and how he occupied himself – that he was very restless. When he sat in the room at Shepherd's Inn he was always writing little notes to himself, considering them as he ate or drank or tapped his stick, and then tearing them asunder and casting them away. He took great long walks – north, south and west of the city, to Hampstead, St John's Wood and Kilburn – which never seemed to tire him or bring him ease. There was a particular street in St John's Wood, very quiet and secluded, with the houses all huddled up behind laburnum hedges, which he walked down several times with a very longing look. He walked down St James's Street looking in at the windows of the gentlemen's clubs there and gnawing at the end of his stick, and along Piccadilly glaring at the shopfronts like a Scots divine who thinks the whole of the West End frivolous and can't for the life of him see why it is permitted.

Once, about this time, as they were sitting together in the room at Shepherd's Inn, looking out at the statue of the shepherd boy behind his iron fence, Mr Pardew said, in such a soft voice that he might have been speaking to himself: 'I was done a bad turn, but it will all come out right again, you shall see.'

And Jemima, not quite understanding the words, and not having heard him talk in this way before, wondered at them, and smoothed her hands very demurely down the folds of her dress, and went away to infuse the tea.

'By the by,' Mr Pardew said, when she returned, 'how should you like to go to Richmond one day?'

And so they went to Richmond, on an April day that was not quite spring and not quite summer, and walked by the river, until it became too cold for comfort, and ate whitebait at the Ship, and looked at the people, and perhaps in the end enjoyed themselves. There was a fog starting up over Richmond Hill as they came back, with the gas lights winking through it and a dull grey twilight descending, and Mr Pardew thought it was like the fog that covered his own affairs and resolved that the bold stroke he was now meditating should blow it away.

Captain Raff called again, and they had a very intimate conversation, at the close of which Mr Pardew sent the Captain away down the staircase with perhaps the haughtiest look he had ever minted. The scheme on which he was now embarked promised a great deal – if it succeeded. But if it were to fail Mr Pardew knew that even little dinners at Richmond, out of season, with the wet grass fouling his boots, would be beyond him. And so life went on quietly at Shepherd's Inn and Mr Pardew continued to meditate on the bold stroke that would blow the fog away.

One Saturday morning towards the middle of April, when there was a faint suspicion of gillyflowers in the Shepherd's Inn window boxes, Mr Pardew dressed himself with more than usual care in a suit of black-cloth taken from the trunk he had brought with him from Boulogne and, with Jemima (who assumed from his appearance that he was going off to dine with a duchess) bidding him farewell, walked off under the arch and into Oldcastle Street looking like an old black rook. The sun had been out and the crowds flocked over the pavement, and it may be that Mr Pardew was troubled by the conspicuousness of his suit – which close inspection revealed to be not of black-cloth but of Oxford mixture – and the silk hat he had on his head, for he seemed to step in and out of doorways and into those places where the crowd pressed thickest. He headed, not north towards Hampstead and St John's Wood and the usual course of his wanderings, but eastwards towards the City, walked down Newgate Street and Cheapside and came presently to Cornhill.

It was by now about a quarter past twelve and the press of people about the Mansion House was very great. Carriages stood waiting on the kerb to scoop up City lordlings as they came out of their temples. A cab-horse had gone down on the corner where Cornhill runs into Leadenhall Street and half a dozen passers-by were offering suggestions as to how it might be righted. All this Mr Pardew saw and noted as he marched up Leadenhall Street. Anyone who saw him pass might have taken him for a gentleman off to see his broker about share-dealings, or a lawyer about his will, but Mr Pardew had no interest in stockbrokers or lawyers. Coming to Mr Gallentin's shop, a vast expanse of plate glass with a hundred rings and gold chronometers winking in the window, he turned in at the door, went straight to a tray of silver-ware and began looking at it quite as if he meant to buy something. One of Mr Gallentin's polite young men, dressed in a suit of black quite as decorous as Mr Pardew's own, stepped up and, having engaged him in conversation, Mr Pardew intimated that he wished to buy a gold brooch of a kind that might ornament a lady's hat. As he made this request, and as various brooches and pins were brought on a tray for him to inspect – Mr Gallentin himself stood by the doorway and looked on approvingly as the tray came up – Mr Pardew looked carefully around him.

The shop consisted of three separate chambers: the showroom in which he now stood with Mr Gallentin's young man and his tray of brooches; a second room behind it, in which Mr Gallentin presumably sat when he was not rallying his troops; and a third room, away to the right, connected to the shop by a metal-plated door. This Mr Pardew assumed to be the strongroom, and his assumption was confirmed when another of Mr Gallentin's young men, carrying a second tray of medallions, passed into the shop, closing the metal-plated door behind him, but offering for a second the glimpse of a small, shadowy chamber dominated by the outlines of what Mr Pardew knew was a cast-iron safe. Fascinating as all this was to Mr Pardew, he was careful to keep his gaze trained for the most part on the tray of brooches before him. Secretly he was calculating the extent of the strongroom, which he reckoned to be about twelve feet square, and the thickness of the metal plate that separated it from the rest of Mr Gallentin's premises. Something seemed to strike him, and, looking at his watch, he announced that there was no helping it, he would have to consult with the lady for whom the brooch was intended – Mr Gallentin's young man would appreciate the difficulty? – and there was nothing for it but to return post-haste on Monday. Whereupon Mr Pardew had himself bowed out of the shop, with even Mr Gallentin condescending to hold the door open for him as he went.

The lunch hour was fast advancing, and the throng of people had begun to lessen. Mr Pardew stood on Mr Gallentin's doorstep for a moment with his thumbs pressed into the lapels of his coat, and an expression of supreme nonchalance on his face, as if his time was entirely his own and he could buy up the entire City for his private fiefdom if he chose. Then, still with the same casual air, he crossed over to the other side of Leadenhall Street to a point exactly opposite Mr Gallentin's doorway. Mr Gallentin's plate-glass frontage, he saw, extended for perhaps twenty feet. To the right was a patch of bare wall, which Mr Pardew assumed to include the strongroom. This suspicion was confirmed by the presence of a single, slit window built into the wall at a height of about six feet and designed, as he knew, to allow any passing constable the means of assuring himself that all was well within. Taking care that there was no one in sight of him, Mr Pardew took out a notebook and made a little sketch of this somewhat unprepossessing vista. Then he stood back and examined the part of Leadenhall Street in which Mr Gallentin's shop lay in its entirety. To the right of the wall that concealed the strongroom lay what seemed to be a steam-laundry, and beyond this a staircase with a number of brass plates by the door leading up to a suite of offices, the profusion of whose windows suggested that they formed an upper storey beyond Mr Gallentin's shop.

Mr Pardew shifted his gaze to the left of Mr Gallentin's shop and saw that it abutted a poulterer's. He went back across the road, looked into the poulterer's window, stared at a couple of dead hares, which looked back at him in a very melancholy way, and then, resuming his former station on the farther side of the street, began to walk very deliberately along the pavement, measuring his steps as he went. A walk of thirty paces brought him opposite the staircase and, noting this, he lowered his head and walked rapidly back over the street to the northern side. Here he stood with his thumbs stuck in his lapels once more examining the clutter of brass plates, and finding that they advertised an insurance agent, a pair of attorneys and the offices of the Equatorial Mining Company, walked up the staircase.

Turning a sharp left, he found himself in a bare, tenantless vestibule with a hat-stand and an expanse of gloomy carpet. A series of rooms, some with their doors shut and manifestly in use, others with their doors open and manifestly not, lined a long, shabby corridor that ran away for a distance of fifteen or twenty yards. Fetched up in this clerical wilderness, Mr Pardew was quite at home. He looked at a calendar on the wall and noted that it was two years out of date. He put his finger on the hat-stand and then brushed off the dirt that clung to its tip. An old clerk in a billy hat and a greasy neck-tie, with ink-stained hands, came hurrying by and Mr Pardew put on his brightest smile and asked: were these the offices of Messrs Gilray, the ecclesiastical commissioners? 'No one of that name here,' the clerk told him, with a shake of his head, and Mr Pardew smiled again and said that he must have been misdirected.

The clerk continued on his way, bound for Shoreditch Station or the Metropolitan Railway, and Mr Pardew watched him go. There was no one else about. He looked this way and that and then, with a little twist of his feet, like Mme Taglioni executing the *pas seul*, danced into a little room that lay opposite, empty except for a metal cabinet and an ancient roll-top desk, and concealed himself behind the gaping door. Somewhere in the distance a clock was striking the hour and Mr Pardew listened to the single stroke, and to other noises that could now be heard along the corridor. There was a general sound of bolts being shot, of cash boxes being emptied and locked, and tramping feet. A couple of clerks came and stood on the far side of Mr Pardew's door and had a bright conversation about Hooky Sam and his chances against the Leicestershire Pippin, and Mr Pardew held his breath and gripped hard on his stick until finally they went away. There was another long silence after which a last pair of feet went scuttling along the passage, like a crab bent on aquarian mischief, and a sound of keys locking the vestibule door.

Mr Pardew waited another five minutes and then stepped out from his hiding place. He was quite alone, with only a little current of chill air blowing along the corridor to disturb the bottoms of his trousers. 'Hey there!' he said, quite loudly, and then 'Hey there!' once again, but the silence echoed around him and nobody came. Where the corridor went down to the left there were half a dozen doorways and empty rooms, and Mr Pardew walked past them, keeping a count of the number of paces he travelled as he went. Someone had left the door of Messrs Stanway & Co., accountants, slightly ajar and he went inside, flicked through one of the firm's account books, which had been left open on the desk, and then walked on. At the other end of the corridor he came upon a pair of large rooms with windows looking out onto Leadenhall Street, which by the smell of them had once formed the headquarters of a tea-broker. When he came to the first of these, Mr Pardew bent down and tapped at the floor with his stick once or twice, assured himself that the ceiling was reinforced, and continued to the second room, where a further series of taps revealed only ordinary plaster and lathe. This suggested to him that the first of the rooms lay over Mr Gallentin's shop, while the second was above the poulterer's.

Had anyone seen Mr Pardew in the empty rooms, altogether alone except for the mice scurrying in and out of the wainscot, they would have marvelled at the peculiarity of his behaviour. First he walked round the perimeter of the rooms as if to ascertain their length and breadth, writing down the calculations in his notebook. Then he knelt on the carpet that lay over Mr Gallentin's ceiling, put his ear to the floor and listened very carefully for several minutes. Then, with a queer smile on his face and the stick gripped tightly in his hand, he stalked back along the corridor, past the melancholy accountant's office and the dusty sanctum of the Equatorial Mining Co., and came out in the vestibule. There he examined the door-fastening, brought out a little metallic device he had in his pocket, twisted it into the lock, snapped it open and re-emerged onto the stairs. There was a difficulty with the door, which could not very well be allowed to hang open, so he pulled it to and, by prodding very expertly with his piece of metal, contrived to make some small part of the mechanism fall back into place. A locksmith would have noticed immediately that the fastening had been tampered with, but Mr Pardew assured himself that whoever opened it first thing on a Monday morning would probably not. This done, he continued down the staircase with a very jaunty air, stamped his feet on the bottom step and came out again into Leadenhall Street. It was about a quarter to two.

*

'So this is where you live?' said Captain Raff, two miles away in Hoxton. 'And not much of a place, neither.'

'I'll thank you to state your business, Captain Raff,' said Mr Lythgoe from the door of the second-floor back bedroom and parlour which he and his family inhabited, 'and then be hoff.'

But Captain Raff was still smarting from his ordeal at the hands of Mr Pardew and determined to make the most of this unlooked-for discovery of someone he could patronise. 'Times is hard, I take it?' he went on, squinting horribly through the gap between Mr Lythgoe's shoulders and the peeling door-frame. 'Bread ain't cheap, nor sugar neither, and what's a man to do? But there's a job here for you, Lythgoe, if you'll but say the word. Just the ticket for a steady man that's known to be reliable.'

'What's that then?' Mr Lythgoe opened the door a little wider, allowing a sight of two small children playing with a heap of toy bricks in front of an unmade grate.

'These your children, Lythgoe?' Captain Raff asked. 'Uncommon nice-looking they are.' Captain Raff lived in rooms in Ryder Street and had no children he cared to acknowledge.

'Certainly they are. And I've a fancy for them to grow up knowing their father's an honest man. What's this job that needs a steady hand? No' – for Captain Raff had made a move towards the door – 'you *shan't* come in. What is it?'

'Hang it all. A fellow can't talk properly standing on a doorstep. You remember that Mr – Abernethy you went and saw for us in Boulogne.'

'His name wasn't Abernethy,' corrected Mr Lythgoe, who had done further research on this subject. 'It was Pardew.'

'Pardew. Abernethy. It makes no odds,' Captain Raff said. 'Well, this Mr Pardew, who you'll recollect, has need of a man to . . . accompany him on a little errand.'

'I'll not do it,' Mr Lythgoe said stoutly. 'And you can tell your Mr Happerton I said so.'

'Times is hard,' Captain Raff said. 'Even harder when a man owes money. There's paper of yours on Mr Happerton's desk, Lythgoe, and you know it. What about that twenty-five pound, eh, owing to the place in Clerkenwell?'

'I'll not do it,' Mr Lythgoe said again, with slightly less conviction.

'What? And be sold up, and end up in the Fleet most likely, and have the family put upon the parish? No, you say yes to this and Mr

Happerton'll say goodbye to the bill *and* come up with something hand-some into the bargain, I shouldn't wonder. Now, are you with us, or are you not?'

Mr Lythgoe gave a blank nod of his head and Captain Raff, taking this as an assent, said he was glad to hear it and plunged off down the stairs, where the busy life of the street picked him up and obliterated him, so that Mr Lythgoe, looking anxiously out of the window a moment or so later with one of the children in his arm, saw no sign of him amid the tradesmen's barrows and the cat's-meat stalls and all the vagrant life that is Hoxton on a Saturday afternoon in springtime.

XI

London and Lincolnshire

Whereupon the sky split asunder, and a black horse, very dreadful to behold, fire-girt, the light around it as red as the sun, did make its way across the country which men call Holdernesse.

Gesta Daemonorum Lincolnensis: Being a new translation: Rev. Adolphus Symonds, late Fellow of Trinity Coll. Cantab fecit, 1783.

There is one person whose part in this narrative we have sadly neglected. How is Mrs Rebecca Happerton, and how has she been getting on? Mrs Rebecca was very well, slept soundly in her bed, had a healthy appetite and despite the responsibilities and cares of the married state was still looking out for her opportunities. Just at this moment – it was about ten o'clock on a morning in late April – she was sitting at the breakfast table with a roll and a cup of tea before her and *The Times* newspaper to hand, staring at a letter that had been brought to her with the teapot. The letter read as follows:

My dear Cousin Rebecca,

It is too bad of you to throw me over! Even Mama says it is a shame how I am never asked to dinner, and you know how she never notices anything. And a girl, you know, must look out for her chances. There are certainly none in this house, nor anywhere near it. Mr Cadwallader comes to tea sometimes, but he is a retired sea captain, and hideous, and in any case wants only to pay court to Mama. But here, you bad creature, let bygones be bygones, and if there is anything that has separated us in the past, let it not divide us in the future. I long to hear about Mr Happerton, and Rome, and Tiberius!

    Your sincerely attached friend

    Harriet Kimble

P.S. Mama and I were so sorry to hear of Uncle Tom's indisposition and trust he is improved.

'Stuff!' Mrs Rebecca said to herself, putting the letter down on the tablecloth and resolving not to answer it. There are some explanations of human conduct that cannot be vouchsafed even to one's most intimate friends, and the explanation of Cousin Harriet's throwing over was that Mrs Rebecca had grown tired of her, was bored by her conversation, preferred her own boudoir to the dusty drawing room at Eccleston Square, with its amorous sea captains, and had certain schemes of her own to prosecute in which she was anxious that Harriet should not interfere.

A woman who has been married nearly ten weeks may be supposed to have acquired some ideas about the marital state, and so it was with Mrs Rebecca. Turning the matter over in her mind, she thought that there were some things that were satisfactory about it and others that were not. As she saw it, she had married Mr Happerton to escape a mode of life that was uncongenial to her – the life lived out in her father's drawing room and at her aunt's house in Eccleston Square – only to find that Mr Gresham's illness had returned her to much the same existence as before. She acknowledged that this was nobody's fault, but it did not make her love her father any the better. As for Mr Happerton, she found that she was slightly puzzled by her attitude to him. She liked his vigour and his frank admiration of her, liked even the smell of his tobacco and the whole clubland scent that hung over him, while allowing the vulgarity of his pins and his tremendous top-boots.

As to what Rebecca wanted from her husband, save those comforts which make every marital hearth delightful, it must be said that if any politician had proposed universal suffrage and then asked her how she intended to exercise it, she would have replied that she intended to vote for her party – that party, in fact, having only a single member, which was herself. And so her attitude to Mr Happerton depended entirely on his ability to serve the interests of the Rebecca party. She liked the idea of Tiberius, because it spoke of enterprise, status and ultimately money. She would have liked other ideas, yet more ambitious than this, had they been proposed to her. She was not in the least concerned that Mr Happerton wanted her father's money, for she fancied that only a very poor specimen of a man marries solely for that reason, and that Mr Happerton was not such a type. Besides, what was old Mr Gresham's money there for other than to supply her wants? What did annoy her was that Mr Happerton seemed to want to take the money and pursue his schemes without taking her into his full confidence. And so she determined that she would set her own schemes in action, not, unless it was absolutely necessary, deflecting Mr Happerton from his chosen path but making sure that she proceeded as far along that path as her resourcefulness and ingenuity could take her.

Meanwhile, there was her cousin's letter to answer. Going over to the bureau in the corner of the room and taking from it a pen, a sheet of notepaper and an envelope, she wrote the following:

Dear Harriet,

I have not 'thrown you over' as you put it, and it is absurd of you to say so. I am afraid papa is very unwell and, in consequence, we are seeing no one. Mr Happerton is at present in Lincolnshire. Rome was very nice [she had been going to write that Rome was very tedious, but did not see why Harriet should not be encouraged to envy her going]. *I know nothing of Tiberius.*

Rebecca Happerton

No sooner had she sealed up the letter and written Miss Kimble's name upon the envelope than her maid slid into the room. It has been said of Mrs Rebecca, by those who did not like her, that she could not keep her maids, and yet curiously between herself and the present incumbent there was a quite marked affinity. It was not that Mrs Rebecca was any softer in her tone, or Nokes any more obsequious in her replies, merely that the looks and gestures exchanged between them were enough to suggest that the junior partner in the transaction knew what the senior partner was about, approved of her wants and would do her best to supply them. Seeing the girl standing before her – she was small and rather sharp-faced – Mrs Rebecca put her head on one side, emptied her tea cup and enquired:

'Was that all the post?'

'There was a letter for Mr Gresham, ma'am, that John footman has taken up with his breakfast.'

'It is odd that Mr Happerton should not have written.'

'Gentlemen are sometimes shy of sending letters, ma'am,' said Nokes, who may have had past experience of this failing.

'How is Mr Gresham this morning?'

Mrs Rebecca was no less assiduous in looking after her father than Mr Happerton had been, took him driving in her carriage most afternoons, brought him his milk-and-arrowroot just as he liked it and afterwards helped him up the stairs to bed with many an injunction to mind his feet against the banister and to beware of the stair-rods.

'I believe he has ate his broth, ma'am, and shall be getting up.'

After this a silence fell upon the room. Mrs Rebecca stared bleakly at the breakfast things and at *The Times* newspaper as if their very presence on the table annoyed her. Her maid meanwhile essayed a little rearrangement of a sideboard that did not perhaps need rearranging, while quietly detaching a little jam-pot for her own private use. In the course of these manoeuvrings her eye fell upon the envelope.

'Perhaps', Mrs Rebecca said, seeing the eye fall, 'you might ask John footman to take this round to Eccleston Square when he has leisure.'

This was civil – for Mrs Rebecca – and Nokes acknowledged the civility by bobbing her head as she took up the white oblong and placed it in her apron pocket.

Whereupon the life of Belgrave Square resumed its morning course, which is to say that Mrs Rebecca first took herself off to her room and dressed herself, looked at her sandy hair in the mirror of her dressing table, and then sat in the drawing room reading a novel. When this occupation failed her she went back up the staircase and stepped into a room which Mr Happerton had recently appropriated for his own use, shut the door behind her and sat down in the solitary chair looking interestedly about her. There was an ancient desk whose drawer she tried, but found locked, and a metal cabinet which for some reason Mr Happerton had left open, and here she turned up a pocketbook and a couple of memoranda that she read through with the greatest zeal. The picture of Tiberius stared down from the wall above her as she read. Once or twice as she browsed she gave a little smile that was not very pleasant to see, but that there was no one to see it. The lunch hour came and she went back down the staircase, pecked up a cutlet in the dining room and drank a glass of Marsala, ascertained from Mr Gresham that he did not feel well enough to take his afternoon carriage ride, contemplated the ride herself and then voted against it, and then went back into the drawing room to resume her novel. Just at the moment when she thought she might die of boredom, and that even Cousin Harriet might be preferable to the ticking of the drawing room clock and the copy of *Marchionesses and Milliners*, there came the butler to announce that Mr Gaffney had called and would the mistress like to see him. The mistress, after thinking about this for a moment or two, said that she would.

Mr Gaffney stood in an unusual relation to the life of Belgrave Square, in that he was the only one of Mr Happerton's friends regularly invited to the house. Perhaps his age and his comparative lustre had something to do with this. Like the members of the Blue Riband Club, he was a sporting gentleman, but of an older vintage, who remembered Nimrod in his prime, and knew Mr Surtees, and seemed to have attended every horse race that had taken place in these isles since the Accession. In appearance he retained just that amount of sprightliness which allows an old man to appear a middle-aged one. As he was, additionally, the younger brother of a baronet, and practised no vice that anyone knew about, ladies liked having him in their drawing rooms, and Mrs Rebecca liked having him in hers. At the same time she thought that there was information she might glean from him which would be worth the having, and without Mr Gaffney knowing that it had been had.

'Didn't know that Happerton was away, upon my honour,' Mr Gaffney said, who always talked like a walking telegraph. 'Shouldn't have come if I'd known. Really.'

'Mr Happerton is in Lincolnshire,' Mrs Rebecca explained, giving the coyest little glance as she handed Mr Gaffney his tea. It might have been observed that in Mr Gaffney's presence Mrs Rebecca was, for her, positively girlish, and the servants who came into the room wondered at it.

'Oh, so this is to see the famous Tiberius is it?' Mr Gaffney wondered.

'Is that its name?' said Mrs Rebecca. 'You will think me very foolish, Mr Gaffney, but I really know very little of my husband's affairs.'

'Not foolish, ma'am, not at all,' Mr Gaffney said. He thought Mrs Rebecca a nice, well-conducted young woman, and wished that his own daughter, who had married a Dissenting clergyman and was very serious, was more like her. 'We must have you at a meeting, and let you see the horse being put through its paces.'

'I am sure I should be very confused,' Mrs Rebecca said, 'and cheer when there was no need for cheering. But I think Mr Happerton said he may enter him for the Derby.'

'He ought to do it, Mrs Happerton. He really ought. The horse is the right age, you see, and I believe was put down as a yearling. Why, he might carry all before him and make your husband his fortune.'

'There is only three thousand pounds, I believe, for winning the Derby,' Mrs Rebecca said very demurely.

'Well, yes. But there is more to winning a horse race, you see, than the prize money. But perhaps I am boring you?' Mr Gaffney's occasional remembrance of where he was, and the duty owed to his hostess, was another reason why the ladies liked him in their drawing rooms.

'Not at all,' Mrs Rebecca said.

And so Mr Gaffney talked some more about the Derby, and Mrs Rebecca listened, and Nokes, returning to the room on some pretext – to fetch a tray that was no longer there, or a phantom duster that had probably never been there in the first place – stood and regarded her mistress with a look of the profoundest infatuation. And all the while Mr Gaffney drank his tea and thought that he was spending a very pleasant afternoon.

*

'So what do you make of it?' Mr Happerton asked Captain Raff in Lincolnshire.

'Doosid quiet place.' They were standing at the lower end of Mr Davenant's garden at the point where it met the wood. 'Plenty to eat and drink, mind,' Captain Raff mused. 'Fine-looking governess, you know.'

Mr Happerton gave a little snort of disgust and kicked at the turf in front of him. Twenty feet away the rooks were swarming over Mr Davenant's gibbet. 'I'll not have you making eyes at governesses, Raff, nor sticking your head into the dairy half a dozen times a day. It ain't that kind of place. No, what do you make of the establishment?'

Captain Raff took his pipe out of his mouth and tapped it against the heel of one of his varnished boots. He looked more than usually put-upon and had complained about the climate and the absence of curaçao in Mr Davenant's wine cabinet.

'Well now, since you ask, it ain't the best I ever saw. No doubt Curbishley knows his business . . .'

'That was a man that rode Sultana in the Oaks in '64, as you well remember.'

'D—— it all,' said Captain Raff resentfully. 'You never give a fellow the time to speak. As I say, Curbishley knows his business. But as for that Jem Claypole, I never saw a boy use a dandy brush so bad. Never pulls his ears neither, not when there's sweat pouring off 'em on all sides.' Captain Raff became quite animated as he pronounced these judgements, and a little redness came into his worn white face.

'Never mind Jem Claypole. We can have fifty Jem Claypoles if need be – or none. What about the horse?'

'Tiberius? Well, very fair you know. A very nice animal,' Captain Raff said, beginning to walk down into the outlying quadrant of the wood. 'Ugh! Why Davenant keeps that gibbet I can't imagine. If this were my place, you know, I wouldn't stand for it, and should tell the keeper to go hang.'

'But it isn't your place,' Mr Happerton reminded him. 'Nor is it ever likely to be. What about Tiberius?'

There was a sound of female voices higher up the garden, and they saw two figures go darting round the side of the house.

'Well, as I said – very fair you know. (Look – there is that girl off on one of her wanderings. I should sooner look at Davenant's gibbet than that white hair of hers.) No doubt he's everything they say he is. Teeth ain't gone yet. Mouth is very distinct. As to wind, I ain't seen him recent and neither have you. What does Curbishley say?'

'Curbishley says they galloped him on the wold the other day and there was nothing amiss.'

'Hm. (How that girl does shriek. I'd give her something to shriek about, that's all.) I tell you what it is, Happerton' – Captain Raff's tones would have been more authoritative had they issued from a face less pale and scared – 'we need to put him through his paces. That's what we need to do. No amount of gallops will get a horse ready for the Derby?'

'Who said I wished to run him in the Derby?'

'Ain't you going to?' Captain Raff wondered, in utter astonishment. A divine, informed that the Thirty-Nine Articles had been reduced, by general agreement, to Thirty-Eight, could not have affected more surprise. 'Why, what's the game?'

'Let us say that it is not quite decided,' Mr Happerton said. He was getting tired of explaining himself to Captain Raff. 'Well, look here. There's a race at Louth just next week. Just a mile or so. I dare say every carthorse in the vicinity has been entered. But I should like to see it. Curbishley can ride him . . .'

'As to that . . .' Captain Raff began, who had perhaps harboured faint hopes in this quarter.

'Indeed Curbishley shall ride him. And as for the dressing of him, why, if Jem Claypole can't be taught to do it, why I should think you might very well condescend to undertake it yourself.'

Quite crushed, Captain Raff followed Mr Happerton up the hill to the house.

*

It was Mr Davenant's habit, during his guests' stay, to keep himself as much out of the way as possible. Although he showed himself at meals, and was occasionally induced to accompany Mr Happerton on tours of the stables or to a neighbouring paddock in which the horse was now and then exercised, at other times he retired to remote parts of the house and was not to be found. Mr Happerton was not in the least put out by these sensitivities. He had things he wished to say to Mr Davenant, and questions he wished to ask. Eventually, having searched fruitlessly in the study and the estate office, he ran him to earth in the gunroom.

'I hope I don't disturb you, sir,' he remarked, extending one glorious top-boot in Mr Davenant's direction and holding out his hand. 'Only I particularly wished to speak with you.'

'No, you do not disturb me,' Mr Davenant said. He was examining an ancient musket, of the kind that is primed by powder and shot being thrust into its barrel, and looked very bleak and cast-down. 'What is it that I can do for you?'

'Well.' Mr Happerton hesitated, saw the expression in Mr Davenant's face and perhaps appreciated something of his disquiet. 'I have been here four days and we have scarcely spoken.'

'If I have fallen short in the obligations of a host, then I am sorry for it, Mr Happerton.'

'I did not mean that.' Mr Happerton wondered for a moment what he did mean. 'It's a nice little establishment you have here, Mr Davenant.'

'It was my father's, and his father's before him,' said Mr Davenant, neither acknowledging or denying the claim.

'I don't doubt it was. Mr Curbishley seems an excellent man . . .'

'I have always found him so.'

Mr Happerton felt oppressed by the coldness of the room – there was no fire – and the gloominess of the surround. The musket in Mr Davenant's hand struck him as a terrible old antique which had much better be lent to a museum.

'How far, I wonder, is it from here to Louth?'

'About twenty miles.'

'And there is a racecourse there, I believe?'

'It is nothing very much. You would not, I think, find it suited to Tiberius.'

'Wouldn't I? Well, we shall see.'

And with that, Mr Happerton raised his hand in the most friendly manner, turned on his heel and left Mr Davenant to his cold, damp gunroom, his gathering darkness and his ancient musket.

*

'That's a fine red mark you have on the side of your head, Raff,' Mr Happerton said as they passed one another in the stable yard. 'I wonder who put it there?'

'Red mark be hanged,' Captain Raff said, in what for him was a tone of quite unaccountable fury.

*

Miss Ellington's father had always said that a young woman should have her resources, and so the governess had hers. There was her

Christian Year, which she read at a little in the early mornings, and there was Mrs Brookfield's novel, which she had by her chair after supper. There were her walks in the garden and in the pasture that lay behind the wood, and there was the drawing-room piano, whose keys, to be sure, were very stiff and yellow. And then, looking through a trunk which sat in the corner of the schoolroom, she found a box of water-colours and an ancient brush or two of black horsehair, which was a source of satisfaction to her, as she had used to paint, both at home – Mr Ellington said she did very well but would do better to clean her brushes – and with her dear girls in Warwickshire. The reds and blues and yellows were all dried up, alas, but as Mr Glenister truly remarked, seeing her at work upon a view of the garden, all one needed for a prospect of Scroop Hall was green, brown and grey. And so with her books, and her walks, and her easel, she had her occupations, which was a comfort.

And then there was Evie, who was the greatest occupation of all. Having had the opportunity to observe her, Miss Ellington could truth-fully say that she was a dear, sweet girl – affectionate, confiding, altogether without malice or guile, but that there was nothing to be done with her. Miss Ellington devised a scheme of study that she thought might entice her: a picturesque scene or two from history that might awaken her curiosity; a little parable or two from nature to make her smile. But it was no good at all: she could not understand it, and the pain of this want of understanding reduced Evie to utter misery. And so the scenes from history and the parables from nature had been given up, and they sat and looked at picture books, and played at spillikins, and talked. Or rather Evie asked the most peculiar questions, plucked from nowhere, like a cloud pulled out of the sky, which it was Miss Ellington's task to answer as best she could. Thus, on a cold morning, with the wind rushing through the tree-tops and the windows rattling in their frames:

'Where is Pusskin?'

'Pusskin is dead.'

'Why is he dead?'

'Why, Evie, we have spoken of this.'

'Will Pusskin go to heaven?'

'Pusskin was a good cat and shall have his reward.'

(Which, by the by, Miss Ellington believed to be true, whatever Mr Fitzgerald may have said in his book about the afterlife being an exclusively human resort.)

Another time – it may have been the same morning, when the wind had abated a little – they were looking at an illustrated paper, full of sketches of ladies' fashions, toxophilites drawing their bows, &c., and she asked, quite mournfully, while pointing at one of these Dianas fixing an arrow to her string:

'Is that my mama?'

'You know very well that it is not your mama.'

'Why does my mama not come?'

'You know, Evie, that she cannot.'

'Where is your mama? Is she here?'

'Alas, she is like your mama, Evie. She is gone from us, and will not come back.'

And then, looking through the trunk in which Miss Ellington had discovered the boxes of watercolours, which was very deep and capacious and would not yield up all its secrets at once, they found a pile of clothing, very ancient, and, she believed, dating from a time sixty or seventy years ago. A time when ladies wore gigots, and paduasoy, and marvellous bonnets from which you would hardly think there were room for a human face to stare out. And so, having nothing else to amuse them, it wanting an hour until tea and the servants gone out, they stopped up the door and arrayed themselves in some of this finery: Miss Ellington in an ivory muslin that might have done for a countess's daughter in the time of old King George, and Evie in a wide-brimmed hat with an ostrich feather on its brim that, when they touched it, broke into three pieces. They fetched mirrors and stared at themselves in wonder, for it was the drollest sight, after which they hastened to put the things away, for it seemed to Miss Ellington – although she could not say exactly where the fault lay – that they had done wrong, and that it would have been better not to set these ghosts a-caper.

For this was a house of ghosts. There were the pictures of Mr Davenant's ancestors in their frames, and there was the portrait of Evie's mama upon the dining-room table. Miss Ellington asked Mrs Castell, who had known her, what manner of woman she was, and received the answer that Missus was the gayest, spiritest lady she ever saw, and, though it was not her place to say so, worth two of Mr D. The wind swept in from the east – from Jutland, Mr Glenister said – with nothing to stand in its way but sea and sky. The trees wavered in the rushing air and the dogs barked in the stable yard. Miss Ellington asked Hester whether she did not think this was a very lonely place and the girl said that she had served at one time in a great house on the coast that had been closed up for the winter while the family was away, with only an old housekeeper for company, and that the two of them went to bed each night at seven and rose at five and saw no one except the grocer with his cart, who called once a week. It seemed to Miss Ellington that such a life must be insupportable, but no, Hester said she had known girls who had gone further and fared worse, and if one trusted in one's Maker – Hester was a very religious girl – all would be well.

Remembering what her papa had said, Miss Ellington resolved that she should make a study, and the things she should make a study of would be their guests, Mr Happerton and Captain Raff. Miss Ellington wondered a little at the propriety of this, but then remembered that we were all of us subject to the observation of those we move among, and were not, she thought, much wounded by it. Besides, what was she to Mr Happerton and Captain Raff, who were London visitors – as different to the people in Lincolnshire as a dish of peas was from one of the mangel-wurzels that lay in Mr Davenant's fields – who were concerned only with Tiberius, and when they quitted Scroop, which Mrs Castell said she believed they would do next week, would bear not the faintest recollection of us back to the metropolis with them?

Of the two, she preferred Captain Raff the less. Mr Glenister, who was amused by him, she thought, said he was an 'old buck', an expression Miss Ellington had never heard before. Why did she not like Captain Raff? Because he fidgeted over his dinner, and swallowed his wine in great gulps, and gave the maids very knowing looks (indeed Hester said she had boxed his ears for some familiarity, and certainly there was a great red weal on the side of Captain Raff's face). To be sure he was very civil to her, raised his hat – a very dirty hat that any other gentleman would have had cleaned – when they met about the place, called her 'Miss Ellington' and so forth, but she did not believe the civility well-meant.

There was a particular conversation that she had with Captain Raff once when they met by chance at the side gate of the house.

'Why, Miss Ellington, you are looking uncommon fresh today. You will think I am waiting here on purpose, I daresay.'

'I think nothing of the kind, sir.'

'A doosid warm day I call this.' (In fact there was a great wind blowing in from across the wold.) 'What do you say to a turn about the garden?'

'It is very cold, Captain Raff, and I am on my way to the schoolroom.'

'Ah, I daresay you think I'm a sad sort of man, Miss Ellington.'

'I think nothing of the kind, sir.'

At which Captain Raff gave an extraordinary wink, like Mr Punch at the seaside immediately before the stick is brought down upon his head, and skipped off along the path in his dirty little boots, so that she almost wished she had a stick herself with which she might belabour him.

Mr Happerton, meanwhile, had won what Miss Ellington's papa, talking of his Oxford days, would have called 'golden opinions'. He quite melted Mrs Castell's heart by presenting her with a box of preserved fruits, and when he sat in the drawing room reading the newspaper Hester and Dora listened out for his bell as if the Prince of Wales himself were quartered there. His letters were brought in ever so humbly on a salver, and there was a special bottle of port in the cellar which he was most insistently urged to try of an evening. For herself, Miss Ellington thought Mr Happerton a loud, cheerful kind of a man, very appreciative of all that was done for him, very civil to those around him, and yet, she thought, rather calculating. He had a trick of reckoning them up which was not wholly agreeable, like a shopkeeper pricing up a turtle for his window: a glance at Mrs Castell; a glance at Evie; a glance at Hester as she balanced the dinner plates on her arm. He had a way of looking at things as if they were not to his taste and he wished to alter them: a glance at the stable yard and the midden that lies beyond it; a glance at the apple trees in the orchard by the kitchen garden; a glance at Mr Davenant's ancestors in their frames.

Miss Ellington's papa would have said that he was not a gentleman, and yet there was, she thought, no general agreement as to of what gentlemanliness consists, and a man might drop his aitches and sit al- together woodenly at the dinner table with his mouth open and still be very highly regarded.

Every day or so the post brought a letter to Mr Happerton which was thought to be from his wife, which he read very attentively and then made a spill of it for his cigar or threw it straightaway into the fireplace, where sometimes it was not wholly extinguished by the flame. At these moments Miss Ellington sometimes had a great urge to gather up the fragments and examine them. He was always striding about the place, pacing the garden, putting his nose into the bins that were kept for the pigs, or strolling over to the church to talk to the sexton as he stood digging, or walking into the village on some private errand that was never revealed.

'Why is it', Miss Ellington asked once of Mr Glenister, as they sat in the schoolroom, where he had come to bring Evie a bag of sugarplums that he had bought in Lincoln, 'that Mr Happerton should wish to make copies of Mr Davenant's signature?'

'Is that what he has been doing?' Mr Glenister demanded, with a sharpness of tone she had not previously noticed in him.

So she explained about her coming upon him in the study, his being called away, the piece of paper that lay on the desk, &c.

'Well, he is a sly one,' Mr Glenister remarked, laughing as he did so, but not, as Miss Ellington thought, without some dissimulation, and she laughed too, though not quite knowing why she did so.

And then came a very strange and peculiar incident, which Miss Ellington thought would exercise them far more than whether they liked Mr Happerton and if he sat in the study copying Mr Davenant's signature.

*

The noises came from outside in the stable yard: a high-pitched cry of anguish; the slam of a door; feet moving rapidly over stone. Then came other voices and other doors banging in their wake. There was someone coming rapidly up the main staircase, and Mr Happerton, who had kept at his toilet, and was now calmly dipping his razor carefully into his shaving-water, was not at all surprised when the feet stopped before his bedroom door, the door was thrown open and Captain Raff, his coat even more dishevelled and his face turned scarlet from the unwonted exercise, fairly flung himself onto the carpet at his feet.

Though he knew that nothing short of an earthquake would have induced Captain Raff to invade his sleeping quarters at ten past eight in the morning, Mr Happerton's first response was that of anger.

'What the devil do you mean, Raff, bursting in here like a dervish? What on earth is the matter?'

'Cut!' Captain Raff pulled himself up from the carpet, where he had come to rest almost on his knees, and repeated the word two or three times. 'Cut!'

'Cut? What is cut? I very nearly cut myself with this razor when you came crashing in. What do you mean?'

'The horse,' Captain Raff gasped, like a fish hauled out onto the towpath. 'Cut. Stabbed. Slashed.'

And then Mr Happerton put down his razor, threw on his jacket, and with the lather from his shaving preparation still clinging to his jaw ran out of his room, down the staircase and through the back parts of the house to the stable yard, with Captain Raff – now very much out of breath and quite wild-eyed – following behind him.

In the stables all was confusion. The rail that stood before Tiberius's stall was half thrown down and the horse stood quivering behind it with his hoofs stamping nervously on the straw. A lamp had been turned over and was leaking oil onto the floor. Jem the stable boy stood half-in and half-out of the stall, not liking to approach any nearer, such was the horse's agitation, but making placatory gestures with his hand.

'Here, maister,' Jem shouted, giving Mr Happerton a nod. 'I's'll not come close if I were you. There ain't no knowing what he might do. Look, he have kicked half his stall away already. Hand us that blanket, will ye, that's on the straw there.'

Mr Happerton's gaze took in the quivering horse, the spilled oil and the raised arm all in a moment. He was horribly afraid – afraid of the blood on the horse's flank, and the terror in his eyes, but a part of him felt also an inexpressible relief. Whatever might have happened, Tiberius was at any rate not dead. 'What on earth has been going on? What is the matter with Tiberius?'

Jem had begun gingerly to pat the horse's flank with the blanket-end, which Tiberius suffered him to do.

'Someone have broke in through the side door in the night – see there how the bolt is forced and the straw all thrown about. Whoever it was has cut Tiberius on the flank, and – here again – on the foreleg. It's my belief it were done lately, too, for when I came in here ten minutes since I heered a noise of broke glass very like a lamp being turned over.'

All this time Captain Raff had been edging forward at Mr Happerton's side, like a terrier anxious to get at a rat. 'The confounded villain,' he now yelled. 'We must search the estate, find him and have him hanged.'

'You're the bravest fellow that ever there was, Raff, and I always said so,' Mr Happerton remarked, almost wearily, and then, addressing himself to Jem Claypole: 'He seems quieter now. See if you can get that bridle around his neck. There, old fellow' – this to Tiberius – 'I shan't hurt you, even if some other scoundrel has.'

Captain Raff looked as if he would like to make another rush, but Mr Happerton pushed him away, went over to the horse, and, taking great care – for the animal reared up at his approach – made a close inspection of his injuries, which were as Jem had described them. There was a great gash on the horse's flank, from which blood oozed forth, and another, lesser, mark somewhere above his forehock.

'Very well,' Mr Happerton said. 'Jem Claypole, I am obliged to you. Heaven knows what might have happened had you come a moment later. Now, you should have the property searched and send someone for the constable.' As Mr Happerton pronounced these instructions, his eye fell on incidentals: a mouse creeping through the dirt a dozen feet away; a line of ancient horse-brasses that hung on the mouldering plaster; a splash of bright blood upon the straw. 'As for you, Raff, you had better ride into Scroop as fast as you can and bring the vet back with you.'

'I should like to take a knife to the d——d villain that did it,' said Captain Raff stoutly. But he consented to saddle up a horse and gallop off into Scroop as he was bidden. Jem Claypole went off to execute his commissions. Mr Happerton, with another glance at Tiberius, whose nervous terror seemed somewhat to have abated, went back into the house to complete his toilet.

*

There is rather a gash in his flank, Mr Happerton wrote to his wife, and no one save Curbishley cares to go near him, but I think he will do. Raff is being very martial and belligerent, saying it is all a plot, and ready to fight a duel with anyone who says otherwise. If you have a moment, you might tell Mr Gaffney that all is well – or nearly well – as I know this is an affair in which he takes an interest. My regards to your father, and tell him I hope that he is comfortable, and that I shall see him before very long.
    Your affectionate husband
    G. Happerton

*

'There is some mischief about the horse,' Mrs Rebecca said to her maid as she looked at the letter next morning in Belgrave Square.

'You don't say, ma'am,' Nokes remarked, continuing to buff away at an area of the mahogany sideboard that did not in the least need polishing.

'Mr Happerton says that someone has broken into the stables and tried to injure him with a knife!'

'Indeed, ma'am,' Nokes went on, demurely polishing, but it is a fact that half an hour later she retrieved the letter from the bureau in which her mistress had placed it. And then a dozen hours later the landlord of a public house on the northernmost side of the park could be heard advising his customers that Tiberius, that everybody thought was such a certainty, had – had his throat cut, been found dead in a ditch, had had all his limbs broke, and whatever he did, alive or dead, would certainly not be competing in the Derby.

Mrs Rebecca, as anyone who has so far considered her character will admit, was a shrewd woman. If the importance of Tiberius to her husband and to the world in general had not previously been apparent to her, then in the next few days it became abundantly clear. A report of the incident appeared in the *Morning Chronicle*. Sporting gentlemen talked about it at their clubs. The Blue Riband was wild with excitement, and half a dozen of its members seriously proposed to hire a chaise and drive instantly to Scroop to hear the story from the horse's – or rather Mr Happerton's – mouth. Mr Gaffney, having heard the news, came straightaway to tea, was shown the letter, patted Mrs Rebecca's hand and went away reassured. Neither was Tiberius the sole topic by which the sporting world now declared itself to be animated. It was one of those times – nobody quite knows how they come about, and can only register the fact of their coming – when the public decides to take a more than usual interest in the Turf. A sporting baronet had been found dead in his dressing room with his brains blown out and a piteous note at his side, and it had been suggested that this tragedy was the result of his owing ever so many thousands of pounds to Mr Macready, the society bookmaker. The police had raided several public houses in the Fitzrovia district and confiscated betting slips sufficient, as one newspaper put it, to paper a drawing room.

All this, unhappily, had led to an outpouring of moral sentiment. A slum missioner, whose duty directed him each day to the rookeries of Whitechapel and Jago Court, maintained that half the population of the East End spent the greater part of their wages on gambling. A bishop inveighed against it in the House, a dozen provincial pulpits allowed his case, and *Punch* was very satirical, both about the proscribing clergymen and the recreation they presumed to condemn. All this Mrs Rebecca saw and wondered how she could make redound to her advantage. Meanwhile, she wrote the most dutiful letters back to Mr Happerton in Lincolnshire, said that she was very sorry to hear about the poor horse, hoped that Captain Raff was not continuing to make a fool of himself, and remained his affectionate wife, R. Happerton. All of which Mr Happerton looked at very keenly and by which he was briefly consoled.

*

The course at Louth is not particularly extensive. If truth be known it is not much more than a large field to which the addition of various posts and barriers has contrived a circuit perhaps half a mile in length, for the sporting gentlemen of Lincoln generally take their horses to Leicestershire or even further afield. There is a little grandstand and a couple of rails for the communality, and a paddock, and it was here that Mr Happerton and Captain Raff stood watching Mr Curbishley exercising Tiberius on the greensward.

'Looks a trifle stiff,' said Captain Raff gloomily. The spring sun was making his eyes water. 'See how he is putting his right foreleg down. Just where that d——d villain stabbed him. The police have no idea who it was, I suppose?'

'None at all.'

'That fellow Abernethy who owns Pendragon is as great a scoundrel as I ever met. It wouldn't surprise me in the least if he sent a man up here to do it.'

'What nonsense you talk, Raff,' said Mr Happerton, not quite as good-humouredly as he sounded, who knew Mr Abernethy to be the meekest little man in Christendom, bullied by his children and seen in the West End running errands for his wife's mama. 'Abernethy would have to be mad to do such a thing.'

'Mad or not, he should be hanged for it,' said Captain Raff fervently.

The horse having now described a circle and returned to the place from which it had originally set off, Mr Happerton called up: 'Well, Curbishley, how do you find him?'

'Well enough, I think,' Mr Curbishley said. He was a lean, strong man with the additional advantage of riding under ten stone. 'There is no one to touch him here, I should say. Have you seen the card?'

'Nothing I ever heard of in my life before. Mr Jenks's "Calliope" is a nice little mare, I heard a fellow say. Who is he?'

'Oh he has good horses enough,' Mr Curbishley said. He sat up in the saddle, feet balanced on his stirrups, staring out across the paddock and the pale horizon beyond it. 'But he don't race 'em so much, you know.'

'Well then, I should go at it gentle-like,' Mr Happerton advised. 'Don't be afraid to pull up if, if – well, you know what I mean.'

Mr Curbishley said he knew what he meant, brought the point of his whip up to his chin, gave a little smile – as a sporting man, his attitude to Mr Happerton was one of complete neutrality, and if Beelzebub had bought Tiberius he would have taken orders from him quite as happily – and began to trot once more towards the paddock's edge.

Mr Happerton, meanwhile, had his eye on the racecard, a little slip of paper, villainously printed. '"The Tin Man: Mr Flaherty. Servitor: O. Jermy Esq." Heavens, Raff. What is the matter now?'

'It is that Curbishley,' Captain Raff complained. 'He will pull so, you know. The beasts can't stand it.'

Mr Happerton found increasingly that there were certain things he could not stand, and that Captain Raff was one of them. For all the mildness of his temper – he had been mild all morning, mild in the carriage that had taken them from Scroop, very mild in the tavern where they had taken luncheon, milder still in his negotiations with the clerk of the course – he was deeply uneasy. Should the race not go according to plan, he knew that a scheme in which he had invested a great deal of time, money and ingenuity would be damaged beyond repair. It might even be doubted how he could refashion his career, should Tiberius fail him. These anxieties burned in his head quite as much as the cries of the old women selling sherbet outside the beer tent and the shouts of the Lincolnshire bookmakers.

'They're uncommon down on racing here, I believe,' Captain Raff said sadly. There was a kind of dull astonishment in his eye, as if he could not imagine how anyone could have a down on the sport of kings. 'Why, the magistrates tried to close the course down last Michaelmas, a fellow told me, on account of drunkenness.'

'Look, there is Curbishley waving,' Mr Happerton said. 'What does he want, I wonder?'

But it turned out that Mr Curbishley wanted only some minor re-adjustment of his bridle, and Mr Happerton sighed with relief. Another five minutes and the race had begun.

It was Captain Raff's immemorial habit, when attending race-meetings, to station himself at the rail with a pair of field glasses, and then, oblivious of the crowds who swarmed around him, relay the finer points of the competition back to the friends he had brought with him. Shoulder to shoulder with the rustic audience, this service he now delighted to perform for Mr Happerton.

'. . . Well now, off they go. Frightfully bad piece of starting, too. Why, the horse was a yard behind the line, at least . . . Now, sir, there is plenty of room for both of us . . . I see Curbishley is taking him away from the rail. Well, I daresay that is the thing to do . . . Indeed, sir, you *shan't* stand there' (it was a marvel how Captain Raff's natural timidity deserted him at race-meetings and he became quite bellicose). 'Now, where has that brown horse come from? Calliope, I suppose. Tremendous little fellow riding her, too. Wonder how he stays on? Ugh! There's a fellow down there – never saw such a lot of potholes in my life. Stuck, is he? No, he is getting to his feet. Come now,

Curbishley. Why does he stay with the pack, I wonder ...? I shall thank you to keep your elbows to yourself, my man ... Now, where are they? If I were Mr Jenks I should not put any wagers on Calliope, indeed I shouldn't. Dear me, but that's a sharp turn – I wonder it's allowed. Why's Curbishley standing up? I declare, he'll fall over. A little grey's making a run – quite a stylish horse. No stamina though – see the foam coming out of her mouth! Looks half done. Here comes Curbishley. That's it, sir! Always very sparing with the whip, Curbishley, but never mind. Three lengths clear, I should say. Is he quickening, do you think, or is it the others fading away ...? My good man, I shall certainly thrash you if you come a step nearer ... Five lengths! That Calliope you see is nowhere – a lot of carthorses. Ten lengths, Happerton, and could have had more ...'

*

In Belgrave Square Mrs Rebecca stood at her dressing table, hairbrush in hand, and thought about Mr Gaffney who, coming to tea again, had disclosed, amid much handpatting and many confidential remarks, that Tiberius was now regarded as a certainty for the Derby and that the price put upon him had fallen to 5–1.

XII

What *Bell's Life* thought about it

I t behoves us to state our opinion of the great Derby race. While we are
happy to vouchsafe this information, we observe that we are not a prophet.
If prophecy is required, then recourse should be made to that modern
seer, Captain Crewe of the *Star*. We insist, moreover, that though we may
note the fact of a horse's entry into a race, we cannot guarantee its appearance on the Epsom course. Only Mr Dorling's cards can do that, and even
they, it seems, are not infallible. Of the smaller fry – and we mean by this
term no disparagement – Mr Abernethy's PENDRAGON is a smart horse
(though whence came his Cornish name, when he was bred up in
Barnstaple, we cannot guess), a trifle finicky and uncertain on his feet –
he threw Joe Darby at Croxton Park and broke that gentleman's thigh at
the hip – but sweet-tempered and generally biddable. Of Lord Martindale's
SEVERUS there is not much to say. Our correspondent, who saw him at
Wincanton early in the season, declared him lively, but with a propensity
to hug the rail. He was got by NECROMANCER of WESTERN STAR and may
be thought not yet to have honoured this noble parentage . . .

DAWN TREADER – a pretty name for an ungainly animal – delighted those who saw him at Newmarket in the March gallops, but is said, like a certain political party, to be ungovernable. He is the property of Mr Cartwright, a gentleman not previously known to us, or indeed to anyone, was brought, obscurely, out of Lancashire and, we anticipate, may very soon be taken back there. Will PERICLES (we confess to being tired of these classical names, and would mention poor Lord Fitzharding, who called his horse after a river in Sparta only to see it ruin itself at a brook in Sussex) run? Mr Grant, his trainer, is supposed when asked this question to have savagely shaken his head, but one can think of half a dozen animals of whom this gentleman has despaired, who have then stepped out of their stalls and done him credit . . .

And then a gaggle of horses of whom no one has ever heard and, it may confidently be predicted, will never hear of again. Mr Coveney's WARWICK LAD was apparently got by SPARTACUS of DAMOSEL, but then the toothache may be got of an over-indulgence in toffee. TELEMACHUS (Mr Duchesne) was given up for dead after his accident at York, but is supposedly recovered. We have seen LONGSHOREMAN run and did not esteem him. Mr Harrison will do no good if he continues to exhibit POTENTATE to the public. Are gentlemen, knowing his habits, expected to back him out of charity? Or because Mr Harrison's attachment to the sport goes back to the old king's day? Alas, sentiment has no place in racing and neither does POTENTATE, next to whom Mr Bellingham's AVOCET might have carried Prince Rupert into battle at Naseby and Lord Havergal's CONQUISTADOR been put to drag an Athenian chariot. BOSKY BOY: a dull horse, never seen to do anything. Won the Tradesman's Plate at Chester, but the field was of three only, and the third horse destroyed. VALENTINE: need not detain us, and indeed in the past has only detained course officials anxious to get home for their dinners. EMPEROR'S FRIEND: why Mr Malplaquet persists with this animal we cannot imagine. AVOIR-DUPOIS: we are reliably informed that Lord Eddington spent the winter attempting to sell this horse, but got no takers. HIBERNIAN: an Irish horse; a shamrock has more novelty. FELIX (Lord Fitzpatrick), his lordship's pride and joy, not thought likely to run . . .

XIII

An Evening in the City

Messrs Gallentin of Leadenhall Street are pleased to advise clients of their recent acquistion of the 'Corinthian' safe. Devised by Messrs Milner, of cast iron to a depth of two inches, the lock – designed by Mr Chubb – consisting of a brass front with steel reinforcements, its manufacturers are confident that no more secure repository has yet been laid before the public.

Advertisement

Spring had finally come to Shepherd's Inn. The gillyflowers were blooming in the window boxes, there was a patch of bright green grass growing in the dust before the statue of the shepherd boy, and the old porter had been sufficiently animated by the joys of the season as to take his chair out into the courtyard and read his newspaper in full view of the passing traffic. Not that there was a great deal of this. April is a rather questionable time in Shepherd's Inn. The half-pay majors don't like it – it reminds them, perhaps, of past glories – and keep to their rooms. The shirtsleeved young gentlemen with their cigars and their pewter pots are elsewhere – down the river at Greenwich, maybe, or at Richmond or Teddington Lock. But the man who did not wish to be called Mr Pardew and the lady who, conversely, was very anxious to be called his wife, saw it and were presumably gladdened by it. The blind was not so often lowered in the window of their lodging, and the lady could sometimes be seen looking out of it in a rather hopeful manner, and the gentleman could sometimes be found descending the staircase of an afternoon to stand in the court-yard, where he sniffed the scent of the gillyflowers, stared rather sardonically at the shepherd boy, on whose shoulders there was perhaps the hint of a bird's nest, and spoke a word to the porter, who, with the half-pay majors quiescent and the shirtsleeved young men down the river at Greenwich (or wherever), was, of all things, anxious for conversation.

It was about five o'clock in the afternoon – still very bright and blust-ery, with little ribbons of wind darting in and out of the alleyways – and Mr Pardew was sitting in his armchair talking to Captain Raff. Spring, too, had had its effect on Captain Raff, who was wearing a blue jacket and a pair of duck trousers that were very nearly white, to the great amusement of his host.

'I declare, Raff, in that get-up I should expect to find you in Oldcastle Street with your hat in front of your feet dancing jigs for halfpennies,' Mr Pardew now said acidly. The stick lay on the table between them.

'No need to insult a fellow, you know,' Captain Raff said. 'It's a nice jacket, ain't it though?'

'I shouldn't wonder if the Prince wanted the name of your tailor,' Mr Pardew said. 'Now, what is it that I can do for you?'

Despite the mockery of his three-guinea coat, Captain Raff thought that he was getting the measure of Mr Pardew. 'Hang it all,' he said. 'You know what we want. Why, May is nearly come and nothing ventured. When's it to come off?'

'Such things don't arrange themselves, Raff, as you very well know.'

'I daresay they don't. But that was another twenty pounds you had last week, and Mr – that is, my people – would like to know when they can see a return on their money.'

Mr Pardew looked at Captain Raff, whose white face contrasted very oddly with the splendour of his costume, at his stick, and at the light streaming in at the window. He wondered how much might be gained by drawing Captain Raff's attention to certain facts that had come his way since their last meeting.

'Seventy pounds, you know, you've had now,' Captain Raff said again, a shade portentously. 'We shall be wondering – indeed we shall – if you intend to carry off the business at all.'

'A sporting gentleman, isn't he, your Mr Happerton?' Mr Pardew enquired.

'Eh? What's that?' Captain Raff demanded, with an expression of stark horror on his face.

'Mr Happerton, who has sent me that seventy pounds, is a sporting gentleman, I believe?' Mr Pardew ventured again.

'I don't know what you mean.'

'Not know about your own principal?' Mr Pardew went on, and Captain Raff thought that he had never hated a man so much. 'Or of Tiberius, that everyone says is entered for the Derby? I suppose you'll be backing him yourself, Raff?'

'I don't know what you're talking about,' Captain Raff said miserably.

'And I dare say Mr Happerton don't know anything about Milner's Quadruple Patent. Perhaps,' said Mr Pardew, almost to himself, 'he means to back it himself. Is that the case, eh, Raff? Well, never mind. You had better tell Mr Happerton, who you don't know anything about but I do – I dare say he paid for that jacket, didn't he, Raff? – that I intend to bring it off within the week. There, will that do?'

Captain Raff, very humble now and with half an eye perhaps on the stick, said that it would do, and took his leave, clattering away down the wooden staircase with such haste that Mr Pardew fairly laughed out loud. After this he sat in his chair for an hour until there came a noise of footsteps on the stairs and Jemima walked into the room with a marketing basket on her arm.

'Gracious,' she said, seeing the attitude in which he sat. 'Have you been sitting here all this time?'

'Well – maybe I have,' Mr Pardew conceded. But he brightened at the sight of the basket, and at Jemima, whose complexion was very fresh, quite glowing from her walk indeed, and thought that there were some pleasures which even Captain Raff could not take from him.

Mr Pardew saw Captain Raff on a Tuesday. On the Wednesday he and Jemima did not stir from their chamber, and on the Thursday the extent of their recreation was a little walk in the sunshine up and down Chancery Lane. But on the Friday, quite early, Mr Pardew put on his best coat, took his stick in his hand and went off to an address in Amwell Street to see a friend from his early days in London of whom, as he explained to Jemima, he had the most pleasant recollections. Mr File, Mr Pardew's friend, was an amiable old gentleman of sixty-two or -three, very small and demure, with a shiny bald head, who had once worked as a locksmith for Messrs Chubb and now lived in the greatest seclusion in a nice, neat house which those with knowledge of a locksmith's emoluments might wonder how he was able to afford. Although it was barely ten o'clock in the morning, Mr File greeted his visitor with a glass of sherry-cobbler, toasted him with his own glass, and then embarked on a catechism so oblique that the bare record of it set down on paper would be altogether mystifying to anyone who read it.

'So it's to come off then, is it?' Mr File asked, settling his spectacles comfortably on his nose.

'Well – yes, I suppose it is,' said Mr Pardew, who did not sound very certain.

'A Milner, you know,' said Mr File, whose respectful tone suggested that he was discussing the antecedents of a great lady.

'I don't doubt Mr Milner knows his business.'

'Reinforced, I believe,' Mr File went on. 'You shall have to take the alderman with you.'

'Well – I dare say.' They might have been talking of a Guildhall dinner. 'Did you ever see a Milner?' Mr Pardew went on.

'Oh, indeed. I saw a jack-in-the-box set on it once, and even then the lock held. But the alderman would do it, I imagine. How shall you get in?'

'Circumnavigation,' said Mr Pardew with a bitter laugh. 'Do you have anything?'

'Well, there is this, perhaps.'

And Mr Pardew smiled and secreted whatever 'this' was in the inner pocket of his coat.

Reaching Shepherd's Inn once more at about twelve, Mr Pardew found that his chambers were empty. Not feeling the need to eat anything, after Mr File's sherry, he sat down in a chair and began to brood. He had told Captain Raff and Mr File that 'the thing was to come off', but in truth he was not so very sure. He had once before pulled off a bold stroke of this kind and he was not certain that it had done him any good. Another bold stroke might do him some considerable harm. And then, even if he succeeded, where should he go? Boulogne was all very well, but Mr Pardew had an idea that, given the boldness of the stroke, Boulogne might not be far enough away, and that even Pau or Lisbon might not satisfy his peculiar needs for quiet and seclusion.

And so he brooded on, sometimes picking up a slip of paper and writing a note on it, sometimes staring out of the window, and sometimes plunging his hands into his trouser pockets and jingling the coins in them. 'Well,' he said to himself, finally, when perhaps an hour had passed, 'I shall have to decide, anyhow.' There was a little pile of silver – quite a little pile – lying on the sideboard, and he selected from it a florin, with that picture of Her Majesty on its reverse side that has so lately been superannuated, spun it in the air, looked at the result – the coin fell heads up – and gave a little smile. When Jemima came back he was sitting once more in the chair with a newspaper open in front of him and apparently in high good humour.

'I think I may not have told you,' he said, 'but I am called away this weekend.'

'Where to?' Jemima wondered, with her eyes open very wide.

'Well – in fact it is that Lord Fairhurst wants to see me down in Hampshire. I really have half a mind not to go.'

'If his lordship wants to see you, then I think you ought to go,' said Jemima very firmly. 'When shall you be back?'

'Sunday afternoon, I imagine.' The expression on Mr Pardew's face as he said this was quite inscrutable. 'But I don't like to think of you here alone. Perhaps you would like' – there was now a particular glint in his eye – 'to visit your sister?'

'Well, perhaps I shall,' Jemima said. She was still considering Mr Pardew's invitation. 'Does Lord Fairhurst have a large establishment?'

'It is just in the normal way of things. There is eighty acres, I believe. But he is very much in debt.'

'You must certainly go,' Jemima said.

*

Saturday morning came and Mr Pardew went quietly about his business. By noon he had been out to make one or two little purchases at an ironmonger's shop in Oldcastle Street – brought back secretly in a carpet-bag – and packed Jemima off in a cab to her sister in Islington. This done, he sat the carpet-bag on the kitchen table, made sure the door of the lodgings was firmly shut, and began to stow into it certain items that would have been looked at very oddly by the manservant who unpacked them at Lord Fairhurst's, had that domestic or his master existed. There was a big three-pound hammer, which Mr Pardew took out of a cupboard and wrapped up expertly in a cloth, and a couple of wrenches, which he concealed in the end of a sheet. Finally he went and looked into one of the trunks that had come with him from Boulogne, and from among several queer items that rose to view, chose a mysterious-looking piece of iron, apparently only twelve inches long, but capable, if manipulated in a certain way, of being extended to a length of five feet. This, too, was put in the carpet-bag, which Mr Pardew then picked up and shook. There was a clanking noise, which seemed to disturb him, and so he went back to the trunk and found a rag or two to wrap round the objects within.

Looking at his watch, he discovered that it was barely one o'clock – a church clock a quarter of a mile away was striking the hour – and he told himself that he had been premature in his schemes, and that there were several hours to fill before he could set about his day's work. What was he to do with himself? There was bread and cheese in the kitchen cupboard, and he ate this looking out of the window at the courtyard, where the old porter was sunning himself in his chair and a couple of undertakers' men were bringing in a coffin on a trestle. Mr Pardew shifted his gaze to take in the rooftops and the smoking chimneys that lay northwards in the direction of Chancery Lane. But there was something about the bright air and the smoky tints that annoyed him, and he let his eye turn back to the room in which he stood. He was struck by its shabbiness. Everything – chairs, table, the profusion of knick-knacks – was set out in the neatest imaginable way, but it was clear that the things had been bought second-hand. Mr Pardew resolved to himself that, whatever happened, he would be quit of Shepherd's Inn. The thought cheered him, and he picked up the carpet-bag, hoisted it over his shoulder, seized his stick in his right hand, stepped out onto the landing, fastened the door behind him and went off down the stairs.

Anyone who followed in Mr Pardew's wake in the next two or three hours would have wondered at his restlessness. He walked up Chancery Lane and looked at the shops there. He stepped into Southampton Buildings and inspected the attorneys' plates and the carriages waiting to take the Chancery lawyers away to their Saturday retreats at Greenwich and Richmond Hill. He went into a bookseller's in High Holborn and stood for so long over one of Mr Trollope's novels that the bookseller asked him somewhat satirically if he intended to buy it. Finally, when all other occupations failed him, he turned through the archway of Warwick Court – very grim and shut up now, with most of its occupants departed – walked through the gates of Gray's Inn and proceeded towards its gardens. There was no one much about. An old lawyer or two sat taking the air, a pair of ladies was being escorted very ceremoniously around the gravel drives by a grave young man in a black stuff suit, and a porter was wheeling a handcart with a pair of long settles precariously balanced on its rim towards one of the legal doorways. An old man in a frock-coat and a pair of pepper-and-salt trousers came rambling out from among the bushes and, seeing Mr Pardew establishing himself on a bench next to the principal lawn, said in a high, cracked voice:

'Do you know, sir, that I have been coming here seventy years?'

'Seventy years is a very long time,' said Mr Pardew affably, rather amused by the quaintness of his address.

'A very long time. That was in my grandfather's day, that won Lady Julia Darby's case against her husband for false imprisonment. You will recollect it, perhaps?'

'I can't say that I do. No doubt you can recollect a great many things.'

'That's about it, sir. A great many. I saw the old king in his coach once.'

'Would that have been King William or the Regent?'

'Neither, sir. It was George III. The German king, we used to call him. That's a nice-looking bag you have there, sir.'

'I find it very convenient,' Mr Pardew said. He thought the old man was a little cracked. 'An old Skimpole,' he said to himself. 'Sitting and walking here and pretending he had some connection with the place. I suppose his grandfather was a pork butcher, and as for Lady Julia Darby, I don't suppose such a creature ever existed.' There was a pause, while the noise of the porter trundling his handcart of settles receded into the distance and the old man stared gravely at the nearby garden beds.

'A rhododendron is a very splendid flower, sir,' he said finally.

'There will certainly be a fine display of them here,' Mr Pardew conceded.

'Why, when I lived at Esher, sir, I had a whole bank of them. One looked out of the window of a morning and there they were. In point of fact – there they were. But all that is over now.'

'Things come and go,' said Mr Pardew. 'That is their way.'

'And yet we don't notice their passing. I'll bid you a good afternoon, sir, if I may.'

Mr Pardew watched him move off down the gravel path with a strange loping gait that every so often looked as if it might develop into a run. In a little while he came level with the two ladies and their escort, and could be seen to stop and raise his hand. 'I'll wager he is telling them about his grandfather and Lady Julia Darby,' Mr Pardew said to himself, and managed a little guffaw, but his heart was not in it. He was thinking of his own past: a little office in a cramped thorough-fare where the language spoken by the people going by outside the window was not English, and himself in it, with a pair of ledgers pushed up close to his face; a great hill somewhere in the north of England with sheep grazing on it and the line of the sea a couple of miles distant; a team of bay horses, somewhere in the West Country, and himself in the carriage behind them, though he could not remember how he had come there, or where he was going. The memory of this irked Mr Pardew and he reached out and slashed savagely with his stick at the empty air, so that the phantoms of the little continental office, and the great hill with its sheep, and the carriage bowling along the Bath Road broke away and disappeared, and all that remained was the green grass, grey stone and bright sunshine.

Presently Mr Pardew rose to his feet and, with the carpet-bag still slung over his shoulder and the stick swishing away at the unseen enemies who barred his path, went out through the south-western gate of Gray's Inn, through Warwick Court and back into High Holborn. It was about four o'clock, and the place thronging with costers' barrows and boys selling newspapers. Setting off east, by Holborn Circus, Mr Pardew made his way in a rather desultory fashion along Farringdon Street and through the little maze of courts and alleyways that abuts St Paul's Churchyard. There was a wedding party, and he stood for a moment with a grim smile on his face – perhaps this, too, reminded him of something – before turning east again to Cannon Street, Poultry and then the approach to Cornhill. Here on the corner there was an eating house with a sign on its gable showing a very fat man in the act of devouring an oyster, and Mr Pardew turned into it, marched up the stair to the upper floor and discovered there, quite on his own at a table at the very end of the room, a small man staring at the remains of a chop.

'Lythgoe, ain't it?' said Mr Pardew easily. 'That came and fetched me from Boulogne. Thank you, miss,' – this to a young lady with a starched white apron who put her head out of a closet to the rear – 'I'll take a cup of tea and some bread and butter if I may.' While the tea was being brought and the remains of the chop taken away, he stowed the carpet-bag carefully under the table, sat himself down on the further side of it and looked Mr Lythgoe in the face.

'Been here long?'

'I was told – five o'clock,' Lythgoe said unhappily.

'Well then, you're a very punctual fellow. Thank you, miss – that's a very nice thumb you have, only I wish you wouldn't put it on the bread. I expect you've got all kinds of plans for Sabbath morning, isn't that right? Some Dissenting chapel in Hoxton waiting to receive you, I don't doubt. Well, you may forget about that, for we shall be here until tomorrow afternoon, like as not.'

'I won't do it,' Lythgoe said, under his breath, so that the serving girl, washing her hands at the tap in the closet, wondered what it was that he would not do.

'But I think you will,' Mr Pardew said. He was tearing up the bread and butter, strip by strip, and plunging the fragments into his mouth, and the glint in his eye was harder than when he had first come into the room. 'And believe me, there is very little you shall have to do. Why, a young lady from a girls' school could probably settle to it, if she had a mind.' Mr Pardew nearly added that the young lady from the girls' school probably did not have her stamped paper in Captain Raff's pocket. 'Now, did you bring those other things that Raff got for you, eh?' It became apparent that Mr Lythgoe, too, had a bag with him – very capacious and heavy it looked – stuck under his feet, and that the having of it was torture to him. Some of the hardness went out of Mr Pardew's eye. He drank the last of his tea and tore up the final piece of bread between his fingers. 'See here,' he said. 'You stand with me, and I shall stand with you. As for Captain Raff, well' – and here Mr Pardew absolutely snapped his fingers – 'we may outwit him yet.'

'How shall we outwit him then?' Lythgoe wondered, altogether fascinated by the turn the conversation was taking.

'We shall see,' said Mr Pardew ambiguously, getting to his feet. 'One and sevenpence, is it miss? Well, here is a penny for yourself. But you must mind that thumb.'

Outside in Cornhill the afternoon was falling away and the streets all but deserted. They set off along the pavement, Mr Pardew issuing *sotto voce* instructions out of the corner of his mouth. 'Now, you may set off. No, there is nothing between us. Walk to the street corner at the end – there by the tavern sign – and wait for me to join you.' Lythgoe did as he was told, the sag of his shoulder as he picked up his bag suggesting that it contained nothing lighter than an anvil, and Mr Pardew watched him go, or rather did not watch him, for he very soon took himself and his belongings – shouldered once more, in a very jaunty way – across to the far pavement, where he sauntered lazily for a moment or two before quickening his pace and finally coming to rest at the point where the south side of Cornhill turns into the mighty expanse of Gracechurch Street. Here he looked northwards for a moment, less interested in the sight of Lythgoe standing dismally beneath the sign of the Porter's Retreat, with a picture on it of a porter so jolly and rubicund that he cannot have existed outside Mr Dickens' imagination, than in the vista of shopfronts and commercial premises that went away on his left-hand side. These were as he remembered them: the steam-laundry shop, the yawning staircase, the black wall behind which lay Mr Gallentin's strongroom, the latter's sparkling frontage, and the poulterer's shop, in whose window, the early evening now being advanced, no poultry remained.

Mr Pardew took another keen look, with his jaw jutting out in front of him like a ship's prow, and saw that the shopmen were at work in Mr Gallentin's window taking out the trays of jewellery and pulling down the blinds. In another quarter of an hour, he told himself, the place would be shut up. Signalling to Lythgoe – he did this with the faintest motion of his fingers, as if he were adjusting his cuff, only that Lythgoe saw it and nodded in return – he moved a few yards along the pavement and turned into a little alley that ran along Cornhill's southern side, always keeping the same few yards of Mr Gallentin's shopfront under a discreet surveillance. Presently the door of Mr Gallentin's shop swung open and a couple of young men came out, settled their hats on their heads as they stood talking on the step and then plunged away in the direction of Leadenhall Street, and Mr Pardew, remembering his own youth and its constraints, rather thought that he envied them. Then, five minutes after this, the door swung open again and Mr Gallentin himself appeared on the step, quite tremendous in a frock-coat and a tall hat with a black oblong case in his hand, and Mr Pardew wondered what he had in it. It struck him as curious that Gallentin's did not put up its shutters, but then, as he reminded himself, no jeweller leaves his goods in the window and therefore shuttering of the kind that ornaments a tobacconist's or a pastrycook's may be thought superfluous. Mr Gallentin's figure was now a hundred yards away, and Mr Pardew crossed the road, not looking at Lythgoe but again signalling with his forefinger, and passed into the shadow of the staircase, where he stood hidden from view, waiting for his accomplice to join him.

'Now,' he said, very briskly and giving his companion's arm a little tap with his stick, 'just you go up those stairs and knock on the outer door you'll find. Nobody will answer it, and when they don't, and haven't done for a moment or so, why, give a little whistle and I shall come and join you. If anyone should answer, which they won't, you're Messrs Gillray the ecclesiastical commissioners' legal representative come to the wrong address, or some such. There's nothing to fear and no danger that can befall you.' As he uttered these reassuring words, Mr Pardew darted his head out of the staircase's entry and glanced back along the pavement, but there was no one there. On the instant, just as it had done in the garden at Gray's Inn, Mr Pardew's mind jumped back and he remembered himself in the van of a train racketing over the viaduct beyond London Bridge, in the company of a man who had been sent to Australia in a convict ship. Mr Pardew smiled, heard the low whistle from above, and went rapidly up the stairs. The dust rose up in little eddies under his feet, the motes hung in the air and the noise made by his boot-tips echoed in the silence.

Outside in Cornhill there had been bright sunshine gently diffusing across the pavements and gleaming off the windows of the Porter's Retreat. Here everything was gathered up in shadow. The door to the set of offices was locked fast and Lythgoe stood uneasily before it, his hand still on the knob. 'There's no one there,' he said superfluously, and Mr Pardew smiled again. 'I daresay you wish there had been,' he remarked. He had a little metal cylinder in his hand like a long, thin pencil, and this he now twisted sharply into the lock, jerked once to the right, once to the left, took out, put back again and gave a final jerk and a stamp with his foot. The door flew open and they stepped inside, Mr Pardew immediately turning and pulling it to behind him. Noting the ease with which they had gained entry, Lythgoe seemed to lose something of his disquiet. 'What kind of place is this?' he whispered as they stood in the ghostly vestibule, with the dust spreading under their feet. Mr Pardew, who had already begun to make his way towards the corridor, said, 'What kind of place? Why, offices, attorneys, clerks – that kind of thing. A tea-broker, too, if my nose don't deceive me. If you've a kettle we might easily sit down and recruit ourselves. Ha!' And Mr Pardew gave an altogether mindless laugh and forged on into the shadow.

It was not quite as dark as it might have been, for here and there a window in one of the adjoining rooms admitted a stray gleam of light into the passage. 'Tea,' Lythgoe said, perhaps recalling certain commercial transactions in which he had taken an interest, 'now, that's an item you need a licence for, if I recollect,' but Mr Pardew did not trouble to answer him. He was calculating the number of hours that it might take to achieve the task before him, and wondering as he did so what aspects of it could be delegated to his assistant. 'I can stay here until Monday morning,' he said to himself, and gave a little swish with his stick at some imaginary policeman who lurked in front of the big rooms – the rooms with whose floors he had been so much concerned – whose doors they now negotiated. 'Not much light in here, is there?' Lythgoe offered, as they tramped into the second and larger chamber. Mr Pardew ignored him. Again, he was deep in thought. The second room was empty, apart from a chair with only three legs, a pile of sacking, what looked like a cast-iron heating apparatus and a portrait of Her Majesty in her Coronation robes hanging on the wall. A lamp, brought in from one of the adjoining rooms and lit with a sulphur match out of Mr Pardew's pocket, cast long, eerie shadows. 'Cheerful kind of place, ain't it?' Mr Pardew laughed again. He had taken off his coat – it was the same coat he had worn on the afternoon Lythgoe had surprised him in

Boulogne – and dropped it over the three-legged chair. 'Now, have the goodness to help me lift up this carpet.'

'Help you do what?'

'Lift the carpet – there, by the ends.'

The carpet was an ancient drugget, much frayed and in places no more than a quarter-inch thick. Peeled back to perhaps half its extent, it revealed a yet more ancient floor, boards stained almost to black by some long-ago exposure to wax. Mr Pardew looked at the boards for a moment, quite judiciously, as if he were a pork butcher planning his first cut, took a piece of chalk from the carpet-bag, which he now put down on the floor beside him, and drew a rough circle, perhaps a couple of feet in diameter, over the wood.

'What's that you're about?' Lythgoe wondered, leaning forward with the lamp in his hand.

'Why, I am sending a telegram to Windsor requesting an audience of Her Majesty. What does it look as if I am doing? You had better give me that bag of yours.'

Mr Pardew's expression as he took up the bag was quite wonderful to see. The manager of a penny-gaff who had happened to pass by would probably have engaged him on the spot, in the certainty that the bag contained a dozen bunches of violets and a brace of pouter pigeons. Instead Mr Pardew took out a short hatchet, with which he instantly made a deep incision in the area of the floorboards within the chalk circle.

'Why, the wood is half rotted,' he exclaimed. 'We should be thankful we haven't already fallen to our deaths.'

Again, it was wonderful to see Mr Pardew at his work. He made one or two dextrous motions with the hatchet, and chopped out a little more of the wood. Then he took an iron spike out of the bag, jabbed it under the protruding surface and twisted it a little more. Somewhere in the middle distance – in Leadenhall Street, say, or Bishopsgate – a clock was striking the hour, and he listened to the chimes with his head on one side. It was six o'clock. There now lay exposed before him an area of off-white plaster, not quite approximating to the area of the chalked circle but perhaps eighteen inches across at its widest point. 'It will do, I daresay,' Mr Pardew said, almost to himself, reaching once more into the bag. The reason why Lythgoe's shoulder had sagged as he picked it up now became clear. Inside, neatly wrapped in a coil of rope, was a twenty-pound hammer. Seizing it in both hands, and bending over the floor like a man hewing wood, Mr Pardew gave the plaster a couple of sharp blows, stepped a pace or two back and, taking the lamp from Lythgoe's outstretched hand, gazed into the jagged hole that had opened up beneath him. This done, he took the coil of rope, bound one end round the stanchions of the heating apparatus, and let the other end down into the hole.

Lythgoe, who had watched these manoeuvrings with mounting unease, and now understood what was afoot, said suddenly: 'I'll not go down there. You'll not make me.'

'Maybe I shan't make you,' Mr Pardew said, still playing out the rope in his hands. 'But you'll go all the same, I fancy.'

There was a wild look in Lythgoe's eye. 'I'll——'

'You'll what?' Mr Pardew said easily. 'Run out into Leadenhall Street and fetch a policeman? What's in that bag alone would be enough to send you to the hulks. You'd do much better to stay here. Now, just take a hold of the lamp – like that, do you see? – while I go down. If you don't care to bring the bag with you, you may lower it.' So saying, Mr Pardew took a firm grip on the rope and with an agility that was surprising for a man of his years began to lower himself into the murk.

Down in the poulterer's shop it was nearly pitch dark, with only a thin shaft of light penetrating the shuttered windows. Mr Pardew felt his boots brush against the stone floor, almost blundered over, but regained his balance and stood taking stock of his surroundings. As his eyes became accustomed to the gloom, he made out the shop's long wooden counter and the assortment of hooks and wires that ran across its further wall. Something blew against his hand and he reached down and saw that it was a feather.

'Are you there? What's amiss?' Above him he could see Lythgoe's pale, lamp-lit face peering through the hole in the ceiling.

'Nothing is amiss. But you must turn down that lamp. There is a crack in the shutter. Now, you had better send down that bag.'

Lythgoe made as if to do this, hauling up the rope and attempting to secure it, but lost his grip and sent the bag crashing down onto the stone floor, very nearly taking off Mr Pardew's head in the process. Mr Pardew swore softly under his breath. As he waited for Lythgoe to descend, which was done with painful slowness, he moved over to the wall of the shop which adjoined Mr Gallentin's premises and struck it hard with his fist.

'What are you doing?' Lythgoe wondered, very dishevelled and with his hair white with plaster.

'It is as I thought,' Mr Pardew said. 'They have reinforced the dividing wall. A metal plate, if I'm not mistaken. I wonder if it goes the whole way?' He made three or four more assaults with his fists at various points along the wall and shook his head. 'Well, we had best explore a little.'

The poulterer's shop was found to consist of the central chamber in which they stood, a smaller room behind it, containing a safe, which Mr Pardew, on examining it, found to his regret to be unlocked and empty, and a flight of steps leading down to a cellar. Turning up the lantern, Mr Pardew went down the stairs. Since he had dug out the hole in the poulterer's ceiling – a long age ago now, it seemed – his mind had not ceased to calculate. It was now, he thought, about half past six in the evening, but time meant nothing to him. No key would be turned in Mr Gallentin's front door until Monday morning. He could spend the whole of Sunday there if he chose. The cellar was dark and airless, but not untenanted. In fact, thirty or forty pheasants in various stages of ripening hung from its walls, together with a brace or two of Norfolk turkeys and several geese. Mr Pardew set down his lantern at a point where he judged it would provide maximal illumination and began to inspect the further wall. This, he was pleased to discover, was made of soft red brick, crumbling in several places and not more than five or six inches thick.

'What is it we've to do?' Lythgoe wondered uneasily. He was

breathing heavily. Stepping too close to one of the birds and feeling the touch of its claws upon his shoulder, he recoiled in horror.

'What are we to do? Why, we are to break through that wall,' Mr Pardew told him. 'That is, unless you want to use a powder charge which would very likely bring the roof down on us.' He saw a flash of the little office in the continental town and the people walking past the window, and a lake set amid green hills with a far-off view of mountains, and he wondered at the distance between the boy he had been and the man he now was. He remembered, too, a house in Kensington and a woman who, unlike Jemima, certainly had been his wife, and the carriages in the street beyond, and the recollection hardened in his mind and made him angry, and he picked up one of the metal spikes that had come from Lythgoe's bag, pushed it into a soft part of the wall where the mortar had crumbled away, took the twenty-pound hammer and struck it with all his force. Still the memory of the house at Kensington played on his mind – the little study where he sat and read his books, and the little kitchen where he ate his breakfast – and he struck at the wall again, while Lythgoe watched and put his fingers in his ears and the lamp danced and all but fell over and the pheasants looked indifferently on.

Presently he came to his senses – how many blows had he struck? He could not quite tell. He laid down the hammer and inspected the damage he had caused. The brickwork was even weaker than he had first imagined. He wondered why no one had attended to it, and told himself that if he had possessed a cellar it should have been regularly looked into. Three or four bricks now lay on the cellar floor beside him. Lythgoe coughed at the brick-dust and passed his hand over his face. 'This will never do,' Mr Pardew said. Reaching into the pocket of his coat, he drew out a bandanna handkerchief and tied it around his mouth. A scrap of paper came fluttering out of the pocket along with the handkerchief, but in his haste he did not see it. The vision of the house at Kensington had almost faded from his mind, but there was no mistaking the fury with which he once more began to attack the wall.

In this way perhaps an hour or two passed, Mr Pardew alternately striking at the brick and resting with his hands on the shaft of the hammer and inspecting the damage done. Lythgoe stood, or occasionally sat with his hands on his haunches, regarding him with an ever more piteous expression. All this Mr Pardew saw, to a certain extent sympathised with, but was also very much amused by. Putting down the hammer once and brushing the red brick-dust off his shirtfront, he asked:

'Are you a religious man, Lythgoe?'

'Certainly I am.'

'And might I enquire' – the red dust was very troublesome and had got in his watch chain – 'how you square what we're engaged upon here with your conscience?'

'It's no fault of mine. I was pressed into it, and shall not be judged for it.' Lythgoe's voice, as he said this, was unusually firm.

'No fault of yours! I suppose you made that fellow Raff a present of your paper, just to give him an income?'

'It is not Captain Raff who has the paper, but that Mr Happerton who directs him.'

'Oh yes, Mr Happerton,' Mr Pardew said, with an attempt at vagueness that very nearly succeeded. 'I have heard of Mr Happerton. And how will he be judged, eh?'

'Why, the Lord will find him out,' Lythgoe said. 'There are men – discounters, people in the bill-broking line – that buy up paper in the way of their business dealings, and that's fair enough, for the money's not certain and no one can be blamed for taking a risk. But this Mr Happerton' – Lythgoe's face as he said this was very white in the glare of the lamp and its dark surround – 'does mischief with his bills. He does. Why, there's half a dozen fellows like me, very near ruined, that he likes to play with as a cat does with a mouse, never quite striking it dead and never quite letting it go neither. It's my belief that he don't want the bills paid up, for then he could do no more mischief.'

'I have known worse than Mr Happerton,' said Mr Pardew, whose late partner, Mr Fardell, had been found dead in Pump Court with his brains knocked out and no one any the wiser as to the identity of his assailant.

'The Lord will judge him, you shall see,' Lythgoe said, very earnestly, and Mr Pardew wondered at his fervour, and the incongruity of the conversation, here amid the flaring lamplight and the swirling brick-dust, and perhaps thought for a moment of Mr Fardell lying dead upon the Pump Court cobbles. If there was anything on Mr Pardew's own conscience, it did not seem to trouble him, for he soon after leapt up and attacked the wall again with redoubled fury. A great piece had been torn out of it now, and by means of some dextrous probing of the mortar he was able to widen it out to the point where a man, if he did not care very much about damage to his clothing, could climb through it into the adjacent room.

'We ain't going through there, surely?' Lythgoe asked.

'You may blame it on Mr Happerton,' Mr Pardew told him. 'Let him be judged for it.' Once more, his mind was lost in calculation. He knew that if he broke through the cellar wall of the poulterer's shop he would emerge into the space beneath Mr Gallentin's show-room. What he did not know was how far this space extended, whether, in fact, he would be forced to undertake some other strenu-ous assault upon a second wall, or a locked door, before he could effect an entry into Mr Gallentin's strongroom. But, as he now saw, taking the lamp from Lythgoe and forcing first it and then his head and shoulders through the ragged gap in the brickwork, he was in luck. The cellar beneath Mr Gallentin's showroom seemed to extend for a considerable distance. Pulling himself through and getting to his feet, he gazed enquiringly round the vault in which he now found himself. There was not, in truth, a great deal to see, merely the squat outlines of one or two pieces of furniture which Mr Gallentin, or someone else, had thought to store there, and, at the cellar's further end, a flight of wooden steps leading up to a metal door-frame. Mr Pardew put his head back through the brickwork, instructed Lythgoe to hand him the carpet-bag, heard a complaint from that gentleman that his mouth was full of brick-dust, and assisted his passage into the cellar by main force, so that he tumbled all in a heap on the damp stone floor.

'Now,' Mr Pardew said briskly, 'there is only a short way to go. You had better follow me, and bring the bags.'

'Gracious heaven,' Lythgoe said, 'I think my back's broken.'

'It is nothing of the kind. But there may be something else broken in a moment or two. Now, stir yourself.'

The security of his cellar was clearly not one of Mr Gallentin's prime considerations. The lock on its door was known to Mr Pardew, and he greeted it like an old friend and made short work of it. Thrusting open the door, they found themselves in a tiny corridor, its right-hand exit, Mr Pardew judged, belonging to the showroom, but with a second door, immediately before them, which, he thought, could only lead to the strongroom. Here the fastening was altogether more secure, but Mr Pardew had his cylinder, and an ingenious instrument made of flattened steel but with a ridge along its side, which he inserted into the space between the door and its frame: in another five minutes the lock snapped open and they tumbled into the room.

'Great heavens!' said Mr Pardew, almost to himself. 'Great heavens indeed.'

Lythgoe caught the note of wonder in his voice. They were standing, as they now saw, in a single, windowless room, lit by the blazing lights of half a dozen gas jets turned up to their fullest extent. This, allied to the three or four carefully angled mirrors that hung upon the far wall, gave the place a fantastic air, as if it would not be wonderful to see piles of precious stones heaped on the floor and a dragon coiled beside them. The safe – a squat metal box, four feet square – stood on a plinth in the very centre. Mr Pardew did not at first approach it. He was taking a survey of the room, noting the angle of the mirrors, searching for the observation slit which he knew let out into the street and could be looked into by anyone passing down Cornhill who had a mind to stare. Having located it, six feet up on the further wall, Mr Pardew's first act was to turn down the gas jets to the point where they made the overall complexion of the room soft red rather than bright orange. This done, he took another look at the mirrors and then at Lythgoe, who was brushing the brick-dust from his shirtfront with stiff little jerks of his white hand.

'Now,' Mr Pardew said equably – he might have been assisting Lythgoe to negus at a buffet – 'there is nothing you can do here. You had better go back the way we have come and wait in the street.'

'And what am I to do if a policeman comes?'

'You may stop looking like a rabbit when it sees a fox. The police come by each half-hour. I have made a study of it. Up from Leadenhall Street. When you see one, give a whistle and then find an alley to hide in until he has passed.'

'What if you don't hear?'

'Why then, we shall find ourselves in Pentonville,' Mr Pardew said, more equably than ever. 'Now be off. In five minutes I intend to begin.'

Lythgoe disappeared. Mr Pardew heard the noise of his retreat: the door slamming in the passage; a faint pattering of feet below; a distant scuffling which seemed to come from the bowels of the earth, but which he knew marked his descent into the poulterer's cellar. Mr Pardew waited until the sounds had faded away almost to nothing and then, with a sigh that had something in it of pleasure mixed with profound anxiety, turned his attention to the safe. Like the lock he had disposed of a few moments before, it was not unknown to him. Unlike the lock, he did not quite know at first what he should do with it. He had a suspicion that his cylinder, and his metal contrivance, would be useless with this behemoth of Mr Milner's devising, and so it proved. The first cylinder he pushed into the lock snapped when he tried to extract it. As for the metal plate, he could not even insert it between the door of the safe and the cast-iron frame. Listening all the while for noises from the street, Mr Pardew reached into his carpet-bag and drew out a small hammer and a couple of thin iron wedges, so thin that they were no more than the size of wafers. These, by dint of a prodigious blow or two, he succeeded in driving into the gap between the door and the wall of the safe. The lock naturally held firm, but Mr Pardew thought that he saw an inconsiderable space where the gap might be thought to have widened.

Encouraged, Mr Pardew took out three more wedges, put the first two in his mouth and hammered in the third, a little further down the door-frame but still not within a foot of the lock. As he did this, a low whistle sounded from beyond the wall, and Mr Pardew instantly dropped to his knees and shuffled away to what he judged to be the safest part of the room – the area immediately below the observation slit. Presently there came a sound of footsteps, a silence, and then the noise of the same footsteps moving away. Mr Pardew counted to thirty, wiped the perspiration from his forehead with the flat of his hand and then went back to inspect the safe. In the soft light it looked unblemished, but Mr Pardew's eye, turning repeatedly on that tiny gap between door and frame, saw that it had widened. For the next half-hour, until another whistle sounded from the street, he went on hammering in wedges. Then, when he went back to examine his handiwork, he saw that the space between door and frame was perhaps a quarter of an inch.

Mr Pardew glanced at his watch and found it was nearly ten o'clock. A part of him told himself that he ought to rest, that he had a whole day and another night before him if he wanted it, but another part of him counselled urgency. He fancied that Lythgoe, if left to his own devices for too long, might very well lose his head, or at any rate draw attention to himself in a way that might imperil the whole enterprise. There was a mirror near at hand, and Mr Pardew stared at his face in it, saw his red eyes and jutting jaw and wished himself at home at Shepherd's Inn. Then he took another handful of wedges and began to hammer them home. In this way a great stretch of time seemed to pass, but still Mr Pardew hammered, aware as he did so that that there had been no whistle from the street. Then, almost at once, three things happened: a clock began to chime the midnight; the gap between the uppermost part of the door and its frame was found to have widened to half an inch; and, advertising his arrival by way of a series of scuffling noises down in the building's heart, Lythgoe appeared in the doorway.

'What is it?' Mr Pardew demanded, his mouth full of wedges.

'There hasn't been no policeman for an hour and a half,' Lythgoe said. 'So I thought I should come back.' He seemed utterly woebegone, saw the safe with the gap opening up in its frame, and shrank back from it with a look of absolute terror.

'There are some nights when the police stop their patrols,' Mr Pardew said. 'Very shocking to a law-abiding man, I know, but there you are. If no one has gone by for an hour and a half, I should think we are pretty safe. Great heavens, man, what is the matter?'

Lythgoe was still staring at the safe. 'I am innocent of this,' he said. 'It was you that made me do it – you and that Captain Raff. And that's what I shall tell anyone that asks me.'

'You had better hand me that bag,' Mr Pardew said, 'and stop talking about your innocence.'

And so the night went on. No doubt the police had stopped their patrols. By two o'clock the gap between the door of the safe and the wall had widened to the point where Mr Pardew could begin to insert a series of much larger wedges into it. By three, the wall of the safe had been forced substantially apart from the lock, and Mr Pardew brought out his 'alderman', the sectioned iron bar against which it was thought that no safe in Christendom could hold out. Lythgoe lay sprawled asleep on the floor, insensible to the noise of the hammer blows, with the red brick-dust still sprinkling his face. Outside there was pale early summer light gently diffusing through the City streets. At ten minutes to five, when the contents of the safe could be plainly seen through the all but shattered door, Mr Pardew gave a final blow and then laughed. Mr Chubb's finest, that no cracksman had ever been able to get the better of, sprang open.

Another man would have instantly plunged his hands into the safe, but Mr Pardew's composure held and he sank down into a sitting position. He was immensely tired. He knew, too, that there was no reason for him to hurry – that hurry, in fact, might be fatal to his chances of avoiding detection. Accordingly he was very prudent and careful. He tidied up the floor a little and removed one or two odd pieces of debris. He counted the wedges back into his carpet-bag and turned up the gas jets. Finally he turned his head towards the safe, inspected what he saw there, gave a little snort of exaltation and began to fill his pockets from the trays of jewellery that lay within. Occasionally he held a particular item up to the light, the better to appraise it. This done, he pushed the door of the safe – very battered it was now, and altogether knocked out of shape – back into position. Mr Pardew wondered whether the extent of its damage would be visible to anyone looking in from the street and decided that the answer was very probably not. With luck, no one would be any the wiser until the strongroom was opened the following morning. As he stepped back from the safe, patting the pocket of his coat, Lythgoe came awake.

'What? Is it all done?'

'All done,' Mr Pardew said. He was examining the strongroom door and wondering how that, too, might be made to look as if it had sustained no hurt.

Ten minutes later – it was half past five in the morning – anyone walking down Cornhill into the dawn (but that there was no one) might have seen a tall, grim-looking man and a small, shabby-looking one, each very pale-faced and somewhat dishevelled, coming smartly along its southern edge in the direction of Leadenhall Street, and that, in addition to the carpet-bag slung over his shoulder, the tall man carried two braces of pheasants on his arm.

'Here now,' Mr Pardew remarked, as they reached the corner of Leadenhall Street, and prepared to go their separate ways, taking down two of the pheasants. 'You had better have these.'

It seemed for a moment as if Lythgoe might refuse them, but then he thought better of it and let the birds slide into his grasp. 'But where am I to say I got them?' he asked. 'That's what I'd like to know.'

'Where did you get them?' In the distance the sun was coming up over the pediment of St Paul's. There was violet sky behind it. Mr Pardew laughed. 'Why, say that Lord Fairhurst gave them to you.'

Part Three

XIV

Hounds upon the Scent

Dear me, London is the queerest place. A man can live in it twenty years and not understand the spirit that animates it, or the odd conjunctions that bring the people who journey through it fleetingly together . . .
London: Its Haunts, Homes and Habitations: A Compendium (1867)

All morning and for much of the afternoon a harsh April breeze had been blowing stiffly across Clipstone Court. Now, in the early evening, it had grown subdued. The cinder-dirt lay in piles where the wind had carried it, and the fragments of packing case had been swept away to form a matchwood reef that blocked up one of the entrances. A drunk woman sat on a doorstep with her head in her hands, shrewdly observed by the proprietor of what had once been the tobacconist's shop – now a desperate grocer's – who stood in his doorway with a look of puzzlement on his face. Beyond the drunk woman and the shopkeeper, the four figures of a street acrobat and his family went slowly over the north-west corner of the court to the culvert that leads into Goodge Street, with the voice of the man occasionally breaking over the noise of their footsteps as he upbraided his little son.

'You understand me, you bad boy! As long as you're with me you got to come under collar. And where'll you be next I *dunno*, a bad creature like you.' Of the four, only the father was dressed in his professional costume: a pair of very dirty silk stockings, a buff-coloured tunic and old-fashioned buckle shoes. Curiously these articles, together with the fact that, like the lachrymose woman on the doorstep, he was slightly drunk, gave him an odd sense of dignity. He walked with a slow, mincing step, raising the heel of each foot higher than required and placing his toes very slightly out of kilter.

'You bad boy,' he said again. 'I can't think what's coming to you. To go and lose a sixpence like that! A creature like you!'

The father loomed above the tiny figure shuffling under his elbow and kept his eyes fixed on him. He was a very thin, sparse boy of seven or eight, who made no sound but cried quietly as he went. He wore a man's cap, a dirty sailor's jacket and a pair of button boots that looked as if they might have been given to him by his mother.

'To go and lose a sixpence!' the man said. He had a gaunt, raw face, and had spent five minutes that morning accentuating his eyebrows with burnt cork and rubbing up his cheekbones with rouge. This gave him a frightful but exotic look, like a Red Indian warrior that had just climbed out of a coal-scuttle. As they came near the grocer's shop, with its mournful display of split-pea sacks, candles, potted tongue and dried beef, he caught the boy a cuff with the side of his hand, and the shop-keeper, thinking that these irruptions of spirit ought to be encouraged, cried out: 'S'elp me father, that's a good 'un. Wallop his trousers.' But the man ignored him, as he ignored the noise of the traffic drifting in from Tottenham Court Road, and the sound of the woman behind him.

'You bad boy,' he said once more. 'Where d'you think you'll fetch yourself, eh?'

The woman, a frail slip of a woman, walked behind them with the smaller child. She took no interest in the lost sixpence, or the view of Clipstone Court or the drunk woman on the doorstep. None of these things disturbed her. Instead she spoke to the child, whom she held by the hand, half a dozen paces behind the man of anger. Then, as they reached the culvert which ran on in Goodge Street, she yelled, 'George, George.'

The man turned round.

'Look after Annie,' she yelled again.

The idea appealed to the man. With a flourish of his arms, and a motion of his front foot that was almost graceful, he swung the child up onto his shoulders and settled her there. As he did so, the boy sidled up to his mother, reached into his pocket and passed her something that only the two of them saw, and the cortège – silk-stockinged father, lofted child, mother and son – moved on and out of Clipstone Court for ever.

*

'You can eat them, you know, if you've a mind, McIvor,' Mr Mulligan said, very graciously to his friend, who sat deferentially regarding the plate of boiled cockles, 'for they aren't to my taste. Rich food ain't sometimes.' There was a moment or two's silence while McIvor applied himself to the shellfish and Mulligan looked attentively around him. In the months since they had last patronised the establishment, an energising brush had swept out some of the antique corners of the Clipstone Arms. There was a sheet of paper pinned to the wall advertising a Whit Monday excursion to Epping, and the posters giving notice of sporting benefits had all been taken down.

'Ugh!' Mulligan remarked, noting this access of sobriety. 'If Tom Huddleston, as was the Dartford Chancer these fifteen years, can't tell of his benefit here, then where can he tell of it? And a brake hired for Whit Monday at Epping! Gracious. Ginger beer all round, I shouldn't wonder, and a prayer meeting to follow. I can't stand these respectable houses. So, McIvor, how has the world been treating you since we last met? What about those books that you've been making up at the Bird in Hand?'

McIvor, whose plate was now a wasteland of cockle shells, and from whose teeth fragments of his meal still hung, did not look as if the world had been treating him particularly well. His coat was dirtier than ever, and there was a raking cut, which perhaps ought to have been stitched, across the back of one of his hands. Seeing the cut for the first time, Mulligan whistled through his teeth.

'That's a fair stab someone's taken at you, McIvor. From the look of it I'd say you're lucky you weren't turned into mincemeat.'

'They're a dreadful rough crowd at the Bird in Hand,' McIvor agreed.

'Ha! Captain McTurk will close the place down one of these fair mornings, and be thanked for doing it. Well, there never was an arrangement that wasn't the better for being settled. How much did the widder bring in then?'

McIvor had a battered brown pocketbook open on his lap and was running his finger up and down a line of figures.

'Seventy-three letters. Of course, a few of them didn't send the full half-crown. Some come in with only a shilling. You'd be surprised, Mr Mulligan, who some of them were from. Two clerical gentlemen, there were. Not to mention Mr Aloysius Barraclough, as is the member for Chadwell Heath.'

'That Barraclough'll have a bailiff stepping up to him at the front door of the House one of these days if he's not careful . . . How much?'

'Eight pound thirteen shillings and sixpence,' McIvor said. There was an odd glint in his eye that Mr Mulligan did not perhaps notice.

'That's fair, I will allow. Next time, McIvor, we shall have to lay out more on the advertising. Costs more to begin with, but it pays in the end. There can't be no more widders though, more's the pity.'

'Why's that, Mr Mulligan?'

'Well –' Mr Mulligan put a finger between his teeth and looked anxiously around the room. 'It's not for me to say, but there's something wrong about that hoss.'

'What do you mean "wrong"? Broke its leg or got the pneumony?'

'You're green, McIvor, that's what you are. No, nothing like that. Why, there was a meeting in Lincolnshire where it well-nigh flew over the line. The *Pictorial Times* had a picture of it in its stall and said it was fit to carry the Prince. But what would you say if I told you Major Hubbins was to ride it?'

'Major Hubbins!'

'I know, I know. Saw him ride at Brighton, why it must have been

196

three years ago, and they near enough had to call for a Bath chair for him when he came in.'

'If you told me you owned a horse and Major Hubbins was to have the riding of it, I should say that you didn't want it to win.'

'That's what folk are saying about Tiberius. But he may do it, you know. That Septuagint is money thrown away.'

'They are saying Pendragon has a chance.'

'An old nag from Devon that would be better off carrying children on the sands.' Mr Mulligan seemed to have lost interest in the Derby. His eye moved restlessly out into the court, where the wind had got up again, and then back to the cover of McIvor's pocketbook. 'Anyhow,' he said. 'Eight pound thirteen and six is eight pound thirteen and six, so we'd best settle up. I've to Clerkenwell at seven, and for once it's not a hoss that's taking me there.' Whatever was taking Mr Mulligan to Clerkenwell was presumably the cause of the green cutaway coat that he wore and the flower that drooped rakishly out of his buttonhole. 'Three quarters to a quarter, didn't we say? I make that six pound ten shillings and a penny ha'penny.'

'It was seventy to thirty,' McIvor said. 'And that ain't fair, neither.'

'Not fair! What do you mean, it's not fair? Who was it that put you up to the dodge, I wonder? Wrote the blessed notice for you and told you where to advertise it and all? Three quarters to the quarter it is, or I shall know why.'

McIvor took out an immensely dirty purse and laid it on the table. 'You can have five sovereigns, Mr Mulligan, seeing that seventy–thirty was what I agreed to, which I was a fool to. Them letters didn't write themselves.'

'And neither did the tale that 'ticed em, which you didn't have the wit to write yourself. Bob McIvor, that drinks up other chaps' leavings at the Bird in Hand, which folk that go there have told me about.'

'It's no more than you do yourself,' shrieked McIvor. He was very angry. 'Five sovereigns and not a halfpenny more.'

'Five sovereigns be d——d.' Mulligan. Then, seeing the publican come striding through from the public bar to enjoin quiet, he lowered his voice. 'This house is like a blessed girls' school,' he said. 'They'll be having 'ymn-singing here on a Sunday night, I shouldn't wonder, with a collection plate going round. You step outside, McIvor, and we'll settle this.'

Both talking at the limit of their voices, and gesticulating with free hands, they tumbled out of the door. Here the light had begun to fade and there were flashes of soot drifting in from above the rooftops. The first casualty was Mr Mulligan's buttonhole, which went into a gutter. The grocer, who had come out to furl up his awning, looked delightedly on. At the court's south-western corner an assault was made on McIvor's purse, which he resisted, and the two of them rolled out into the Tottenham Court Road, where a policeman saw them and, blowing a whistle to summon his colleagues, came running to investigate.

*

There are some conversations that are too private even for the library of a gentlemen's club. And so it chanced that, perhaps a week after the burglary at Mr Gallentin's shop, Mr Happerton and Captain Raff might have been seen walking towards each other on Westminster Bridge. No one who saw them could have predicted that they meant to meet. Neither gave the other so much as a look, and both kept to opposite sides of the bridge, so that their view was every so often cut off by the passing hay-carts and the other miscellaneous traffic rolling in from Lambeth. But somehow, a moment or two later, they could be found leaning together on the rail and staring down the river towards Battersea, where three or four lighters and small craft were engaged in the task of getting a moribund tug to turn into the current. It was a brisk spring afternoon and the wind had got up, so that in the distance the smoke from the Kennington factory chimneys drifted north in little clouds and eddies, and it was clear from the demeanour of the two persons on the rail that one of them burned to confide some choice piece of information while the other was curiously reluctant to hear it. The person who burned to do the confiding was Captain Raff, who fidgeted, winked at his companion a couple of times and then, apparently defeated, stared down the river again, where the tug was moving slowly upstream towards Putney or Richmond or Teddington Lock – all places that Captain Raff, to judge from the bleakness of his expression, would have preferred to be rather than perched on Westminster Bridge, with the wind blowing into his face. Then, after what seemed an eternity, and the passage of at least a dozen more hay-carts, Mr Happerton remarked:

'Gracious, Raff, what have you been up to? You look as if you had been dragged through a hedge.'

'What's that? What is the matter with me?'

'Only that your face is all of a colour with your shirtfront.'

Captain Raff rocked uncomfortably on the heels of his boots, one of which looked as if it might be about to part company with the sole. In fact the colour of his shirtfront was grey.

'Well, it was deuced late I got to bed, I don't mind telling you. A fellow is bound to look a little pale sometimes, you know.'

'Never mind that. I daresay you're not so young as you were.' Mr Happerton lowered his voice. 'Where has he gone?'

Captain Raff looked cautious. 'I hardly like to say.'

'Well, try anyway. Where?'

'Vanished! Disappeared!' Captain Raff said. 'Won't show his face.' And then: 'Richmond, I believe.'

'And the goods?'

'The goods?' Captain Raff lowered his voice to a level only just commensurable with its being heard. 'Well, it was the most awkward thing you ever saw. There is that fellow in Whitechapel that has known me a dozen years positively refused to do business. Think of it! A nasty Jew not wanting to do a gentleman a service.'

'I'm surprised you stood for it, Raff. But go on.'

'It is that policeman McTurk, you know. They say he has agents everywhere. It was the same in the West End, and that is usually quite a different thing. Quite a different thing,' Captain Raff repeated, almost piteously, as if the wickedness of the world was altogether beyond him.

'And that man Savory says he does not deal in stones any more, for the jewellers are all being watched.'

'Things have come to a pretty pass when a man like Savory won't deal in stones. What does he deal in, I should like to know?'

'They have fallen off deplorably,' Captain Raff said, with a really impressive gravity. The tug was almost out of sight now, moving into the shallows of Battersea Bridge. A flock of gulls sprang up in its wake, like a handful of paper scraps flung suddenly into the air. 'I tell you what it is, Happerton. Why, if things go on like this a fellow won't be able to make a living, no matter how hard he tries.'

'There are other places than the West End,' Mr Happerton said.

'And some of them d——d queer,' Captain Raff said bitterly. 'Ugh! Those men in Clerkenwell. I don't know how a fellow is to stand them.'

'It seems to me you stand most things pretty well, Raff. Never mind. If the goods are disposed of, we needn't worry. But no one is to do anything foolish, mind.'

'What? Put them on display in the Commercial Road, or offer them back to Gallentin at discount? I should say not,' Captain Raff remarked, in pious horror.

There was a silence. The tug had disappeared and the gulls vanished in its wake. The sun shone through misty, grey-white clouds, very melancholic and mournful. Mr Happerton was thinking about the substantial sum of money that had now come into his hands, and how it might best be laid out. Captain Raff, meanwhile, licking his lips nervously, looked as if he might be about to speak, subsided, was silent for a moment, and then, all in a rush, said:

'See here, Happerton, now that there are – funds available, I take it you'd like me to lay them out. There is a fellow in Regent's Park still offering sixes on Tiberius, you know. At least he was when my man Delaney was there the other day.'

Mr Happerton smiled, but it was not a very nice smile. 'That's very civil of you, Raff, but I shall be doing the laying out myself. A fellow is always better placed in the matter of odds when he does it himself, I think. Now, are you going anywhere?'

'I thought – to the club,' Captain Raff said miserably.

'Ah well, we had better say goodbye then, for I have to see a man at Tattersall's.'

And Mr Happerton took his leave, sauntering back across Westminster Bridge with his hat tipped very jauntily on the back of his head, while Captain Raff stood gnawing the inside of his cheek and wondering why a service he had previously performed so punctiliously for his employer should now be so unaccountably denied him.

*

How is a newly married young lady to fill her time when her husband is at his place of work, or in Mr Happerton's case at the Blue Riband Club or standing by the ring at Tattersall's? To be sure, there is the management of her house to take an interest in, but the establishment at Belgrave Square was very neatly administered by the old butler and the housekeeper, and as Mrs Happerton could not have cared less what she ate and how often the curtains were taken down and sponged, this sphere was rather closed to her. Then there are one's relatives to cosset and conciliate, but Mrs Happerton was frankly bored by her father's company, and her aunt's house at Eccleston Square was a torture to her. There is, of course, that infallible resort, light reading, but Mrs Happerton thought she had read enough novels to keep Mudie's in business for a year. And so she was forced back to that time-honoured expedient – as common to a duchess's mansion as a woodman's cottage – of inviting her acquaintances to tea.

Even here, though, there was a difficulty, for tea parties can only take place if there are people who can be asked to them. Mrs Happerton, looking down the list of her friends' names which she kept in the neatest little calf-bound book that Mr Happerton had given her, together with sundry other tokens of his regard, on the day of his marriage, was conscious that it was neither particularly extensive nor particularly enticing. A husband, when he marries, generally introduces his wife to the society of his male friends, but Mr Happerton had played her false in this regard. No doubt some of his friends had wives, but they were not the kind of people who were invited to Belgrave Square. The majority of the names in Mrs Rebecca's book, consequently, belonged to middle-aged ladies who had known her mother in their salad days, and these she did not think she could bear. Accordingly she returned to the milieu in which, for however short a time, she had moved with her cousin Harriet. She invited Mrs Venables, and took great delight in snubbing one or two little suggestions that this lady made about the drawing room and its decor. But there was a limit to the fun that could be got out of snubbing Mrs Venables. And then she remembered Mrs D'Aubigny, whom she had met at one of Mrs Venables' luncheons in Redcliffe Square, and was a younger, milder version of their hostess, and asked her to tea.

Mrs D'Aubigny came on a cold, wet afternoon in early April, in a carriage which her husband, a lawyer who worked in Mr Screwby's office on Cheapside, was not supposed to be able to afford. But she was a nice, humble, modest girl who, in addition to her niceness and her modesty, was a fund of interesting information. She knew what the Prince was supposed to have said to his mother when they met at Balmoral. She knew what Mr Dickens might be supposed to be reading to his audiences at Edinburgh. She had an opinion of Mr Frith's new picture. But best of all she knew a great deal about Mrs Venables and the life of Redcliffe Square.

'Of course it is such a pity about Mr Venables,' she began at one point when, the initial pleasantries having been concluded, the two young ladies were rather wondering what to say to each other.

'Why is it a pity about Mr Venables?' Mrs Rebecca wondered, who had perhaps heard a little of Mr Venables' recent difficulties but was under no compulsion to say so.

'Well, John' – John was Mr D'Aubigny – 'says that his association with Lord Pitching was very unwise. And now they think that he is going to have resign his seat.'

'Papa always said that Lord Pitching would destroy himself and anyone who made the mistake of lending him anything,' Mrs Rebecca said sententiously. She was bored by Mrs D'Aubigny, but for private reasons of her own rather interested in the fate of Mr Venables.

'John says that the real difficulty is that Mr Venables has not been very discreet.'

For Mr Venables, in whom one or two Conservative newspapers had begun to take an interest, had recently made a little speculation. This in itself was not enough to condemn him – how many parliamentary gentlemen are there who do not speculate in some way? But it was thought that Mr Venables had rather overstepped the mark. He had allied himself with a mining company whose affairs had been shown to be fraudulent, and he had done so under the auspices of Lord Pitching, a gentleman whose reputation in polite society was not much more than that of a ravening wolf. Even then he might have got out of the business unscathed, but Mr Venables represented the Chelsea Districts, and it was thought that the fine independent sensibilities of his electors wouldn't stand for it.

'Mr Venables is a radical, is he not?' Mrs Rebecca enquired, rather artlessly.

'Well – it is not quite certain.' Mrs D'Aubigny's familiarity with politics was almost equal to her knowledge of *I Promessi Sposi*. 'Of course he is for extending the suffrage, but John says it is all a sham and he would just as soon sit down to dinner with Mr Disraeli, if Mr Disraeli would have him.'

It was about four o'clock in the afternoon and the carriages were circling the square.

'And will some other radical gentleman obtain the seat?' Mrs Rebecca wondered.

'John says there is bound to be a row. They are still having an enquiry into Mr Venables' conduct at the last election. John says he spent three thousand pounds bribing the publicans. So there is a good chance that a Conservative may get in. At least that is what Mr Dennison told him.'

Here Mrs Rebecca was entirely mystified. 'Who is Mr Dennison?'

'Oh, he is the gentleman . . . well' – Mrs D'Aubigny smiled – 'perhaps he is not quite a gentleman – who manages the seats all along the river.

He is only an attorney, but they say the party can do nothing without him. But perhaps', Mrs D'Aubigny said, fearing that she had let her enthusiasm run away with her, 'you do not care for politics?'

'Well, maybe not. Papa is an old Tory.' And here Mrs Rebecca smiled a smile of such paralysing sweetness that her father would have marvelled at it, had he been there to see. 'He would have the Corn Laws back, I think, if it were left to him.'

'I daresay old gentlemen are rather set in their ways,' Mrs D'Aubigny proposed. She was a nice, modest, humble girl.

It was remarkable how after this Mrs Rebecca's interest in the conversation stalled. Mrs D'Aubigny tried her with the Irish Church Bill and the portraits in *Vanity Fair*, but it was no good. When she got up to go – it was still raining in the square – she said, all in a little breathless rush:

'I am so glad we have met. You will not mind my saying so, but it is so rarely that one meets anyone that one – likes. We – that is, some ladies of my acquaintance – are engaged in arranging a sale of work. It would be so nice if you could join us.'

'I am afraid I am very busy,' Mrs Rebecca said, with an infinitesimal shake of her head, 'what with Papa and the house. But it is very kind of you.'

Mrs D'Aubigny left the house with a faint suspicion – one that she could not for the life of her have put into words – that the afternoon had been a failure in some way or other. Mrs Rebecca, on the other hand, rang for the footman, ordered that a fresh pot of tea should be brought in, and settled down amid the sofa cushions in what for her was high good humour.

XV

Captain McTurk Takes Charge

It is remarkable how the police have grown respectable. In Sir Robert Peel's day the representatives of Her Majesty's force would sometimes be hard pressed to distinguish themselves from the malefactors they pursued and harassed around the streets of London. Now, mysteriously, they are men of education, tenacity and resolve. They are invited into polite drawing-rooms; their portraits are in newspapers; romances are written about their exploits . . .

Some Thoughts on our Contemporary Malaise (1865)

The burglary at Mr Gallentin's shop was a nine days' wonder. Mr Gallentin himself discovered it when he came to unlock his strongroom at eight o'clock on the Monday morning. Thereafter the news of it spread like wildfire, was taken up to the West End by all the City Croesuses who lunched there, and by late afternoon had made its way into most of the evening newspapers. Mr Gallentin, picturesquely interviewed by his shattered safe, was loud in his expostulations. He had done everything in his power to protect his property – locked it into a safe and put the safe on general view – but he proposed that the police had not done enough. The value of the stolen goods was put at £6,000 – an extraordinary sum. There had been no robbery like it in living memory, people said, not since the Duke of——'s plate had been snibbed from his strongbox in Grosvenor Square while the family lay asleep, and Mr Fogle, the celebrated cracksman, been taken on Hay Hill with a coronet absolutely in his knapsack. The next day's newspapers were full of it, and the political gentlemen talked about it in Westminster

Great Court. And before long, the City police being baffled by its complexities, it was taken back to the West End again and presented to the commander of the metropolitan force, Captain McTurk, for his particular delight and edification.

Quite what Captain McTurk made of this forensic gift was anyone's guess. He was a tall, spare, middle-aged man with a blue chin that no razor could ever subdue, who had filled his present post for upwards of a dozen years. There was a Mrs Captain McTurk and half a dozen little McTurks living at a villa in Fulham, but most of Captain McTurk's days were spent in an office in a greystone building overlooking one of those melancholy courtyards on the western side of Northumberland Avenue. He was sitting in this office now, in a high-backed chair, with a cigar smoking between his fingers, a pile of correspondence on the japanned desk before him and a secretary in a closet nearby awaiting his summons, but in truth the cigar had ceased to interest him, the pile of letters was so much camouflage and the secretary had not been called in for half an hour. At the same time, he could not be said to be ignoring the world around him, for every time a door slammed in the corridor or there came a clattering of footsteps in the middle distance he raised his head and stared intently at the doorway. Finally, there was a noise of footsteps more purposeful than any he had previously heard, and a demure-looking man with a tall hat pushed to the back of his head came striding along the passageway. This was Mr Masterson, Captain McTurk's confidential assistant.

'So you have been to Cornhill?' Captain McTurk demanded.

'Certainly I have been there,' Mr Masterson said, as suavely as if Captain McTurk had asked him if he had been to Margate for his holiday.

'It is a confounded imposition. How are we likely to see anything that Major McGarry's people have not seen? I suppose they have been down there and trampled everything. I never knew such a man for interfering with things as Major McGarry.'

'There has been no trampling, I think,' said Mr Masterson. 'At any rate, there is not a great deal to trample. Everything has been left just as you would wish it, I believe.'

Captain McTurk's stare relented a little. 'What does Gallentin say?'

'Oh, he is in a fury. Says that McGarry must have stopped his patrols that night, and McGarry cannot deny it. There is talk of an action for negligence.'

'You have seen the room?'

'Certainly I have,' Mr Masterson said. 'A thoroughly professional job, I should say. Indeed, they came down into the poulterer's shop next door and then up through the cellar. I should think it will take the best part of a week to make good the damage. As for the safe, I gather Mr Milner is in despair.'

'That's what comes of calling your things "invincible", or whatever was said. They came at it with a torch, I take it?'

'By no means. In fact, the lock held. It was done by main force, I should judge.'

Captain McTurk thought about this, and stared out of the window where an ostler in the stable yard below was turning over a pile of straw with a fork.

'Gallentin can say precisely what was taken?'

'Oh precisely. I took the liberty of obtaining a list.'

'And is that the extent of the damage?'

'Well – Mr Henley – that is, the poulterer who has the shop next door – earnestly desired me to tell you that there are two brace of pheasants gone missing from his storeroom.'

If Captain McTurk was amused by this, he did not say so. 'Is that all?'

'There is this.' And here Mr Masterson produced what looked like a sheet of notepaper, faintly tinged with blue, and placed it face down upon the pile of letters. 'It was found on the floor of Mr Henley's cellar, and Mr Henley knows nothing about it.'

'Doesn't he?' Captain McTurk picked up the sheet of notepaper, looked at the three or four lines that were written on it, appeared to make nothing of them, and put it down again. He asked no further questions, seemed to pass into a state of dazed abstraction, and Mr Masterson, who was used to his superior's moods and fancies, crept silently from the room.

A minute or two passed after he had gone before Captain McTurk woke up. He first stared out of the window – the same ostler was still forking up the same pile of straw – and then set about making an inventory of the items on his desk. The letters to which he had been attending, or not attending, when Mr Masterson arrived he folded up and placed in a tray. The list setting out the contents of Mr Gallentin's plundered safe he now arranged in front of him. The fragment of the letter that Mr Masterson had found on the cellar floor he took up again and closely inspected. It was, as he now saw, a rather curious document, written in a distinctive but almost unintelligible hand, had no salutation and no signature, and seemed to consist of a pair of questions: would the recipient be interested in performing a certain task? And on what date did he (or she) think that it might conveniently be performed? After this there were a number of crossings-out and the start of a sentence that presumably continued onto a second sheet of paper which Captain McTurk did not possess. Captain McTurk stared at it, held it up to the light to examine the watermark, and then put it down again, thinking that if he could find the author of it, much less the person to whom it had been sent, then he would have the answer to his mystery. Then, seeing by his watch that it was about half past twelve o'clock, and that the secretary in the adjoining cubby-hole had so despaired of being called that he had gone off to his lunch, he locked up his desk, with the sheet of notepaper in it, took his hat, descended into the courtyard, nodded at the ostler and passed out under the archway into Northumberland Avenue, where he hailed a cab and had himself taken off to Cornhill.

There was a crowd of people scurrying around the door, and a constable on duty, who touched his hat, and Captain McTurk felt his spirits sink. 'That confounded Gallentin will do nothing but wail at me,' he said to himself. But having discovered from the constable that Mr Gallentin was away in Lothbury consulting his insurers, he made his way into the shop and, having declared himself to one of Mr Gallentin's young men, was immediately ushered into the strong-room. What he saw there, though it corresponded exactly with

208

Mr Masterson's description, interested him very much. The safe had been taken down from its plinth and now lay in the middle of the floor with the twisted door pulled back to its furthest extent. Bending down to examine it, Captain McTurl inspected the lock and saw, as Mr Masterson had told him, that it had been pulled out by main force. Then he took a small optical glass out of the pocket of his coat and held it against the door-frame, noted the countless tiny abrasions that ran along its length and then put the glass away. This done, he inspected the observation slit in the wall, and the angle of the mirrors that flanked it, and then walked slowly around the perimeter of the room, paying the closest attention to the floor and the wainscoting. There was not a great deal to see, but Captain McTurk thought he had the measure of what little there was. Coming back out of the strongroom into Mr Gallentin's shop, which was full of people making not the least pretence of buying jewellery, he did trouble himself to walk out into the street, up the flight of stairs adjoining the strongroom and into the warren of offices that ran above it. There were men at work patching up the gaping hole in the poulterer's ceiling, and Captain McTurk smiled at them, asked a question or two, looked thoughtfully at the unfurled carpet, and then went down to his waiting cab.

There was a street conjuror at work on the pavement before the Mansion House, and Captain McTurk watched the half-dozen coloured balls that he spun making their variegated descent and thought of the other conjuror and the £6,000 he had spirited away. What struck him about the robbery was not merely the technical skill brought to bear on Mr Gallentin's safe but the audacity of the person, or people, who had committed it. Captain McTurk was not perhaps a very advanced student of criminal psychology – his interest in wrongdoers extended only to catching them and locking them up – but he believed that most of them were, above all, fearful of exposing themselves. This led him to reason that only a very bold man would have robbed Mr Gallentin's shop in this manner, and he spent the remainder of his journey back to Northumberland Avenue wondering who that bold man might be.

Arriving back at his office, where the view from the window disclosed the same ostler still apparently forking up the same pile of straw, he instantly routed out the secretary and had Mr Masterson summoned to him from the nook he occupied at the corridor's further end.

'I declare', he said, as Mr Masterson came into the room, 'the fellow there has been turning over the straw for the last half-hour at least. What can he mean by it?'

'I believe there is very little for them to do,' Mr Masterson said apologetically. 'Do I take it you have been to Cornhill?'

'Certainly I have been there. So has half the City. It is quite as you say. I wished merely to see the premises. The safe was wedged open, I suppose, or an iron bar driven in. There is no more information?'

'We have had a report of two men possibly seen in Eastcheap at about half past five in the morning on the Sunday.'

'And no one arrested them?'

'The constable who saw them declares that they were some distance off and that he had no reason to suspect their behaviour.'

'I should suspect anyone's behaviour that I met in Eastcheap at half past five in the morning. I don't doubt those were the two men. But there is no use crying after spilt milk. You have asked our people?'

'It would be difficult, I think, for anyone to offer one of Mr Gallentin's pieces without our coming to hear of it. Certainly not in London.'

'They may be in Paris now, for all we know.' Captain McTurk put his hands in his trouser pockets and jingled the money in them. 'Well, we had better make out a list. Do you suppose Maggs could have done it?'

'Hardly. I believe he is very infirm these days.'

'What about the fellow who took the insurance certificates from Finsbury Pavement?'

'I think not. The case went unproven, if you recall. Since then he has turned very respectable. Lives in Kensington, I believe, and has set up as a wine merchant.'

This litany went on for some time and was not very enlightening. It was remarkable, in fact, how many of the capital's criminal fancy had been temporarily detached from their livelihoods. Mr Slater, the great Whitechapel cracksman, had been seized at a West End gaming club six months since and was currently Her Majesty's guest at Wandsworth. Crewkerne, who had robbed Lord Baker of his rubies, disguised himself as a footman and left the house by the front door in broad daylight, was thought to be in Antwerp. By the time Captain McTurk had reached the end of his catechism, it might have been wondered exactly how the crime had been committed, seeing that there were so few people left in London capable of committing it.

'That Frenchman, perhaps, M. Jambon,' Mr Masterson suggested. 'He could have been brought in from Paris, and no one the wiser.'

But Captain McTurk shook his head, suggesting that whoever had perpetrated the crime would have needed several weeks to make their preparations, and that such an absence from his Parisian haunts on M. Jambon's part would have been remarked.

'What was the name of that man who robbed the mail train going down to Dover?'

'Pardew wasn't it?' Mr Masterson offered, who was still determined to prove that M. Jambon, spirited into the country by nocturnal ferry and then spirited out again the following day, was the guilty man.

'Pardew it was. I recollect the case' – Captain McTurk remembered every case he had ever had a part in solving. 'Took a hundredweight of bullion off the train and melted it down . . . The coolest fellow I ever saw – or didn't see.' Mr Masterson nodded his head at this admission of defeat. 'What happened to him, I wonder?'

'There was talk of him on the continent. Did we not send a man to Leghorn?'

'Pshaw. Leghorn!' said Captain McTurk. 'If every villain supposed to have gone to Leghorn had been taken there, we should have no room left in any gaol in England. There were accomplices, were there not?'

'There was a man died in the street,' Mr Masterson said. 'Ran into a cart or some such. And another fellow lagged – transported. But Pardew was his own man, I fancy.'

'Not quite, I think. Didn't that File have a hand with the tools?'

'I believe Mr File lives a very quiet life these days,' Mr Masterson suggested. 'Hands round the plate at church. Never sees any of his old friends. That sort of thing.'

Captain McTurk made a little gesture with his hand, showing that he did not at all believe in the idea of Mr File's retirement. He was, although he did not say so to Mr Masterson, perplexed by the whole affair, perplexed by the audacity with which it had been carried out, and perplexed by the coldness of the trail. Still, he thought there were things he might do and opportunities that he might avail himself of.

'You had better go and see File at his house,' he said finally. 'Don't, whatever you do, say anything that might alarm him. He may very well levant. He has done that before. Just – well – go and see him and hear what he has to say. And then take this paper' – he produced the fragment that had been found in the poulterer's cellar – 'and see if you can find where it came from.'

'It is rather a long shot, surely?' Mr Masterson ventured.

'And so was the bullet that took Nelson at Trafalgar,' said Captain McTurk, 'but he died of it all the same.'

Presently there came a message to say that Captain McTurk was wanted by the Home Secretary, and Mr Masterston took his hat and went off to execute his commissions.

*

Mr Masterson had the reputation of a thorough man, but he became aware, as he went about his tasks, that his thoroughness was of no help to him. Mr File, found by his parlour fire in Clerkenwell, was extremely courteous, but that was all he was, declared himself absolutely in retirement, seeing no one and utterly forsaking the associations that had previously brought him to Captain McTurk's notice, and was supported in this view by his wife, who declared that Mr Masterson was cruel coming to browbeat folks as had been lying in bed of a quinsy this past fortnight with never a thought for anything beyond it.

'What about that fellow Pardew?' said Mr Masterson, thinking to spring the name on him unaware, but Mr File was ready for him. 'Dear me,' he said. 'I had thought I might be spared this. Really, you know, when one is' – there was a church over the way from Mr File's bow-window, and if he did not actually gesture at it he gave Mr Masterson to understand that it was there he knew his duty to lie – 'when one is, well, I shan't say any more about it, but, well, it is hard, you know.' Mr Masterson knew that he was dealing with a hypocrite, but somehow he could not bring himself to say so, with the subscription card from the Distressed Housepainters' Guild lying there on the mantelpiece to rebuke him.

'I think Pardew had better look out for himself,' Mr File suggested to his wife when Mr Masterson had gone.

'I never did like that Pardew,' Mrs File volunteered, who was perhaps not very genteel.

'Maybe not. But I think he had better look out for himself.' And Mr File went to the church on the next Sabbath and sang the hymns in a very loud voice.

Having no luck with Mr File, Mr Masterson took himself to a stationer's in High Holborn. Here he had better fortune, for the stationer not only recognised the weave but gave him the address of the firm in Kennington that manufactured it. The paper was of a very superior kind, he learned, in a conversation with the firm's director. They took pleasure in supplying half a dozen shops in Mayfair and in Kensington and Brompton beyond it. Indeed, there was a move to colonise Fulham and Putney too, as the wives of the clerks who lived there wrote confidential letters to their friends just like grand ladies in Grosvenor Square. And Mr Masterson knew that his enquiry could take him no further, that he could probably compile a list of every stationer in the West End and the City, but that a record of their customers, not to mention samples of their customers' handwriting, would probably be beyond him.

All this plunged Mr Masterson into a thoroughgoing ill-humour. He had sent his agents out into the highways and byways of London – into Hoxton jewellers' shops, and discreet little emporia in the Pimlico Road – all those myriad places where the goods offered for sale are sometimes not very scrupulously obtained, and the agents had come back empty-handed. Nobody, least of all the Jewish gentlemen in Hoxton and the Pimlico capitalists who offer limitless credit in exchange for the bearer's note of hand, knew anything about Mr Gallentin's safe, who had robbed it, what was in it, and how the items might have been disposed of. There was a rumour come to Captain McTurk from one of his continental spies, and an emissary was sent to Boulogne, but the cottage by the sea was locked up and had part of its roof stove in by the equinoctial gales, and it was soon proved that Mr Pardew was long gone from there, if indeed he had ever been. Meanwhile, Captain McTurk had other things to trouble him. Two off-course bookmakers had knocked each other's heads in outside a public house in Soho; a veritable epidemic of betting slips had blown out across the West End; and the superintendent of the Surrey Police had written an urgent letter demanding his assistance in frustrating the upsurge of criminality which always attends that great sporting celebration at the Epsom Downs, Derby Day.

XVI

What *The Star* thought about it

'Paddock Pencillings' by 'Captain Crewe'

... There is a mystery about PERICLES. Mr Grant, his trainer will say
nothing, and the animal has not been seen. The 100 to 7 being offered
is, in these circumstances, money ill-spent. Of TIBERIUS, on the other
hand, it can confidently be stated that the horse will run, having distinguished itself – in modest company, admittedly – in Lincolnshire.
THE SPARTAN, belying the austerity of his name, has fed a little too well
over the winter – gentlemen *will* over-feed their horses: can nothing
be done to stop them? – and shall, we hear, do nothing. GUILLEMOT
(an extraordinary name, but then the upstart vulgarity of the age
knows no bounds) has tumbled over a mole-heap in the Breckland
and had to be destroyed. SEPTUAGINT: that noble adherent of the Sport
of Kings Lord Trumpington is cautious, which may be an omen. Your
correspondent saw PENDRAGON at exercise lately, thought him dainty,
well-set-up, an ornament to the Cornish line that sired him, and
undervalued at twelves.

XVII

At Home and Abroad with Captain Raff

When I hear about a villain and his wiles, my first thought is for that villain's associate. Where does he lay his head? How does he occupy himself when not engaged on villainy? What ravens feed him, and who launders his clothes? What are his innocent recreations and where are they indulged?

A London Charivari (1862)

Captain Raff lived in practised seclusion up three flights of stairs in Ryder Street. The chambers he inhabited were an artists' rookery, where the gaunt old men in frayed collars marching along the corridors were as likely to be portraitists' models as duns, and the traffic of the hallway was ripe to be interrupted every so often by a picture being taken downstairs to a waiting cab. There was a general air of bohemian laxity, of which Captain Raff warmly approved. The name beneath the street bell was not, of course, his own; the door of his apartment had a very sound lock; and behind it Captain Raff quietly luxuriated. It was a small room, under the eaves, with a skylight and several yellow-looking plants in pots which he sometimes remembered to water and sometimes did not, so that they dwindled away in consequence. There were sporting prints hung on the walls, and gauzy dancers, and a portrait in charcoal whose frame noted that it had been hung at the Academy fifteen years ago, captioned 'Head of an Officer', whose incongruity, in a room given over to bachelor dissipation, grew less marked when one realised that it was a younger version of Captain Raff himself, 'taken off' by Anstruther, RA, on a long-ago evening in the regimental mess. When he read about Anstruther in the newspaper, Captain Raff envied him his luck.

It was a Saturday morning in Ryder Street, not at all early, with the bolt drawn across the door and the skylight half-open – each an infallible sign that Captain Raff was at home – and the Captain, very negligently swathed in an ancient dressing gown, with one bare leg dangling over his chair, was making a late breakfast of a plate of oysters brought in from a neighbouring cook-shop and a bottle of soda-water. People who set foot in Captain Raff's chamber – an inconsiderable number – said that he really should not keep that 'Head of an Officer' on the wall as the contrast with the second head that laboured beneath it was so very marked, but Captain Raff was proud of his portrait. 'Anstruther, sir,' he would explain, 'why, he simply dashed it off – just dashed it off. And fellows who know me say it's the most sovereign likeness.' Captain Raff liked to say that he was a free spirit and went about as he pleased, but in fact there were several things lying on the table next to the litter of discarded oyster shells and the Tabasco bottle that had the ability to constrain him: a bill from his laundress; a letter or two containing columns of figures and respectful compliments; and a heap of sporting newspapers – *Bell's Life*, *The Field* and *The Sportsman's Magazine* – over which Captain Raff was intermittently poring. Every so often, finding some paragraph that interested him, he would take a pen from its holder on the desk, wipe it carefully on the hem of his dressing gown, and make a calculation on the back of the laundress's bill.

Presently there came a noise of footsteps in the passage and a smart double rap on the door. Starting up from his desk, but taking care not to make the slightest sound, Captain Raff made his way not to the door but to an upturned bucket that lay slightly to one side of the doorframe. There was a crack in the uppermost part of the wood, and by mounting the bucket – this, again, he managed without making the slightest noise – he was able to observe the person standing in the passage. This done, he shot the bolt and admitted into the room a fat, dull-featured man wearing a coat that was perhaps too warm for the time of the year, and a very battered tall hat.

'You've been a long time letting me in, Capting,' this gentleman observed. 'There's money owing I suppose?'

'A trifle. A guinea or so. That man McPherson, you know.'

'Landlords is always a bother,' said the visitor, putting his hat down next to the pile of oyster shells. 'Anyhow, I dare say there is business to do, eh?'

Somebody once remarked that however low a man's position in life, there is usually to be found some other man prepared to cling to him and do his bidding with a deference that it is very gratifying to his wounded vanity. And so Mr Delaney – this was the visitor's name – for reasons which no one had ever been able to fathom, clung to Captain Raff. He ran errands for him. He negotiated his little bills – at three months, six months, or even a year – and took sixpenny commissions. He went to race-meetings and hung about the enclosure gates while Captain Raff toadied his acquaintances in the ring. There were people who said that Captain Raff owed Mr Delaney money, but this was not borne out by Captain Raff's attitude to his protégé – which was at all times patronising – or Mr Delaney's response to it, which was deferential in the extreme.

'Well, now,' Captain Raff said, retreating behind his desk – it was the only chair in the room, and Mr Delaney had to stand – 'let's see what you have been up to. I've seen all the papers.'

'Yus indeed, Capting.' Mr Delaney regarded the copies of *Bell's Life* and *The Sportman's Magazine* with professional distaste. 'But the papers is always so behind-hand. Coming out for Lord Garroway's Hecate when everyone knows the beast has an habcess on its hock. That McIvor, down at the Bird and Hand . . .'

'McIvor?' Captain Raff must have heard Mr McIvor's name before. 'What does McIvor have to say?'

'Well.' Mr Delaney looked very knowing. 'It's not much of a book that Whalen lets him make up . . . You know they had the police in there again the other day and a whole heap of slips got thrown out the windy? But he does know what is being said. Now, McIvor has Tiberius at fives.'

'No more than he ought,' Captain Raff broke in again.

'That's what I said myself, Capting. As nice a hoss as I ever saw. Leave that Belchamber, that everyone was talking about a month since, in its tracks. But then, that's down from four. Baldino's at eight. And Septuagint – that's Lord Trumpington's horse, that nobody thought would ever run, at nine. And yet there's money going on Baldino all the time. Why, McIvor swore he knew of a single stake of two thousand pound on Baldino only the other day.'

'Two thousand pounds! And Tiberius going out from four to five?'

'I know, sir. And "Nimrod" in *Bell*'s saying how he was the certainest thing he'd seen in a month of Sundays. It's all very queer.'

'Very queer,' said Captain Raff. He was thinking hard about Mr Happerton, and what Mr Happerton might be doing with the capital that had come into his hands in recent weeks. The idea, in so far as Mr Happerton had been prepared to convey it to his associate, had been that the money was to be staked on Tiberius. And yet here was the price lengthening, while someone had placed two thousand pounds on Baldino!

'What do people say about Mr McWilliam's horse?' he now enquired.

'Baldino?' Mr Delaney looked as if he was trying to remember a lesson from school. 'A nice little hoss, certainly. Might do well with a fair wind and someone who knows how to ride him on the seat – he's got a nasty way of chewing his bit and veering off towards the rail which even Dolly Walker, as rode him in the Two Thousand, could do nothing about, you recall. But he's no match for Tiberius . . . Anything the matter, Capting?' For Captain Raff's face had turned more than usually pale.

'One of those confounded oysters, I'll be bound. You'd better excuse me.'

While Captain Raff was in the water closet parting company with the bad oyster, Mr Delaney made a little tour of the room, leered at the unmade bed, grinned at the laundress's bill, picked up the sporting newspapers that he had previously disparaged and looked at the marks Captain Raff had made in their margins. 'A market 'oss if ever I saw one,' he said to himself. 'But do the capting know? That's the question.' Then, hearing sounds that suggested the captain had finished his ablutions, he returned to his position in the centre of the room.

'Who's to have the riding of Tiberius, I wonder?' he asked, as Captain Raff fell back into his chair.

'Ugh! I'll have that man summonsed, indeed I shall . . . What's that?'

'I said: who's to have the riding of him?'

'It's not quite decided,' said Captain Raff, who had a horrible suspicion that it might have been without his knowledge.

'Well, it had better be decided quick, with the race to be run in a month, and Sam Collinson already booked for Septuagint, if what I hear's correct.'

There was just slightly less deference in Mr Delaney's voice as he said this: perhaps it was the sight of the laundress's bill that did it.

'That's enough of that,' Captain Raff said. He looked horribly seedy. 'Here, there is something you can do for me. Did you ever have any dealings with Mr Handasyde, who keeps the Perch in Dean Street?'

'Know the 'ouse, Capting. Don't know the gentleman.'

'Well, take this paper to him, and tell him – in point of fact – tell him I shall be glad to renew at three months.'

Mr Delaney picked up the bill from the shaking hand that Captain Raff extended to him, gave it an odd look that suggested Mr Handasyde might have his own opinion, and put it in his pocket. 'I shall stick with him till the race,' he said to himself. 'But after that, well, there are safer bets, Delaney my boy, and you knows it.'

When he had gone, and the door had been carefully locked behind him, Captain Raff exchanged his dressing gown for the pair of white duck trousers and the royal blue coat with brass buttons that made him look rather like a nautical man and sat down in his chair. The portrait by Anstruther, RA, caught his eye and he thought about the young man he had been. Those had, in fact, been the days. And now he had crows'-feet under his eyes and there was thirty shillings owing to his laundress that he could not pay. It was very hard, Captain Raff thought, as he turned over the matter of Baldino and the two thousand pounds that someone had wagered on him and the subsequent lengthening of Tiberius's odds. He suspected that Mr Happerton was playing some game from which he was being excluded, but he could not quite see how he was to bring his suspicion out into the light. 'Two thousand on Baldino,' he said to himself once or twice. The sunshine, streaming in from the skylight, sparkled off his brass buttons and wreathed the officer's head in a little golden halo, and in this way Captain Raff's courage renewed itself.

At about half past twelve he put on his hat, unlocked the door and stepped cautiously out into the passageway. There was no one there and, swaggering a little, with odd shafts of sunlight from stray windows above and behind him gleaming off his brass buttons, Captain Raff went down his three flights of stairs out into the street. There was no one much about at the Blue Riband – it is very quiet on a Saturday, for the sporting men are all gone into the country – but there was a waiter carrying a liqueur glass on a tray up the stairs to the library, and Captain Raff followed hopefully on his heels.

'Holloa there, Happerton. Fancy seeing you here.'

'Well, it's a place I'm generally to be found, I suppose,' Mr Happerton said. He was sitting in an armchair, his legs encased in a yet more brilliant pair of top-boots, looking at an album of equine prints. 'Are you going to sea, Raff? You look like a midshipman.'

'It is just a navy coat that I happen to have,' Captain Raff said, wishing that he had left his brass buttons at home. He was conscious that Mr Happerton did not think his arrival at the Blue Riband coincidental. 'Mrs Happerton is well, I take it?'

'Never saw her better.' There was a silence.

'And the old gentleman?'

'Takes off his milk-and-arrowroot every night like a man. We are getting on famously. But you're very full of questions, Raff. I'm on my way out, as it happens. Is there anything else you'd care to ask me?'

'Well –' Captain Raff thought he might as well be hung for a sheep as for a lamb. 'I was at Tattersall's this morning, you know, and some of the fellows were asking who is to ride Tiberius?'

'Were they? That is very kind of them.' Captain Raff could not tell if Mr Happerton was annoyed, or satirically amused. 'Well, I can tell you the answer, and you may tell them. It is – Major Hubbins.'

'Major Hubbins!'

'Don't tell me you've never heard of him?' Mr Happerton was holding the liqueur glass in his right hand, halfway to his mouth, and the sunlight caught the liquid and illumined it.

'Of course I have heard of him. But . . .'

Captain Raff had not only heard of Major Hubbins, but met him, talked to him and been bought glasses of brandy-and-water by him. There was no one in the Blue Riband – not even the knife-boy or the girl who laundered the tablecloths – who had not heard of him. His name had been spoken of in sporting circles for nearly thirty years. He was a short, white-haired and very nearly elderly man who had once, riding Lord Fellowes' Danton, won the Cesarewitch, but the riding of it had been a long time ago.

'But what?' Mr Happerton demanded.

'Well. He . . . he ain't very young, you know.'

'Cantrip won the Derby at fifty-seven.'

'He's not so very far short of that, I should say.' Privately Captain Raff was enraged. A part of him suspected that Mr Happerton was actively conspiring to lose the race, and that the two thousand pounds staked on Baldino had come from the robbing of Mr Gallentin's safe. The morality of this intrigue did not concern him – Captain Raff had known a great deal worse in the dainty sporting circles in which he moved – but he was furious that it should have been begun without his connivance, and he suspected that this concealment boded very ill for his status as Mr Happerton's confidential adviser. 'As you say, Cantrip was fifty-seven. He may do very well.' Still, though, Captain Raff could not entirely bid farewell to his professional judgement. 'His knee isn't strong, you know. Not since he went down under Pyramid that time at Uttoxeter.'

'I happen to know the bone was reset,' Mr Happerton said. 'He is as strong as an ox.'

'He'll need to be,' Captain Raff said, in what might have been taken for a humorous tone, 'if he's to ride Tiberius.'

'Well, that is what has been proposed. In fact, I am just going off to see him. You had better come with me, if the prospect charms you so much.'

Major Hubbins lived in rooms above a public house on the north side of the park, where he was made much of and got his glasses of brandy-and-water gratis. Sitting in the cab as it trundled along High Holborn – Mr Happerton said nothing and stared out of the window – Captain Raff found himself transfixed by misery. He knew that his position in life, such as it was, depended on Mr Happerton, and now it seemed as if Mr Happerton was about to throw him over. Captain Raff thought of the things on which his association with Mr Happerton depended – they included his subscription to the Blue Riband, his rent at Ryder Street and one or two private things which it is not necessary to go into here – and fairly groaned. He was enough of a realist to know that if Mr Happerton abandoned him, the path thereafter could only lead down, down to the debased hostelries where the McIvors of this world plied their trade. In this wretched state his imagination began to play tricks on him. He thought of adamantine rock, dark caverns far underground, white, nacreous jewels in clustered profusion. There was a pair of street acrobats turning somersaults on the pavement, a grey-haired man and a boy who, judging from the set of his features, was his son, and he stared at them unhappily, not liking the patterns they made or the sight of the boy's head emerging from the space where a split second ago his feet had been. Something of Captain Raff's unease communicated itself to Mr Happerton, who turned in his seat and said:

'What's the matter, Raff? There's no press-gang come to take you to your ship, surely?'

The dark caverns, far underground, with their clusters of garnets, had been replaced by a flux of black, oily water that rushed over a landscape of bleached and broken stone. Try as he might, Captain Raff could not avoid the water. He ran away from it, stepped smartly out of its path, but still it followed him and threatened to drag him down. It was worse when they came to Bayswater, for Captain Raff swiftly divined that Major Hubbins was a superior version of himself. The rooms were just like his own – the same mess and confusion – only larger and better appointed. There were the same sporting prints on the wall, only the sheen of the panelling gave them respectability, and on the desk, instead of the laundress's bill, there was an earl's *carte de visite*. All this depressed Captain Raff horribly. So, too, did the sight of Major Hubbins, who they found not lounging elegantly by his deal table, as Captain Raff remembered him, with a dog-whip dangling out of his pocket and the emerald pin that the Duke of Grafton had given him in his white stock, but sitting with his feet in a hot mustard bath looking simultaneously ancient and comic.

He is like a little old clergyman, Captain Raff thought as he bent to shake Major Hubbins' hand, and smelt the bear's-grease on his sleek white hair, *a little old clergyman bobbing up with the sacrament at some altar-rail in a country church with a few old women waiting in the pews*. It was twenty years since Captain Raff had taken the sacrament, but the image was very vivid to him and for a moment the tide of black water ran elsewhere. 'I think I can do it,' Major Hubbins was saying in response to some polite enquiry of Mr Happerton's. 'Indeed it's very kind of you to think of me. Lord Mountjoy' – Major Hubbins was famous for introducing aristocratic names into his conversation – 'was saying only the other day that he wondered I did not get my chance.'

What weight was he riding at, Mr Happerton innocently wondered, and Major Hubbins said he believed it was eight stone five, and Captain Raff smirked horribly. The smell of the mustard was very strong. They stayed there an hour, without, it seemed to him, discussing anything of note, talking of ancient Pegasuses and their exploits, how Desdemona had won the Oaks, with little Jack Simpson, who weighed only six stone, hanging on to her for dear life, and Lord Fawcett's seizure, which everyone said was on account of his having backed Gladiolus, only Major Hubbins swore that it was not, for he had seen the paper and it was some other horse, and Captain Raff frankly despaired. The sporting prints nagged him with their splendour, the earl's *carte-de-visite* winked at him from the table, and he remembered his own room at Ryder Street with the unmade bed, the litter of oyster shells and the providential lock.

When they came out into the street it was well on in the afternoon, and Captain Raff, seeing the bustle and clamour of the streets, thought that there was no world of which he was a part and that the black tide would surely carry him off.

'We must get him up to Scroop without delay,' he said. 'I doubt he's sat on a horse for a twelvemonth.'

'I've no doubt he'll come to Scroop,' Mr Happerton remarked. 'He told me he is going to stay with Sir Harry Creighton at Towcester. I dare say we shall see him after that.'

'You know, Happerton,' Captain Raff said easily, as if he meant it for a joke, 'there are people who might think that you meant to use Tiberius for the market, and that – well – you favoured some other horse all along.'

'It is amazing what people will think,' Mr Happerton said.

'And yet, you know, it will do you harm if they go on saying it.'

'They may think what they like,' Mr Happerton said.

*

Two miles away in Soho someone else was thinking it.

'No, I won't renew,' Mr Handasyde of the Perch in Dean Street was telling Mr Delaney. 'I don't want Captain Raff's paper at three months, nor even at six for twice the interest. I want what's owing. And if the Captain don't like it, why, I've a friend in Cursitor Street who'll be happy to make his acquaintance.'

'There's no need for bailiffs,' Mr Delaney said. He was wondering to himself if Captain Raff's game was worth the playing any more. Then a thought struck him. 'Now see here,' he improvised. 'You renew at two – and if I know the capting and how he's placed he'll settle, indeed he will – and I'll give you a tip for the Derby.'

'What sort of a tip?' Mr Handasyde wondered. He had a sneaking regard for Mr Delaney's opinion that the shadow of Captain Raff had never quite displaced.

'Shall you sign?'

Mr Handasyde signed his name across the bill with a flourish. 'What is it?'

'Well – that Tiberius that everyone talks of so much, it's my belief that he's been bred for the market, and that the man who owns him has his money on Baldino.'

'What? You mean he'll be ridden to lose?'

'I mean he won't be ridden to win.'

Mr Handasyde said something under his breath, and Mr Delaney, grinning in spite of himself, put the bill in his pocket and took it back to Ryder Street.

XVIII

The Triumph of a Modern Man

It is the rain that makes us melancholy – that, and the localities we inhabit.

A Lincoln memorial (1853)

Sitting in his armchair with a blanket drawn round his knees, drinking his milk-and-arrowroot, preparing to be despatched to his bed for the night, stumbling his way up and down staircases with the old butler supporting his arm, Mr Gresham had ample time to reflect on the question of his daughter. His illness – there was still this fiction that he was getting better from it – had done two things to him. It had made him querulous, very anxious that his blankets should be drawn up properly, that his milk-and-arrowroot should be hot enough – but not too hot. But it also gave him leisure of a kind that no previous part of his life had ever afforded, and he determined to use this leisure to explore one or two mysteries that he had never satisfactorily solved, the greatest of these being his daughter.

First there was the business of her marriage. Mr Gresham did not like Mr Happerton, although he appreciated his courtesy, but he knew the kind of man he was. His daughter he felt he did not know at all. He had watched her once at dinner as Mr Happerton, coming in late with some choice morsel of intelligence that he wished to share, had bounced over and placed his arm on his wife's shoulder, and Mrs Rebecca had stared at the hand as if it were a bat that had just flown in out of the stilly night. And yet it could not be said that she fell short in most aspects of that wifely regard by which newly married gentlemen set such store. She accompanied Mr Happerton to such social occasions as he proposed happily enough. She liked to hear the horsey talk with which he occasionally favoured her. But all the time, Mr Gresham fancied, there was calculation in her. Worse, perhaps, was the fact that he knew this calculation extended to her dealings with himself. He would catch her looking at him sometimes as they sat in the drawing room – she on her sofa, he in his chair – and he could not help but think that the glance she gave him was not unlike the glance that M. Soyer gives the mock turtle, seen in a provisioner's window in Piccadilly, that he intends to render into that night's soup. Her eyes at this juncture seemed very green, and the twists of hair gathered up in the corner of her mouth were very disagreeable.

He tried to conciliate her, to pass small remarks that she might find amusing, but still the green eyes stared calculatingly back. He had nothing to complain of materially. He had his cushions, and his blanket, and his meals brought in hot-and-hot, and his carriage-ride in the park – he was bored by that carriage-ride – and for these he was grateful. But his enfeebled state made him miserable and in his misery he told himself that if his daughter's peculiarities – her detachment, her calculation – had any root cause, it must lie in his treatment of her. He had not been what he ought to have been to her, and the green eyes staring at him from the sofa were the result. The consciousness of his failings – that was how he saw it – made Mr Gresham indulgent and perhaps explains a conversation between the two of them that took place at this time.

'Papa,' Mrs Rebecca said – they were in the drawing room, he with a newspaper, she with a novel – 'may I ask you something?'

Mr Gresham put down the strong article he had been reading on Irish disestablishment. He could not remember the last time his daughter had asked him anything.

'What is it?'

'Do you think that it would be a good thing for George to go in for politics?'

It was all Mr Gresham could do to establish who 'George' might be, so outlandish did this proposal seem. But a look at his daughter's face told him that she was in complete earnest.

'What do you mean? That he should try for a seat in parliament?'

'I suppose that is what gentlemen generally do when they go in for politics.'

'I thought George was more exercised by winning the Derby.'

'That doesn't signify at all, Papa. Plenty of people who own horses have a seat in the House.'

Mr Gresham acknowledged that it didn't signify. He was entirely nonplussed. But still, there were the green eyes staring at him. In ordinary circumstances he would have assumed that his son-in-law had asked his wife to make this intercession. But it now occurred to him – he did not quite know why – that the thought was Mrs Rebecca's own.

'Does George know that you have asked me this?'

'Why should he know? It is not his idea.'

This struck Mr Gresham as so comical that he almost laughed.

'Great heavens, Rebecca. Gentlemen who take seats in parliament are generally consulted about it the first place, don't you know. At least that has always been my experience.'

Mr Gresham had never been a political man. Some gentlemen in Hertfordshire with strong views about tariff reform had once invited him to be their candidate against a sitting Liberal and he had declined. That was as far as it had gone. But still he was not insensible of the advantages that a seat in parliament may confer on its incumbent. Privately he could not imagine anyone less likely to distinguish himself in the House than his son-in-law. Then again, he told himself that many persons with much less outward distinction than Mr Happerton had made brilliant careers for themselves there. And all the while, as these thoughts passed through his head, Mrs Rebecca stared at him.

'Horse racing is all very well,' she said suddenly. 'But it won't do in the long run.'

'And so you would have him go into the House?'

'I should like to have him distinguish himself in some way.' Mrs Rebecca's expression as she said this was wonderfully stern. 'Not to sit in an office like cousin Henry, and be made KCB when he is eighty. But to do – something – that the world will take notice of.'

Mr Gresham marvelled at her. He saw that, on the one hand, she was in deadly earnest, and that, on the other, her scheme was entirely vicarious. She wanted Happerton to succeed, whether he himself wanted that success or not, and the nature of that success, even the side of the House on which it was achieved, was indifferent to her. The psychology rather baffled him, but there was no doubting its intensity. A part of him admired this resolution; another part was merely shocked. Still faintly amused by the thought of Mr Happerton in his equine pins attempting to catch the Speaker's eye, he said:

'You will find that such things cost a great deal of money.'

Mrs Rebecca did not say anything, but the look on her face suggested that she regarded money as the least of her worries.

'You have discussed – well – some of this with George – with your husband.'

'He knows nothing of it,' Mrs Rebecca said.

And Mr Gresham felt again the twinge of guilt that seemed to afflict all his dealings with his daughter. He did not approve of her, or what she did, but he fancied that the flaws in her character were the result of his neglect.

'If there is money needed,' he said, 'then I suppose it shall be forthcoming.'

'Thank you, Papa.'

Mr Gresham looked hard at her, but he could see no glint of calculation. He picked up his newspaper once more and went on with Irish disestablishment.

*

In Lincolnshire the weather has changed. The spring gales have been and gone, leaving half a chimney smashed and two trees down in the orchard, and now the rain has set in. The fields are awash in lapping pools of water, grown bigger by the day, and the butts are overflowing and would be emptied if there were anyone to empty them. The sky is mostly gunmetal-grey, salmon-coloured around the edges at dawn, then shading into slate. There is a word for all this, Mr Davenant thinks, though he cannot for the life of him imagine where he found it, a word for all these inundations and damp, mournful air: *deliquescent*. The road beyond Scroop Hall is all but impassable; the sheep are huddled up in the dips at the fields' ends; even the rooks are hunkered down under the tree-tops. Somehow the horizon seems further away than usual: a grey wall of cloud, out beyond the wolds and the coastland, from which inexplicable protrusions of light occasionally bounce and glimmer, as if there were a battle being fought far out to sea. Like much going on here, it is all faintly mysterious, ineluctable, out of reach.

Mr Davenant watches the rain from his study window. Pinned down by this torrent of water, his estate takes on fantastic shapes, becomes unrecognisable and haphazard. There is a sense that everything is inert, tethered to its foundations. Over the stable doors, where the drainpipe has come away, the water falls in a cataract: he can hear it at night, roaring through his dreams. The trees flap in the wind; the evergreens in the shrubbery have turned livid and arsenical. It has been very quiet at Scroop, although Dora the housemaid has gone, on the excellent grounds that Mr Davenant cannot afford to pay her quarter's wages, and Evie has been restless. She has a habit of plucking at his sleeve when they meet in the hall before dinner, a way of fussing with the strings of her pinafore dress. Mr Davenant is uncertain about Evie. There are times when he wonders whether he has done his duty by her, whether it might have been better to have sent her elsewhere. But what is 'elsewhere'? Besides, he has a feeling that Evie's moon face and her pink eyes – though he is her father he knows that they remind him of the white rats he had as a boy – are a judgement sent by God. It is difficult to tell.

Just now Mr Davenant is making notes on one of the scraps of paper that litter his desk. Like the estate, battened down beneath the rain, the desk has turned haphazard. There are newspapers on it a fortnight old, plates and glasses, trays of old pipe-ash that no one has taken away. It is hard to know exactly of what these notes consist. Sometimes they are little columns of figures, always petering out before they reach their end; sometimes they are memoranda; sometimes drawings of bridles, stirrups, foxes' heads. Perhaps Mr Davenant scarcely knows himself. Also on the desk, amongst the plates and the drawings of foxes' heads – wonderfully sharp and lifelike, with pointed ears and serious, vulpine eyes – are several letters, for if Scroop has been very quiet of late it has not gone unvisited. Mr Silas has come again, to the ruination of his patent-leather boots, and Mr Jorkins and his mail-cart. Some of the letters have London franks; some are unopened. Not all the people who have written to Mr Davenant are known to him. It is a new thing, he supposes, this urge to communicate with someone you have not met, this torrent of respectful salutations, esteemed compliments and lurking menace, pouring down upon his head. Like the rain, it seems to have settled in, to be here for the duration.

Something has gone wrong in his life, Mr Davenant thinks, and he cannot work it out. Other men have owned horses that destroyed themselves, and properties that are embarrassed, but somehow they have not turned out as he has. He has always been fascinated by his ancestors – the yellow faces in their gilt frames, the grey tablets in Scroop churchyard – but now they haunt him. There was a moment the previous week when he found himself in the drawing room just before dawn with a candle in his hand, staring at the Caroline clergymen and the Georgian squires, as the rain cascaded over the gloomy garden and a pale, jerky shadow went bounding off across the lawn. Even now he cannot quite say how he came there, what impulse he was attempting to subdue. Like the lights, glinting through the horizon, it is all slightly out of reach. No doubt the Caroline clergymen, preaching their Assize Day sermons, and the Georgian squires, riding into Lincoln for news of the Jacobite rising (which stopped only seventy miles away at Derby), believed in fate. Perhaps, Mr Davenant thinks, it is simply fate that is marshalled against him.

Mr Happerton's latest letter is face-down on the desk, somewhere beneath the memoranda and the foxes' heads. In some ways Mr Happerton in the flesh is preferable to Mr Happerton on paper. The man himself is somehow less insinuating, less poised to do harm. It is curious that Mr Happerton's demands – they are never called demands, everything is offered up in a spirit of absolute amity – should always be brought up in Jorkins's mail-cart rather than spoken to his face. He wonders how his ancestors would have judged Mr Happerton, and suspects that they would think him simply an adventurer from London, vulgar and ungentlemanlike, as out of place – and as negligible – amid the Lincolnshire fields as a duke's brougham. None of this, he concedes, is bringing him any closer to the matter of Mr Happerton's letter, which proposes that the Scroop estate should be made over to him in settlement of his debt, and what should be done with it, such a shocking and terrible thing that Mr Davenant cannot bear to examine it whole but prefers to dwell on its incidentals, or on the wider currents of the world that flow behind it. Mr Happerton, he thinks – and he has grasped this from his conversation, his dress and his slang – is a modern man, and it is this modernity that has brought about his triumph.

There is a brass paper-knife in the shape of a scimitar on the desk, and Mr Davenant picks it up in his left hand while balancing Mr Happerton's letter on the thumb and forefinger of his right. Even now, though, his mind is not really on Mr Happerton, and the dreadful blow he has struck him, but on the forebear – Mr Davenant cannot precisely locate him in the confraternity of the drawing room – who is supposed to have looted the knife after the battle of Plassey. For all its century spent in a Lincolnshire study, the blade is still keen. There is a little red streak on it that might be blood, or rust, or some other substance. For a moment Mr Davenant forgets Mr Happerton and the other persons who follow in his wake, takes a sulphur match from his pocket, places it on the desk and watches, entranced, as the scimitar cuts it in two. It is a remarkable thing, he thinks, and shall stay with him, whatever else at Scroop may have to be given up.

Outside there is a gap in the rain. Mr Davenant is sensitive to these interludes, and can trace the sounds of dripping water that dominate them back, as it were, to source, to particular trees and defective gutters. He thinks – and the thought rather surprises him – that he will not trouble himself with Mr Happerton's letter, that he will roust Evie from the schoolroom and take her for a walk in the woods. Then he recalls the last walk he took with Evie – she has an odd way of flitting from tree to tree like a white ghost that is somehow disagreeable – and thinks that perhaps he will leave her to Miss Ellington. Miss Ellington is an excellent young woman and is making great strides with Evie, if only she were not so restless and did not fuss so with the strings of her pinafore dress. He wonders where this vexation with Evie has come from, and thinks that it must have something to do with his present troubles, that if Mr Happerton were not oppressing him he would be able to take his daughter for walks in the woods and not think her a hopping white ghost. In the distance there are clouds coming in from across the wolds, and Mr Davenant knows that if he wants his walk he will have to be quick about it. In his haste he drops the point of the scimitar onto his thumb and watches as a little bead of red blood falls onto the edge of Mr Happerton's letter.

Mr Davenant is used to the sight of blood: pigs screaming in terror as their throats are cut; the scarlet sheen of a stable floor beneath two fighting cocks. All the same, the sight disturbs him. As a young man, subduing a hedge, his right forefinger was nearly severed by a springing saw-blade, and a surgeon had to be called from Lincoln to staunch the wound. We are none of us *safe*, he thinks. A defective saw-blade, a horse's wrecked foreleg, a ton of sand dug out of a field: each has the capacity to tear our legs from under us and leave us sprawling. There are more grey clouds moving in above the garden. The wind is getting up. A flock of rooks, becalmed for a moment on the sodden grass, takes unexpected flight and goes soaring off over the wold. Mr Davenant stands uncertainly behind his desk, which has become a thing of terror to him, craving diversion but not knowing where it can be found. The little scimitar knife gleams up at him and he slides it into the pocket of his coat. It will be a useful thing to have with him, he thinks, at night, in a dark house.

*

At Glenister Court, Mr Glenister is restless. He has begun the day in his study with a newspaper, continued it in the morning room with Mr Gosse's *Omphalos*, and extended it with a walk in his fields, where there is nothing to see but waterlogged wheat, but none of these things has brought him comfort. The newspaper is two days old and has lost its novelty. Mr Gosse's book, which suggests that when God created the world he also created the fossils that appear to pre-date that world's existence, he finds implausible. The wheat will very likely be ruined. Mr Glenister knows that this uneasiness of spirit has to do with Scroop Hall, dimly visible from his bedroom window, half a mile off through thickets and trees. He is rarely invited now and has to find pretexts to visit his friend. A copy of *The Times* that Mr Davenant may want to consult; a brace of partridges that Mr Davenant may want to put on his table; a book that Evie may care to read, or stare at: each of these errands in the past fortnight has taken Mr Glenister over to Scroop, and none of them has been sufficient to prolong his stay beyond twenty minutes. Mr Davenant is polite – he is always polite – but also distant, or rather more distant than before. There is something wrong between them, and Mr Glenister cannot see what it is. Or rather he can see, but chooses not to. A man's wounded pride is for its victim to deal with, Mr Glenister thinks. The second reason, more tangible but no less troubling, is the mass of paper that lies on his desk. Mr Glenister is a resourceful man, and he has been putting these resources to work on his friend's behalf. If Mr Davenant knew of these endeavours he would doubtless be deeply disapproving, and Mr Glenister does not intend that he should. Or rather, not yet. There are advantages in proceeding with stealth, Mr Glenister thinks, of which Mr Davenant, brought up on plain speaking and plain dealing, may possibly not be aware.

Mr Glenister sits at his desk and riffles the papers, which are already thoroughly well ordered, into a new and yet more fascinating arrangement: like a mosaic in which each successive piece is incremental to the design. Mr Glenister is a tallish, fair-haired man of thirty-five, rough-complexioned but with surprisingly dainty hands. At various times over the past dozen years attempts have been made to marry him off. A brewer's widow from Grantham, a young lady recently discharged from Miss Smollett's establishment at Stamford, and even a daughter of the Earl of Gainsborough have been proposed for this endeavour, but none of it has come to anything, and Mr Glenister sits in Glenister Court unmolested, plays patience of an evening and takes solitary walks in his wheatfields. He is a *crackit,* people say, a useful Lincolnshire word meaning a bachelor fond of his comforts, resistant to change, or even fearful of the married state.

The papers, for all their fascination, are still not quite arranged to Mr Glenister's liking, and for a moment or two he shuffles them, holding them close to his chest before dealing them out again onto his desk like a pack of cards. People who do not know Mr Glenister well – most people, that is – sometimes declare that he is an idle young man who would be better off in a government office or an Inn of Court. The brewer's widow is supposed to have said as much. Mr Glenister is amused by these reports which stem, he imagines, less from moral dissatisfaction as simple pique. Unlike Scroop Hall, Glenister Court has a kitchenful of Dresden china, a studyful of books and not a tile out of place on its roofs. Mr Glenister knows that had he been a more forceful man, he would have pressed his friend Davenant not to start that lawsuit and not to buy those horses, but he is not forceful, and Davenant is headstrong. There is nothing you can do with such people, Mr Glenister supposes, save to let their folly work itself out and to manoeuvre stealthily behind their backs for its redress, to help them without conveying to them that they are being helped. Hence the pile of papers, which, dealt out a second time onto the desk, are – unlike himself and the brewer's widow – fulfilling the roles allotted to them.

There are nearly two dozen letters. Some from Mr Silas, the Sleaford attorney. Three from tradesmen in Lincoln. Several from gentlemen – and one or two people who are not gentlemen – in London. The subject of all this correspondence is Mr Happerton, and taken together they make quite a dossier. It is remarkable, in fact, what Mr Glenister has managed to discover. He knows, for example, how Mr Happerton came to marry Miss Gresham, and what Mr Gresham thought about it. He knows about his business dealings with Mr Solomons in the office near Hatton Garden. He knows that he has – no, that he is associated with, a woman who is not his wife. And he knows something, if not everything, about the series of interventions that led him to Tiberius. If it comes to it, Mr Glenister even has one of Mr Davenant's bills on his desk, bought from a broker in Great Turnstile: although the signature says 'Saml Davenant', Mr Glenister is not certain his friend wrote it. That is the trouble with bills, he thinks, together with lame horses and advice in lawsuits: you cannot be sure that what you pay for is sound.

Mr Glenister's restlessness has begun to leave him. It is afternoon now, a time he prefers, when no one calls, the house is silent and he can please himself. For a moment he wonders whether to find some excuse for walking over to Scroop, and then thinks better of it. He will be happier here, he thinks. Besides, it is all very well accumulating information. The problem is how to put it to use. Mr Glenister is aware that what he knows about Mr Happerton is not conclusive. It might interest a lawyer – it might conceivably interest a police inspector – but it will not convict him. He wonders what Miss Ellington would make of it, who has lately become rather a confidante of his. Mr Glenister thinks Miss Ellington is a nice, well-spoken girl, rather nervous and given to talking about the family she worked for in Warwickshire, who sound dreadfully dull, but not for that reason to be disregarded in any estimate of Mr Davenant's affairs. She wears curious clothes – little ancient shawls and pelisses, a dress made of stiff, shiny fabric that he thinks may be that legendary substance, black bombazine – but then, as he reflects, it is highly probable that she is not being paid anything.

For a bachelor, living on an estate in Lincolnshire, Mr Glenister has

237

had quite extensive dealings with women. He has danced with them, sat next to them at country-house dinners, bowed to them in the Lincoln shop doorways and once or twice sought them out in other places, but he has never met anyone like Miss Ellington, who is always shooting nervous glances into empty rooms, makes odd gestures with her fingers as she talks, and tells Evie queer stories about will-o'-the-wisps and boggarts, who live far underground and go flapping through their tunnels in search of children who have strayed there by mistake. Mr Glenister thinks that Miss Ellington has a fervid imagination, a thing not altogether to be despised. He is not sure if he pities Miss Ellington, whose past life is clearly something of a burden, or thinks that only the withholding of pity will help her to prosper. It is difficult to tell.

Outside the rain has begun to fall in torrents, dancing up from the lawn and almost obliterating the line of currant bushes twenty yards away. Mr Glenister wishes the rain would stop. His wheat can stand or fall. It is of no consequence to him. There are other, immemorial livelihoods at stake. This is an ancient part of the world. There are people here, in this corner of England, next to whom the Davenants are brazen interlopers, people who have farmed land for six hundred years. 'Scroop' itself is Old Norse, but there were settlers here before that. A year since, one of Mr Glenister's men found a coin in an upturned furrow, which a Lincoln antiquary dated to the reign of the Emperor Constantine. It sits on the study mantelpiece, along with a tobacco jar sporting the arms of Mr Glenister's Cambridge college and the portrait of his mother. Mr Davenant must not lose his estate, Mr Glenister thinks. As to why he must not lose it, he cannot exactly say. Because he is a good man and Mr Happerton a bad one? Who can tell? Not even the paper on Mr Glenister's desk can answer that. Because something long-standing, infinitesimal in itself but part of that wider pattern of solidity and substance, should not be lightly broken up? Here Mr Glenister thinks he is on firmer ground.

*

The schoolroom is at the top of the house, under the eaves. As well as being used for educative purposes, it is also a repository. At some point a variety of oddments – two cabin trunks, an harmonium, a saddle – have been dragged up here and pushed into corners where, when there are more than two persons present, they occasionally do service as chairs. There is, additionally, a blackboard, a set of globes, some ends of chalk and a curious instrument, like an inverted dome, which Miss Ellington supposes is an antique sundial. Even if one's pupil were not Evie, it would be difficult to teach in such a room, she thinks. There is a strong smell of damp, and the rain rattles the windows with an extraordinary violence. The rooks cry in the sodden garden and the wind, coming in through the cracks in the frames, sounds uncannily like a human voice – or a voice that is perhaps not human. Just at this moment the chalk is back in its box and the blackboard dusted over, and Miss Ellington is telling Evie a story of her own devising. It is about a creature who lives on an island in the middle of the Wash and fishes for sprats with a rod made from a parasol. The creature may be human, or may not be: this information Miss Ellington keeps purposely withheld. It is difficult to know what effect this invention is having on Evie, who is unresponsive at the best of times. Just now, she is sitting on a tall, stiff-backed chair with her head on one side and her eyes lowered, making little restless movements with her hands.

The story has ceased to interest Miss Ellington. All her stories do in the end. They start well and then fizzle out: a consequence, she thinks, of her not possessing any true imaginative power. The creature who sits on his little island, fishing with his parasol, is called Lancelot, merely because she has been reading Tennyson, and will not, she thinks, do. Not, she concedes, that Evie is capable of distinguishing between a good story and a bad one. On the other hand all stories, good and bad, seem to awaken an interest, which poetry and recitations on the cracked drawing-room piano have not so far been able to produce. Coming to a passage in which Lancelot, walking the perimeters of his island, is gripped by the suspicion that it is actually a huge, floating fish, Miss Ellington takes a sidelong glance at Evie, who fascinates, depresses and rather scares her. She has a habit of asking questions that bear no relation to the world she inhabits. 'Is it far?' 'Will he come?' 'How did it get there?' She is still interested in Pusskin, a bowdlerised version of whose fate has several times been vouchsafed to her. Taken out on a walk, when the weather permits, she wanders in a kind of dream from plant to plant and gatepost to gatepost. The island, on which Lancelot has so innocently loitered, has started to sink, the waves come lapping menacingly over the rocks and crevices, Lancelot himself hanging terrified from the branches of a tree. Now the water is at his toes. Now at his ankles. Perhaps Evie has registered this transformation, and is moved by it? Who knows. Sometimes Miss Ellington wonders what is to become of Evie.

If it comes to that, what will become of them all? Miss Ellington has several times found herself asking this question, which is in truth of more interest to her than the fate of Lancelot, now assuming his true, bat-like shape and preparing to take wing from the tree-top. Mr Glenister says that the estate is to be sold, that its new owner is Mr Happerton, but that there may be some delay before he comes to claim his property and that he will very likely suffer Mr Davenant to remain as his tenant. This information is troubling, and there is no one with whom she can discuss it, certainly not Mr Davenant. Indeed there is not a great deal that anyone can discuss with Mr Davenant, who keeps mostly to his study, but can sometimes be seen walking in the fields, not seeming to care which way his feet take him. Lancelot has flown off into Yorkshire, taking his dinner from a pastrycook's tray in an unguarded window, and Miss Ellington decides to leave him there. 'Where have they gone?' Evie demands suddenly, and they stare uncomprehendingly at each other, while the rain rattles agitatedly at the window, the pools of water gather in the wild garden and the wind whips under the eaves.

She hears, rather than sees, Mr Glenister arrive – doors opening and closing a long way off; feet drawing steadily nearer on the creaking staircase; the handle turning in the door – but there he is suddenly, nodding his head, smoothing back his hair and giving her his hand to shake. Miss Ellington is not sure what to make of Mr Glenister. The Lincolnshire squires are not generally prepossessing. There is an old man three miles away with seventy acres at his command who is said scarcely to be able to read. Mr Glenister can certainly read – there is usually a book poking from the lip of his coat-pocket – but, still, Miss Ellington does not know precisely what manner of man he is. She is used to complimentary attorneys, crimson-faced boys, clerical gentlemen requiring to be offered sherry. Warwickshire society is very polite. Mr Glenister, who lives in solitary, wifeless comfort, attended by a couple of serving maids, and can sometimes be found sitting on tree-stumps reading a copy of the *Athenaeum*, is a little much for her.

'How is Evie?' he asks as he comes into the room, and Evie, who likes Mr Glenister, starts up and says words that might mean *The man has gone into the wood*, or might not, and Mr Glenister smiles and pats her on the shoulder (she puts her hand there after him, as if she does not know what the gesture means). Miss Ellington has been to Glenister Court once – they went as a family party in the days before Mr Happerton's shadow came to disturb them – and found it odd, full of queer decorations and paintings and pieces of tapestry, and not at all what a Lincolnshire gentleman should have in his house.

'Tell me,' Mr Glenister says – he has very long legs that as he sits in a chair rise almost to the level of his chest and make him look like a grasshopper – 'how is Mr Davenant?' And Miss Ellington knows that they are to have one of their little coded conversations about Scroop and its prospects, and the peculiarities of its owner, in which more is implied than is stated and less demanded than inferred. 'Mr Davenant is mostly in his study,' she says, and Mr Glenister nods into his tea cup, gives Evie something to play with that he finds in his pocket, and goes on:

'They say there is a man coming to ride Tiberius.'

'I thought that it was Mr Curbishley who was to ride him?' Miss Ellington knows only a little about horse racing, which was thoroughly disapproved of in Warwickshire.

'This is the man who will ride him in the Derby. Major Hubbins, he is called.'

'And who is Major Hubbins?'

'Rather a dog in his day,' Mr Glenister says, with a peculiar little smile. 'But that day was rather a long time ago. There are people saying that Tiberius is to be used only for the market.'

'For the market?'

'Forgive me. It means that a person who enters a horse in a race does so with the aim of talking up its chances, but all the while he is secretly staking his money at better odds on his rival.'

'Does Mr Davenant know this?'

'I think not. But it would break his heart if he thought Tiberius was being used for some low game. Though I expect it is all the same to Mr Happerton.'

While Mr Glenister talks, Miss Ellington thinks of other men she has known. Once, in the drawing room at Warwick, one of these – one of the complimentary attorneys – had absolutely taken to his knees and asked her to marry him. Flattered by this declaration, if ultimately disapproving, she had also been startled by its incongruity. It was not, she thought, that complimentary attorneys should not be permitted romantic feelings, merely that the expression of them, in a room full of chintzes and subscription cards and embroidery, seemed so very odd.

Mr Glenister is still talking about Tiberius. 'He would be certain to win the race if he were ridden properly, Miss Ellington, you see, and that Major Hubbins is fifty-five years old.'

Miss Ellington has forgotten who Major Hubbins is and has to force herself to remember. He is quite animated, she thinks, as she has previously seen gentlemen animated by politics, or Sir Charles Lyell's discoveries among the stones, or suffrage petitions.

'And how old should a man be to ride a horse?'

'Well, there is an old gentleman of eighty still rides to hounds with the Sleaford pack. But fifty-five would be thought rather old for the Derby, for all it is such a short course. Why, if Major Hubbins were to be thrown or ridden down by another horse one would fear for his life.'

Evie is nodding her head, and crooning over the ball of string

Mr Glenister has given her. Miss Ellington looks out of the window at the dripping caryatid, the long expanse of gravel drive and the wild fields beyond. She thinks of Pusskin, stretched out on the gamekeeper's gibbet, with his eyes staring from his head, and his tail pinned up beside him, and another story told to Evie — she does not quite know where this one came from — about a black dog with live coals for eyes and claws like steel talons that prowls the wolds. Lincolnshire, she thinks, is beginning to oppress her. There are live things in the roof — they make a pattering sound that does not sound like any rat or bird that ever lived — which haunt her sleep.

'It seems to me,' Mr Glenister says — he is choosing his words carefully, looking at Evie's white face and the little agitated movements of her hands, like doves, he thinks, pinioned in a net and striving to break free — 'that Mr Davenant is not quite himself. Men who are in such a condition may do things that they come to regret. They brood upon their misfortunes and feel nothing 'but their immediate hurt.' Mr Glenister has never had any misfortunes worth speaking of, and felt no hurt, but still he is sorry for Mr Davenant.

'I suppose they may,' Miss Ellington says. She thinks — she is surprised at the snappishness of her thoughts — that she has no patience with men who are not quite themselves, and that 'being oneself' is itself a suspect phrase, for of all things that self is horribly uncertain.

'What will Mr Happerton do?' she asks.

'What will he do? Well, I doubt he will come to live here permanently. He is a London man, I believe. A Lincolnshire winter would finish him off, I fear.'

The question that has not been asked, but which hangs in the air between them, is: what shall Mr Davenant do, and his dependants? Mr Glenister gets to his feet, glances at Evie, who is still occupied with the string, takes his pipe out of his pocket, puts it back, and suddenly asks: does she remember the occasion when she discovered Mr Happerton in Mr Davenant's study and the file of facsimile signatures under his hand?

'Certainly I remember them,' Miss Ellington says. She wants nothing to do with Mr Davenant's signatures, Mr Davenant's study, or Mr Happerton, but she has been brought up to believe that gentlemen's questions are there to be answered.

'There is a great deal of paper in Mr Davenant's study,' Mr Glenister says. 'A great pile of it stacked up next to the desk. Old newspapers. Bills.' Mr Glenister made a little twist with his face as he said the word 'bills'. 'Might they not be there?'

To this Miss Ellington has no answer. Who knows where anything is at Scroop, she thinks, where there is no salt in the salt cellars and no logs in the grate and no one to cut the grass beyond the window.

'I should give a great deal to have that slip of paper,' Mr Glenister says. He is not looking at her, but beyond the windows at the fields, where there is a black scarecrow flapping dismally in the wind. 'Could you find it for me? I cannot go myself, for Davenant is always there. But you – you are not so constrained.'

And rather to her surprise, Miss Ellington finds herself agreeing to examine Mr Davenant's study for evidence of the sheet of facsimile signatures. It will very probably have to be done at night, Mr Glenister says, and she nods her head, bemused by what seems to her the effrontery of the request, and her own bewildering haste in agreeing to it. 'Where did it go?' Evie says suddenly, which for once is rather apposite. They stare across the room, a little conspiratorially, and Miss Ellington thinks of Pusskin with his bloody fur, and Lancelot, parasol in hand, wings sharply extended, taking flight from the island that vanishes beneath his feet over the grey North Sea.

*

Scroop Hall by night is a mystifying place. The angles disappear. There are great banks of shadow that conceal solid objects or, in certain cases, nothing at all. Some of the passages are so dark that not even a candle can penetrate the murk. There are also inexplicable shafts of light glimmering from banisters and picture-frames, curious scufflings behind the wainscot and, it sometimes seems, in the walls themselves. But still, here she is, in her nightgown and shawl, quietly descending the main staircase to the pitch-dark hall. It is just gone midnight – the grandfather clock in the vestibule struck five minutes ago. The house is asleep. Evie has a queer way of sleeping, half-in and half-out of consciousness, asking questions of the curious people who populate her dreams. Of Mr Davenant there is no sign. The hall is so black as to be almost unnavigable, but gradually her eyes grow accustomed to the lack of light and she presses on. She is not afraid of the dark, but she has a horror of something she cannot see scampering over her feet. Once, in Warwick, someone put a mouse in her bed for a joke and she astonished herself by attacking it with a poker. There were no more mice, and no more jokes.

The door creaks and is difficult to open. Outside the wind is careening over the garden. Mr Davenant's study is in chaos. There are wineglasses all over the desk, and a map of Lincolnshire has been spread out over the carpet and trampled over by someone with muddy feet; one or two of the pictures on the walls are slightly askew. For a moment she worries that the chaos will extend to the mass of old papers, but there it is, gathered up in shadow, apparently unchanged. Holding the candle in one hand, she bends cautiously down to examine the pile. At first she finds nothing except copies of the *Agricultural Gazette* and old receipts, but after a while there are other things: letters; a Grantham seedsman's catalogue; a Corn Law pamphlet; pages out of a book that must have displeased Mr Davenant, for they have been ripped halfway through. Moonlight is streaming in through the window now, which makes her job easier, but also alarms her, for there is something ghostly about the prospect before her: the spines of the books gleaming on their shelves, a stuffed falcon under glass gazing cruelly down from a recess in the wall. Once or twice she finds paper on which Mr Davenant has begun, and abandoned, letters, in which he urges his correspondent to certain courses of action, offers *prompt reassurance*, and in one very terrible passage *throws himself on their mercy*. She wonders what effort it took Mr Davenant to write them, here in a room where Davenants have written letters for two hundred years. She is tearing on through the pile – the candle is on the carpet by her side and may very soon go out – as the dates of the newspapers grow more and more ancient, and the receipts more dusty, and then, all of a sudden there it is, half of a foolscap sheet, nearly hidden beneath a newspaper that almost swamps it, in handwriting which is like Mr Davenant's and then again curiously unlike it, a dozen representations of his name – *samuel Davenant. Sam. Davenant. Samuel Davenant Esq.* – running on to the page's end. She places the sheet in the fold of her shawl, bends to her knees and restores a little of the fresh disorder she has created.

And then, suddenly, in the passage – she has gone barely two yards and the door is scarcely shut behind her – is Mr Davenant, still in his day-clothes, very pale in the face, bustling towards her. She does not scream, for she has no breath, and even in the split second of apprehending him, she realises that he does not quite see her. There is a little gleam of something in his hand, on which the light shines for an instant, and then nothing. The candle falls to the floor – it is about to go out – and Mr Davenant picks it up and stares wonderingly at the tiny flame. The wind pours against the window and she hears herself making some excuse: a toy of Evie's needed to quieten her. Mr Davenant stares blankly at her and does not, she thinks, properly take it in. She leaves him standing in the passage, with the queer look still on his face and the light flickering under his nose, and hurries away into darkness.

And so it is done, and in the morning Mr Glenister has a sheet with a dozen approximations of Mr Davenant's signature on his desk for him to ponder.

XIX

Visitors

Even in the best-regulated establishments, where all is sweet amity and conjugal bliss, a gentleman needs his sanctum. The newly married young lady will find that her husband, when sequestered in his study, will be as chary of interruption as a lion in its den . . .

A New Etiquette: Mrs Carmody's Book of Genteel Behaviour (1861)

On a particular Wednesday afternoon, towards the end of April, when there were only five weeks remaining until the day of the great Derby race, Mr Happerton had two unexpected visitors to his study.

The Pardews were gone from Shepherd's Inn. A butcher's boy, calling there with a bill for thirty-five shillings, found the door wide open and a cat tearing a newly killed mouse in half on the mat. The porter knew nothing about it. In fact, the Pardews had removed to Richmond – not to the mansion with its bright lawn running down to the Thames which stretched itself through Mr Pardew's imaginings, but to a terraced house in a little thoroughfare off the high street. There was no carriage, but the woman who called herself Mrs Pardew – there was already a doubt about this in the neighbourhood – sometimes had herself driven about in a fly. All this suggested a need for prudence and quiet economy. Mr Pardew was actually the proud possessor of seven hundred pounds – a lot of money, but not enough for Mr Pardew, and some of it was already spent, not least on the house, which, unlike the rooms at Shepherd's Inn, had been taken unfurnished. It was a pleasant house to begin with, and by judicious purchases in Richmond High Street Jemima made it more so, but Mr Pardew was uneasy in it. He thought that seven hundred pounds, or rather the six hundred pounds that remained, was a poor reward for the labour put into getting it, not to mention the trouble that might lie in wait. For her part, Jemima was quite happy. She had sent a ten-pound note to her sister in Islington, and did not notice Mr Pardew's depression of spirits.

Mr Pardew found that the seven hundred pounds – the six hundred pounds – and the move from Shepherd's Inn, which had been done rather late at night, noiselessly, in a covered wagon, had made him restless. He made one or two trips into the City in an omnibus but did not stay there long, and he joined a club at an institute on Richmond Hill to read its newspapers. He was always reading newspapers, particularly the police reports. He had a habit of sitting in the parlour, or the kitchen, or wherever Jemima had gone to occupy herself, and staring at her as she went about her work. It occurred to him that, in all the years he had known her, he had never inspected her closely, had no real idea of the person she was. He saw, as he watched, that she was very adept at her household tasks. He thought that he liked the way her hands moved over the objects around her. Once at this time he said:

'We could go away from here, if you wish.'

'Do you not like Richmond?' She was shelling peas into a white earthenware bowl, and he watched them as they fell. 'You always said that you would like to live here.'

'I like Richmond very well. It is just that – there are other places.'

But Jemima was happy in Richmond. She had a budgerigar in a cage, for which she bought seeds at a naturalist's shop, and the sound of the hired fly creaking up to the gate was a tonic to her. Seeing this, Mr Pardew determined to conciliate her.

'By the by,' he said once, as they sat together in the parlour, 'I saw Lord Fairhurst the other day.'

'How did you find him?' Jemima asked.

'Oh he is no better, I dare say. It wouldn't surprise me at all if his uncle, who made him his heir, outlives him. Stranger things have happened.'

'I expect they have,' Jemima said.

And so the time went on, spent in omnibus rides to and from the City, in the parlour of the little house off Richmond High Street, and in reading the newspapers at the Institute, and not at all satisfactorily. Mr Pardew had kept but one souvenir from the evening in Cornhill – a quaint blue pin in the shape of a butterfly, which he wore sometimes in the lapel of his black stuff suit.

And then one day something dreadful happened. Coming down Richmond Hill with a bag of provisions in his hand Mr Pardew saw a woman's figure bent over a shopfront. He knew instinctively that there was danger in this apparition, something to do with the set of her shoulders and the umbrella jutting from her elbow, and the woman turned towards him and he saw that it was his wife. What happened in the next half-minute he could not quite remember. He had an idea that some words had been said, that she might have spoken his name, and he said something in response, but then he was flying down Richmond Hill to the more densely populated streets beyond it – the bag of provisions went rolling off into the gutter – not looking behind him until he reached the safety of his own garden gate. Here he was able to recover himself and, assuming a nonchalance he did not in the least feel, stood for some time looking back the way he had come. There was no one there, and, after another moment or two, with his heart still pounding beneath his ribs, he let himself into the house. Here all was genteel domesticity. The bird was singing in its cage and Jemima was rolling pastry for a pie. When she saw him she said:

'You are home very soon.'

'There are too many people about. What is the point of a pavement if one is pushed off it every two minutes by some fellow's elbow?'

'Did you call at Grieveson's?'

'Ah,' said Mr Pardew, with a very passable imitation of good humour. 'I knew there was something I had forgotten. I shall go out again later.'

When he reached his bedroom he found he was very nearly shaking with fear. Looking at his face in the mirror, he saw that it was stark white. He told himself as he sat there that fate had singled him out, that nothing else could explain the monstrous coincidence of walking down Richmond Hill and discovering the one person in the world with the capacity to do him harm. Presumably, he told himself, she lived in Richmond, would now look out for him and, such is the nature of suburban life, be bound to see him again. This thought enraged him so much that he got up from the chair into which he had thrown himself and roamed desperately around the room, pulling at his chin with his fingers, wishing that he were not so conspicuous, that his dark hair and his jutting chin were gone, that he was a meek little man of five feet four with a bald head and spectacles that no one looking into a crowd ever saw. There was a china vase sitting nearby on an occasional table and he seized his stick – he had been carrying it all the while on his walk – brought it down upon the willow-pattern and smashed it into three pieces.

After this he was not so angry. He put the stick down on the bed, tidied up the fragments of the china vase, loosened his collar, sprinkled a little water on his face from the ewer, and settled down to consider the situation. On the whole, he told himself, turning the matter over in his mind, things were not as bad as they might have been. He had seen his wife, who had undoubtedly recognised him – he remembered now that she had spoken his name – for a split second on Richmond Hill. It might be – Richmond being so very full of visitors at this time of the year – that she was passing through the place, might already be gone from it and have no intention of coming back. Even had she wanted to pursue him – and it might very probably be that she did not – she did not know where he lived and had no means of finding out. All this was very consoling and quite cheered Mr Pardew's spirits. But then what if, having seen Mr Pardew on Richmond Hill, she had decided to share this intelligence with a third party, with Captain McTurk, say, or one of his satellites? For the moment the bedroom in which he sat – it was a pretty room, lined with pink, sprigged paper, with cupids smiling from an embroidered screen – altogether fell away, and he was back in a house in Highgate twenty years ago picking apples in an orchard with a curly-haired child and a woman who . . . But that way lay madness, Mr Pardew thought, and he sprang up from the bed, rearranged his collar and composed himself.

They were very quiet at supper that night, and if Jemima wondered at the silence, and the absent china vase, she did not say anything about it. Mr Pardew felt that his nerves jangled him. Halfway through the meal there came a knock at the door. It was only a neighbour come to issue an invitation, but he found his hands grasping the table in fright. Several times he turned the encounter on Richmond Hill over in his mind – the woman's figure in silhouette, her turning towards him, that terrible moment of recognition – but there was no way of recasting it that he found satisfactory. The even tenor of his days had been destroyed and he knew it. Later that night, brooding into the small hours as Jemima slept comfortably beside him, he had decided on two courses of action. The first was that he and Jemima should leave Richmond forthwith. They would go abroad, he thought – to Pau, or Leghorn, to any place, in fact, where Mrs Pardew would not come looking for them. The second was that the money needed for this resettlement should come from the person who, in Mr Pardew's judgement, was most likely to be induced to supply it. That person was Mr Happerton. And so the next afternoon Mr Pardew put on his best hat, took his stick, walked down to the stand in the high street and took an omnibus into the West End. He was quite nonchalant as he did this, believing that Mrs Pardew was by this time quite likely forty miles away. And then a strange woman, looking up from the corner of the omnibus, seemed to stare at him in a very marked manner, and he took up his newspaper and hid his head for the remainder of the journey.

Mr Pardew was not in the least intimidated by the house in Belgrave Square, and walked up its grey stone steps quite as if he owned it. There was a little trouble with the butler, but rather like Mr Happerton himself Mr Pardew had a way with seneschals and chatelaines. Besides, there were at this time, in the weeks before the Derby, any number of messengers and emissaries going back and forth from Mr Happerton to the City, the Blue Riband and other places, and the butler had decided that if he had to err, it should be on the side of laxity. And so there he was in the doorway of Mr Happerton's study (or rather Mr Gresham's study, since expropriated) not at all discountenanced by the domestic who was bringing out Mr Happerton's breakfast tray – Mr Happerton had taken to breakfasting in the study, as he found it more convenient. The butler waved him in and Mr Happerton looked up from the desk.

'It is very good of you to see me,' he began. 'My name is Pardew.'

'Can't say I know it,' Mr Happerton said.

'I think you do,' Mr Pardew told him. 'At any rate Captain Raff knows it.'

Mr Happerton sat back in his chair and stared at his visitor. He thought that Mr Pardew was an odd-looking man, like the subject of a painting that has stepped out of its frame. What he saw was a man of middle age, perhaps in his later fifties, but still vigorous, distinctly tall and dressed in a rusty black suit that rather emphasised his height and a blue butterfly pin sticking incongruously out of his lapel, with a prognathous jaw that a beard and side-whiskers did not at all disguise. He was carrying a stick under one arm, and Mr Happerton thought that he did not like the stick in the least, and that he would have preferred it to be left in the hall with Mr Pardew's hat. But stick or no stick, Mr Happerton thought he could deal with Mr Pardew.

'Captain Raff knew that you were not to come here,' he said. 'Did he tell you?'

Mr Pardew was looking round Mr Gresham's study, with its profusion of legal bookcases and its three white wigs on their stands. He knew, or he believed that he knew, that Mr Happerton was an interloper here, and he wondered if there were some way he could remind Mr Happerton of this. The stick twitched in his hand.

'I suppose,' Mr Pardew said, setting off on a different track, 'that everything has been disposed of by now.'

'I really don't know what you are talking about,' Mr Happerton said, wondering whether to ring for the butler.

'I think you do,' Mr Pardew told him again. He was examining Mr Happerton as he sat in his chair, wondering what kind of man he was. A thought occurred to him, and he said:

'I see Tiberius's price is falling. Really, I think if I were a betting man I should be inclined to put my money on Septuagint.'

And then Mr Happerton knew that he could not ring for the butler, and that he had better be careful. But he also thought that in his time he had met, and dealt with, many visitors more unpleasant than Mr Pardew. Thinking, too, that he knew what Mr Pardew was about, he said in a less hostile tone:

'Now that you're here you had better tell me what you want. You have been paid in full, I think?'

'Certainly I have been paid,' Mr Pardew said. 'And no doubt in full. There's been no chiselling off of percentages, I dare say. Raff is too poor a fish for that.'

'Then what do you wish me to say? That it was a job well done? That I look forward to offering further opportunities in the future? That I shall be happy to provide a reference? If you have come to blackmail me, you had best say so.'

Mr Pardew grinned. He thought he knew what kind of a man Mr Happerton was. 'Suppose,' he said, 'I were merely to offer you an honest opinion on which horse I should lay out my money – if, of course, I were a betting man?'

'You could be d——d,' Mr Happerton said, in what was really a very friendly way. 'If you want money, I can tell you that there isn't any. It's all disposed of, for the moment. Expose me and you expose yourself. I suppose that has occurred to you.'

'Well, perhaps it has. Although one of us might be more alarmed by that exposure than the other,' Mr Pardew said. 'The fact is, I am minded to go abroad. In fact, there are excellent reasons why I should leave London and not come back. And so, I have come to – throw myself on your mercy.'

Mr Happerton thought about this. A part of him knew that a Mr Pardew who was safe in some continental hiding hole would be far more pleasant to him than a Mr Pardew who stood in his, or his father-in-law's, study talking about throwing himself on his mercy. He swung his chair round from behind his desk, crossed one of his top-boots over the other, and said, almost confidentially:

'It's true about the money. It is all laid out. Heavens, there is a jockey out there sending in his bills who don't know the meaning of being frugal. I dare say you know the necessity of cutting your coat according to your cloth?'

'No one better,' Mr Pardew assured him.

'How much would do it?'

Mr Pardew had an idea that Mr Happerton was telling the truth. 'Three hundred.'

'Can't be done. There isn't two hundred in the house.' Here Mr Happerton may not have been telling the truth. 'Would you take a bill?'

'I don't like paper. Paper never bought anyone a steamer ticket.'

'No more it did. Look! If I give you a bill and you take it into the City, they may give you two hundred on it, perhaps even two hundred and twenty. Take it to that Jew in Hatton Garden – Solomons – and see what he says. But I'll not see you again, do you hear? Raff's a poor fish, as you say, but there are others who're not.'

The stick twitched again in Mr Pardew's hand, but he merely nodded his head. And so a piece of paper was produced from Mr Gresham's drawer on which Mr Happerton attested that he intended to pay Mr R. Pardew of Richmond in the County of Surrey three hundred pounds three months hence, stuck a penny stamp under the words and signed his name across it. Mr Pardew put the paper in his pocket.

'And so it's not to be Tiberius?'

'You can draw what conclusions you like,' Mr Happerton said, who was doubting whether Mr Solomons really would give him 70 per cent of the bill's worth.

'I suppose he has backed Septuagint to the hilt,' Mr Pardew told himself. Later that morning he took the bill into the City and, if he did not quite raise the sum that Mr Happerton had advertised, at any rate procured enough of it to fulfil Mr Happerton's chief requirement of their meeting, which was that he never wanted to see him again in his life.

*

The second visitor was Mrs Happerton.

Mr Gresham had now been ailing for nearly three months. His doctor, who came thrice-weekly, pronounced that he was not so very ill, but not so very well either. Indeed, it was difficult to work out what the trouble was, beyond languor and fatigue. He sat about in his room or on chairs in the drawing room, alternately sleeping or waking into querulousness, and the querulousness was a trial. The chambers at Lincoln's Inn had been shut up and the clerk discharged, and the papers in the Tenway Croft case had been given to Mr Gissing, Mr Gresham's great rival in the Equity Courts for forty years. Nobody came to dinner, for dinners are troublesome when there is an invalid in the house, and nobody went out to them either (Mr Happerton still being very solic-itous of his father's welfare) and things were very dull. The silverware that was brought out on great occasions lay in its box – Mr Happerton still had the key – and the piano had not been opened since Christmas.

If Mrs Rebecca was made unhappy by this state of affairs she did not say so, but she was certainly very cross, and her crossness had a habit of breaking out in conversations with her father. Perhaps Mr Gresham hardly realised. As his weakness had advanced – and he still did not think it was advancing; he thought he was getting better – his attitude to his daughter had softened. He found, as he now had little with which to occupy his mind, that he was more interested in her, and yet, with the waning of his mental powers, his interest was vaguer and more beneficent. He made little jokes to his daughter about the married state, and his son-in-law's political career, which were excruciating to her, and got very sharp answers back, which perhaps he did not prop-erly notice. There were times in the afternoons when he slept two or three hours at a time, and when he was not quite lucid. He would say more than he meant, or intended, and not realise that he had said it, and his daughter would say more than she meant, knowing that what she said would not be understood. They were not pleasant, those afternoons in Belgrave Square, with the old servants bringing in the tea with grave faces and Mr Gresham nodding over his blanket, and Mr Happerton, for all his solicitousness, kept away.

'So, my dear,' Mr Gresham said on one of these occasions, with a sudden access of paternal spirit, 'how do you like being a married woman, I wonder?' There was something almost indelicate about this, which Mrs Rebecca did not at all like: Mr Gresham had never been indelicate in his life. She put down the illustrated magazine she had been reading, or not reading, and said:

'How do I like being married? It is the same as any other state, I suppose. One sits here, and people come to see one – that is, they don't come – and because one is a woman nothing is explained to one and life goes on quite mysteriously as if it were all sealed up in a black box, and – in a few years we shall all be dead.'

Mr Gresham understood scarcely the half of this, but he thought that things like it should not be said. 'I suppose George is very busy at his work just now.'

'Oh, George is a prodigy. George is an Admirable Crichton. George has purchased the freehold of Buckingham Palace, and if I am very lucky I shall allowed to see it. Will I ring for tea, Papa, or have you not finished sleeping?'

Mr Gresham drifted back into sleep – there was something intensely pathetic about the sight of him huddled up in the armchair beneath his blanket – and his daughter sat furiously on the sofa staring at the illustrated magazine gripped in her hands. Her fury had a single source. It lay in what she imagined was a want of confidence on her husband's part. As she saw it, she had done a great deal for Mr Happerton. She had consented to marry him, she had listened to his schemes, she had found him money, and although the finding had certainly produced Tiberius in his stable at Scroop she was wholly ignorant of her husband's plans. There had been one or two other things which perhaps she did not care to remember. And Mr Happerton, for his part, had kept silent.

Or rather there had been a series of little hints and allusions by which his wife had felt patronised, and in the end slighted. Of all things, Mrs Rebecca did not want to be patronised. Suspicious of the motives of nearly everyone who surrounded her, she found, somewhat to her surprise, that she did not want to be suspicious of her husband. She found that she approved of his schemes, in so far as she knew what they were. It was the being kept in ignorance that irked her, and to this end she had made enquiries in all kinds of directions that would certainly have alarmed Mr Happerton had he known about them. She had several times consulted Mr Gaffney, and even gone down to the kitchen to borrow a sporting newspaper from the tall footman. And what she had discovered annoyed her even more, for it seemed to her that Tiberius, the horse on which Mr Happerton had set his heart, and which, she had been told, should wear her colours if it ran in the great race, was to be set aside in favour of some other horse, or horses, which Mr Happerton thought would serve him better.

All this might have been tolerable if Mr Happerton had explained it to her. She sometimes thought that if he had engaged an elephant for the Derby, along with a mahout to ride it, she would have been satisfied had she only been told how he proposed to decorate the beast's howdah. And so Mrs Rebecca chafed, and fretted, and returned sharp words in answer to her father's questions, and, able to bear it no longer, appeared in Mr Gresham's study about ten minutes after Mr Pardew had left the house with Mr Happerton's bill for three hundred pounds at three months in his pocketbook. Installed in the study, from which Mr Happerton could not very well evict her, where she sat, uninvited, in a chair and looked around her with the keenest interest, Mrs Rebecca began:

'Who is that man whom John footman has just let out into the street?'

'He is Mr Pardew,' Mr Happerton said, not thinking there would be any harm in letting the name be known.

'And what does he do?'

'I believe he runs errands for Captain Raff. Certainly that is why he came to see me.'

Mr Happerton looked hard at his wife. Her green eyes were blazing under her sandy hair. He suspected that she was angry, but he could not imagine the source of her anger. Mrs Rebecca, meanwhile, was staring critically at the wall behind his desk.

'Why has the picture of Trinity Great Court where Papa went as a young man been taken down and that other thing put up in its place?'

Since colonising his father-in-law's study, Mr Happerton had made one or two little adjustments to its decor. He had substituted a picture of Eclipse in his glory for the print of Trinity College, and there was a dog-whip or two lying on the mantelpiece among the legal invitations.

'I didn't know you cared about it,' he said, rather meekly.

'Well I do. And Papa would be cross if he knew.'

Mr Happerton was tired of this. There were a dozen things needing his attention. Major Hubbins was in Lincolnshire and complaining piteously about its privations; the livery stables he had engaged to transport Tiberius south wanted ten guineas in advance; he was anxious on account of Captain Raff, who had not been seen for several days. And now his wife was annoyed because a print had been taken off the wall of her father's study. Raising his voice slightly – but only slightly – he said:

'Papa does not need to know anything about it.'

'And I am to be like Papa, I suppose, to be kept in ignorance and made a fool of, and to be put in the dark without candles and told things only when the people think it is safe for me to be told them.'

Mr Happerton thought he would have preferred Mr Pardew back in his study. Mr Pardew had only wanted money.

'What is all this about?' he asked weakly.

'It is about me.' The fingers of the hands that Mrs Rebecca clasped in front of her were white to the knuckle. 'How I am never to know. *You do not tell me things*. But people say that you do not want Tiberius to win the race. That it is all a sham, and Major Hubbins could ride him into a ditch and you would be delighted.'

'Major Hubbins will do no such thing.'

'He is nearly sixty, Mr Gaffney says, and not to be trusted with an old mare in the park. You had better tell me what you propose to do, or – or I shall go to Papa and tell him what became of his two thousand pounds.'

'Papa's two thousand pounds is perfectly safe. You may be assured of that.'

'But it has not been spent on Tiberius.'

'It was as good as spent on him!' Mr Happerton was recovering his good humour. He thought he had never seen anything as spirited as his wife in her fury. 'As I recollect, it was spent in buying up Davenant's bills.'

'And now you wish him to lose, so you can win money on Baldino, or Septuagint, or – some other horse.'

'Is it Gaffney you have been talking to? Or Raff? What have they said?'

'Mr Gaffney says you are playing a dangerous game.'

'Mr Gaffney knows nothing about it. Listen to me, Rebecca.' He saw that she was looking at him intently. 'Certainly I put myself in the way of Tiberius thinking that he might win. But I don't think that now. I think one of the two horses you have mentioned will win. There's no room for sentiment, you know, in these affairs. It's a question of establishing how much money can be made and the right way to go about making it. Do you understand? I am not trying to vex you. I am trying to make our fortunes. But there is an art to this. All through the spring people said that Tiberius was bound to win, and a great deal of money was staked on him, and so the odds shortened. Now people are saying Baldino or Septuagint will win, and their odds are shortening. But my money was laid out earlier, at seven or eight to one. There's no going back from it.'

'And what if some other horse should win?'

'That's something that doesn't bear thinking about. But don't fear. Baldino is a certainty. Tiberius is a nice little horse – you can see the arab in him, rather than being told it's there – but he ain't got the stamina, that's what I think, and there's more to be gained by letting him lose. I'm sorry he won't wear your colours, but it's the difference between five thousand pounds and twenty. Now, do you understand?'

He thought to himself as he said this that he did not have the least idea how his wife might react. She might throw herself upon his shoulders or hurl the fire-irons at him for all he knew.

'What are Baldino's odds now?'

'Five. Five-and-a-half. There was a heap of money followed ours. I dare say one could get six if the funds were in dribs and drabs.'

'If I could get another two thousand pounds from Papa, it would help?'

'Certainly it would.'

'Then you shall have it,' Mrs Rebecca said. Mr Happerton looked at her wonderingly. He thought that he had made a mistake about her, that the boldness he brought to his business dealings was something that excited her. The light had come into her eyes, he noticed. Trying to placate her further, he said:

'There's another thing. I've decided to take that place in Lincolnshire. Davenant is nearly bankrupt and it can be bought for a song. Should you like to go there?'

'How far is it?'

'About a hundred miles. The train reaches Lincoln.'

'Certainly I should like to go,' Mrs Rebecca said. And Mr Happerton, elate with the promise of his two thousand pounds, thought that, finally, he had begun to understand his wife.

*

'Well, here is news,' Mr Masterson said, walking into Captain McTurk's room at the back of Whitehall Court. 'That man Pardew has been seen in London.'

'Seen in London, was he?' Captain McTurk stood up from his desk. Outside in the courtyard the same melancholy ostler was shovelling up the same pile of dung. 'Who has seen him?'

'His wife, by all accounts. Came across him on Richmond Hill, and went straight to the station to report the fact.'

'A very public-spirited lady. There was some mystery about her, was there not?' Captain McTurk wondered. 'Knew nothing about bullion robberies. Thought her husband was a bill-broker. Lived respectably in Kensington and was never so surprised in her life when it all came out . . . Might she have been mistaken, do you suppose?'

'I think not. He is supposed to be of very distinctive appearance.' Mr Masterson had a portrait of Mr Pardew in his hand, an artist's rendering that had appeared in the illustrated papers two years previously, and the two men stared at it.

'No,' Captain McTurk said after a while, 'there would be no mistaking him, I think. Did she have any idea where he went?'

'Only that he turned and fled down into the town. It was all over in an instant, I believe. One could not very well expect her to give chase.'

'I suppose not. Of course, it may only be the merest coincidence. I mean, he may only have been visiting the place. Where does his wife live?'

'At Teddington, I believe . . . I have told the people at Richmond to keep their eyes open.'

'And I don't suppose they will see anything,' Captain McTurk said. 'He is probably twenty miles away by now. Certainly nowhere we shall find him.' Mr Masterson thought Captain McTurk was unusually pessimistic about the case. 'Have any of the pieces been found? That is, the things from Gallentin's safe?'

'There was a necklace recovered in Paris the other day. How it got there, no one knows.'

'I don't doubt it changed hands half a dozen times, and was bought by the Prince along the way.' Captain McTurk was really very gloomy. 'What about the notepaper?'

'There are a dozen shops over the West End that sell it, I'm afraid. You would have to bring in half the householders in Chelsea and ask them one by one.'

Captain McTurk looked as if he would be quite delighted to summon half the householders in Chelsea to his office and ask them questions.

Then his eye fell on the litter of papers on his desk – letters from honourable members, complaints about tide-waiterships and toll-bridges, all the things, he thought, which conspired to oppress him. Down in the courtyard the melancholy ostler had disappeared, but the dung still lay in a heap.

'Tell me' – it was Captain McTurk's habit to ask unexpected questions – 'did you ever hear of a horse called Tiberius?'

'Certainly I did. If he doesn't win the Derby in three weeks' time there will be a great many people regretting that they ever backed him. Why do you ask?'

'It is just that wherever I go his name seems to jump up at me. There were a couple of men taken in the Tottenham Court Road the other day – tipsters, you know, brawling in the street, one of them had his brains nearly knocked out – and his was the name you got in exchange for your half-crown. And now there is a man in Lincolnshire writing to say that the horse was unfairly come by.'

'I believe a man called Happerton owns him now,' Mr Masterson said, who took an interest in the turf.

'The fellow who married Gresham's daughter?'

'That is him, I think.'

'Odd kind of man to marry an Equity Court lawyer's daughter,' Captain McTurk said. 'But then somebody told me the other day that the Dean of Christchurch was set on marrying his cook, and the Fellows were up in arms. But was there ever a horse changed hands that did so fairly? There is always some debt or obligation hanging over it. You had better take the letter and see what can be done. As for that other business, you ought to go down to Richmond and see if they have missed anything. It is quite possible that Pardew is living in a cottage at the end of the superintendent's garden. At any rate stranger things have happened.'

Not at all averse to a pleasant afternoon in the countryside, Mr Masterson spent the remainder of the day in Richmond. Here, as an emissary of Captain McTurk's, he was made much of. A constable was sent to show him the exact spot where Mr Pardew had been seen.

Mrs Pardew's deposition was produced for his inspection, and it was proposed that a cab should be sent instantly to Teddington to fetch her back. This offer Mr Masterson declined. He did not think there would be the slightest benefit in having Mrs Pardew brought over from Teddington, he explained, at which the Richmond constables looked sulky. They had expected a greater fixity of resolve from Captain McTurk's lieutenant. Instead, Mr Masterson walked about Richmond on his own. He went back to the spot on Richmond Hill which the constable had shown him and traced the path for a good half-mile or so, casting little glances into the nearby lanes and once or twice picking up a fragment of discarded paper from the ground. He walked into the town and put his head in at the door of the institute, which was empty except for an old gentleman reading the *Academy*. There was a butcher's shop further down the hill, and Mr Masterson strode into it, examined the pile of saveloys and the trays of kidneys on display and engaged the proprietor in conversation. At the end of this excursion, which lasted almost until the early evening, Mr Masterson felt that he had learned a great deal about Richmond but almost nothing about Mr Pardew. The twilight began to descend over the trees up on the hill and the fading sun burned off the surface of the water, where there were skiffs and rowing boats out in the gloaming, and Mr Masterson thought that he had spent a very pleasant afternoon.

At the station he stopped and bought a copy of the *Star*, which had a great article by Captain Crewe about the Derby and told him that while the odds on Tiberius had lengthened those on Baldino and Septuagint had shortened to five and six to one. Mr Masterson put the newspaper in his pocket, and in the same preoccupied manner that he had brought to his tour of Richmond, went off to his train.

*

It was not so very long after this that the scales fell – or were induced to fall – from Captain Raff's eyes. He was recruiting himself of an evening at a club in Dover Street when he chanced upon a friend – not one of the intimates with whom he dealt in the management of horses and the laying-off of bets, but a man who had known him twenty years ago and who perhaps remembered something of his inglorious military career. The club was not very select, and neither perhaps was the friend, whose name was Mr Howarth, but even the Captain Raffs of this world are allowed their innocent recreations – and their friends. Anyway Captain Raff, who had drunk a great deal, was pleased to see Mr Howarth, all the more pleased, perhaps, in that he did not hail from that part of the world through which the captain customarily strode. There was a certain amount of reminiscent talk about what the regiment had done at Belfast and a bygone steeplechase in which both men had performed to great advantage that was very agreeable to Captain Raff. But then, at a very late hour, just as the club was closing for the night – if such establishments can ever be really said to close – Mr Howarth fixed his friend with a look and said:

'Now, what is the mystery about this horse, Raff?'

'What horse would that be?' Captain Raff wondered jocularly. He had drunk seven glasses of curaçao and was off his guard.

'That Tiberius that you and that man Happerton are up to your necks in. I've ten guineas on him myself or I shouldn't be so interested. Only the fellows are saying that Happerton has bred him up for the market, that – in point of fact – he don't mean him to win.'

'Oh, there is nothing in that,' Captain Raff said. 'Fellows always say that kind of thing before the Derby you know.'

'And then there is that Major Hubbins who is to ride him. A man who last won a race when they were bringing the bodies back from Scutari.'

'It was not so long ago as that, surely?'

'Never mind that, Raff. The point is that Happerton don't mean him to win. He has put four thousand on – what is that other horse's name? – Baldino. I had it from a groom. And I don't say that Hubbins ain't thoroughly above-board, and as white as Miss Coutts's underskirts, but he's no Derby winner, not at his age, or I'm the Prince's valet.'

'You're quite wrong, you know,' Captain Raff said feebly.

'Am I? Well, let us hope so. Gracious heavens, man, you'll break the tumblers if you spill them on the floor like that. Let us see if they can get you a cab back home to Ryder Street.'

When Captain Raff got home to Ryder Street it was two o'clock in the morning, but he knew that there was no prospect of sleep. His laundress had left her bill twisted under the door-knocker, and he clutched it absently in his hand as he fumbled for a match to light the candle. In the half-darkness the room loomed up eerily at him and he sat down grimly in the armchair and stared out into the shadow. Still Captain Raff was trying to soothe his anxieties. He did not want to believe that Mr Happerton had thrown him over and so he sought for evidence that would disprove what Mr Howarth had said. But as he did so he remembered half a dozen little hints and insinuations – moments when Mr Happerton had lowered his eye or averted his gaze when some question about Tiberius had been put to him. The more Captain Raff thought about it the more he recalled the peculiar circumstances in which Mr Happerton had not allowed him to lay out the money realised by the burglary at Mr Gallentin's shop, and the stronger was his suspicion that Mr Howarth had been correct.

'Five years, by God!' he said once or twice. Five years had been the period of time he had known Mr Happerton, an acquaintance begun when Mr Happerton was a great deal less prosperous than he had since become. 'Five years!' he said again. They seemed very long years. He tried to remember them, but he could recall only days spent looking at horses, desultory afternoons at the Blue Riband and elsewhere, and a part of Captain Raff regretted these bleak profitless hours and wished they had been put to better use. He had a vision of himself sitting in a little cottage in Herefordshire, fishing for trout in the Wye, and going to evening service like a respectable man, but it was a dreadful vision, for he knew it would never be realised. What should he do? Where should he take his grievance? 'I shall have it out with him by God!' Captain Raff said out loud, but another part of him shrank from confronting Mr Happerton with his treachery. He fancied that if he went to Belgrave Square, Mr Happerton would very probably have him thrown out into the street, and Captain Raff did not want to give Mr Happerton this pleasure. What then? There were things he knew about Mr Happerton, compromising things, some of them, which, properly explained, would probably bring him to a police court, but Captain Raff had an idea that the explaining might very well incriminate other people, not least himself. He fancied that he could not soil Mr Happerton's reputation without defiling his own.

All this was torture to him. Three or four hours came and went, the dawn rose slowly above the Ryder Street chimney-pots, and the sound of one or two pleasure-seeking artists coming back from their nocturnal revels echoed across the passages, and still Captain Raff rocked back and forward in his armchair. By this time a certain amount of his courage had returned to him. He found the half of a bottle of brandy in a cupboard, drank some of it and felt braver still. He would essay some bold stroke, he thought, make some gesture that would not only redeem himself but show Mr Happerton the mistake he had made. After this he grew serious again, took a sheet of paper from his desk and various bills that littered the floor beneath it and began to compile a list of his assets and liabilities. It was a disagreeable task, and when he had finished it Captain Raff heaved a sigh and stared wildly about him. By chance he caught sight of himself in the glass and marvelled at how pale his face was and how bloodshot his eyes.

The calculations were not to his taste. In fact they showed that his liabilities exceeded his assets by the small matter of two hundred and twenty pounds. But still Captain Raff was not discouraged. He pulled down an old tobacco tin that lay upon the mantelpiece and fished out a twenty-pound note that he had hidden there long ago against such an eventuality as this. Then he looked into a pot that stood nearby and extracted a Crimea medal and a gold watch chain. The gold watch chain had belonged to Captain Raff's father. 'And a precious lot he gave me, but for this,' he said to himself. It was past breakfast time now, but sleep was altogether beyond him. Instead, at about ten, he stole down to a pawnbroker's in Jermyn Street and exchanged the medal and the watch chain for two ten-pound notes. Then, a little later, he took a cab to Putney – the cab-man wondered at his staring eyes – and drove up to a little villa on the edge of the heath. What he said to the lady he met there, and in what relation that lady stood to him, is not recorded, but at any rate he emerged with another twenty pounds. Ten pounds of the sixty Captain Raff kept for himself, but the other fifty he placed on Baldino at odds of six to one. Three hundred pounds! He had never seen such a sum. The thought drew him out of his misery. Later, after he had finally permitted himself to sleep for an hour or two, he shut up the room in Ryder Street and walked off in the direction of Soho. He would lie low, he thought, and consider his opportunities. In any case it wanted only a few weeks to the race. He went on through the crowded streets, his feet dragging behind him and a peculiar expression on his face, so that the people that he passed took pains to avoid him, and turned to look back at him as he went by, until the Soho pavements swallowed him up and he was gone.

XX

More from *Bell's Life*

As the great day nears ... Mr Gulliver, a gentleman without whose attendance no race meeting in the north of England is truly complete, has sent us this account of BALDINO: 'A very chaste horse, and dainty, who caused a sensation at the Bolton handicap, where he was very nearly bought up by a syndicate, only that his owner, Mr McWilliam, stood firm. Very neat on his toes, minds the whip, but is not its slave. Mr Solloway rode him previous and may well do again. Will sit upon the rail, if not steered elsewhere. Lost against COALHEAVER in March but carried a stone and was full of running at the finish, and Mr Solloway confessed an error on his part, viz fearing he was blown early on. He was got by EXCALIBUR of DAWN'S DELIGHT, whose victory in the Oaks may be cordially recollected. I have heard it said that he lacks application, but have never seen so ...' We are obliged to Mr Gulliver for his report, a model of judicious impartiality that may be favourably compared with some of the dubious encomia offered up elsewhere for our inspection ...

For SEPTUAGINT we have nothing but praise. In a packed field, he is discreet but effective, will seem not to be there yet rise suddenly to out-distance the throng. In a procession he will move stealthily, fix his sights upon the next impediment to his progress and swiftly overhaul it. Mr Gladstone has not more staying power, and Lord John not less poise. We have seen him make up a dozen yards in a furlong and maintain a four-length advantage with a dozen Pegasuses on his tail. Lord Trumpington – a very modest and circumspect man – is to be credited with not overusing him or ruining him through premature growth in the equine forcing-houses to which so much of the sport of kings are now unhappily given up. We should proclaim him a certainty, were it not for a slight stiffness in the hindquarters and the consequent un-wieldiness that is its inevitable companion . . .

. . . Of Mr Happerton's TIBERIUS much has been written and said. Was a finer-looking horse ever seen on Newmarket Heath in recent years? But then how many fine horses have been rendered down into cat's-meat a year beyond their pomp? He *will* toss his head, to his rider's disadvantage, but there are graver sins than this. Dan Wickens, who rode him for Mr Davenant, his *quondam* owner, kept him on the tightest bridle imaginable, and seemed to prosper. Full of vigour, running, spirit, etc. Bred up by Mr Curbishley, of whom all the world knows, in Lincolnshire. A strong horse, no doubt, but we have seen him wearied by his exertions. He is to be ridden by Major Hubbins, whose best days are behind him, it has been averred, but then the same was said of His Grace the late Duke of Wellington at Waterloo. We observe again that we are no prophet, and that those in search of financial gain should straightaway take themselves off to the warm embrace of Captain Crewe, and yet experience, foresight, history and intuition decree that the race will be fought out between TIBERIUS and SEPTUAGINT, with BALDINO's ability to interfere in this Herculean contest by no means to be discounted . . .

XXI

The Governess's Tale

There's many a wretch
Shall meet Jack Ketch.
And many a wight
Struck down in fright
And fear in the brook
That a dozen has took
Sing hey for the Lincolnshire Crowner!
The Lincolnshire Songbook (1819)

If they lived once in a dark house, now it was darker still, with a crêpe wreath upon the door, to silence the knocker and black-edged cards on the dining-room table. The rooks mourned with them, and the cries of the birds echoed their own.

Scroop was gently disintegrating under the rain. Half a chimney had fallen away in the March gales, and the stone still lay on the gravel where it fell. There were holes in the roof-tiles that nobody came to mend. But if there was no occupation, except for the safeguarding of the schoolroom carpet, then at any rate its inhabitants were not alone. Indeed it sometimes seemed that the place was nothing but a giant magnet drawing people towards it, and in this power lay the root of their distress. Mr Silas the Sleaford attorney had come, by whom Mr Glenister had been so amused and whom Mr Davenant hated so much, and his clerk. A pair of lawyers from Lincoln, dressed in black and looking very like the rooks, followed him, and Mr Happerton too, and then a long, low equipage with a couple of black-dyed horses to draw it, and a pair of very discreet men in subfusc to unload from it the object that now lay in Mr Davenant's study, lengthwise upon a trestle.

*

It seemed to Mr Glenister and Miss Ellington, when they discussed the matter, that the moment of Mr Davenant's decline could be fixed to a visit that Mr Happerton paid them at about the end of April. The rain had ceased, and the sun come out – or what passes for sun in Lincolnshire – and with it came Mr Happerton, bringing with him the celebrated Major Hubbins, who was to ride Tiberius – this fact was conveyed to them out of *Bell's Life* in the Scroop kitchen – in the Derby. It was apparent that Mr Davenant was made yet more wretched by Mr Happerton's appearance, and when the latter offered him his hand – for he was always very civil – absolutely refused it, and slunk away, the same treatment, Miss Ellington later saw, being meted out to Major Hubbins, when he went over to him upon the lawn to offer some polite word. As for Major Hubbins, Miss Ellington thought she had never seen such a sedate old gentleman, or one so careful that his feet should not be wetted by the grass, or his glass of negus brought to him hot and with cinnamon in it. 'Surely,' she remarked to Mr Glenister, 'there is some mistake, and this is Mr Happerton's butler or his uncle?', but no, Mr Glenister said that it was Major Hubbins right enough, and indeed, a day or so later, they saw him out in the lanes upon Tiberius, and a great deal more purposeful, but still, Miss Ellington thought, wishing that he had stayed at home with his old wife and his grand-children to play about his knees. His hair was quite white, and he talked like Mr Spectator in the old books and said he was obleeged, and was quite harmless, and yet it was plain that Mr Davenant could not stand to look at him, and that his presence near the stables – where Mr Davenant sometimes lurked of a morning – was simple torture.

Mr Happerton, like Major Hubbins on his horse, was exceedingly purposeful. He had a surveyor come over from Lincoln with a map, and the two of them paced out the boundaries of the estate. He went down to the cellar and brought up the hogsheads that lay there. Seeing that Mr Davenant shunned his company, he asked Mr Glenister to accompany him (Mr Glenister thinking, as he told Miss Ellington, that he might serve his friend by this attendance, although he knew Mr Davenant would resent it) and was, Mr Glenister said, remarkably shrewd in his judgements. *Imprimis*, he had a plan to cut down part of the wood and to drain certain of the fields beyond it. Did this mean, Miss Ellington asked Mr Glenister, being very struck by the seigneurial air with which Mr Happerton went about the property, that he was now its owner, and Mr Glenister confirmed that the legal papers had been signed the previous week. And something of the pathos of Mr Davenant's situation was brought home to the governess, and she regretted that her master should have to skulk around the back ways of a house that he had called his own for twenty years, while a man in bright top-boots strode about his gates and made notes in a pocket-book.

And then came two incidents that no historian of the last days of Mr Davenant's discomfiture could fail to omit.

There was an old man living in the village, half-blind but with an amiable disposition, who came to the house sometimes of an evening with his fiddle, and was helped into the back-kitchen by Mrs Castell, given his supper and permitted to play for whomever was sat there. While he ate, Mrs Castell catechised him as to the progress of his family: had Martha any more children? Was Jane married? Was Peter – a notorious scapegrace, famous in the neighbourhood – to be brought once more before the bench? All this roughly, but with a genuine charity. And they were assembled there one night – Mrs Castell, Miss Ellington, Hester, Evie half-asleep with her head upon her shoulder – listening to this modest entertainment, when the door was flung open and Mr Davenant strode in, very pale and grim, with the queerest expression on his face, to say that he would have no music, the sound was a torment to him and the man must go. To all of which instructions they instantly acceded, though with reluctance and, on Mrs Castell's part, an exceedingly bad grace, she remarking that it was all very well a bankrupt sending a poor old man out into the night without his supper, but there might come a time when he would want supper himself.

And then, the next afternoon, walking with Evie in the garden, Miss Ellington observed the most painful scene. It appeared that Mr Happerton, having inspected the wood and the fields, had now turned his attention to the house, and together with the surveyor was standing on the lawn examining certain of the stone buttresses. It being a warm day, he had his hat in his hand, which had some bearing on what followed. Mr Davenant had not been seen all day – it was thought that he had locked himself in his study, or perhaps gone over to Glenister Court – but suddenly, with a kind of jerky precision, like a little wooden puppet whose strings are suspended from above, he emerged out of the wood and, seeing Mr Happerton and the surveyor on the lawn, started instantly toward them. Whether Mr Happerton saw him or not, or had merely (being so engrossed in his architectural survey) determined to ignore him, Miss Ellington did not know, but at any rate Mr Davenant came almost within a yard of him before Mr Happerton so much as raised his hand, and stood there, as it seemed to her, spluttering with rage. 'Well Davenant,' Mr Happerton now said, having registered the fact of his presence, 'what is it that we may do for you? I am afraid we are rather busy here.' Whereupon Mr Davenant, not caring for the sensibilities of anyone who might be passing, shouted that he was a villain and he would see him d——d. 'Indeed,' Mr Happerton said, who did not seem very put out by this irruption, 'why am I a villain?' 'You have pulled down the gibbet,' Mr Davenant shouted at him. 'Pulled it down and burnt it.'

'Why certainly I have taken it down,' Mr Happerton told him – the surveyor had backed away a little by this time, but Mr Happerton still stood in his original attitude. 'A badger's head and half a dozen polecats nailed to a couple of fence-posts. Who would want to see that while walking round a gentleman's garden?' 'It was there in my great-grandfather's day,' Mr Davenant told him, now fairly shrieking, and Mr Happerton, turning back to the surveyor with a gesture indicating that they should resume their work, said that his great-grandfather had probably worn a wig and gaiters, but that was no reason for him to wear them. What Mr Davenant said Miss Ellington did not hear. There was a moment when she feared he might absolutely assault him (and would have come off the worse for his pains, for Mr Happerton was a well-made man and perhaps two stone the heavier) but then, thinking perhaps that some symbolic gesture would suffice, he seized Mr Happerton's hat, threw it down upon the grass and fairly trampled it beneath his feet. Then he went back the way he had come, still with the same disjointed movements, back towards the wood, where he soon disappeared into the trees. 'He is not quite right in the head, I am afraid,' Mr Happerton said, picking up the ruined hat from the lawn and ruefully regarding it, and the surveyor, wondering perhaps at the spectacle, raised an eyebrow and the work was resumed.

Later that evening, when Evie and Miss Ellington were sitting in the drawing room playing at spillikins, with Mr Happerton and Mr Glenister talking together in the corner, Mr Davenant appeared suddenly in the doorway, said something in an undertone which sounded like an apology, shook Mr Happerton's hand, gave Evie a very longing look, which she, staring up from the tray on which the pieces were set out, quaintly returned, and then was gone. Mr Glenister started from his chair, made as if to follow him and then recovered himself and resumed his conversation.

On the next day he was gone: his bed had not been slept in, Mrs Castell said, who had the care of it; his study locked up and the key vanished, but no sign of anyone behind the window; no trace of his whereabouts inside the house or out of it. At first no great fright was taken at his absence. Somebody remembered that the horse fair at Sleaford fell on that day, which he was in the habit of attending; Hester recalled that he had asked for his boots to be brushed on the previous night, which was thought significant in this respect. But then, at teatime, when no word had been heard of him and a neighbour, back from Sleaford, reported that he had not been seen there, a council of war was held in the kitchen, at which Mr Happerton, Mr Glenister, Mrs Castell and Miss Ellington discussed what ought to be done. 'He has gone on one of his walks, I daresay,' Mr Glenister said, 'but all the same it is inconvenient of him not to have given us notice.' 'I confess I did not like the look on his face that time yesterday,' Mr Happerton said, who of the two perhaps seemed more anxious. 'What do you suppose is in that study of his?' The key still not being to hand, Mr Happerton and Mr Glenister broke down the door, but there was nothing there – only a great mass of papers thrown over the desk, and – which Mr Glenister said privately that he wondered at – a Bible open on a chair. But when Miss Ellington ventured in there later she found a miniature of Mr Davenant done when he was a boy cast on the floor with its frame cracked that alarmed her greatly.

There was a wind that evening, and a storm that flattened the tops of the trees in the wood and smashed a chair that had been left out on the lawn into matchwood, and Mr Glenister said that it was a bad night to be out in, but he had no doubt that Mr Davenant had taken shelter somewhere. Miss Ellington was left with the task of comforting Evie, whose distress was very pitiful to see, although it seemed to the governess that what had happened was in some measure beyond her understanding, that she grasped at its shape in the air above her but could not bring it down. This thought had occurred to Mr Glenister. 'Do you suppose she knows?' he asked Miss Ellington at one point, who said that she thought she did, whereupon Mr Glenister brushed up his moustaches, offered to dance a hornpipe, imitate a pig, &c., all impostures that generally had Evie shrieking with laughter, but on this occasion fell sadly flat.

On the next morning Mr Glenister had his men search the estate and make enquiries in Scroop, but all to no avail. There was another storm that night, and a great rattling of windows – the trees dancing up beyond the panes like a forest of imploring hands – but Mr Glenister said nothing about it being a bad night to be out in.

And then came a curious time at Scroop, quite three days at least, of people going about their tasks in the most regular way, but knowing all the while that a great cloud of disquiet hung over their heads, the post earnestly examined but bringing nothing, the least stir of gravel on the drive calling faces to the window to see who might be coming and what they might bring.

On the evening of the third day they found Mr Davenant in a little stream that runs to the north of Scroop, drifted up against a copse of alder trees that hangs over the water. Miss Ellington saw him lying on the rail, by which they carried him up to the house, his face all white and mottled from the river.

He had a little scimitar paper-knife in his hand, which she remembered from his study.

His eyes staring up at nothing.

And now they were all as lost as he . . .

Part Four

XXII

Mist

At Glenister Hall the mist is rising. For half an hour now Mr Glenister has stood by the window in his study watching it roll up from the fields behind his lawn, and Edgard Dyke, which lies to the back of his birch wood. There is always mist in Lincolnshire. Even on fine summer mornings it lurks in the spinneys and the water meadows' edge: a dense white halo, ghostly, like fine-spun cotton. The local myths and legends are full of it. The _Gesta Daemonorum Lincolnensis_, a monkish scribble on the flyleaf of a tenth-century psalter kept in the vault of Lincoln Cathedral, talks of a great fog clouding the sky from _Sliofor ad Luthe_, which Mr Glenister, who has seen the psalter, thinks is the land between Sleaford and Louth. Out of this fog, according to the author of the _Gesta_, a winged steed, coal-black and with flaming eyes, periodically emerges to gallop the night sky with a pack of spectral hounds yammering at his hoofs. There are similar myths in Norfolk, forty miles away beyond the Wash; antiquaries – Mr Glenister is a member of the Lincolnshire Society – think them derivative. It is the

Pegasus of the Lincoln psalter who rode here first, out across Spurn Head above the grey North Sea. But it is a second black horse, which interests Mr Glenister now: Tiberius, in point of fact, who only a fortnight hence will be taken down to London for the great race. For reasons he cannot quite fathom, Mr Glenister has determined to be present, even if – Derby Day being what it is, and no lodgings to be found within a dozen miles of Epsom – it means staying in a London hotel. It is all to do with Mr Davenant, he thinks, Mr Davenant and, more generally, the tribute that the dead exact from the living, in this case the obligation to travel a hundred miles to watch a horse run in a race that will last two and a half minutes in front of a hundred thousand people.

There is something ominous about the mist, Mr Glenister feels, watching now as another dense cloud or two comes stealing up from the birch wood, if not uncanny. A human figure suddenly engulfed by it – he has seen his keeper so surrounded – does not disappear but is rendered frailer and less substantial. The idea of frailty makes Mr Glenister think of Mr Davenant, on whom, since the body was brought up from the stream on a rail ten days since, he has not ceased to focus his mind. It is known to everyone – everyone, that is, except the Coroner, who charitably diagnosed mischance – that Mr Davenant destroyed himself. And it is thought, from the evidence of a paper found in Mr Davenant's study, that it was Mr Davenant in his rage and misery who attempted to destroy Tiberius, killing the thing he loved so that no one else could possess him, or perhaps did not mean quite to destroy him, or he would have chosen a better time and a better weapon. To Mr Glenister, who reads books and newspapers, who is a Lincolnshire man but with affiliations beyond the flat fields and the lowering sky, all this is curiously symbolic. The world is changing, he thinks, and it is leaving Mr Davenant and his sort behind. It is not enough, now, to live in a house that your grandfather inhabited, in sight of fields that his grandfather walked, in a periwig, for there is a tide sweeping over the Lincolnshire flats that no amount of ancestry can damn or divert. Tiberius, Mr Glenister thinks, is caught up in this tide, although a part of him knows this to be nonsense, for gentlemen have always run horses and crowds come to watch them, if not at Epsom Downs then elsewhere. And now, by destroying himself, Mr Davenant has made that tide run a little faster, ensuring that a crowd of other things will be swept away on it just as he has been swept himself.

It is only ten days since Mr Davenant slipped into the stream – whose banks, as the Coroner pointed out, were caked in mud and unusually steep – and already he has been buried, and memorialised in the *Lincolnshire Chronicle*, and if not forgotten then is of no account in the new arrangements that mysteriously prevail. The will was read out at a lawyer's office in Lincoln to an audience consisting of Mr Glenister, Mr Davenant's brother, Mr Happerton and his London attorney, and was, everyone very soon agreed, quite otiose, seeing that Mr Happerton had in his pocket a bill of sale of the Scroop property with Mr Davenant's signature on it. 'It is all to do with that horse, I suppose,' Mr Davenant's brother remarked, with whom Mr Glenister subsequently ate his lunch. 'There is more to it than that, I think,' Mr Glenister said, not knowing what he could decently say in such circumstances. 'And this Mr Happerton,' the cousin complained. 'How did he come to get such a hold on him, I wonder?' 'He should never have begun that lawsuit, I fear,' Mr Glenister said, again not liking to say all he knew. 'Poor Sam,' Mr Davenant's brother lamented. 'Ruined for a horse and a sandpit that someone dug up in one of his fields. It is very hard.'

The rooks do not trust the mist, Mr Glenister notices. At the first hint of it they return to the tree-tops. These, Mr Glenister thinks, look like the masts of fog-bound ships. In winter the Humber would resemble a forest, were it not for the clanking hulls. And yet, for all Mr Davenant's brother's complaint – he is resigning his Fellowship to be married and perhaps needs the money – Mr Happerton has, in the matter of the will, been surprisingly gracious. The incidental legacies – £30 to Mrs Castell, a carriage clock to Hester the housemaid – have been handed over. Mr Glenister himself is already the proud possessor of a steel engraving of the Battle of Culloden, at which some Davenant is supposed to have distinguished himself. To the starker questions – what will happen to Evie and Miss Ellington – there is, as yet, no answer. Mr Happerton is at Epsom: the fate of his tenant's child and her governess is of little moment to him. Doubtless, like the servants' wages and piles of mouldering timber, it will be dealt with at the proper season. Mr Glenister has discovered, somewhat to his surprise, that he is to be Evie's guardian. He is not certain how he feels about this, liking Evie but wondering whether this liking may not be stifled by her constant proximity.

Since her father's death Evie has fallen into a decline, rambling around the place like a pale white ghost and having to be brought back from woods and meadows into which she has strayed. Mr Glenister, whose advice has been sought, has suggested that laudanum should be mixed into her milk. But one cannot always go on administering laudanum to a fourteen-year-old girl, he thinks. He wonders what it would be like if Evie came to live at Glenister Court, and foresees a future of cats persecuted by her ineffable love, white muslin in hasty transit over the wet grass, the red eyes which remind him of a rat's staring up from the kitchen table. It is all a question, Mr Glenister feels, of determining where responsibility lies.

Just at that moment there is a knock at the study door, and the maid opens it to reveal Mr Silas, the Sleaford attorney, raising his legs, one knee at a time, in a kind of jogging motion, and twisting his hat in his hand. In the past few weeks Mr Glenister and Mr Silas have become remarkably intimate, in so far as intimacy can ever exist between a Lincolnshire squire and the deacon of a Dissenting chapel. Mr Glenister knows that his late father, a Canon of Christchurch, would have refused to enter a room if Mr Silas sat in it. There are people who say that Mr Silas, whose feet are still moving nervously up and down as if he walked some invisible treadmill, is another part of the tide sweeping in across Lincolnshire and the world beyond it, but Mr Glenister thinks not. There have always been Mr Silases, he believes, demure but self-conscious little men skipping about the coat-tails of the great, and not so great, and charity (in Mr Silas's case expediency) requires that they should be honoured. Mr Silas, he sees, is somewhat changed from his usual appearance, and the difference lies in his dress, specifically in the substitution of his black jacket with a kind of antique frock-coat, frogged and emerald green, but with a hint almost of purple. Mr Glenister thinks his father would have been seriously offended by Mr Silas, with or without his coat, whereas his son is merely amused.

'Come in, Silas,' he says now. 'It is very good of you to come and see me.' The coat, he finds, is too big to be ignored. He cannot avoid looking at it, nor can Mr Silas avoid the slant of his gaze. 'That is a very extraordinary garment you have on.'

'I don't know that it's so very remarkable,' Mr Silas says nervously. 'But then, us attorneys are always supposed to go about like rooks, you know.'

'You have not brought Mr Jones with you, I think,' Mr Glenister says, looking into the doorway as if Mr Jones might still be lurking in the corridor.

'Well – no. Jones is a very useful man, you know, but when the business is confidential, I like to come on my own.'

Mr Glenister is suddenly aware of colour, both in the room and without it. The imperial sheen of Mr Silas's frock-coat; the red wax seal on the sheaf of legal documents he now takes out of his case; a damasked chair-back; the whiteness of the mist, now receding a little on the virid grass. The *Gesta*, he recalls, has the same variegated palette: black hounds, red eyes, golden stars flung over the horizon. Mr Silas, meanwhile, is stirring in his chair. Without Mr Jones to cajole and bully he is less sure of himself, and somewhat humble. The legal documents are strewn across his lap.

'A terrible business,' he says suddenly, out of his nest of papers. 'I take it there's no doubt that the poor gentleman ... did away with himself?'

'Every doubt,' Mr Glenister tells him, who privately has none, but is not prepared to allow this point, 'with a bank as steep as that. A regiment of dragoons could have tumbled down there in the dark and not climbed back again.'

Mr Silas has his own ideas about the river bank, which not even his respect for Mr Glenister can subdue. 'And then that Mr Happerton. He's a low fellow, that one, bringing a London attorney up to settle the affair when any one of us could have done service.'

'I think it is only that gentlemen prefer to use their own men of business,' Mr Glenister demurs.

'In case questions are asked that can't be answered. I've no doubt you're right, sir,' Mr Silas says. 'I suppose there's no doubt about the bill of sale?'

'None. It was all laid out in the usual way, I believe. Mr Statham' – Mr Statham sits in the House for the county – 'was one of the witnesses.'

'A nasty Liberal, that never should have been set over us ... Well, I have done what you asked, sir, and here is the result, sad as it is. But perhaps you would like to see a schedule?'

Sometimes the ghost horse of the *Gesta* carries a warrior in black armour. At other times he is riderless. Some antiquaries have identified this figure with the Norse god Tyr. Others think it a fanciful tribute to Offa, the Mercian king.

'No indeed,' Mr Glenister says. 'I should like to hear anything you have to tell me.' There is a fire bursting up in the grate for all it is May, whose red coals would do for the ghost horse's eyes. Mr Silas moves his hands out in front of him like a pair of pincers, looks for a moment as if he will seize up the ink-bottle on Mr Glenister's desk, but in the end merely presses the tips of his fingers together. He is quite in his element again.

'Well, sir. There was a great deal of debt. But you know that. None of it considerable in itself, perhaps, but a terrible amount when put together. There was money owing to the lawyers. Half a dozen tradesmen in Lincoln and elsewhere too. Now, in the normal course of things a shopkeeper that knows his man and has a bill will keep that bill going – take his interest, have it renewed, that kind of thing. And country gentlemen's the best kind to have the paper of, sir. There may not be ready money, but there's property. Two acres with a dozen cows in it's worth far more to a man with a bill than a grand pianner or a wardrobe of Dresden silk. But that London attorney of Happerton's, he went around buying up debt. And he did it a-purpose. Times he'd pay pretty near all that was owed on a bill – 80 or 90 per cent – just to get his hands on the paper. There was a bill owing to Edric, the Lincoln corn chandler, which Edric, to give him the credit, didn't want to give up, out of respect to Mr Davenant whose father helped set up his father in his shop, which he paid face value for, and that's not natural, for there's no profit in it.'

'You are saying that Mr Happerton deliberately set out to ruin my friend Mr Davenant?'

'I don't say that, sir. Bill-broking's a free trade. Any man can set up in it if he wants and pay what he likes for such paper as comes his way. Who's to say what's the value of a thing? If we all knew that we'd be as rich as Dives. What I'm saying is that Mr Happerton went to a deal of trouble to get his hands on Mr Davenant's property, which he did by bringing all the debt together, so there was only one creditor. And then ...'

'And then what?'

Mr Glenister is still thinking of the *Gesta*, in which the ghost horse with the pack of hounds yammering at its tail has been replaced by Tiberius, with the figure of Major Hubbins clinging to his back. He will go and see Tiberius at the Derby, he decides, in the hope that it was something his friend would have wanted. He wonders what extremity of passion it was that inspired Mr Davenant to attack the horse in its stall. But then there is no knowing what a person may do when afflicted by circumstance. There is a man whom Mr Glenister once knew – he is in the Hanwell asylum now – who, when a young lady wrote to him breaking off their engagement, severed his own finger at the knuckle and sent it back to her in a bloody envelope by way of reply. No, there is no knowing what a person may do.

'Well, when a man's in debt and signing his name to paper all the time there comes a day when he don't know what he's signing. Or when what's signed isn't his, if you take my meaning.'

'You mean that some of the paper wasn't Davenant's, but it had his name on it?'

'Who's to say, sir? But if a man's signed twenty bills, he may not jib at the twenty-first. There's nothing more lowering than a mound of paper. Now, take a look at this. I got it – well, I'd best not say how I came by it – but you'll see the promise is to Lovegrove, that saddler, which between ourselves is not an honest man. Did Mr Davenant have dealings with Lovegrove? May very well have done. Who's to say? But here's his name on Lovegrove's bill.'

'But surely all Mr Davenant's bills were bought up by Mr Happerton?'

'Well then this one was overlooked. Put to one side and forgot. You'd be surprised how often that happens. Why, I knew a house once that was about to be sold – new owner had his cows already grazing on the meadow, and measuring up the sash window that he wanted took out – when they found the place was entailed and couldn't be sold at all.'

'I should give a great deal,' Mr Glenister says, 'to have that bill.'

'I can't let you have it, sir. Indeed I can't. It should be in our safe, that's where it should be.'

The mist is receding now, and there are rooks out on the grass. Again, a part of Mr Glenister's mind is wondering what plans Mr Happerton has for Evie and Miss Ellington. He will do what he ought, he thinks, for this is what he has always done.

'By the way,' he says, 'there is sad news of Lady Mary Desmond.'

'I am sorry to hear that, sir. Truly. What is the matter with her ladyship?'

'Well – it is all very delicate. I fear she has quarrelled with the Reverend Toms at St Julian's. A rather high establishment, I should say.'

'As high as they come, sir,' Mr Silas agrees. 'Why they'd lower down a stuffed dove on Whit Sunday if they could get away with it. It's not a place I ever visit, but they do say that you can scarce see the altar for smoke.'

'Exactly. And Lady Mary, as you doubtless remember, was raised a Quaker. Of course it is early days, but I have heard that she was speaking very favourably of your congregation.'

'Was she, sir? Well, we shall be very glad to welcome her. And the old Earl, too, if he's a mind.'

A moment later and the saddler's bill is in Mr Glenister's hand. Again, he thinks of his father. The Canon of Christchurch would have disdained these subterfuges. But then he did not live in such an age as this, Glenister thinks. We must adapt ourselves to the world we inhabit, or we are lost. The signature on the bill is like Mr Davenant's, but in some way curiously unlike it.

'Now look at this,' he says, drawing out of his desk the sheet of paper that Miss Ellington retrieved from Mr Davenant's study. For some reason the memory of Mr Davenant's face staring up from the rail is very vivid to him: white, sightless and curiously indistinct — as unfathomable, Mr Glenister thinks, as the signature on the bill.

'What's that then?' Mr Silas asks. He looks thoroughly animated, even more so than at the prospect of Lady Mary Desmond visiting his red-brick chapel and sitting next to the pink-cheeked tradesmen's wives in their Sunday bonnets.

'An attempt at Mr Davenant's signature, I should say,' Mr Glenister tells him. He puts the saddler's bill face down on the desk. 'Let us see if any of them tally.'

'The third, maybe,' Mr Silas says. He is breathing heavily, like Tiberius, or perhaps the ghost-horse as it gallops the night sky.

'The fourth, I should say,' Mr Glenister corrects him. 'Look how the line drops down under the "D" in "Davenant".'

And Mr Silas looks at him in admiration.

＊

Not more than a hundred miles away Captain Raff wakes up in an attic bedroom looking out over a series of low, grimy rooftops. The dome of St Paul's looms over the skyline. The sun shines uncomfortably through the open window. There are no sheets on the bed and the mattress is yellow with age — and other things — but Captain Raff is more concerned by the absence of the water jug which has vanished mysteriously during the night. He suspects that the landlord of the premises, to whom he is beholden, has taken it in spite. For a moment he stares around the room in search of it, looks at the bare floorboards and the solitary chair that supports his clothes, but there is no sign. Of all things in the world, aside from Baldino's victory in the great race, the receipt of his £300 and his revenge on Mr Happerton, Captain Raff thinks that he desires a glass of water the most. A mouse runs over the boards towards the wainscoting and he watches it slide itself, with furious motions of its paws, into an aperture that the naked eye would not have known was there. The thought strikes him that he, too, is a species of mouse and this is his hole.

For a week or more, Captain Raff has been lying low. He has lain low in Soho, and he has lain low in Fulham. Just now he is lying low in Clerkenwell. The state of Captain Raff's linen and his personal appearance is a testimony to this concealment. There is a fragment of mirror balanced upright on the chest of drawers which is the room's only other ornament and while he dresses Captain Raff stares into it. As he stands twisting his greasy black neck-tie in his fingers there is a commotion on the staircase beyond the door and an old woman in a black dress whose lower fringes are quite encrusted with dirt, as if she were a kind of market garden, puts her head in the door and says, with a dreadful mock-solicitude:

'I suppose you'll be wanting your breakfust, Capting?'

'Breakfast? Of course I shall be wanting breakfast,' says Captain Raff, whose haughty tone is quite wonderful to hear. 'What on earth is the time, anyhow?'

'It's jest gorn about half past eleven.'

Try as he may, Captain Raff cannot account for the last fourteen hours. He knows that some of them have been spent in the sheetless bed with its views of the grimy rooftops, but of at least half that time there is no trace. As he pulls on his boots, which are even dirtier than ever and are missing a heel, a thought strikes him.

'Has anyone – has anyone called for me?'

For on the previous afternoon, growing tired of his solitude and wanting fresh information about the race, Captain Raff had sent a message to Mr Delaney.

'No one's called. If they had, I'd have sent them up. This ain't Buckingham Pallis, where folks sits about at levvys.'

'Wait there – wait I say,' Captain Raff shouts out, but the old woman is already halfway back down the stairs. There is a purse in the captain's pocket which, unearthed and shaken out onto the mattress, produces a groat, two silver threepenny pieces, a farthing, a piece of sealing wax and the ticket which will either settle his debts or send him to perdition. As he stares at these miscellaneous items a scheme springs into his mind that will allow him to eat the breakfast and avoid paying for it. But all this is suddenly cast aside – blown away – quite banished from his head – by the realisation that once he has paid his bill in Clerkenwell, there will be no money to take him to Epsom. 'Hang it all,' Captain Raff says to himself, with an attempt at jauntiness, 'fellows have got to the Derby before without an omnibus to take 'em, and there's a week to make the trip.' But somehow the fight has gone out of him and the legs that go tottering down the staircase to a back-kitchen where what smells very like a haddock is being broiled up are surmounted by a face that anyone who saw might have thought to have resembled that of one of the condemned men, who steps up to the block at Snow Hill, where Mr Ketch, or his successor, can supervise his passing from this world to the next.

XXIII

Stratagems of Captain McTurk

We are not, heaven knows, an advocate of female suffrage, but there is one sphere in which feminine influence should be paramount: we refer, of course, to the domestic. If a newly married young lady cannot command her establishment, choose her callers and entertain the guests of her own desiring, then what, it may be asked, can she command?

A New Etiquette: Mrs Carmody's Book of Genteel Behaviour (1861)

In Belgrave Square Mrs Happerton was entertaining a visitor. He was a rather unusual visitor for Belgrave Square and indeed he had almost been repulsed by the butler and brought back only at Mrs Rebecca's urgent insistence. But still, there he was in old Mr Gresham's drawing room cracking his knuckles as the parlourmaid brought him his tea, looking eagerly about him, and by no means discountenanced by the ambiguity of his reception. This gentleman was Mr Dennison, whom the political world esteems so much but whom the old butler, knowing nothing of the way in which aspiring Treasury lords are brought to their electors, had very nearly cast out into the street.

Mr Dennison was a short, sallow man of perhaps fifty-two or fifty-three with very black hair cut close on the top of his head who worked as an attorney in the Borough. This, however, was not his chief distinction. His singularity lay in the fact that he was the Conservative Party's leading source of intelligence, influence and manipulation in those parts of the capital where Conservative candidates – successful Conservative candidates, that is – are not generally to be found. Modest in his demeanour, frowned on in polite drawing rooms for that irrepressible habit of knuckle-cracking, Mr Dennison was nonetheless a titan in his way. Had he not taken Mr Carstairs – a man whose candidature had previously been despaired of – to within thirty votes of victory at the last election? And had he not unleashed such a volley of insinuation against the Liberal candidate in Limehouse that this gentleman had absolutely retired from the fray? People said of Mr Dennison, if they wanted to praise him, that he was not perhaps a nice-looking man but that he knew his business.

Quite what Mr Dennison's business was in Belgrave Square, he did not exactly know. He had received a letter and now here he was drinking his tea and cracking his knuckles in Mr Gresham's drawing room while Mrs Happerton stared at him from the other side of the fireplace with her gooseberry eyes.

'A shame your pa – your father – can't join us, Mrs Happerton,' Mr Dennison said in a voice in which the scent of cockney was very much pronounced.

'I am afraid my father is too ill to leave his room,' Mrs Happerton remarked. 'But he asked that I should give you his compliments.' In fact, Mr Gresham had not been told of Mr Dennison's visit.

'A gentleman that is very much respected in his profession,' Mr Dennison said, still angling for some hint as to why he had been asked to warm his feet at the fire of a drawing room in Belgrave Square. 'A great pity he can't be here. But perhaps Mr Happerton will be coming?'

'I am afraid my husband is at Epsom, Mr Dennison.'

'With his 'oss, of course, that we hear so much about,' Mr Dennison said encouragingly, cracking one set of knuckles off like a cap-pistol. 'Nero, ain't it?'

'He is called Tiberius.'

'I never read much in the classics, Mrs Happerton. It's a failing in me, I daresay.' Still thoroughly mystified, Mr Dennison decided that he ought to lay his cards on the table. 'Now, what is it that I might have the pleasure of doing for you?'

Mrs Happerton hesitated. She had thought long and hard about what she might say to Mr Dennison, whose appearance and accent she heartily disliked, but now that the moment had come she found that she could not properly frame the words.

'There is to be an election soon, I believe, in the Chelsea Districts?'

'Certainly there is. What with that Mr Venables disgracing himself and losing his seat.' Being invited to talk about his favourite subject, Mr Dennison lost his reserve and became quite animated. 'Not that anyone will have a clear run, I daresay.'

'The Liberals will not be putting forward a candidate, I hear?' Mrs Rebecca enquired, who had done a certain amount of research in this field.

'Liberal candidate?' Mr Dennison's knuckles went off again like a series of raps at the door. 'An himpossibility. The men can't agree and the borough won't support 'em. Why, they say that Mr Huckleby, that everyone was so sweet on for the nomination at York, walked down the King's Road the other week and had a dead cat thrown at him out of a window.'

'And what about the Conservatives?' Mrs Happerton's expression as she said this was horribly intent, and her eyes sparkled.

Still Mr Dennison was mystified. Much as he appreciated the comfort of the Belgrave Square sofa cushions, the warmth of the fire, into which his lacquered boots were very nearly plunged, and the excellence of the tea, he could not quite see why he was being asked these questions.

'Well – I don't mind telling you that there is a difficulty there too. Sir Charles Devonish, who could have had the seat last time round for an old song, has gone and taken a wife, and it's said she don't approve of the game – the women don't, sometimes, begging your pardon. And then that Mr Fitzmaurice who was so thick with the publicans has gone smash over those railway shares. They say Alderman Savage wants the nomination, but between you and me, Mrs Happerton, he ain't quite the thing. Couldn't make a speech to save his life, not if the Chartists were at the door waving pitchforks.'

And then Mr Dennison stopped and looked at her enquiringly with his tea cup halfway to his lips as if to say: it is time, my dear madam, that we cast aside this pretence and you were so good as to inform me why you have brought me here.

'What would . . .' Mrs Happerton paused, and he saw how finely dressed she was, and how decisive in her gestures, how smartly she rattled the tongs when she put sugar in her tea, and how sharp her eye seemed. 'A d——d fine woman, anyhow,' he said to himself. '. . . Would there be any chance of my husband coming forward for the seat?'

'Mr Happerton?'

'From what you say, there is a vacancy. Why should he not do as well as – Alderman Savage?'

There was something very like contempt in the way she pronounced Alderman Savage's name, which did not escape Mr Dennison's sensitive ear.

'Why not indeed? I daresay pretty much anyone could do as well as Alderman Savage. But – you won't mind my saying this, Mrs Happerton – what's his connection with the place?'

'Mr Shipperley was elected at Richmond without ever having gone near the borough, I believe.'

'That's so, Mrs Happerton, that's so indeed!' Mr Dennison was delighted at this sally. He wished some of the men he dealt with were as well informed. 'But you see Chelsea is a very different place to Richmond. And the folk do like to see the candidate, and think he's one of themselves. All nonsense, of course. A drayedful low lot they are down there. But, well, it is something they sets store by.'

Mr Dennison's initial mystification, since appeased, had been replaced by a newer unease. Now that he thought about it, there was nothing outlandish in Mr Happerton seeking the nomination for a parliamentary seat, but he could not work out why it was that Mr Happerton's wife was doing the seeking.

'But you think that he would have a chance?'

'If that 'oss wins the Derby, Mrs Happerton, he would be dragged through the place in a coach-and-four. Best dodge in the world. Better than fighting bare-knuckle or flogging your opponent with a horse-whip. But that isn't the whole of it, I'm sorry to say. No one ever got in for the Chelsea Districts – Liberal or Conservative – without spending a deal of money.'

'How much money?'

Mr Dennison hesitated. He was, according to his lights, an honest man. Certainly no more than 20 per cent of the expenses in any single election campaign went into his own pocket. And he was favourably impressed by Mrs Happerton, even if he could not understand why she was her husband's proxy. So he decided to tell the truth.

'It couldn't be done for less than three thousand.'

'If it is to cost three thousand pounds,' Mrs Happerton said, 'then the money will be forthcoming.'

'And am I to hear Mr Happerton's own intentions?' Mr Dennison wondered, rather alarmed at the turn the conversation was taking.

'You had better come and see him after the race. I shall have him write to you.'

And Mr Dennison's knuckles went off with such force that the old butler, coming into the room with a fresh tray, stopped dead in astonishment, as if half a dozen firecrackers had suddenly been flung at his feet.

*

Looking out over the ostlers' yard, from a desk piled high with papers, and with sufficient tea cups to hand to furnish a caterer's canteen, Captain McTurk was sadly perplexed. Over a month had gone by since the assault on Mr Gallentin's shop and the identity of the thief was still unknown. Certain items of the stock that had been taken had lately been recovered from commercial premises as far apart as Brighton and Prague, but no one knew how they had got there, and it was allowed that the collection had been very cunningly dispersed. Worse still, in the weeks since the robbery a dozen other outrages had come clamouring for Captain McTurk's attention. A Cabinet minister had been robbed of his watch and chain almost on the steps of his house in Hyde Park Gate. A dozen tide-waiterships in the Port of London had been found to be fraudulently come by. And amid all this excitement – the Cabinet minister had nearly been garrotted into the bargain – the mystery of Mr Gallentin's shop in Cornhill had rather fallen by the way. But Captain McTurk had not been idle. Fascinated by the report brought back from Richmond by Mr Masterson, he had taken the opportunity to journey down to Teddington himself and call, quite unannounced, on Mrs Pardew.

This had not been very satisfactory. Captain McTurk had found Mrs Pardew living in the most modest of retirements, in a tiny villa next to a slaughterhouse, and it was clear from the moment of his entry into the house that his visit was a source of stark terror to her. But Captain McTurk had persevered. Was there any known particularity of Richmond that might have driven Mr Pardew to it? Any relative who lived there or pleasant association that he might have wished to rekindle? Had he ever tried to contact her since – since those unfortunate events of two years before? Did his appearance seem in any way different to her recollection of it? To all these questions Mrs Pardew answered no, and Captain McTurk, impressed by the smallness of the room in which she sat, the sparseness of the furniture and the stink of the slaughterhouse, which seemed to permeate every corner of the building, very soon took his leave.

A week later, when the fuss about the Cabinet minister had receded and a man had been apprehended who, it was hoped, might be charged with the assault, he paid a second visit in connection with the Gallentin case. This was to Mr File at his house in Amwell Street. Captain McTurk knew that the safe in Mr Gallentin's strongroom had eventually been broken open by main force, but it seemed to him very likely that the person responsible would have consulted an expert authority about the lock, and it seemed even likelier that the authority consulted would have been Mr File. Again, the visit had not been very satisfactory. Captain McTurk found Mr File lying ill in bed with the counterpane pulled up to his nose, so ill, his wife said, that he had not left the house for a fortnight, and had been despaired of. However, his wife having taken a message from the visitor that he had better stir himself if he knew what was good for him, he consented to appear in his front parlour, wrapped in a dressing gown.

'You're not very well, I see,' Captain McTurk said, who thought Mr File deserved anything he got.

'I should be better if I were allowed back to my bed,' Mr File said modestly.

'I dare say. You heard about that business at Gallentin's shop?'

'What business would that be?' Mr File meekly enquired. 'We are very quiet here, you know, and scarcely see a newspaper.'

After that Captain McTurk gave up and contented himself with questions about Mr File's doctor, which were answered very cordially. But he made a point, before he left, of staring very sharply at the invalid and saying that he thought Mr Pardew had been seen in London. Mr File opened his eyes wide and shook his head, as if to say that invalids should not be bothered with such things, but he could not suppress a little involuntary tremor of his hand, which the Captain saw.

'I'll swear he and that man Pardew have seen each other,' he told Mr Masterson when he got back to Northumberland Avenue, and such was his conviction that a policeman in plain clothes was sent to pace up and down Amwell Street to see if anyone went into Mr File's house or came out of it. For two days no one did either, and then on the third morning a fly rushed up from the livery stables nearby and took Mr File and his wife away to, of all places, Richmond. When Captain McTurk heard about this he sent Mr Masterson and a brace of constables off in pursuit in a closed carriage, and had them lurk for four hours in the shrubbery of the house where Mr File was being entertained, only to discover that he was innocently dining with his cousin. After this Captain McTurk despaired of Mr File and gave up all pretence of watching his movements, so that the old locksmith could subsequently have burgled half a dozen houses and gone rolling home in a coach-and-four without any notice being taken of him.

And then came something else which looked as if it might further distract Captain McTurk from the robbery at Mr Gallentin's shop, and the probable part played in it by Mr Pardew. This was a letter from Mr Glenister – not the first letter Mr Glenister had sent, but sufficiently interesting to require more than a courteous acknowledgement. In fact, Captain McTurk read the letter three times and made a little summary of its principal points on the obverse side of the envelope. At first his interest was no more than speculative. He had heard of Tiberius – everyone had heard of Tiberius – and he had heard of Mr Happerton. He had even, in a small way, heard of Mr Davenant, news of whose unfortunate death had been reported in the London papers. And now here was a man, Mr Davenant's intimate friend, the grandson of an earl (Captain McTurk had looked Mr Glenister up in a peerage), saying that there was some mystery about the circumstances of his death, insisting that the horse had been fraudulently acquired and insinuating that the deceased had been driven to his own destruction.

'You remember that fellow Happerton we spoke of?' he asked Mr Masterson.

'Certainly I remember him. There was something about him yesterday in a newspaper. Not to do with the horse, but saying that the man he bought the horse from had tumbled into a ditch in Lincolnshire.'

'Of course, everyone is so uncommonly polite when a man kills himself,' Captain McTurk said. 'Well, here is another letter from that man who lived next to him saying that Happerton drove him to it.'

'Should you like me to go Lincolnshire?' Mr Masterson asked, when he had read the letter, but Captain McTurk shook his head.

'I think not. The fellow who half-killed Robinson on his doorstep with the butler a yard behind the door is to be tried in a week, and I particularly want a conviction. No, I think I shall go and see Mr Gresham. It was his daughter Happerton married. No doubt I can find out a good deal more from him than could be got by asking Happerton questions which he mightn't like to answer.'

Of course Captain McTurk knew Mr Gresham. How he could not know him? Everyone knows everyone else. The butler in one house nods to the butler in the next as he passes him on the street. The Mayor of Norwich knows the Mayor of Ipswich and bows to him at municipal dinners. General Smith of the Buffs knows Colonel Jones of the Blues, for they were at school together. It took Captain McTurk ten minutes to think of some legal point on which he needed Mr Gresham's opinion, to have a letter written and a messenger ordered to take it round to Belgrave Square. It was then quite late on Monday evening and so the letter, although received by the butler, was not given to Mr Gresham until breakfast time on the Tuesday morning. Here, as might be expected, it was generally discussed by those present – Mr Gresham, Mr Happerton and his wife.

'It is from Captain McTurk,' Mr Gresham said, putting on his spectacles, the better to read the note.

'Oh indeed' (Mr Happerton). 'There is nothing amiss, I hope?'

'There is a Chancery case he wants my opinion on. Though why he should come to me when there are a dozen Home Office lawyers to advise him, I can't imagine.' Mr Gresham had never thought very much of the Home Office.

'You would hardly like to receive him in your current state of health I think, Papa,' said Mrs Happerton impartially.

Mr Gresham was certainly rather frail. It was a bright early summer morning, but he sat huddled in a dressing gown and complained of cold. Though pressed by his daughter to eat, he had managed only half a cup of tea and the end of a roll. His infirmity, such as it was, had lately begun to declare itself as a kind of vagueness. When brought downstairs he would sit looking out of the window or drowsing over the newspaper. Once, emerging from one of these stupors, he had mistaken his daughter for her mother. The awareness of this mistake, when it was brought home to him, had been very painful. But he was interested in Captain McTurk's letter, and his hand shook less as he held it up in front of his spectacles.

'I have heard of Captain McTurk,' said Mr Happerton, who was eating kidneys as if he had been half-starved. They had been very lightly cooked, and spots of blood dripped from the end of his knife. 'Wasn't he the man who took Morley the cracksman in full view at Shoreditch Station?'

'If you like, Papa, I shall write to Captain McTurk and say that you are not well enough to see him,' Mrs Happerton volunteered.

'And such a busy time, too,' Mr Happerton said, in the most genial way. 'I wonder Captain McTurk has the leisure to pay calls in Belgrave Square.'

But Mr Gresham thought that he would like to see Captain McTurk, and could not be gainsaid. And so a letter was written by Mrs Happerton inviting him to call. *I am afraid that my father is distinctly unwell*, Mrs Happerton wrote in a codicil that Mr Gresham never saw, *and we greatly fear that such a visit would not repay your trouble*. Nevertheless, Captain McTurk said that he would call, and such was his enthusiasm that he arrived on the very next afternoon.

There were a great many visitors to the house in Belgrave Square these days, among whom Captain McTurk did not perhaps seem so very significant. Horsey-looking gentlemen came to confer with Mr Happerton. Emissaries from livery stables and the sporting press were regularly entertained in the servants' quarters. Major Hubbins had been twice to dinner, stepping very cautiously on his injured knee (he hoped, he said, that the weather would keep up and they should have a nice, bright day of it, as had been the case in '43 when he had done great things – but not, alas, the greatest thing of all – on Lord Emley's Kingfisher). The only absentee from this cavalcade of pundits, hay chandlers and horsebox proprietors, curiously enough, was Captain Raff, but Mr Happerton, though puzzled by his disappearance – when a man decides that another man shall be dropped, it is generally he that wants to do the dropping – and his disregard of a message or two sent to Ryder Street, did not particularly regret this desertion. He had had enough of Captain Raff. If Captain Raff wished to vanish into the ether, then that was up to Captain Raff. At the back of his mind was the fact that Captain Raff knew certain things about him that he would not wish to be made public knowledge, but at the same time he could think of no reason why Captain Raff should betray him. In the meantime he was very busy – Tiberius was now at some stables near Cheam and required daily visits – and, like Captain McTurk, the mystery of

Captain Raff's disappearance did not loom so very large as it might have done.

He did not altogether like those visits to Cheam. Some of the people in the streets and the public houses knew who he was and saluted him, and the recognition pleased him and he returned the salutes. But going into the stables where the rival horses were kept – he did this incognito, standing at the back of the crowd with a newspaper held up to his hat-brim – a serious look came over his face. He thought Mr Abernethy's Pendragon an absurd horse, that a Tiberius without the encumbrance of Major Hubbins on his back would beat by the length of the finishing straight, and that Lord Trumpington's Septuagint had not been properly trained up and would suffer for it. And the odds, which he saw each day in the sporting papers or surreptitiously chalked up in the doorways of such public houses that had reached an accommodation with the police – Tiberius was at eight now, and you could get five on Baldino – made him shake with vexation. At these times he would go to Tiberius' stable and stare at him as he stood in his stall, think that he was a true Arab, unlike these hybrid monstrosities that the world now favoured, and that it was a shame he could not have his due.

And so the afternoon of Captain McTurk's visit came. If he had hoped to have a private conversation with Mr Gresham he was not disappointed: Mr Happerton, clad in his brightest pair of top-boots and with a carriage waiting in the square, was on his way to Cheam and, meeting Captain McTurk as he passed through the hall, merely shook his hand and remarked on the fineness of the weather; there was no sign of Mr Gresham's daughter, and Mr Gresham was alone in the drawing room. In fact, Captain McTurk had no such end in mind. His object in coming to Belgrave Square was merely to look about him, examine the world in which Mr Happerton moved, and try to establish what kind of man he was. Here he proved unexpectedly successful.

The questions which Captain McTurk had brought for Mr Gresham took a minute to ask and twice that time to answer, after which the talk lapsed into pleasantries. 'Heavens how these old men fall away,'

Captain McTurk said to himself as he helped Mr Gresham arrange himself upon his cushions and fill his tea cup.

'You're not very well, I believe?' he said. It was the same question he had asked Mr File, but put with considerably more grace.

'Well no, I suppose I'm not. Do you know, I never had a day's illness in my life before, and now I feel as if I could sleep the whole afternoon?'

'And yet you're well looked after, I hope?'

'Oh certainly. Why, I sometimes think I should have no visitors at all if it were left to my daughter, she is so solicitous of my health.'

Meanwhile, Captain McTurk was looking around him. There was not, in truth, a great deal to see, one gentleman's drawing room in Belgravia being much like another's, but he noticed the picture of Tiberius, which now hung above the mantelpiece, and one or two other horsey items, including a copy of *Post and Paddock* left open at a very flaring article about the Derby.

'I see your son-in-law is set to distinguish himself in the great race,' he said, meaning to be polite.

'Happerton? Yes, I suppose he is. I am afraid I hear very little about it,' said Mr Gresham, who very soon afterwards fell fast asleep. Another visitor would perhaps have pulled the bell-rope and taken his leave, but Captain McTurk seemed disposed to linger. He spent a moment or two examining the line of invitation cards upon the mantelpiece, in which Mr and Mrs G. Happerton were bidden to evening parties and operatic recitals and Lady Fantail's *fête champêtre* at Ponders End, looked at a bookcase in which Sir Walter Scott's novels, their pages mostly uncut, very much predominated, and then proceeded by degrees to a sideboard covered with small pieces of china and other ornaments. Here Captain McTurk stopped and stood on his heels. There on the sideboard lay a silver salver on which two or three letters, clearly intended for the late afternoon post, stood awaiting collection by a domestic. Captain McTurk stared at them without much interest, switched his gaze to a painting of some Yorkshire scenery (Fauntleroy, RA) and then, almost without comprehending the instinct that drew him back, found himself staring at one of the letters again. Something in the superscription nagged at him, but he could not for the life of him determine what it was. A snore from the armchair made him raise his head, but Mr Gresham slept on. Again he looked at the writing on the first envelope, which was unorthodox and irregular, but somehow distinctive and familiar. Where had he seen it before? Then, like a lightning bolt falling out of a clear sky, the answer occurred to him: on the scrap of paper found on the floor of the poulterer's cellar in Cornhill! There was a sound of movement beyond the doorway, rustling silks, a patter of footsteps, and in the split second left to him Captain McTurk picked up the letter and stuck it in the inner pocket of his coat. Then he turned on his heel, just as Mrs Happerton came into the room.

'You must excuse me,' Captain McTurk said – his hand was still in the pocket of his coat. 'But your father has fallen fast asleep. I was about to take my leave.'

'He is not very well,' Mrs Happerton said, with what might have passed for a smile. 'It is unfortunate that he had to be disturbed.'

'He seemed pleased to see me,' Captain McTurk said in mitigation.

'Papa is pleased to see anyone.'

If Captain McTurk remembered Mrs Rebecca, it was as a pale girl scarcely out of the schoolroom. Now, looking at her as she stood in the doorway, he was startled by the passage of the years. Her hair was sandier than ever and her green eyes blazed. He thought she was a fine-looking woman, but that Mr Happerton was welcome to her.

'You will give him my compliments, perhaps, when he wakes?'

'Oh certainly,' Mrs Happerton said, with what to Captain McTurk sounded complete indifference.

And Captain McTurk went back to Northumberland Street, steamed open the letter he had brought with him (which was a reply to a corn chandler's bill and of no interest whatever) and satisfied himself that the man who had written it, and the man who had written the letter found on the cellar floor in Cornhill, were the same person, and that this person was undoubtedly Mr Happerton.

*

Captain McTurk sat in his room looking out over the grey stone yard, where the same lugubrious ostler was shovelling up the same pile of dung, while Mr. Masterson lingered in the doorway.

'We cannot arrest a man because his handwriting looks like the writing found on a sheet of paper at the scene of a burglary. Do you imagine Happerton robbed Gallentin's shop?'

'I cannot think that he did it himself,' Mr Masterson said. 'But it is perfectly possible that he employed someone else.'

'And who was that, I wonder? Here we are racking our brains to find that man Pardew – there are half a dozen men wandering around Richmond as I speak – and yet he may be entirely innocent. Of this particular crime, I mean. You had better have Happerton watched. He will be down in Surrey, I dare say, before the race. Have someone see what he does. Do we know whom he associates with?'

'Racing people of course,' Mr Masterson said, who had already done his researches in this area. 'There is that new club in Thavies Inn – the Blue Riband. They call it a new club, but they began with the Megatherium's subscription list, I believe, and the dust hangs there just the same. I gather he is there pretty regularly with a Captain Raff.'

'I don't think I ever heard of Captain Raff.'

'I believe he sold out of the Rifles. It is all very discreditable. You remember that affair of ——?' And here Mr Masteron whispered a little failing or two of Captain Raff's, over which Captain McTurk half-humorously shook his head.

'Well, let us talk to Captain Raff in a friendly way. That, at any rate, can do no harm. Another specimen of Happerton's handwriting would be a great thing to have, but I don't suppose this Captain Raff carries them in his notecase. As for Pardew, you might let the papers know we have him in mind. We cannot drive him further from us than he is already, and it may prompt someone to recollect him. Have them put out his likeness, if you can.'

Mr Masterson went off to execute these commissions, leaving Captain McTurk seated in his chair. For all his caution with Mr Masterson he was quite convinced, first, that Mr Pardew had robbed Mr Gallentin's safe of its contents, and, second, that there was at any rate some connection between the robber and Mr Happerton. At the same time he could, as yet, see no way of proving this connection. The piece of paper found on the cellar floor had said nothing about Mr Gallentin's jewellery. Though the handwriting might be shown to be Mr Happerton's, it could not be proved that he had dropped it there, that it had been addressed to Mr Pardew, or that Mr Pardew had dropped it there himself. As so often, the evidence that Captain McTurk had before him was thoroughly suggestive, but inexact.

Mr Masterson's thoroughness, meanwhile, did him great credit. First he summoned an assistant, on whom he was accustomed to rely, and instructed him in the matter of Mr Happerton's surveillance. Then he called the secretary who sat in the booth beyond Captain McTurk's door and gave him the names of three or four newspaper editors who might be interested in a chronicle of Mr Pardew's life and accomplishments. Finally, having consulted one or two files and a scrapbook that lay in a neat pile of such items on his desk, he put on his hat and walked across St James's to Captain Raff's lodgings in Ryder Street. It was a fine, bright afternoon, and one or two of the artists were about in the corridors – a model dressed as Charlemagne was being helped out of a cab as he arrived – but there was no sign of Captain Raff, nor anyone to answer his knock upon the door. And thinking that Captain Raff's chambers looked very much as if no one lived in them, and that there were at least half a dozen messages written on villainous scraps of paper and stuffed under the foot of the door, Mr Masterston shook his head, gave one final, unanswered knock and went back the way he had come.

XXIV

Mount Street and beyond

*Who lives in Mount Street? Nobody knows. The directory may be full of the
most distinguished names, it is just that none of them is ever at home there.
It is, consequently, a shy place, full of maiden ladies in comfortable sequestration, noblemen's mansions looked after by housekeepers while the family
is away, and a quantity of young women whose business there can only be
guessed at . . .*

The London Gazetteer (1868)

'And am I to accompany you to Epsom?'

The room in which this question was asked was a neat little feminine chamber on the first floor of a house in Mount Street. The person
who asked it was a young woman of perhaps twenty-three or twenty-
four, fashionably dressed and with very white teeth. The person to
whom it was addressed, sitting on a little sofa with his hat in his hand
and a Pekinese dog sniffing round his ankles, was Mr Happerton. It
was about three o'clock on a May afternoon, and from the open window,
whose frame glowed picturesquely in the sunshine, came the sound of
carriages rolling through Mayfair to the park.

Did Mr Happerton look round the room with a faintly proprietorial
air? He certainly seemed at home there. It was one of those rooms that
one sees a great deal in the illustrated papers, and over which fashionable decorators swarm. There was fresh paint on the door and new paper
on the walls, and everything in it, the pair of lovebirds simpering in the
cage by the window and perhaps even the young woman herself, looked

as if it had been installed there only the other week. A bookcase by the far wall testified to somebody's fondness for novels got from Mudie's circulating library, and a round occasional table hard by confirmed that person's interest in knick-knacks and ornaments of all kind. An arbiter of domestic fashions would have pronounced it 'chaste', but this was not perhaps an adjective that could have been applied to the young woman asking Mr Happerton if he would take her to Epsom. Was there something foreign about her? It was difficult to tell, and perhaps Mr Happerton had not gone into it. She was wearing a dress of watered silk from which the neatest little white slippers stuck out beneath, had very black hair and was as striking as one of Mr Leighton's Attic portraits.

'Am I to come with you?' she asked again.

Mr Happerton gave a half-smile, picked up the Pekinese in one hand and tried to place it on his lap, but got snapped at for his pains. He was looking at the heap of trinkets on the table – tiny bejewelled brooches in the shape of butterflies, little ivory fans from the St James's arcade – and calculating how much he had paid for them. The smell coming in from the window was a horsey one, mingled with the scent of hay, and that reminded him of Tiberius and a dozen other things that pressed on his mind. Had he overreached himself? And was his presence here in the room in Mount Street, with the sound of the maidservant's foot-steps going down the stair and his feet sprawled out over a Turkey carpet that had come from Mr Delacroix's shop in Bond Street, a part of that overreaching? Mr Happerton thought not. He was master of himself, and he would come and go as he pleased. But still he did not care to answer the question that had just been put to him. Instead he picked up his tea cup and looked squarely back at the black hair, the red mouth and the white teeth.

'Am I?' the young woman asked a third time. She did not look aggrieved, so much as satirical, like the young woman in the play whose fiancé has just been disinherited by his uncle the wicked earl, or shanghaied into the navy.

'You can go to Epsom any day you like,' Mr Happerton said comfort-ably. 'I shall be going there tomorrow morning, as it happens.'

'You are very provoking,' the young woman said. She seemed slightly less satirical and more annoyed. 'You know very well what I mean.'

'Well, perhaps I do,' Mr Happerton said. He had known for a fortnight that this request would come, but had still not decided how to respond.

'Surely', the young woman went on, 'this is a day when anyone can accompany anyone anywhere without the least impropriety?'

Mr Happerton went on staring at the butterfly brooches and the ivory fans. He was not a fool about women, however much the tray of knick-knacks might have cost him, and he knew that to appear at Epsom racecourse on Derby Day with Rosa – that was the young woman's name – on his arm would involve all manner of subterfuges and deceits.

'Not the least impropriety,' he agreed. 'I suppose Lord John goes there with his scullerymaid. But if you're expecting to be taken to the Derby in a carriage and picnic on the hill and so forth, then it can't be done. I've a horse to attend to and a jockey to get to the course.'

'It doesn't seem,' Rosa said, rather archly, 'as if you wished me to come with you at all.'

'I should like nothing better. You know I should. But you see, I am not there to stroll upon the concourse and shake hands with people. I am there to do business.'

This was not strictly true. In fact, Mr Happerton intended to do a great deal of strolling and to shake hands with everyone he met.

'Well, it is a great shame,' Rosa said. 'Why, London will be all but empty, for the whole town flocks there.' There was a pause, and the lovebirds scuffled in their cage. 'I dare say I shall have to join Sir George Archer's party.'

'Sir George Archer!' Sir George was a sporting baronet, who was supposed to have lost two thousand pounds on the previous year's favourite.

'Kitty Davey said she was sure they could find a place in the carriage, and Sir George takes her advice on everything.'

'Sir George is . . .' Mr Happerton wondered exactly what Sir George was, and whether some of the baronet's habits differed greatly from his own, and rather lamely concluded, 'very dissolute.'

'Well, I think he is very nice,' Rosa said. 'And we are to put up at the Bell at Cheam, Kitty says, and have all kinds of fun.'

'I absolutely forbid you to go the Derby with Sir George Archer,' Mr Happerton said, who had no real power to effect this other than having paid for the clothes Rosa stood up in.

'Well, it is very hard on a young woman if she is to stay in London on a day when everyone else is enjoying themselves. Sir George has a thousand guineas staked on Pendragon, Kitty says.'

'He'll lose it then. Pendragon would not beat a donkey on Ramsgate sands.'

When he left Mount Street an hour later, Mr Happerton had agreed to a carriage to the Derby. Indeed, Sir George Archer's plans, if in fact they ever existed, were quite in disarray. He walked back to Belgrave Square across the park where three or four of the riders and the gentlemen sauntering by the rail nodded at him, but he returned only a faint wave of his hand, and people said that Happerton was pre-occupied by the race, and no wonder, as Tiberius' odds had fallen to six and were expected to fall further still.

*

In Richmond Mr Pardew saw the picture in the evening newspaper and frowned at it. He was not particularly put out by this representa-tion of himself – in fact he had expected something like it to happen – but still the sight of it unnerved him. For a moment he put the paper aside and dared not look at it. Then, telling himself not to be a fool, he picked it up once more and looked at it and the letterpress that ran beneath it with minute interest. It was not quite an accurate portrait – the set of his chin was exaggerated, and the eyes set too far back in the face – but still he knew that it was near enough like him to promote the idea of a resemblance to anyone who saw it. What was he to do? Richmond – its high street, its riverside walks, its verdant hill – had been distasteful to him since the day he had stumbled into his wife. Now he could not bear to set foot in it – at least not by daylight. He had taken to walking at night, with his hat pulled down over his eyes and his stick grasped firmly in his hand. Once a drunk man, reeling out of a culvert, had tried to take his arm, and Mr Pardew had nearly stove in his skull, such was the pit of fear into which he had plunged. After this episode he did no more walking, but sat around the house and sent Jemima out on errands that had formerly been his exclusive province. Policemen were a torture to him. If one walked past the gate he would hide behind his newspaper or, alternatively, stare belligerently from the window as if defying the man to arrest him. Jemima registered neither the nervousness nor the belligerence, but she did take note of the sequestration.

'I declare,' she said to him once at about this time, 'it is three days since you left the house.'

'Is it? I suppose I have got tired of walking about.'

'You should go and call upon Lord Margrave, seeing that he is always inviting you.'

It was on the tip of Mr Pardew's tongue to say that Lord Margrave did not exist, but he saw that this would be wounding not only to his own pride but also to Jemima's, so he merely shook his head and said that he thought his lordship was sailing off the Norwegian coast. That night they were very comfortable, and had a late supper by the fire, and Mr Pardew did not start up when two men in tall hats went past the house and looked as if they were peering into its garden, but stared out benignly into the evening air. But all the time he was calculating: the amount of money he had at his command; discreet parts of the world that might receive him without enquiring into his history; Jemima, and what he might say to her. That night it rained hard and she complained at the winds that buffeted the house, and Mr Pardew thought that there were other storms brewing up which it would be prudent for him to evade. And on the next day, he went up to London and presented himself once again at the house in Belgrave Square. There was a difficulty with the butler, who perhaps had had orders not to admit Mr Pardew, but in the end he prevailed. 'It is about the horse,' he explained, in his civillest manner, which was after all true, if only obliquely, and after a moment or two was shown into the study. Mr Happerton, looking up from the desk as he came into the room, shook his head and sprang to his feet.

'You cannot come here,' he said. 'It is quite out of the question. I shall have you turned out.'

'Who by, I wonder?' Mr Pardew said. 'The policeman in the square? Try calling him, and see what he says.'

'What do you want?'

Mr Pardew stopped to consider this. What did he want? He was tired of Boulogne, Dresden, Prague, Pau – all the places he had been in Europe, and the other Englishmen who gathered there, nearly all of whom had a tale to tell that was the equal of his own – he might even be tired of Jemima. The stick he had brought with him twitched in his hand.

'Since you ask,' he said, 'I should like five hundred pounds.'

'You shan't have a penny. You have had – what is it – nearly twelve hundred already.'

Mr Pardew felt old and tired. Looking at Mr Happerton, whose face spoke of comparative youth, unalloyed prosperity, and the freedom to stay in bed until whatever hour he chose, he felt a pang of envy. The stick twitched in his hand again.

'There are pictures of me printed in the newspaper,' he said. 'Very bad pictures, but pictures nonetheless.'

'I have seen them,' Mr Happerton said. He was watching the stick with a fascinated expression. 'A very bad likeness, I should say. Hadn't you better take yourself off to a place where such things can't find you?'

Mr Pardew stared at him. He knew he was playing a dangerous game, and that it would be very difficult to betray Mr Happerton without betraying himself, but he had played many dangerous games in the past and usually emerged triumphant from them. He thought, too – and he was correct in this – that Mr Happerton who was anxiously awaiting the result of a great horse race that might make his fortune or lose it, was a better prospect than a Mr Happerton who knew how it had turned out.

'I shall be candid with you,' he said. 'I am leaving England. There are good reasons why I shouldn't stay – not all of them to do with our little piece of business. Five hundred will see me gone and settled.'

'What guarantee do I have that I shan't see you again? You might come and plague me for the rest of my life.'

'You will just have to take my word for it. I never betrayed a man yet, you know. Raff can tell you that, if you ask him.'

'I can ask Raff nothing. He has entirely disappeared. Have you heard of him?'

'Not a word. He keeps peculiar company, I think. Perhaps it became too peculiar even for him.' And here Mr Pardew gave a look that was almost frightful in what it insinuated. 'But Raff is neither here nor there. Five hundred pounds, and you will never hear of me again. Come, you shall have the name of the ship I sail on and the passenger list if it suits you. And then the pictures in the newspaper will be forgotten too.'

'I won't have you threaten me,' Mr Happerton said, but not, Mr Pardew thought, with any great force.

'No one is being threatened,' Mr Pardew said, very civilly. 'If you imagine you are being forced to act against your will, then you had better do something to prevent it. What will you do? Send Captain Raff – if you can find him – to cut off my head? I don't think Captain Raff could do it. In fact, I fancy Captain Raff might find his own head cut off instead. And the same goes for all those other Captain Raffs.'

There was a silence, and Mr Happerton shot him a look of absolute fury, but Mr Pardew thought he knew his man.

'You will have to take it in bills,' he said. 'There is no money in the house. Really – there is not. Two hundred and fifty now, and the rest in a day or so. Zangwill shall take them. He has enough of my paper.'

Mr Pardew said that he should be delighted to do business with Mr Zangwill, knowing that gentleman of old, and the two bills were written, stamped and signed. One of them Mr Pardew stuffed into the inner pocket of his coat. The other Mr Happerton was about to place in his desk drawer, but Mr Pardew shook his head.

'No,' he said. 'If I take a second bill to Zangwill it will be all I can do to raise two hundred. You can send me the rest in cash. After the race.'

Mr Happerton gave a queer kind of half-smile. 'You seem very certain of my success.'

'I don't say that you will win. I said only that you will be successful.' There was a sheet of blank notepaper on Mr Happerton's desk, and he picked it up and scribbled something on it. 'Here is the address.'

'There are people in London who would give a great deal of money for this,' Mr Happerton said.

'And for things which I could tell them,' Mr Pardew said. 'But shall not.'

XXV

Inside Information

It has frequently been remarked how in the days before the Derby race, London society is altogether broken up and dispersed. Gentlemen are no longer at their places of business, but at Epsom; ladies disappear on errands; great houses are given over to cats and caretakers; and servants are everywhere triumphant.

A History of the Derby (1867)

It was a Sunday evening in Belgrave Square, a week before the great race, and exceedingly quiet. On the further side, towards Victoria, a carriage was delivering guests to an evening party, and a faint – a very faint – sound of music could be heard drifting on the early summer air. In a house on the eastern corner somebody lay dying, and there was packed straw down in the street and a muffler hung over the door-knob, but these precautions were quite superfluous: it was exceedingly quiet. Northwards in the direction of the park the light was bleeding out of the sky in crimson and purple flourishes in a way that Mr Turner might have painted, but there was no Mr Turner to see it, no one at all, except a pair of elderly ladies with umbrellas over their arms – for May can be so very inclement, you know – and Watts's hymnals in their hands walking to evening service, and a policeman benevolently surveying them as they passed.

In Mr Gresham's mansion, upon whose upper windows the light darted and flashed like knives, something of a holiday spirit prevailed.

Mr Happerton had gone down to Epsom two days before and not been seen since. Old Mr Gresham still shuffled about the house, drank his tea in the drawing room and asked after his newspapers, but as the servants remarked to each other, lor' bless you, *he* was no trouble. The great dining room was shut up and the chandelier extinguished under brown paper, pending refurbishment. The butler and the old house-keeper were recruiting themselves at Margate, and in their absence Nokes, Mrs Happerton's maid, reigned supreme. Mr Happerton's letters – a great many of them – were piled up on a silver salver awaiting his return. Mr Gresham's newspaper was taken away and ironed the moment it came through the door. There were other accomplishments which perhaps only Mrs Happerton noticed. Miss Nokes's distinguishing mark, it may be said, was her unobtrusiveness. She came in and out of a room with a step so soft that people wondered how a woman weighing eight stone and standing five feet two inches could move so silently. She hovered in hallways with an almost frightening assiduity. No bell rang without her hearing it; if you walked up a staircase you would see her coming down it, and vice versa – Mrs Happerton found her very useful.

At present her usefulness to Mrs Happerton was merely vicarious, for Mrs Happerton, too, was away from home. Robbed of its human traffic, the house assumed an aquamarine air: the deep banks of shadow welled up in the hallway like water, and the shafts of sunlight that issued in from the high windows were lost in it and subdued, so that Nokes might have been a fish moving quietly on its placid current, or perhaps only some siren of the seabed, gone off to her silent cavern where the bodies of drowned mariners repose, to gnaw a bone or two. In fact, just at this moment Nokes was not quite alone. She was sitting in the basement kitchen, with a teapot steaming on the table before her and the half of a Dundee cake on a pewter plate, opposite a tall, dark-haired gentleman in a tremendous waistcoat and a billycock hat, which he preferred for some reason to keep on indoors, and exchanging what is known as 'chaff'.

'Nice little crib,' the gentleman now said, casting his eye around the table, its profusion of pans, ironmongery and stacked china, and rattling his tea cup in its saucer. 'Very.'

'Get on with you,' Nokes retorted. She was not quite easy in her manner, and glanced occasionally at the little cluster of bells that hung over the doorway.

'Nothing like a house that's shut up,' the gentleman continued, 'with the fambly away, the skivvy to gammon about, and no one to answer to except yourself.'

'There's an old gentleman lying asleep up two pair of stairs.'

'And can ring his bell if he wakes up, and very likely be attended to, I shouldn't wonder.'

'Sauce,' Miss Nokes said. She was about thirty, with a severe expression somewhat softened by these juvenile flourishes. There was a silence, during which each looked surreptitiously at the other. 'I dare say you'd sooner be at the Bag o' Nails along with the other chaps.'

'I can't say that I should. Too much talk about horses, you know, which is all very well if you're a betting man. But I'm not, you see. Feminine society, that's what I prefer. Who's the old gentleman that's asleep upstairs?'

'Mr Gresham, his name is, and that's his tea you're drinking.'

'Well, fair play to the old gentleman. Thought you said your mistress was called Happerton?'

'So she is. Mrs Happerton is his daughter – lives here with her husband while the old gent's ill.'

'Ill is he? What's the matter with him?'

But Miss Nokes was not interested in the infirmities of her employer's father. Instead she produced an illustrated magazine and drew her friend's attention to the female costumes depicted within, unpicked a brooch from the front of her dress and invited him to inspect it, and, as these manoeuvrings went on, relaxed the severity of her expression a little.

'That Happerton's a racing man, isn't he?' her friend enquired.

'Owns Tiberius,' Miss Nokes conceded. 'That he's brung down from Lincolnshire.'

'Think he'll win?'

'Thought you said you weren't a betting man.'

'I'm not. But there are fellows who'd like to know.'

'The less they know about it the better' – this very pink-faced.

All this went on for nearly half an hour, as the bells ringing the faithful to evening service sounded across the square and the shadows rose higher into the stairwells, and the kitchenmaid pursued an errand in the attics, and was very pleasant, but that by the end of it Miss Nokes looked less like a fish and more like an angler. Then, unexpectedly, a bell jangled loudly in its bracket, and Miss Nokes started up guiltily from her comfortable chair.

'That'll be the old gentleman wanting his tea.'

'Old gentlemen don't mind being kept waiting, I dare say.'

But Miss Nokes was determined to do her duty. Pouring some water from a kettle that stood on the range into a teapot and arranging pot, cup, saucer and milk-jug on a tray, she set off up the kitchen stairs. Her friend, whose name was Allardice – though this was not the name Miss Nokes knew him by – smiled to himself, took another piece of Dundee cake and crumbled it between his fingers. Presently, this occupation having failed him, and with his billycock hat jammed down over his forehead, he too set off up the stairs and presently emerged into the great hall of the house. It was quite empty, and having assured himself that Miss Nokes was attending to Mr Gresham, he began on a tour of the lower rooms.

It was remarkable what interested him. He took no notice of the pictures on the walls of the drawing room, or the half-empty decanter that Miss Nokes had omitted to return to its tray, but he spent several minutes turning over Mr Happerton's letters in their tray, and a little blue notebook propped up at the end of a bookshelf went into his pocket. All the while Mr Allardice kept his ear cocked for descending footsteps. He had just wandered into the hall to examine a pile of horsey appurtenances that were lying in a heap by the grandfather clock when there came the noise of a cab pulling up at the door, and a sharp-faced but undeniably pretty woman could be seen stepping down from it onto the pavement.

Mr Allardice turned on his heel and went rapidly back into the drawing room, where he took the precaution of hiding himself behind one of the drawn-back velvet curtains. A bell jangled again, nearer at hand. Realising that his idyll with Nokes had come to an end, along with his chance to inspect Mr Happerton's letters, a part of Mr Allardice was all for disappearing down the kitchen staircase and up the area steps as soon as was convenient. Another part, however, told him not to be hasty, and instead he kept his place behind the curtain, and his eye trained on the door. For perhaps five minutes silence prevailed. Then came a noise of footsteps in rapid transit; two voices, one high to the point of stridency, the other meekly subdued, in conversation; and another set of footsteps drawing nearer by the second. The door of the drawing room was thrown open and Mrs Happerton strode over the threshold.

Plainly there was some urgency in Mrs Happerton's sortie to the drawing room, for she was still wearing her bonnet. Advancing into the centre of the room, she saw the decanter on the table – as redolent of mischief to a vigilant householder as a broken window-catch – and sniffed at it. But it did not seem to Mr Allardice that she was much interested in the thought that her maid had been recruiting herself with spirituous liquor, and that her air of preoccupation had quite another source. There was a little earthenware mug in her hand, steam rising from its lip, which she now set down upon the sideboard. Mrs Happerton now reached into one of the sideboard's compartments and brought out a jar of brownish powder in which Mr Allardyce thought that he detected cinnamon or possibly arrowroot. 'Nightcap for the old gentleman, then,' Mr Allardice thought, watching Mrs Happerton stir the powder into the milk.

And then Mrs Happerton did what, to Mr Allardice, jammed into his hiding place behind the curtain with the back of his head squashed up against the window pane, seemed a peculiar thing. Going across to a neat little desk by the bookcase, she took a key from the bunch that hung from the wall to one side of it, unlocked one of the desk's several drawers and, looking very cautiously to right and left of her, produced a little green sack, whose fastening she now opened, and a pinch of whose contents she now sprinkled over the contents of the mug. She then rapidly shut up the desk, put the key back on its ring and, carrying the mug very carefully before her (just as if it was a candlestick, Mr Allardice thought to himself) went back out of the drawing-room door. He heard her feet moving up the staircase, and then they pattered away into nothing.

Mr Allardice came out of his hiding place and looked around the empty drawing room. In replacing the key that opened the desk drawer, Mrs Happerton had – very unhelpfully, he thought – stood directly in his line of vision, but he was an experienced man with keys and a moment or two's experiment had the drawer open and the sack in his hand. The grey and faintly sandy powder inside intrigued him. He rolled a speck or two on his finger and sniffed it cautiously. He weighed the sack in his hands and, finally, took an empty matchbox from his pocket and shook a little of the powder into it. A bell was jangling somewhere in the middle distance, but there was no sign of Miss Nokes. 'No one at home,' he said out loud. The kitchen, to which he returned a moment or two later, was quite empty. There was still some tea in the pot and he drained off half a cup of it and crammed another slice of Dundee cake into his mouth as he went. 'Bella Nokes,' he said to himself, with what might have been a faint rustle of amusement. And then he was gone up the area steps, into the square and out among the people coming back from evening service, nodding at a policeman who stood motionless on the street corner as the crowds swarmed around him and seemed in some quaint and mysterious way to acknowledge him. And Miss Nokes, returning finally to the kitchen, found only the empty tea cups and the last fragment of Dundee cake on its salver and the unfastened door swinging gently in the breeze.

*

'Well, we have half a dozen samples of that man's handwriting in a notebook, at any rate,' Captain McTurk remarked to Mr Masterson.

'Thank Allardice for that.' They were sitting in the office high over the ostlers' yard examining the items brought back from Belgrave Square.

'He has not compromised himself, I hope,' Mr Masterson wondered. 'No banns being read, or anything of that sort?'

There had been an occasion when Mr Allardice's professional zeal had very nearly resulted in a breach-of-promise suit.

Captain McTurk smiled. 'There is no doubt about it,' he said. 'Happerton is the man who wrote the fragment of the letter which was found on the cellar floor. Look here – see how he curls his "a"s. It is quite distinctive.'

'I dare say it is,' said Mr Masterson, who was of all things a realist. 'And yet it might have got there quite innocently you know.'

'A scrap of a letter found in a basement next to a jeweller's strong-room the morning after he is discovered to be burgled! How so?'

'It could have got there in a dozen ways, and have nothing to do with whoever committed the burglary – a man whose identity we don't yet know.'

'I think that I know it.'

'Your opinion is one to which I habitually defer' – Mr Masterson was courtesy itself on these occasions. 'But at any rate there is nothing that connects Happerton to the man Pardew. All we know is that Pardew was last seen at Richmond. That is all.'

'I wish we could find that Captain Raff.'

'Vanished off the face of the earth,' Mr Masterson said, 'and neither his landlord nor his laundress any the wiser.'

'It may be that he is down at Epsom.'

'It may very well be. But no one has seen him there.'

Captain McTurk shrugged his shoulders in a way that suggested Captain Raff did him the gravest discourtesy by not keeping him constantly informed of his whereabouts.

'There is something else, though, that Allardice brought back. What do you make of this?'

Mr Masterson inspected the little box of grey powder while the story of its finding was explained to him.

'I should say,' Captain McTurk elaborated, 'that my old friend Mr Gresham has been taking it with his nightcap.'

'It may well be medicinal.'

'Allardice said it came out of a sack locked in a drawer, and that Mrs Happerton herself mixed it into the milk.'

'Why should a woman not prepare her father's hot milk?'

'Why not indeed? But all the same I should like to conduct a little test. You might tell Hopkins to come in here.'

Hopkins was the secretary who sat in the closet next to Captain McTurk's office. While Masterson was fetching him, Captain McTurk picked up the cup that had held his morning coffee, found that the dregs were still warm and, placing a little of the powder on the end of a spoon, sprinkled it over their surface.

'Now Hopkins,' he began as the secretary came into the room. 'I take it you have no objection to helping us try a little experiment?'

'None in the least,' said Mr Hopkins, who was an amiable young man.

'Well, just drink up this coffee will you? It shan't do you any harm.'

If Mr Hopkins had imagined that he was to be let in on some great secret he was gravely disappointed, for no sooner had the coffee been drunk up than the cup was taken from his hand and he was sent back along the corridor to resume the work on which he had been engaged.

'Ten to one it is nothing,' Mr Masterson said.

'Not such a bad price. Why, you may get that almost on Happerton's horse, which was such a certainty a fortnight ago.'

'I did hear,' Mr Masterson said, 'that a great deal of money has been placed on Baldino and another horse – Septuagint, I think it is.'

'I wonder who placed it?' Captain McTurk remarked. 'What else do we know about Happerton? About him personally, I mean?'

'Oh, he is a regular sporting gentleman. Rather a swell, you know. An agreeable man, everybody says.'

Captain McTurk considered the question of Mr Happerton's agreeability for a moment and then strode rapidly into the doorway of his office and jerked his head along the corridor. 'Well,' he said, coming back into the room and clasping his arms triumphantly over his chest, 'I should say that ten to one was good odds after all.'

For Mr Hopkins, although grasping a pen in his right hand, and with his left extended to retrieve a sheet of foolscap, had fallen asleep at his desk.

*

Two evenings later Miss Nokes, in her best pinafore and cap, stepped out to the Bag o' Nails in West Halkin Street in the confident hope of finding Mr Allardice smoking his pipe on the oak settle before the fire-place, but found him absent. Nor, to her great disgust, did he ever come again.

*

For a week now Tiberius had been at Mr Mountstuart's establishment in Cheam. The stables were in some sense semi-public, and gentlemen who came there in the hope of seeing the horses were not very often turned away, and the grooms who permitted these inspections had something of the vanity of the artist's model. Mr Happerton, who had installed himself at an inn a hundred yards from the stable door, was in two minds about these visitations. He liked people praising his horse because it reflected well on his judgement in buying it, but in these circum-stances – with half a dozen men gathered round Tiberius' stall to discuss his points – the thought that he wanted the horse to lose was a torture to him. At this stage odds of seven or eight to one could still be procured – Baldino and Septuagint were at three and four – and there were times when Mr Happerton's mind harboured wild schemes of raising another three or four thousand pounds and staking it on his own horse.

A moment's thought was enough to convince him that his affairs were too far gone for this to be practicable, but still the idea that his pride and joy, the animal whose picture he had carried with him on his wedding tour and clutched under his arm like a talisman as he burst into Mrs Venables' drawing room, might not win the great race was simple torment, however great the promised reward. He had totted up his likely earnings, should Baldino or Septuagint take the garland, and they stood between fifteen and twenty thousand pounds. What would happen if neither of the horses succeeded, he did not quite like to think about, but he was confident that they would not fail him. He had watched Tiberius very carefully in the practice runs he had taken and assured himself that his original diagnosis was correct, that the horse lacked stamina, and there was additionally a weakness (Mr Happerton was sure that only he had noticed this) in his left hindquarter. And this was to ignore the further impediment of having Major Hubbins to ride him.

But there were other phantoms disturbing Mr Happerton's sweet repose, beyond professional jealousy. First there was Captain Raff, whose disappearance continued to puzzle him. For the Captain's vanishing had been so mysterious. No letter had been sent, and no meeting called for. Mr Happerton had been to the chambers in Ryder Street – missing Mr Masterson by half an hour, although he did not know it – but found the door shut up and a sheaf of tradesmen's bills twisted around the knocker. None of Captain Raff's artist neighbours knew where he was, and he was discovered to owe the old woman who looked after his linen thirty shillings. More annoying, perhaps, than the circumstances of this disappearance was Mr Happerton's gradual awareness that Captain Raff had really been very useful to him. He had run messages. He had interviewed that class of person with whom, in the general way of things, Mr Happerton was not prepared to deal. He had tolerated, or suffered, Mr Happerton's slights and aspersions. In Raff's absence this role had to be filled by Mr Mountstuart, and Mr Happerton found that neither he not Mr Mountstuart liked it, for Mr Mountstuart was not a Captain Raff.

He was a big, stout man of forty who had once, it was said, knocked a groom senseless for answering back to him, and he would sooner have submitted to some of the indignities forced on Captain Raff than Mr Bradlaugh consent to be appointed chair of an evangelical mission to the South Seas. And so it was Mr Mountstuart who negotiated with stewards, who led deputations to Mr Dorling, the celebrated clerk of the course, and flattered him, and paid bribes to gatekeepers, and the doing of it irked him – not because he was ashamed, but because he thought it constituted a reversal in his life, like a Cinderella married to her prince, who discovers on the very next morning that she is expected to come downstairs and lay the fire. Mr Mountstuart did not, Mr Happerton assured himself, know very much about horses. Still he knew enough, Mr Happerton also assured himself, to be faintly suspicious of Mr Happerton's motives.

'I think you have made a mistake with that Major Hubbins,' he said one morning when they were making certain arrangements in respect of Tiberius' transportation to the Downs on the morning of the race.

'I never knew a better man in the saddle,' Mr Happerton protested, conscious, as he did so, of the want of civility in his voice.

'Well, that's as may be, Happerton, but I tell you, if he falls off that animal he'll not get back onto him again.'

This seemed to Mr Happerton so indisputably true that he merely frowned, and began instead to talk of some enticing mash that he wished to be prepared for Tiberius on the evening before the race day. There was, he knew, no logic in his annoyance. He wanted his horse to lose, but the realisation that lose he might continually depressed his spirits. He knew that the prospect of his horse losing depended on his being ridden badly, but whenever anyone suggested that he might be ridden badly he grew angrier still.

And then, to add to the problems caused by Captain Raff's disappearance, there was the question of Major Hubbins. Like Mr Happerton, and like Tiberius, and like half a hundred people connected with the race, Major Hubbins was now installed at Cheam. He, too, was staying in an inn, a sporting inn, where the landlord, knowing who he was, made much of him. In fact, Major Hubbins was very comfortable. He had hot water for his feet, which were delicate, and embrocation for his knee, and his glass of negus, and Mr Happerton to call upon him – yet none of this was satisfactory to Mr Happerton. On the one hand

Major Hubbins, who had ridden horses for the old king, and had once been complimented on his ability by the Duke of Wellington, could not be patronised. Mr Happerton had tried this once, got a little rebuff for his pains, and not liked it. On the other hand there was a lack of world-liness about him that Mr Happerton thought that he could not quite believe in. He could not, it went without saying, tell Major Hubbins that he wanted him to lose the race; but he assumed that Major Hubbins must have some faint inkling of his plans. In fact, the merest conversation with the Major assured him that he did not.

'So, how do you think we stand, Major?' he had enquired one morning a week before the race as he stood in the Major's room at the Brood Mare. Major Hubbins was very comfortable. He was looking at a selection of sporting prints, sent to him gratis by a print-seller in High Holborn, and deciding which ones he would like, and a bowl of broth, brought up by the landlady, was steaming at his elbow.

'I think we shall do very well,' Major Hubbins said. 'He pulls a little, you know, and is flustered, perhaps, when there is anyone near him, but really I don't know when I rode a nicer horse. By the by, you might tell Maitland' – Maitland was Mr Mountstuart's groom – 'that his withers need looking at. He was pretty ragged when I took him out yesterday morning.'

'And you are well, I take it?' Mr Happerton wondered, thinking that Captain Raff would have known about the withers. Major Hubbins said he was very well and went on drinking his broth.

But there was another thing about Major Hubbins, set next to which his refusal to be patronised and his apparent lack of worldliness faded into nothing. Watching him put Tiberius though his paces, seeing him approach the horse in the stable yard, Mr Happerton feared that he had made a mistake. There was no denying Major Hubbins' advanced age, or his troublesome knee, or the various other ailments that vexed him, but there was a thoroughness about him that belied his years. One morning out on the Downs, unprompted, the Major had decided, as he put it, 'to give Tiberius his head', and Mr Happerton, as he watched the horse thunder across the bright turf, thought that he would not have cared to do such a thing himself. Dick Tomkins, of whom great things were predicted, was to ride Septuagint, but Mr Happerton suspected that even Dick Tomkins would not have handled the horse a great deal better. Again, wild schemes flitted through his head – he would find some pretext for dismissing Major Hubbins, he would find someone else to ride Tiberius – but he knew that the time for this substitution had passed, and so he stayed silent.

And then again, and in some sense dwarfing all the anxieties of short odds, horses and their riders, there was the problem of Mr Pardew. Mr Happerton had seen the picture of Mr Pardew in the newspapers and been frightened by it. Again, this was an area in which Captain Raff could have helped him. Captain Raff would have advised, sent emissaries and conducted interviews. But now there was no Captain Raff, only Mr Pardew and his stick, infesting his study and demanding bills at three months. There were times when Mr Happerton looked at the matter of Mr Pardew dispassionately. He told himself that there was nothing to connect him with the burglary at Mr Gallentin's shop, and that there was nothing Mr Pardew could gain from betraying him, as the betrayal would also involve himself. He told himself, too, that he had believed Mr Pardew when the latter had sworn that he intended to leave the country. But a small part of him worried that Mr Pardew might not leave the country as he had promised, or that he might do so but then come back, and that any material rewards that accrued to Mr Happerton might be compromised by Mr Pardew's finding out about their existence.

It was an odd kind of life that Mr Happerton led, here in Cheam in the two or three days before the Derby, with its crowds of miscellaneous men – sporting hangers-on, wine-sodden old bucks in green jackets and gaiters – stepping up to his table to confide things heard at the stable door, and the latest sporting intelligence being put into his hand, and Mr Mountstuart coming in to say first that the weather was presumed to be bad and second that it was alleged to be good, and all the time these anxieties about Captain Raff and Tiberius and Major Hubbins and Mr Pardew preying on his mind.

It was to the inn that there came, only three days before the race was to be run, by train from Victoria and then stepping up along the crowded pavements of the high street, the final source of Mr Happerton's anxiety. This was his wife. Mr Happerton had not been much at home of late, for the entering of a horse in the Derby requires a great deal of incidental administration, but he had by no means neglected his responsibilities in this department. A basket of little delicacies had been sent back to Belgrave Square, and a note or two, and a nosegay of flowers from a hothouse nearby, and Mr Happerton thought that he had done his duty. There had been some slight question of Mrs Rebecca herself lodging at the inn, but this had been quickly dismissed. Gentlemen did not generally have their wives by them on these occasions, Mr Happerton explained, and besides it would hardly do to leave old Mr Gresham. To these arguments Mrs Rebecca had assented, but now here she was – not quite unexpectedly, for there had been a note sent up the previous evening – laying down her parasol on the table in Mr Happerton's apartment alongside the copies of *Post and Paddock* and other fragments of sporting intelligence, casting her eye around the room – which was not, in truth, very genteelly furnished – with that sphinx-like expression on her face which had so perplexed Mr Happerton when she wore it on her wedding tour and caused him to think that he could not make her out.

What did Mrs Rebecca think as she stood in her husband's lodgings, looking at the sporting magazines, Mr Happerton's razors laid out on the dressing table – there was a little touch of blood on one of them that had not been wiped away – and a flamboyant frock-coat, hung up on a hook, that had sent the landlord of the inn into raptures but which frankly disgusted her? There were ways, she thought, in which that recent political marvel the Rebecca Party was coming into its own and threatened to carry all before it, but there were also ways in which its triumphs seemed to her hollow and not worth the having. She thought that in the business of the race, and her father and her father's money, she had behaved well – very well – and that her connivance at the schemes Mr Happerton had been forced to explain to her did her the greatest credit.

But she had an idea that there were other schemes afoot which he had not explained, and this annoyed her. She was conscious, too, that, in the course of her married life, her husband had underestimated her, not given her credit for the things of which she was capable. What he would make of the very significant thing she now proposed to bring to him from her conversation with Mr Dennison she could not quite anticipate, and this annoyed her even more.

There was a part of him that almost feared her, she realised, and this, while gratifying to her sense of power, offended her feelings about how men ought to stand in relation to the women they had married. The moment when he had explained his plans for Tiberius had been a revelation to her, for she saw that he had expected to be rebuked, and that her silent approval had contradicted certain assumptions that he had made about her. And, although she was thoroughly in favour of the money that might be made from Tiberius's defeat, a part of her wished for the reflected glory of his triumph. Which was the better, she wondered. To be the wife of the man who had publicly won a small fortune from the Derby, or the wife of a man who had silently acquired a much larger fortune by not winning it? This confusion further annoyed Mrs Rebecca, and explained the tone she brought to her conversation.

'How is your father?' Mr Happerton asked, when she had offered up her cheek for him to salute.

'He is very tired.' Rebecca did not want to talk about her father. 'He has slept most of the time this last day or two.'

'I expect he finds the warm weather troublesome.'

'Papa never minds about the weather. He is just tired.'

There was a coolness about this that puzzled him. He had never established Mrs Rebecca's real opinion of her father, and there was something in the way she talked about the old man that discouraged him from making the attempt. Having seated herself in an armchair, and drunk half a glass of iced soda-water which the landlord's wife had brought up on a tray, and looked round the room again with a gaze that seemed horribly penetrating, she said:

'I suppose everything is in order?'

'Certainly,' said Mr Happerton, half jocularly. He did not know whether to make a joke out of it or not. 'As in order as it is in my power to arrange.'

'And Septuagint or that other horse will win?'

For all that the greater part of him wanted this to happen, he wished that she would not say these things.

'There is no guarantee of anything in horse racing, I daresay, but – yes, it seems likely.'

'In the train coming up there was a man who said that he had wagered five guineas on Tiberius. It was on the edge of my tongue to tell him he was a fool and had wasted his money.'

He did not know what to make of this. He had an idea that she was reproaching him, but her face as she said the words was quite expressionless.

'People who wager money on horses are taking a chance. It is the nature of the thing.'

She considered this for a moment, and then nodded her head. A wisp of sandy hair had fallen from her chignon onto her shoulder, and reaching for it with her hand she twisted it into the corner of her mouth.

'Am I to accompany you to the race?'

Mr Happerton gave a start. They were almost the same words that Rosa had used in Mount Street.

'Well ... On the whole, I think not. You see, it is not very genteel. I saw Lady Burnett the other day and she said she would not think of letting her girls go. It is such a scrum on the hill, and sometimes the carriages cannot even get through.'

'If that is what you say, then I had better go by it. But I should have liked to see Tiberius. When we were to be married, you said that he was to wear my colours.'

He wondered if she was teasing him. She did not look as if she was. 'Surely you would not wish to see Tiberius lose?' He knew he ought not to have said this, but there it was.

'I should like to see you get the thing which you desire.'

There was an odd, humble look about her face as she said this that startled him – almost as much as the question about the race. He wondered why on earth he had made that promise in Mount Street and whether, even now, Rosa could not be thrown over. He saw, or he believed that he saw, that she genuinely wished him to succeed in his plans for the race, and the realisation was somehow exhilarating to him, but also rather shocking. He had an idea that women – the women who walked through those high, elegant mansions of his imagining – did not behave like this. A part of him luxuriated in the thought that she wanted him to win the thing he coveted, but another part of him wished she were at home in Belgrave Square fetching old Mr Gresham his milk-and-arrowroot and knowing nothing about it. Not quite knowing what he was doing, he took her hand and pressed it against the lapels of his coat.

'Tell me again,' she said. 'If Septuagint should win, or – or that other horse, how much money will there be?'

'It is difficult to say exactly. But perhaps sixteen or seventeen thousand.'

'And what shall you do with it?'

He thought that he had never seen her like this. 'I shall see that it is there first.'

Another strand or two of hair had come loose from her chignon, and she twisted them between her fingers.

'If you wished . . . If you wanted to become a parliamentary man, I am sure Papa would help.'

'A parliamentary man! What end would that serve?'

'It is something gentlemen generally wish to do. It is something I would wish you to do.'

'And how might I go about it, I wonder?' He was smiling as he said this, until he saw the look on her face, after which he ceased to smile.

'There is to a by-election in the Chelsea Districts. They say a Conservative could win it if it were managed correctly. I have spoken to Mr Dennison, who arranges these things.'

Again, he was quite astonished. He stared at her again, and was struck once more by the look in her eye. It was calculating – that he could see – but the calculation, surely, was on his behalf. He fancied – something he had never previously thought – that he could do anything with her, propose any scheme and have her meekly acquiesce. The sixteen or seventeen thousand pounds was indisputably his. It was as if he saw the money in bright golden shoals laid out before him. And now she wanted him to be a parliament man and had even gone so far as to intervene on his behalf. He did not know if he was angry or flattered by the interference, but something in the scheme appealed to him. He was an ambitious man, who had previously confined his ambitions to making money and owning horses, but there was no reason, he thought, why they should not be carried through into a grander sphere. The house in Grosvenor Square where in his wilder moments he had liked to imagine himself grew more tangible. He could see himself in its orangery, with the bright fruit growing next to his shoulder, and Mrs Rebecca pouring tea at his side.

'D——it, Rebecca,' he said, again half-smiling. 'Do you mean to say that you have arranged a constituency for me, and all I have to is present myself at Chelsea Town Hall to shake hands with my electors? And all this without enquiring if it suits?'

In fact, he was charmed by the idea. He reached out his hand and let it fall on her neck, and she looked back at him and gave a bold little twitch of her sandy hair. He remembered the day he had come upon her in Mrs Venables' drawing room with the portrait of Tiberius in his hand and itched to return there, and he wished they were in a little cottage in Hampshire with a bright stream running through the meadows beyond and no Mr Mountstuart or Mr Hubbins to torment him.

'You are a dear good girl,' he said, absolutely meaning it, and stroking her face with his hand. She did not resist. He felt her skin twitch under his fingers, and thought of the cream-coloured walls of their Venetian apartment and the nymphs in Mr Etty's paintings. 'But I can't think of these things now, do you see? Let it wait until after the race, and then we shall see how we are situated. Do you understand me?'

'Have I done wrong by speaking to Mr Dennison?'

'Done wrong? No, I don't think so. Of course a fellow likes to know what is being arranged for him. You ain't promised him any money, Rebecca?'

His wife shook her head.

Not very much more was said, and presently Mrs Rebecca took her leave, having extracted from her husband a promise that he would telegraph the result of the race directly it was known. Mr Happerton watched her go from the window of his room, a small, intent figure moving by degrees into the crowd, privately resolving that whatever the result of the race, and however much money fell into his hand, and whether or not he became the member for the Chelsea Districts, he would never set foot in Mount Street again.

*

In the week before the great race Cheam was very full of people: grooms on bang-up ponies taking messages from stable to stable; horsey-looking gentlemen promenading along the high street with their canes; ladies of no particular reputation being driven in hired barouches. If the tradesmen of Cheam did not especially care for this tumult of visitors, then they were at least prepared to make money out of them. The town's shops and hostelries had gone Derby mad: there were favours on sale in the haberdashers' shops; the stationer's by the omnibus halt had come out in a rash of sporting prints and calendars; and the restaurant rooms next to the station were offering Derby cake alongside their usual confectionery. Everything, in fact, seemed temporarily to have increased in volume. There were more policemen, more red-faced men standing outside public houses with pewter pots in their hands, more traffic on the roads, more Gypsies and their dogs, more odds being shouted by one passing horseman to another, more rowdiness and more expectation. All this Major Hubbins saw from the window of his chamber at the Brood Mare, where he had now been living for nearly a fortnight.

Above all things, Major Hubbins liked comfort. He liked soft, warm beds and himself asleep in them. He liked a seat at the play and a carriage to take him back to his lodgings afterwards. Although he was not, by the nature of his profession, permitted to eat a great deal – he weighed eight and a half stone and was as vain of his figure as a duchess – he liked hot meals sent up three times a day. He was a spoiled, indolent, lonely man who had made a living out of horses for over forty years – ever since his bankrupt father, having intended to send him to Rugby School, instead apprenticed him to a livery stable – and these deficiencies of character, if such they were, could be safely attributed to his upbringing. He was, for example, entirely mercenary. If one man offered him more than a second man to ride a horse for him, he would incline to the first man. If a sporting nobleman invited him to his country seat, he would cheerfully throw over the friend who had asked him to his suburban villa. But if he was mercenary, he was not duplicitous. He might sooner ride a rich man's horse than a poor man's, but once he had made a bargain with the poor man he stuck by it. Having engaged himself to Mr Happerton, he considered himself obliged to do his best, even should his knee – that terrible afflicted knee of his – altogether give way beneath him. He had two hundred pounds in the bank, no living relatives, a cottage in Westmorland where he never went, and no one, knowing what he did for a living, would insure his life. This was Major Hubbins.

As well as liking comfort, Major Hubbins liked society, and in this he was quite promiscuous. If there was no sporting baronet to be found, he would just as happily talk to the ostlers in the yard. On this particular morning, two days before the race, with a crowd out in the street below his window, and *The Sportman's Magazine* reporting a rally to Pendragon and Skylark quite out of the betting, sitting in his room at the Brood Mare, he was indulging this weakness for small-talk and fellow feeling with the landlord, who stood in the doorway holding the empty tray that had borne Major Hubbins's glass of negus.

'No doubt you'll remember Thornaby,' the landlord was saying, 'that was Windhover's son out of – was it – Maharini?'

'Andromeda, I think you'll find,' Major Hubbins corrected.

'The very same. Second favourite at fours, with threes laid on the Vizier. But then that Sharpe from Russia was brought in to ride the colt, and Matt Dawson, as was his trainer, and Mr Maxwell as owned him came to blows in the paddock before little Custance was given the nod.'

'No they didn't,' Major Hubbins said equably. 'And in any case, Sharpe did very well. Made the running on Northern Light.'

'So he did. And then, when Dawson happened to call on the Monday morning, meaning to be civil, Mr Maxwell give him a thousand pound.'

'That at any rate I can swear to,' Major Hubbins said, 'for I was at Tattersall's when Dawson brought it in.'

'Were you now?' said the landlord admiringly. 'Well, I expect you've had thousand-pound notes in your time, Major, and shall do again.'

Major Hubbins smiled. He liked this kind of talk and did not care if it was not scrupulously accurate. And he remembered Thornaby, Mr Maxwell's colt, and how Custance had just touched him with the whip a furlong from home when the Vizier was in front. All this awakened in Major Hubbins the pleasantest train of recollection, and he sat there in his chair, with the sun streaming in through the window and the noise of the people in the street buzzing beneath him and the glass of negus in his hand, thinking that his affairs could have turned out a great deal worse. There had been a Mrs Major Hubbins, but she was dead in Westmorland twenty years since, and Major Hubbins, recalling her now – he had a memory of her embroidering his caps with her head very low over the needle – smiled again, if not quite so cheerfully, and thought that it was strange how life worked out.

'And Tiberius,' the landlord said now. 'That's a fine horse if ever I saw one.'

'It is a nice horse, certainly,' Major Hubbins said. 'Indeed, I don't know when I ever rode a better one.'

'Although I did hear in *Post and Paddock* that he was very near coming to grief that time in Lincolnshire.'

'There was nothing much in that,' Major Hubbins said mildly. 'A little weakness in the foreleg that a week's rest soon cured ... Have you anything on him?'

'Why yes I have, Major.' In his excitement, the landlord seized the metal tray that had held Major Hubbins' glass and held it before his chest like a cuirass. 'Five guineas in all, here and there.'

'Well, I shall do my utmost to see that the five becomes thirty.'

'And the house will open to you gratis ever after if you do, sir. But it's not that.' The landlord lowered his voice. 'There are people saying that Mr Happerton don't want the horse to win.'

'Do they?' Major Hubbins shook his head. 'People always say such things. It was said of Cupid's Delight that Mr Poplar was offered £5,000 not to run – you recollect how they took the linchpins off the box in which he went to Epsom? – and yet he beat Kingmaker by a couple of lengths.'

'That's what I thought myself, sir. And in any case, as a gentleman who was in the bar the other evening said: Why, if Mr Happerton don't want him to win, he'd not have picked yourself to ride him.'

Major Hubbins smiled again, a little more wanly than when he had thought about his dead wife, and the landlord retreated. Though liking his comfort, his two hundred pounds in the bank and the flattery of sporting gentlemen, Major Hubbins was not a fool. He, too, had heard the rumours and in the considerable leisure allowed to him had turned them over in his mind. That the odds on Tiberius had first shortened and then lengthened, he did not think particularly significant. A man can place a thousand pounds on a horse at a whim. He remembered a noble acquaintance of his offering 30,000 to 1,000 against Hecuba in the Oaks six times over, for no other reason than the excitement of the wager. He had ridden Tiberius a dozen times now and knew him to be a good horse, certainly a horse that with a fair wind behind him, and barring accident, would stand as good a chance as any of winning the race.

And yet, turning the matter over in his mind again, he acknowledged that if Mr Happerton did want the horse to fail, then the instrument of that failure could only be himself. Again, Major Hubbins' fondness for the good things in life did not preclude his being a realist. He knew that men of his age were not often asked to ride champion racehorses. At the same time, in asking him to execute the commission, Mr Happerton had made much of him, told him that Jones and Robinson, and other leading jockeys of the day were as nothing compared to him. This Major Hubbins had been glad to hear. But a small part of him wondered now if he had been made a fool of.

Major Hubbins greeted this suspicion with the equanimity that he brought to every compartment of his life. When he had finished his negus, smoked a cigarette and glanced at a French novel he had lying by, he went down to the Brood Mare's dining room and had his midday meal in great comfort, and to the delight of the sporting gentlemen who sat nearby entertained them with accounts of Lord Zetland's Vortigern and how he won the Doncaster Cup, and Priam that lost his syndicate £12,000 in '34 and other reminiscences from the old king's day. And yet afterwards, when he stepped down to the stable, it was noted that he cursed the stable boy – something he had never been known to do in his life before – and that Tiberius, whom he had engaged to take for a gentle canter on the Downs, came back with a wild eye and the sweat pouring off his coat. 'Lor' bless you, Major,' the groom had said. 'The race ain't until Saturday, you know, not this afternoon,' and Major Hubbins had given a laugh, which may have signalled to anyone who heard it that, in the matter of the Derby, he was very much in earnest.

*

Captain Raff went south along the Brighton Road. It was about three o'clock in the morning of the day before the great race, but the lateness of the hour had not occurred to him. He supposed that he had been walking all day. He had a dim memory of waking up in a lodging house in Whitechapel and staring very acutely at a man who lay dead drunk on the floor beside him, but he could not have said how he came to the house, nor who the man was. There was a great deal which

Captain Raff did not know. He did not know why he walked south along the Brighton Road – there were street signs every now and then which told him that he was not so very far from London – but the walking comforted him, and the noise of his footsteps set up a little rhythm in his head which he rather liked. He did not know if he was aimed for Brighton or some other place. Sometimes the things he saw were the things around him – the houses by which he passed, wide village greens with the water lying black and cold under the moon – and sometimes he saw the things in his head, which were more ominous. Sometimes it seemed to him that he wandered underground, and that the shutting-off of the light would altogether extinguish him. At other times he seemed to traverse some high point, where cold night air hung upon his shoulders and the wind plucked at his forehead. The things in his head fascinated him. It would not have been correct to call them visions, for they had no substance. Rather, they were intimations, hints of other things: a slither beneath a rock; a glint of light on a nest of serpents seething in the darkness; a hatchet-blade descending on a chicken's neck; a horrible lidless eye with a little nictating membrane at its corner; odd flutters of chill breath and sinister movement.

It was not in the nature of things that Captain Raff's progress should go unobserved. A policeman watched him stutter down a village street, but, seeing that the shop windows and the door-fastenings that he passed were of no interest to him, allowed him to proceed. Three drunk men rose up out of a hedge, capered around him and would have claimed him as one of their own, but there was something ominous and detached in Captain Raff's eye that deterred them and they stole away. At about four, just as the first streaks of dawn were showing over the horizon, it began to rain and he took shelter in a grim old churchyard under a canopy of dark, ivy-clad trees, where the moonlight glinted off the flints in the tower and the ferns grew up under the darkling windows. The inscriptions on the graves interested him very much, and he stood staring at them as the rain dripped off his hat and onto his forehead, wondering what, if he were to die, anyone might say about him. The dawn was showing blood-red now, and something cried out brokenly in the hedgerow near by and then fell silent. There was an old man curled up in the church porch who, when he saw Captain Raff among the stones, came out from his lair and began to talk to him, and Captain Raff grinned horribly back, saying nothing, until the old man shook his head and went away. There were shadows moving through the mist beyond the elms, cows huddling together for shelter, and he examined them placidly for a while as if he had never seen a cow before and could not imagine what function in nature it might perform. He had a sudden vision of himself as a figure of antlike insignificance crawling across a stone ledge set at angles to the wind, from which the breeze might soon dislodge him.

And so, as the rain moved off towards the Surrey hills, he went on: through tiny villages asleep in the mist, past ploughed fields full of glistening stones that fell away into the pale aura of the horizon, where scarecrows hung, as it seemed to him, like dancing men on gibbets, by meres and streams and thickets of sedge, very dark and cool in the early light, the original silence of the world ever more prey to noise and disturbance, the ring of a horse's hoofs on a metalled road, the wheels of a gig rattling towards him, a train's whistle sounding across the fields, moving on, past the wide, double-fronted gates of great houses facing onto the road, past a workhouse made of neat grey bricks with a double row of bleary porthole windows and a porter yawning at the door, past endless hedges twisted about with loosestrife, past rows of cottages with thatch roofs gleaming with dew and spiders' webs stretched out across their porches, but all the time with a curious sense of apprehension – doom, destiny, design, a terrible, irremediable fate – that he could not quite fathom, drawing closer to Epsom and the downs that ran beyond it, where something waited for him whose outlines, try as he might, he could not discern.

*

For some reason the vicinity of Epsom Downs on the day before the Derby is the quietest place in the world. The horses are in their stalls, being fed up on oats and fresh hay. Their owners keep to their hotels and lodging houses, dine frugally off porridge and a plate of sprats with only a little brandy-and-water to wash it down, and send anxious messages via their aides-de-camp. The landlords are in their cellars reckoning up the number of beer barrels, hogsheads and so forth, their wives are counting out knives and plates, Epsom High Street is as empty as Charterhouse School on the first day of the holidays, and a coach-and-pair rattling down it in the middle of the afternoon is seen as the height of vulgarity. There are a dozen people at Evensong, and the little whist club at the town reading room sickens and dies for want of custom. One or two young men in loud jackets and top-boots attempt to get up a song at the bar of the Dancing Pony and are quickly shushed. There will be plenty of time for that, the landlord advises them, when the race is done.

*

How many millions of people, preparing for bed on the evening of the great race, are affected by the thought of what the morning may bring? In Epsom everything is in turmoil, with ten thousand visitors crowded into a town that usually holds eight hundred. The inns are crammed to the rafters and there are people sleeping in the fields beyond Cheam and Ewell village. In London and its surround a hundred thousand go to sleep with the thought that at four, five or six o'clock they must rise up and make haste for the railway station, or the cab stand, or the road. Beyond this – beyond the Home Counties, beyond England even – there are sportsmen making uneasy calculations about the procurement of evening newspapers and their proximity to telegraph offices. The court knows about it. Half of parliament at least will be attending it. The bench of bishops will not go unrepresented, and the diplomatic embassies cannot be kept away. M. Dubois, the French ambassador, has announced his intention of being present at the race. The Mayfair dinners and the Belgravia routs have been aflame with it for weeks. A radical politician has condemned

338

it, and a Methodist divine preached against it, but one might think that something which unites a widow in Kensington Square, an apothecary in St John's Street and the wife of a Hoxton chandler is more democratic than the reverse. Chelsea is going, in carriages and coaches-and-four. Clapham is going in tax-carts and bang-up ponies. Kennington and Brixton are going by way of the Southern Railway or a succession of omnibuses, and Whitechapel and Poplar will be arriving on foot, for what is a sixteen-mile journey under the June sunshine when there is Saturnalia in view?

With such a profusion of people comes, inevitably, a scarcity of resources. There is not a pig or a sheep or a fowl to be purchased anywhere in Cheam or Dorking, for the publicans and the cook-shop proprietors have bought them all. Likewise tea, butter, flour and dried fruit for the delicacies known as 'Derby Buns', which every cottage on the road offers to passers-by. What sugar remains in the grocers' shops on Epsom High Street has been carefully sanded, and the lake of beer distributed among its hostelries stealthily watered down. A newspaper has made a computation of the thousands of loaves, pies and sweet biscuits that will be eaten on the course and the hundreds of thousands of glasses that will be emptied in its near vicinity. A Dissenting chapel has announced that it will be throwing open its door to repentant sinners, but no one much is expected to come. It is as if, all across Surrey and beyond, a great play is in the process of being put together, and although the actors have yet to arrive the scenery lies everywhere about. Five score Gypsy caravans and their owners are camped up on the Downs and have been there a week. So has the fairground with its cockshies, its carousel, its sealed booths advertising werewolves, the corpse of a two-headed baby in a formaldehyde jar, and a pair of young ladies able to recite the multiplication table and speak the French language but joined together at the hip. There are a dozen artists and illustrators from the pictorial papers lodged in Epsom with instructions to take the race, or some part of it, off, and forty or fifty newspaper-writers ready to transmit something of its splendour to the world beyond. There are also three hundred policemen installed in a makeshift barracks at Cheam and a temporary magistrate's court set up in the corner of the Grandstand for dispensing summary justice.

*

Among those gentlemen of the press came Mr Pritchett of the *Pictorial Times*, who had taken the precaution of going down to Epsom by train the night before and reserving rooms at the Perch, Ewell, three months previous.

'It's a thing I always do,' he explained to his assistant, who sat meekly at his side as the train rattled through the Surrey twilight. 'Why, there was one year when that Priestley of the *Illustrated* came at the last minute, found every room taken, had to spend the night under a hedge on Banstead Common and turned up with loosestrife in his hat.' The train was rather full of people – gentlemen in black-cloth suits on their way home from the City, other men clearly bound for the racecourse with mysterious packages under their arms – and Mr Pritchett regarded them with a caustic eye. 'Now', he instructed the meek assistant, 'there will be a great deal for us to do and you had better listen carefully. First you must call at Mr Dorling's house for a copy of the racecard. They'll tell you it ain't ready, I daresay: if that's the case, say that Mr Pritchett of the *Pictorial Times* wants one special. Then you're to go to Pickering's stables at Cheam village for word on Septuagint. If the place is shut up, well, it can't be helped. As for tomorrow, here's my instructions. If anyone from the *Illustrated* wants to know where I am, you ain't seen me and can't tell. And look out for impostors. There was a chap came up one year, said he was Lord Mancroft, the owner of Zebedee and had a tale to tell, and would you believe he wasn't Lord Mancroft at all? Don't go near the card tables or the refreshment tents under the hill – you'll have your wallet taken and it shan't be me that fills it again – give the fellows at the grandstand gate a shilling when you come to fetch me after my luncheon and if anyone gives trouble say you

340

are on a particular errand for Mr Pritchett of the *Pictorial Times*, and see how that suits . . .'

*

As for the principal players in this drama, they are still widely dispersed. Mr Dorling sleeps soundly in his bed, leaving the last preparations to his subordinates, although Mrs Dorling is still hard at work making curl-papers for her daughters and granddaughters. The owners, and part-owners, and the vague-eyed men who have what is known as an 'interest', are dining at their inns, rather subdued and querulous and liable to argue their bills. Their jockeys are smoking pipes in stable yards, exchanging final words with grooms and attendants and setting out their gear. Mr Happerton has forsaken both dinner and the society of Mr Mountstuart and sits alone in his room making calculations with an ink-pen on the back of an envelope: such is his air of zealous concentration that the cigar between his fingers keeps going out and has to be relit from a spill kept ready on a saucer. Major Hubbins is at the Brood Mare, very comfortable with a glass of sherry, some devilled chicken and a biscuit. Rosa is in Mount Street setting out her things for the morrow. Very lavish and fine they look, lying on the coverlet of Rosa's dainty bed, and Rosa's maid thinks that she never saw so much silk and muslin and convent lace in her life.

In Belgrave Square Mrs Happerton goes to bed early, having tucked old Mr Gresham away earlier still. Nokes is nowhere to be seen. Captain McTurk is still in his eyrie above Northumberland Street, and Mr Masterson with him, although candles have had to be called for. Mr Hopkins the secretary has fallen asleep in his chair, although on this occasion quite naturally, and there is fresh information, just arrived, which may have some bearing on tomorrow's affairs. Mr Glenister is at his lodgings wondering what costume might be thought suitable for a racecourse and settling in the end for a linen coat and a soft hat. In Lincolnshire, where the rains have started up again, Miss Ellington stands at the window staring out into the warm, sodden night. Captain Raff is – who knows where Captain Raff is? Captain Raff does not know himself. In Richmond Jemima has long since retired to her fragrant pillow, but Mr Pardew still sits in front of the empty fireplace, hands pressed down against his great knees, musing on his opportunities. The stick rests a foot from his side.

XXVI

Derby Day: Begun

The most astonishing, the most varied, the most picturesque, and the most glorious spectacle that ever was or ever can be, under any circumstances, visible to mortal eyes.

Illustrated London News, 1863

The day dawns bright and clear, more or less. The grey clouds that have hung over Dorking and Reigate pull away northwards and the land opens up: field upon field, like the squares in a patchwork quilt. Over Charnwood the mist gently disperses in little wisps and eddies, like spun sugar borne on the air. From this height – the Hogsback say, from which it is possible to see all the way to London – everything resembles something else. The little villages – Banstead, Coulsdon, Ewell – look as if they were made with the bricks from a child's nursery. The rivers are thin blue lines. The Queen of Brobdingnag, were she paying a call in Epsom High Street, would be an ant. And across the land, even at this hour, move occupying armies. There are caterers' wagons out over the edge of the concourse and a forest of tents to accompany the pastrycooks and beer-sellers and roast-beef providers that Mr Dorling has seen fit to accommodate there. Early carriages are joined up axle to axle, with gentlemen in loud waistcoats and cockades in their hats breakfasting off sandwiches and boiled eggs covered up in handkerchiefs. There will be no racing for seven hours, but the visitors are unabashed.

A gentleman can do a great deal on Epsom Downs if he has a mind. He may go and lose his money at thimblerig, or he may go and drink rum shrub at sixpence the half-pint. He may stop and admire the acrobats and the tumblers and the sellers of prints of famous horses, or he may purchase a tract from one of the serious-looking frock-coated men and read about the Angel Gabriel's flaming sword and Lot's Wife, the implication being that Epsom is a modern Gomorrah with all its patrons ripe to be turned into pillars of salt. He may go and ogle the ladies in the carriage ring – there are not so many of them yet, as the morning is rather young – or he may go and see what the Old Firm, William Latch, The Black Swan, Shoreditch, has to offer him in the way of odds. There are a score of bookmakers and their clerks here already, and more arriving every moment to jostle for places on the hill, all of them highly picturesque – dressed in suits of violent check, with ties made out of yards of flaring green silk, field glasses slung over their shoulders and boots with heels three inches high. The policemen, walking two by two among the multiplying crowd, are tolerant. A man has to be very outrageous, or drunk, or vicious, to get himself arrested on Derby Day. Somewhere on the edge of the crowd there are trumpets sounding. A carriage with a ducal coronet on the door rolls by, past a banner announcing that, in a tank specially designed for the purpose, Miss Delavacquerie, whom the illustrated papers have been admiring this past fortnight, will dive for soup plates at twelve o'clock sharp. The sun continues to rise into the summer sky.

*

In Derby week the Epsom landlords make no difficulties about the sharing of rooms, or overcrowding, or the smuggling of additional guests up the back-stairs, and there were at least seven young ladies arraying themselves in print dresses and feathered hats or combing out their back hair in an upstairs chamber of the Spread Eagle. An eighth, who still lay face down upon her mattress, was thought to be rather spoiling the fun for the majority.

'I declare, Bella, you had better get up unless something ails you. You've been lying there like a bolster this past half-hour.'

'I never felt so bad in my life. You must go on without me.'

'What? And lose your place on the hill?' This remark was somewhat obscured by a mouthful of hairpins. 'Why, the chaps from the Bag o' Nails said to be there bright and early. And there's your odds to take on Tiberius, too.' The party from the Spread Eagle were very sweet on Tiberius, and several of them wore his colours – these were quarters of blue and green – on the sleeves of their dresses.

'I don't want any odds on Tiberius,' Miss Nokes announced from the pillow. 'Catch me throwing my money away.'

'Why's that, Bella?' said the other girl. 'Why shouldn't you back Tiberius when everyone says that Baldino can't stand the hard ground and that other has injured himself?'

'Why?' Miss Nokes wondered, finally consenting to raise her somewhat livid face to the light and beginning to pull on her stockings. 'Because he is going to lose, that's why. Haven't I told you a dozen times? Master's put all his money on Septuagint, which you will too, if you've any sense.'

Sobered by this evidence of the sporting world's rapacity, the party went down to breakfast.

*

Mr Pritchett of the *Pictorial Times* strides purposefully through the crowd gathered beneath the hill. He is a tall, thin man, as tall as the bookmakers in their steeple-heels, and like the bookmakers carries a pair of field glasses slung around his neck. As he strides he throws out observations to the meek young man who follows a yard behind him, with a pencil in one hand and a notebook balanced on his hip.

'. . . Blessed if there isn't ten thousand people here already . . . You'd better give me the grandstand tickets, Johnson' – Johnson is the name

of the meek young man – 'for I don't trust you not to lose 'em ...
Heavens, there is that Miss Abercrombie from the Theatre Royal. I
wonder she dares show her face after Sir John Fortescue threw her
over when his wife found the billet-doo under the antimaccassar ...
Ugh! The look of those Gypsies. I wonder Dorling lets them in. Some
nonsense about common ground, I daresay ... Who is that fellow in
the gig who keeps waving at me, Johnson? Is it Lord Cardew? Not his
lordship, you say ... ? Well, the impudence of these people is astonishing. Here, you had better take this down: *Among a spirited and genteel
crowd, whose early arrival at the course betrayed their especial interest in
the outcome, I observed the delightful and accomplished Miss Abercrombie
of the Theatre Royal, Drury Lane, exquisitely dressed in* – just run up to
her carriage in a moment, will you Johnson, and see what the woman
is wearing – *The Duke of Grafton, who granted me the honour of several
moments' conversation, recalled that this was his forty-fourth Derby and
that he had first been taken here on a pony by his grandsire in '26 when, as
he wittily put it, Lord Egremont's Penguin swam home in fine style* – you
had better check that in *Ruff*, Johnson – *Lord Egremont, as my readers
will remember, once fought the old Duke in a duel, but His Grace assures
me that he bears no grudge ...*'

*

There are a number of convenient ways of approaching Epsom from
London. Depending on your taste, and income, you may hire a phaeton,
a gig, a barouche, a four-in-hand, a brake, a Tilbury or a donkey-cart.
You may make the journey in a single stretch – it is fourteen miles
from Trafalgar Square – or, in the manner of many an honest traveller,
you may stop along the route – at the Swan at Clapham, or the Bell at
Sutton, at both of which places you may very well end up so becalmed
that you find yourself asking the name of the winner from the crowd
surging back after the race is done. Old-fashioned people take the
railway to Surbiton and walk the intervening five miles with good
grace. Only in the last few years has an enterprising railway company

constructed a line that comes right up to the Downs. Mr Happerton had sent a groom up to Mayfair for Rosa. The man arrived promptly on her doorstep at eight o'clock but was compelled to wait half an hour in the kitchen by the maid.

'Mr Happerton distinctly said I should be fetched at nine,' Rosa told him crossly as she came downstairs in a hat that had taken a Hay Hill milliner nearly a week to concoct.

'We had better be off direct, ma'am,' said the groom, who had a pretty good idea what Rosa was, and did not like it. 'Else you and he will miss your place.'

'Well, if that is what Mr Happerton says I am very grateful to him,' Rosa observed. 'Where is the carriage?'

But there was no carriage, only a cab hired from the rank a furlong away, in which the groom proposed to carry her to Waterloo. At this Rosa frankly sulked, but there was nothing to be done about it. The cab bowled away through Mayfair, along empty streets where water carriers were out damping down the dirt, and came eventually to the station, where a great crowd of people swarmed over the concourse – young men, mostly, but with girls' dresses showing spots of colour in the grey morning. Here, safely accommodated in a first-class carriage and with a porter to tip his hat to her, Rosa began to recover her spirits, but the route from Waterloo to Epsom is not very inspiring. They passed by open spaces filled by cranes, old iron, stacks of railway sleepers and giant gasometers rising fat and black in their cages and altogether dwarfing the distant church spires. At Clapham Junction there were horsey men lining the platform in grey overcoats with race glasses slung over their shoulders. They dawdled by bits of common, and then the houses began again, with sordid little gardens coming up to the track and white clothing set out to dry over the currant bushes, and Rosa wrinkled her nose. But then, after an hour, they came to Epsom, where the groom stepped up smartly from his third-class compartment and led her along the platform to where a gig stood waiting.

'Where is Mr Happerton?' Rosa wondered, who had expected her lord and master to be there to meet her.

'Mr Happerton sends his apologies, only he has particular business with the horse. I'm to drive you to the course, ma'am, if you'll step up.'

The gig swept off into a pleasant lane, overhung with chestnut trees, where the white blossoms stood up like candles, and thence up a long hill leading to the Downs. The crowd made way for the vehicles, and the young men in blue and grey trousers and their girls in white dresses turned and watched a tall drag ripe with London fashion and a brake filled with fat girls in pink dresses and yellow hats. The cottage gates were crowded with folk come to see London going to the Derby. At last the trees stopped and they came out onto the hilltop in a flare of sunlight, on a patch of worn grass where a pair of donkeys were tethered.

'Is this the Derby?' Rosa asked, in a voice like a little girl's. 'Where are all the people?'

'You'll see them presently, ma'am,' the groom volunteered. His attitude to her had softened, and he explained that the white building was the grandstand and that the winning post lay a little further beyond the hill.

'Where is the start?' Rosa wondered.

'Where you see that clump. They run through the furze right up to Tattenham Corner.' A vast crowd seethed over the opposite hill, and beyond this she saw open downland rising to a belt of trees which met the horizon. 'They comes right down the hill and finishes up opposite to us. By Barnard's Ring. The police will push them right back, don't you fear.'

They pressed on into the heart of the crowd, past a boy on stilts eight feet high who lowered his cap to receive the flung pennies, and along the rail where rough men lay asleep with pipes in their mouths, and there, miraculously it seemed to Rosa, was Mr Happerton, with a red rose in his buttonhole, reaching out his hand to her, dismissing the groom, who thumbed his hat, took the proffered sovereign and vanished on the instant. He took the reins with one hand and her arm with the other, so that she stopped thinking of the sun's heat burning through her muslin gown, or the dullness of her journey and the sordid little gardens of Clapham that had so disgusted her, and began, slowly yet gratefully, to give herself over to the pleasures of the day.

*

Along the rail, stretched out between poles, hung strips of bleached white linen, stitched with gold and silver letters.

> *Jack Dobbs. Marylebone. All bets paid*
> *Tim Wood's famous boxing rooms, Epsom*
> *Henry Allen, Commission Agent, London*

'On the Derby, on the Derby, I'll bet the Derby. To win or a place, to win or a place. Seven to one bar two or three. Seven to one bar two or three. The old firm, the old firm . . .'

*

Having thrown balls for coconuts, inspected a lady who claimed to be the fattest woman in Surrey and sampled the beer at the refreshment tent, the party from the Spread Eagle had all but reached the summit of the hill. Theirs, however, was not a harmonious spirit.

'Gracious, who is that snivelling? What have you got to cry about, Bella, I should like to know?'

'It's none of your business.'

'If it's that chap from the Bag o'Nails you're mooning over then you've no worries on that score, for Joey Norris that works in the bar says he is a police detective.'

This, for some reason, was not to be borne, and after a half-minute or so of name-calling – very edifying to the surrounding crowd – the two women went tumbling down the hill together while the onlookers whooped and cheered and a nearby bookmaker offered short odds on 'the 'un with the pink dress' – this was Miss Nokes – emerging

349

victorious, which, with several handfuls of her adversary's hair as a trophy, she eventually did.

*

Society is supposed to have turned homogeneous these days, and all the people the same: the same tradesmen in their neat houses; the same shabby clerks streaming across London Bridge to the City; the same fat aldermen jowling their dinners at Guildhall banquets. But the people at the Derby are never the same. There are swells in frock-coats with German dolls, bought from the Gypsies, tucked into their hat-brims. There are tiny, starved boys urging Mr Dorling's racecards – 'Dorling's genuine card list', 'Dorling's correct cards here'. There are butchers' wives from Shoreditch, in vulgar ribbons and their stays out, enjoying the spectacle. There are apprentices in cheap imitations of the fashion, being gulled out of their sixpences at thimblerig. There are persons in the last extremity of poverty huddled up in ditches, recumbent by the rail, or frankly begging along the course.

Amongst the crowd march the personalities on whom Epsom depends for its savour: Mr Dorling, who has come down from his grandstand to supervise the selling of his cards and shake his head over the error that has seen 'Jezebel' printed with only two 'e's; Sir John Bennett, who is not Sir John at all, but a jeweller from Cheapside who saunters along on his cob drinking the health of anyone that asks him; old Mr Maccabee, who has been at the Derby sixty years and remembers the Prince Regent strolling with his friend Mr Brummell. And just as every ramification of society is represented, so each has an echo in the attractions of the fairground. There are peep shows of St James's Park with the Horse Guards out on parade; Spanish bull-fights; the House in session. And all the while the buzz of a thousand conversations and shouted odds and tipsters' jargon coalescing into a single, unintelligible roar. 'Blue to win, and the favourite to be beat ... On the Der-by, on the Der-by ... The Paradise Plate for all-comers.' This last is a mock-race advertised by some evangelical girls dressed as bookmakers with 'Salvation' and 'Perdition' on their satchels.

*

'Of course,' Mr Pritchett tells his assistant, 'the crowds are nothing like what they used to be. It is that d——d electric telegraph. Folk can find out the result now without leaving their parlours. Why, I remember taking two hours to walk a mile once, and there were people who never got there at all. It is very different now ... See that carriage there? That is the Earl of Tredegar, if I'm not much mistaken. The tall man with the eyeglass. Now, just you run up to the coachman, give him this half-crown and tell him that if His Lordship has an opinion on the race, then Mr Pritchett of the *Pictorial Times* will be very glad to hear it.'

*

Captain Raff, turning out of a country lane into the approach to the hill, and not quite knowing how he had got there, fell into the body of the crowd as if it were the most natural thing in the world. The great press of humanity interested him, and he accommodated the rhythm of his walking to theirs. The fact that he had become part of the Derby crowd – a place he had been a dozen times before – registered only faintly with him. Then, after a moment, his eye began to pick out landmarks: a white-painted cottage, larger than its neighbours, that aggrandised over the road; an outhouse where men sold beer and pitchers of lemonade. Although he did not notice it at first, there were others like him in the crowd: gaunt and unnaturally weather-beaten men with their faces bent on the road and not much shoe-leather. A woman came distributing tracts and pressed one into his hand. Several of the people near him who had been similarly blessed ground the slip of paper angrily beneath their feet or tore it in two, but Captain Raff,

351

holding it up to his face, learned, somewhat to his surprise, that each step on the path to Epsom Hill was a step along the road to perdition, that on the grass square beyond Mr Dorling's grandstand lay a hell on earth, and that Tiberius — the tract had been printed before the odds had lengthened — was a snare of the Devil's that would see him damned.

*

'There's that Pritchett of the *Pictorial Times*,' Mr Priestley of the *Illustrated London News* said to the confidential friend who accompanied him. 'Gracious, what a liar that man is. You know how he is always talking of Mr Yates and the Garrick and how he dines there and is wanted for the committee and so forth? Well, I was at supper there with Lord Plinlimmon only the other week, and no one had heard so much as the mention of his name. Now, who is that young man with him? Somebody's illegitimate son, I've no doubt . . . Good day to you, Pritchett. A fine morning, indeed. You came down yesterday, I take it? A wise precaution. Now what do you think of Severus? There was a man in the office yesterday positively begged me to put a ten-pound note on him. Remember me to His Grace, won't you, if you see him.' And Mr Priestley and his friend passed on towards a part of the course where, let us hope, there were no liars and nobody's illegitimate sons.

*

Major Rook (late of the Hussars) and Mr Pigeon bowl up in an open carriage, the cost of whose hire will be charged up to Mr Pigeon's account at the Park Lane livery stables, which is already pretty considerable. With them are Maria, a blooming young lady of thirty-one who gives out that she is twenty-four, and a mincing old woman named Miss Chitterlow. Miss Chitterlow is Maria's companion and they live in the neatest little house off the Row. As for Maria, there is no need at all to say what she is.

'Law, Rook,' Maria says now, peering languidly down at the throng of passers-by. 'That's Lord John there in the tall hat, surely?'

'Nonsense,' says Rook. He is a solid-looking man of forty with a hard grey eye. 'It's Tom Bowling who I took for two hundred sovs at the St Leger three years back, and devilish unhappy he was about it too. Now, see here Fred, you positively must decide who you're to back. You shan't hold off any longer, indeed you shan't.' There is a wonderful jocularity about Major Rook as he makes this observation. 'Now, which shall it be?'

Fred – Mr Pigeon – is a faded young sprig of twenty-two, with a feeble little attempt at side whiskers and ever so many thousands of pounds at his account with Messrs Rowdy & Son, Cheapside, and a complexion the colour of cold boiled veal because he *will* sit up until four in the morning playing *écarté*, smoking cigars and indulging in other manly pursuits with Major Rook.

'Pendragon's a pretty name,' Maria says, who has perhaps received some hint in this matter from Major Rook.

'Nonsense, Fred,' Major Rook demurs, with the ease of a man who has half a dozen of Mr Pigeon's notes of hand in his breast pocket (for if young men of twenty-two sit up playing écarté with Major Rook they will lose their money – that is all there is to it). 'I was at Tattersall's the other day, and Rawlinson – you'll recollect him, I daresay – said that the Duke had put a thousand on The Coalman.'

Poor Mr Pigeon. He has already been induced to drink three brandy-and-sodas and an unspeakable liqueur at the Bell at Cheam, and his poor weak head is giving him as much trouble as his poor weak eyes in the sun, but he is still in awe of Major Rook, just as he is of Maria, Miss Chitterlow and the little house off the Row, which has been furnished entirely at his expense. Major Rook chose the armchairs, and the wine – and the servants. There is nothing that Major Rook, with his spotless white shirtfront and his hard grey eye, can't turn his hand to if he's a mind. And so Pigeon (he is one of those Hertfordshire brewing Pigeons, you know, whose papa died and left him a fortune in the 3 per cents) nods his weak little head and says he don't mind a bet, and Maria laughs and takes a sniff at her scent bottle, and Miss Chitterlow marvels at all the people, and Mr Trant, Major Rook's particular friend, who just happens to be strolling in the vicinity of the carriage, comes up to shake Mr Pigeon's hand and register the stake (Mr Pigeon wants it to be £200, but Major Rook says d——, he has that on himself and he is a poor man, so why not make it £400?) and another little brick in the wall of Mr Pigeon's ruination is quietly cemented down.

*

What sorts and conditions of men are gathered here! Entire families – meek papa, flustered mama, half a dozen children in short jackets or their best pinafores – come down from Sutton and Cheam and Dorking to see the fun. Grave old North Country gentlemen with faltering steps, very much put out by the glare of the sun, who would surely be much better off by their comfortable hearths with their wives to tend them. Mysterious lonely women, not so very young perhaps, nor yet so very old, whose eyes flit shrewdly around them as they prowl the course. Soldiers in scarlet tunics with gay girls on their arms. A Treasury Lord with a vigilant secretary at his side and a determination to back his friend Lord Trumpington – whose estate adjoins his own in Hampshire, you know – to the hilt. Mr Savory the prize novelist, whose last book, *Whimsicalities*, Mr Dickens is thought to have admired, is there, and Lorriquer, the fashionable poet, whose *Attic Dawns* caused such a stir among the reviewers, simpering into Lady Delacave's carriage and ogling her daughters, together with fifty thousand people whose names will never appear in a newspaper, unless it is the section reserved for court proceedings, whose lives are unsung and whose destinies unworthy of report.

*

Major Hubbins was made much of at the Brood Mare. The landlord himself brought him his breakfast muffin, and his whip, cap and colours were reverently returned to him by the landlord's daughter from the salver on which they had lain for the admiration of the establishment's guests. There was a crowd of well-wishers at the door to see him off – the landlord absolutely scorned his attempt to settle the bill – an injunction 'not to forget the old place' once his victory was won – and a fly to take him to the stables at Cheam. All this was very gratifying to Major Hubbins, but it did not heal the injury that he thought had been done to him. He thought – and one or two enquiries among the cognoscenti at the Brood Mare had convinced him of this – that, in some sense, he had been made a fool of, that Mr Happerton had hired him to ride Tiberius because he expected him to fail. Major Hubbins did not consider himself to be a virtuous man. If asked, he would have declared that the profession he followed excluded virtue by its very nature. Certainly, in his forty years in the saddle he had colluded in various little conspiracies that, in certain company – not necessarily very choice – he would happily have admitted to. He had ridden horses that he knew to be unsound. He had cheerfully lost races that a little more dexterity on his part might have won. Most of that two hundred pounds that lay in the bank had been honestly come by, but a certain proportion of it had not.

None of this much alarmed Major Hubbins. It was how the world worked, he thought, and he had known worse. One has always known worse. But somehow what he believed to be Mr Happerton's duplicity infuriated him – not because he considered himself to be Mr Happerton's moral superior, but because the scheme turned on his own unfittedness as a rider. As the fly brought him to Cheam this feeling grew. He thought that the grooms sneered at him behind his back, and that even the man who swept up the muck in Tiberius' stall knew of the deception and laughed at it. 'Here be the horse, Major,' the head groom said, leading up Tiberius – very smartly got up and as neat as one of his owner's equine pins – by his bridle, and Major Hubbins rocked a little on his boot-heels and remarked, yes, he had seen a horse before, and immediately began to find fault. He complained of the snaffle, which he said was throttling the horse, he complained of a shoe, which a blacksmith had to be summoned to file down, and he complained of the setting of the stirrups, and the grooms, who had previously thought him a benevolent old gentleman, fell over themselves to set things right. Mr Mountstuart, who had been watching from a window, came down into the stable yard and said sardonically: 'You are a regular tartar, Major,' and Major Hubbins gave a faint little smile and said he feared things at the stables had got very slack, and Mr Mountstuart, whose stables they were, goggled at him.

And so eventually the procession set off – the head groom leading Tiberius on a short rein, and Major Hubbins in the saddle, with the other men to clear a way and Mr Mountstuart following behind, and such passers-by as recognised horse or rider cheering as they went. They came up behind Septuagint, whose groom knew Major Hubbins of old and hailed and chaffed him, but Major Hubbins grasped his whip and stared straight ahead of him, and Mr Mountstuart, seeing the white roof of the grandstand looming before him, wondered for the first time if his friend Mr Happerton had made a mistake.

*

Mr Glenister walks idly around the course. He has come over early from Dorking, having stayed the night there with a friend. 'You won't mind if I don't keep you company?' the friend has asked – he is the vicar of a Dorking church, and a little amused by this excursion – and Mr Glenister has said, no, he does not mind. Mr Glenister is not an unworldly man, by and large, but even so the Derby perplexes him. He supposes, when he thinks about it, that there is something to be said for standing about in the hot sun with your friends while two dozen horses run a race which you cannot properly see lasting all of two and a half minutes, but he cannot precisely imagine what it is. Just lately he has read some remarks of M. Taine's about the English crowds. M. Taine, being a Frenchman, finds them undemonstrative, bovine, drifting. A French crowd, he implies, would sooner storm a prison, fling a nobleman from his battlements, lay siege to a city.

Mr Glenister both assumes that there is a communal impulse, and suspects it. As a young man, as a dare, he once attended a public execution at Snow Hill, finding at the moment of despatch that he preferred to look not at the condemned man but at the spectators. There is a horse not far away being led to the saddling enclosure by the grandstand, and for a moment he imagines that it is Tiberius, only for proximity to reveal that the animal is a bay with colours of magenta and light blue – Pendragon, he discovers from the racecard bought from a tout at the entry to the Downs. There is a way, Mr Glenister thinks, watching the swarms of people taking up their places on the hill, and the rattling carriages, in which all this is faintly artificial. Only Lincolnshire is real, with the rooks screaming in the elms, and Miss Ellington and Evie coming towards him over the wet grass. For a moment he tries to recall Evie's face, but emerges only with a doughy blur of white flesh. Evie has been better of late, but such terms are relative. Miss Ellington, on the other hand, he can remember: light brown hair, a weak chin, blue eyes. No, Mr Glenister tells himself, they are brown.

*

At Belgrave Square Mrs Rebecca woke late and languid. Despite repeated tugs upon the bell-rope there was no sign of Nokes, whose loyalty in these matters was generally beyond question, and in the absence of the old servants she was absolutely compelled to descend to the kitchen and rout out the kitchenmaid to have her hot water sent up and set her breakfast bohea to brew. The house was otherwise deserted – Mr Gresham rarely came downstairs before eleven – but Mrs Rebecca, reaching the empty hallway and finding nothing in it but a white cat and a few strands of sunlight moving over the polished floor, was not unduly displeased. She liked silence, and she liked solitude, and she would just as soon eat her breakfast without Nokes to attend her or husband to observe her as she crunched up her toast. So, having received her tray from the kitchenmaid, she took it into the parlour and sat over it considering something which had first occurred to her a day or so before and had continued to exercise her mind through the intervening period. This was the identity of the man she had seen coming out of her husband's study four days before and whose features she was sure that she vaguely recognised.

At first this faint air of familiarity had not troubled her. The traffic that passed through her husband's study was both regular and exotic, and she assumed merely that the man had come this way before and been seen by her on a previous visit. Still, though, there was something about the man – something about his demeanour – that seemed to separate him from the equine ragtag of Mr Happerton's daily round. Above all, it seemed evident from the way in which he had strode through the vestibule of the house, and from the almost contemptuous look on his face, that he regarded Mr Happerton almost as an equal (none of the horsey men would have dared cultivate such a look). This intrigued her, and she found herself wondering half a dozen times where she might have seen him before. Then she thought that she might have seen his picture in an illustrated paper, but there was something in that look that told her he was not a politician, or an actor, or a man of fashion. It was all very mysterious, and Mrs Rebecca could not work it out. The white cat came into the parlour as she drank her tea and she took it onto her lap – why the cat seemed reluctant to be so enticed she could not imagine – petted it for a moment and then gave a little twist with her finger, after which the animal sprang gladly away.

She was about to give the mystery up in favour of the great race and what might happen in it, when she caught sight of a newspaper lying on the sideboard. In the normal course of events the newspaper, which was several days old, would have been taken away and disposed of, but in Mr Happerton's absence, and that of the old servants, rather a Saturnalian air had fallen upon the house at Belgrave Square and more than one thing had not been done which perhaps ought to have been done. All this was of less import to Mrs Rebecca than an awareness – a very slight awareness, but suggestive all the same – that something in the newspaper connected it to the man who had walked out of her husband's study. Putting down her tea cup and rising to her feet – the cat saw her from the doorway and moved a little further out of range – she scooped up the paper and began to riffle through it. Some speculations on the composition of the new Cabinet and a very learned essay on tariff reform were soon dispensed with, along with a criticism of Madame Delacourt's recitation, but there, suddenly, in a pen-and-ink sketch, not terribly like him, perhaps, but not wholly unlike him either, was the face that she sought. Staring at it, and at the paragraph or two that accompanied it, she learned that it belonged to a man named Pardew, to whom the police were anxious to speak in connection with the assault on Mr Gallentin's shop, together with yet more picturesque details of a burglary Mr Pardew was supposed to have perpetrated on a mail-train going down to Dover three years previously, and of the murder, many years before, of his then partner in business, a Mr Fardel, of which Mr Pardew had been acquitted but over which some suspicion still hung.

Naturally all this was set out in the most suggestive manner, and Mrs Rebecca read it with the keenest interest. She had no doubt – not the slightest – that this was the man she had seen. In fact, had someone been able to prove to her satisfaction that this was not the man she had seen, she would have been deeply disappointed. As to why Mr Pardew might have been calling on her husband in his study, she presumed that the visit had something to do with the burglary at Mr Gallentin's shop. What she thought about this she could not exactly determine. That her husband might have been in league with a jewel-thief hardly troubled her. There was a way in which this recklessness was very agreeable to her. It spoke of a piratical spirit that she admired, and that her father and most of the men she had known before she met Mr Happerton conspicuously lacked. But what if Mr Happerton's dealings with Mr Pardew should come to the attention of the police?

Again, this did not greatly trouble her. Her faith in her husband's capacities was not infinite, but it was very strong. She told herself that Mr Happerton must have known what he was about, that the connection with Mr Pardew could only have been predicated on some greater

359

good, for which money was required. As she thought about it, it occurred to her that this greater good must have something to do with the events at the Derby. All this both excited her, in its suggestion that she sat at the heart of momentous events, and alarmed her, in that she wondered what harm Mr Pardew meant to do her husband, or whether there was any harm that he could do. Thinking this, she gave a little laugh, which there was no one to hear, smoothed out the paper before her on the parlour table and stared at it again with such intensity that the postman knocking at the front door had to go away unconsoled, and Mr Gresham, waking late and fretful, found that his bell, though it rang violently through the house, went unanswered.

*

'Now who's this then?' a voice said. 'And with a blessed banner showing, too, I'll be bound.'

And Mr McIvor, looking up from the two poles he was attempting to secure to the rail on either side of a square of stationer's card that read *Rbt. McIvor, The Bird in Hand, Soho, all bets paid*, and which was the pride of his life, saw a raw, red face and a pair of watery eyes staring at him from beneath the irregular brim of an ancient billycock hat.

'You lay a hand on me, Mulligan, and there's Joey Blacker, whose chaps are up on the hill and is a particular friend of mine, will have something to say about it.'

But Mr Mulligan, who had perhaps taken a glass of wine, shook his head. He was got up in the most tremendous Derby costume, consisting of a green frock-coat, a neck-tie that dazzled in the sunshine and a silk umbrella that doubled as a shade, and on his arm marched a red-haired lady, not perhaps in her first youth and somewhat deficient in teeth, but quite as strikingly attired in a dress of canary yellow with a bright green sash. 'As to that affair, McIvor, I'm prepared to let bygones be bygones, if you'll shake hands. I'll give you a word of advice even, if you'll listen to it.'

'What advice might that be?' Mr McIvor wondered.

'What odds have you for Baldino?'

'Fives,' McIvor said. 'Taken a good bit of money, too, for all his foreleg's not said to be sound.'

'Well take my tip and lay a trifle of it off on Tiberius. A fellow I know has just seen Hubbins down at the paddock and said he looked as fierce as a Bashi-Bazouk, and that no one could understand it.'

*

'Which is that horse?'

'I believe it is Caractacus, that Lord Rufford owns.'

'And the little black one that is pulling at its groom?'

Mr Happerton inspected the racecard. 'That is Bandolero, that Mr Mountjoy bought for a song in Dumfriesshire last autumn. I wish I had been there before him.'

They were standing by the rail in front of the grandstand watching the horses being paraded up and down, Rosa dandling her short parasol around the back of her pretty neck, Mr Happerton with his hat pulled down low over his forehead. So far they had done all the correct things. They had eaten cold chicken and drunk champagne on the hill and watched the crowd surging round the concourse; they had sauntered along the part of the grandstand where the owners and their entourages are disposed to gather; they had found Major Hubbins and his attendants and shaken his hand; they had watched Tiberius being taken down to be examined and approved by Mr Dorling's assistants; and Mr Happerton knew that he had made a mistake. As they had resumed their places in Mr Happerton's gig, having stepped down from it for a moment at Tattenham Corner, a sporting nobleman whom Mr Happerton had met and been recognised by a dozen times at racecourses, at Tattersall's and several other places, had walked by, nodded his head to Mr Happerton, seen the person beneath the parasol and then marched off without delivering the word of greeting that had clearly sprung to his lips. And Mr Happerton understood that he had done wrong to bring his mistress to the Derby while leaving his wife to amuse herself in Belgrave Square. They had rolled on towards the grandstand, and plenty of other people had come to pay their respects to Rosa — several of the Blue Riband's finest had hastened across to grant themselves that privilege — but Mr Happerton knew he had made a mistake. This turned him sulky and discontented, and to Rosa's blithe suggestions that they should shy for coconuts or stroll along the entertainment booths he had returned only shakes of his head.

'Who is that *distinguished*-looking man at the gate?'

Mr Happerton looked. 'That is Mr Gliddon, Mr Dorling's secretary. I don't know why you think a man who writes another man's letters is particularly distinguished.'

'Oh, is that all he does?'

Rosa, too, was a little sulky. The heat was rather oppressive, the crowds seemed to surge uncomfortably close, and she was aware, without being in the least able to quantify this awareness, that in some way she had fallen short of the standards expected of her. And so they walked a little more amongst the horses and their grooms, were greeted by one or two faintly disreputable men who remarked 'Well, Happerton, how are you my boy?', bickered about matters which no gentleman out walking with a lady at a racecourse should bicker about, and came finally to that part of the course where the bookmakers had set up their poles.

'Of all things,' Rosa declared from beneath her parasol, 'I should like to bet on Tiberius.'

'Nonsense,' said Mr Happerton, finding himself suddenly disgusted by the place in which he stood: the drunks lying asleep under the rail; the red-faced men crying odds; a boy acrobat turning somersaults almost under his feet. He told himself that whatever happened in the course of the afternoon, there should be an end to Mount Street. Why had he not brought Rebecca with him to the Derby, who seemed to care only for his interests and who would not have made ridiculous remarks about the horses as they paraded before her in the enclosure or simpered over little Mr Gliddon, Mr Dorling's secretary? It occurred to him that he had underestimated his wife, that a wiser man would have confided in her, and been less suspicious of her motives. All this chastened him and depressed his spirits. He found himself weighing up a series of inner resolutions. He would be more virtuous, he thought, should the day turn out to his advantage. Perhaps he would go in for politics, as his wife had suggested. And he would certainly cultivate some greater understanding between them. Why, they should be as Darby and Joan together and that little cottage in Hampshire should be their bower of bliss!

For a moment he almost forgot the bafflement which Mrs Rebecca had several times bred up in him and concentrated on this vision of soft words and marital harmony. He would give up Mount Street this very afternoon, he decided. The thought cheered him so much that he resolved, for civility's sake, to be courteous to the companion whom he intended to throw off in three hours' time, and so, selecting at random one of the loungers at the rail, a tall old man with a battered hat and a cast in one eye, he twitched Rosa's sleeve and remarked:

'Now, there is someone far more distinguished than Mr Gliddon.'

'Who is it?'

'I believe it is Mr Cadman from the whips' office. They say the Earl can do nothing without him.'

And Rosa bridled, as at the wildest compliment.

*

'Heavens, Johnson, what a time you take. And all to fill a flask ... Now, who else is there? Lord John ... ? No? Well let us say that we have seen him. He is hardly likely to write to the paper and deny it ... Mr Disraeli ... ? I wonder he don't go and join the other Hebrews shouting odds by the rail ... Now, there goes Mr Dorling ... Take this down, Johnson ... *Among many old friends seen on the course, I had the pleasure of several moments' conversation – this in a respite from the count-less duties that surround him – with Mr Dorling, the Clerk of the Course. To be sure, the racegoer has much to be thankful to Mr Dorling for, in whose family the management of the affair has lain these past forty years.*

Why, half the myriad who flock to the Downs on the Derby Day would know neither the names of the horses, nor the weight and colours of the riders, were it not for Dorling's Card, printed feverishly through the night in the shed next to the family's house and sold the next morning by hoarse vendors stationed at every likely point ... He's a confounded rogue, you know, Johnson. Why, his father hired out pianos ... Leases the grand-stand, runs the course, monopolises the entire place ... They say Lord George Bentinck lent him £5,000 once ... Now, are there any artists here? Not seen any? There is bound to be someone. Take this down ... *One of the regular delights of the day is the number of artistic gentlemen come down by early train with an easel determined to take off some aspect of the proceedings. It is ten years, to be sure, since Mr Frith produced his stupendous representation of the concourse, but Mr Phiz has been here too, and I have it on good authority that Mr Doré is about the place with the aim of transferring the contents of his sketchbook onto some exquisite canvas* ... All gammon, Johnson, you understand. Why, I saw Cruikshank's *The Road to the Derby* the day they unveiled it. Six feet long it was, and you would have wept to see the mess he made of it ...'

*

Gradually a change comes over the Derby crowd. The drunken men have been woken up, none too kindly, and dragged away from the rails, and the police are at work clearing the course. The voices of the carousel attendants and the rifle-gallery proprietors grow vainer and more wistful, for their patrons are moving off. The road that runs from the station is still black with people, but the hill is swollen to bursting point. Beneath it the crowd stretches out to the grandstand and beyond it. The canopies of the cook-tents and the restaurant rooms sparkle in the sun. Above them, white birds soar and eddy like scraps of paper.

*

In the enclosure Major Hubbins is remarking many an old acquaintance: Jem Sorrel on The Coalman, whom he has raced against these past twenty years; Bulstrode on Pendragon, who was given up for dead once at Newmarket but somehow recovered. There is a boy on an unknown horse who is young enough to be his grandson, he thinks. The jockeys grin, bow in their saddles, press the handles of their whips against their foreheads. 'Luck, Major!' 'Fair play to you, Sorrel!' Little Tomkins, who is to ride Septuagint, and been compelled – so rumour has it – to lose a stone in the past week, is very pale about the gills and being fortified with brandy. Major Hubbins is grateful for the egg beaten up in a glass of sherry that he consumed half an hour before. His mind focuses, as it always does on these occasions, not on the ordeal before him but on incidentals: the pennants that flutter by the grandstand steps; the shine of his boots; Tomkins, who shakes in the saddle and whose discomfort the Major notes and approves; the rasping breath of the horse beneath him. Some of the other jockeys are demanding how long, staring at the hands of the big clock face on the grandstand's turret, but Major Hubbins does not follow their gaze. There is plenty of time. And nothing, he knows – they are having to right little Tomkins on Septuagint now, for he is in danger of slipping off – can take place without him.

*

On the Derby, on the Derby, I'll bet the Derby. To win or a place, to win or a place. Seven to one bar two or three, seven to one bar two or three. The old firm, the old firm ...

XXVII

Derby Day: Concluded

*. . . gives all London an airing, an 'outing', makes a break in our overworked
lives and effects a beneficial commingling of the classes.*

Gustave Doré and Blanchard Jerrold 'The Derby',
in *London: A Pilgrimage* (1872)

Mr Pardew stalks warily through the Derby crowd. He is not quite
sure what impetus has driven him here: nonetheless the urge, conceived
over the breakfast table in Richmond, has proved quite irresistible.
'Here is news,' he had said to Jemima, feigning to read from a circular
letter plucked from the morning's post. 'Lord Fairhurst wants to know
if I will join him at the Derby. Apologises for the short warning, but
will meet me at the Bell in Cheam. Well, that is very civil of him.' 'Is
His Lordship a racing man?' Jemima had wondered, buttering bread
with the loaf clasped under her arm. 'Indeed yes,' Mr Pardew had
assured her. 'Ran half a dozen horses from his place in Leicestershire,
only I believe his uncle disapproves, you know.' 'You must certainly
go,' Jemima had said.

There are times when Mr Pardew wonders if Jemima is quite sane
in the matter of Lord Fairhurst, Lord Pevensey, the Earl of Grantham
and other bogus noblemen brought out for her edification. Mr Pardew
supposes, in his heart, that his coming to the Derby derives from an

instinctive curiosity, that he is here because he wishes to see Tiberius, on whose destiny so much in his recent life has hung. On the other hand, the anonymity of the crowd is very comforting to him. He is dressed in his habitual black, with his stick wedged up under his arm like a military man, and the butterfly-pin resplendent on his lapel, but not, he imagines, conspicuous. There are all sorts and conditions here at Epsom: drab, white-faced men who look as if they have spent their lives in tunnels far underground, and have only now been let out into the paralysing light; butchers' boys in bloody aprons come straight from the slaughter-yard.

All this interests Mr Pardew, while confirming to him his solitariness. His ideas of life admit no solidarity, none at all. He thinks that perhaps he ought to have brought Jemima with him, who loves an outing, but that the business of Lord Fairhurst would have caused a difficulty. The greater question of what he is to do with himself beats down on him with the same vigour as the sun shining over Epsom Hill. For all his talk, there is a part of him that does not wish to leave England. He has a vision of himself in some country village, where the post comes but once a week, but never to him, and there is no trace of his former life to disturb him, no one to summon him back, merely sky and fields and little white houses gathered under the hills. No Lord Fairhurst, no Mr Happerton, no Tiberius, nor any other burden, real or imagined. The sun is getting up now; the carriages are rolling down to the ring. The crowd surges, divides and regroups, and Mr Pardew, stick in hand, follows where it leads.

*

Captain Raff was thinking about his schooldays. He had not thought about them for thirty years, but somehow there they were. It was extraordinary, he thought, how much he could remember: the great grey schoolyard with the bare Cumberland hills rising beyond it and ominous crags brooding in the distance; the stony sky above the lake; the faces of his schoolmates. He wondered where they had all gone and what had become of them: Devereaux, who had wanted to go to sea, and Willoughby, whose father had fought at Trafalgar, and Baker, who was reckoned a great fellow on account of his being able to bring down crows from the roof with a sling-shot. Then he remembered himself playing cricket on the big field, with fat Lakeland cattle looking on from their pasture, and sitting in the schoolroom while rain fell on the window pane. 'But I was a devilish idle fellow when I was at school,' he said to himself, thinking of the boys who had not been idle and had presumably won great places for themselves. He supposed that some of them would be ... what would they be? Attorneys and clergymen and ships' captains. Well, they were welcome to these employments. And so he wandered on, brooding over these visions of his former life, and Baldino, the instrument of his destiny, with his blue jacket all pulled down on one side, so that the people who saw him go wondered what heavy object he might have concealed beneath it.

*

Such a quantity of items already lying in trampled profusion on the squashed grass. Remnants of food and their containers. Pocket handkerchiefs. Little trails of buttons which the urchins pick over, thinking them to be coins. Ripped-up copies of Mr Dorling's racecard. Newspapers. Hairpins. Stout bottles and a spirit-flask. A St George's medal. A defunct parasol with the spokes hanging out. A Coronation mug. A volume of Praed's poems dropped out of somebody's coat-pocket. Fragments of hard-bake off the tart-women's trays. Opera glasses. A watch-and-chain. Some seals off somebody's waistcoat. The tattered strings of ladies' dresses in muslin, taffeta, watered silk and other materials. A shoe. Several walking sticks. A bottle of Daffy's Elixir. Numberless cigar-ends. A cheap edition of *Pendennis*. A file of legal briefs done up in red string and sealing wax ...

*

At Belgrave Square things were very quiet. Old Mr Gresham, having been given his breakfast, went straight off to sleep again: Mrs Rebecca thought he looked very ancient and worn as she pulled the coverlet back from under his chin. Nonetheless, as the old man had chewed his toast and Mrs Happerton moved restlessly around his room picking up little odds and ends and then returning them to their resting places, a conversation had struck up between father and daughter.

'Where is Happerton?'

'He is at the Derby, Papa.'

'Will the horse . . .' – it was an effort for Mr Gresham to remember his name – '. . . will Tiberius win?'

'The people seem to think so.'

Mrs Rebecca had noticed that, in his infirmity, her father had become more direct in his questions to her. Now he looked at her very keenly and demanded:

'Are you happy? Happy that you married him, I mean?'

'Heavens, what a question to ask, Papa. I suppose any girl that gets married is happy with her husband, otherwise she would not get married.'

'But there are plenty who are not.'

'Well, they must be very foolish,' Mrs Rebecca said, pulling up the coverlet – it was pulled up very tight, so tight that Mr Gresham could probably not have got out from under it even had he wished to – and hastening away.

It was now about eleven o'clock. Belgrave Square was almost empty, and the white cat had gone to sleep on a cushion on the drawing-room sofa. It occurred to Mrs Rebecca that the day was her own and that she could do what she chose with it: walk into the West End, if she had a mind, and set half a dozen milliners and dressmakers scrambling at her feet. But to do this, she knew, she would need money. Accordingly, she repaired to Mr Happerton's study, knowing that there was a drawer of his desk in which loose notes and sovereigns sometimes lay, and it was here, scrunched up among a heap of silver coins that she found that other note. It was the most innocuous scrap of paper you ever saw, cerise-coloured, with the words written on it in a neat, slanting hand, saying something about being eternally obliged, pleasantly delighted and so forth. It was plainly written by a woman – what man ever says that he is eternally obliged or pleasantly delighted? – and it was signed *Your own R.W.* Mrs Rebecca read the note through three times before its implications occurred to her, but then they took her by the throat. *Your own R.W.* There was no doubt about it. She threw the scrap of paper – which had now become a hot thing – down on the desk-top, as if the very touch of it might contaminate or burn her hand. There was a poker among the fire-irons next to the grate and a cut-glass representation of a racehorse on the mantelpiece, and before Mrs Rebecca properly knew what she was doing she had seized the poker and sent the little statuette flying into smithereens. The noise of it – in the silence of the deserted house it seemed like an explosion – rather frightened her, and she let the poker drop to the floor.

Your own R.W. There was no getting away from it. Her first thought was a vast, implacable resentment. She had placed her trust in someone, and compromised herself in all sorts of ways on that person's behalf, and that person had betrayed her. Some of the fragments of the glass horse were lying on the carpet next to her foot and she kicked at them. Then, suddenly, some of the complexities of the situation occurred to her and she began to think about Mr Happerton and his plans, the money that had been acquired on his behalf and the schemes in which she had been confederate. She no longer doubted that he and Mr Pardew had been in league. Why else should Mr Pardew have come to the house? Where else had Mr Happerton got the money that had not come from her? All this was very terrible to her. She knew that while a part of her hated Mr Happerton for his deceptions and his *Your own R.W.*, another part of her admired him for his stratagems. At the same time the brooding, ruminative side of her nature would not release her from its grasp. It was as if the whole affair – her marriage, Tiberius, Mr Happerton's striving after money, Captain Raff, Mr Pardew and the vacancy at the Chelsea Districts – was simply a gigantic puzzle crying out for her to solve. Still standing by the desk, she found herself instinctively trying others of its drawers. Most of them were locked, but on this occasion Mrs Happerton was equal to locked doors. There was a key lying on the mantelpiece, hidden under a pair of horseshoes, and pretty soon she had the drawers open and their contents spread out over the Turkey carpet, and herself seated beside them with her skirts hitched up to her knees and an expression on her face in which fury and cunning zealously commingled. If Mr Happerton himself had appeared at the study door and seen what was going on inside it, he would probably not have dared to enter.

After an hour Mrs Rebecca got to her feet. There was a little attaché case resting against a chair, and she picked it up, turned out its contents into the grate, and began to fill it with documents pillaged from the desk. A little later, with the case clutched tightly in her hands, she strode out into the hallway, ordered the kitchenmaid to summon her a cab, marched through the front door and into the square and had herself driven off eastwards towards the City.

*

The noise is quite overpowering: every visitor to the Derby remarks it: coach-horns sounding from the drags; the scrape of carriage-wheels on the broken turf; the cries of the cook-touts; bookmakers shouting their odds; half a dozen native dialects and a dozen foreign tongues mingled promiscuously together. Mr Pardew thinks, in no particular order, of Mr Fardel, his late associate, with his head stoved in upon the Pump Court cobbles, the Dover mail-train drawn up at London Bridge station, policemen's whistles in Carter Lane, the red brick-dust on Mr Lythgoe's shirtfront. The memories are distasteful to him, but he cannot slough them off. He will get out of this, he thinks. What dream of conquest was ever worth a rose garden in the sun, or dawn striking a water meadow? And for a moment the stick in his hand falls not upon a patch of once green grass trampled grey by a hundred thousand feet, but on a Wiltshire lane, leading on into chalk hills, nothingness and soft oblivion.

*

QUESTIONING OF THE WOMAN HAPPERTON:
BY CAPTAIN McTURK: MR MASTERSON ATTENDING

Captain McT: You say that Mr Pardew came to your house, and was interviewed by your husband. Did he ever come before?

Mrs H: Not to my knowledge. He may have done. There are many people wanting to speak to my husband.

Captain McT: What kind of people? Come, you need not be shy.

Mrs H: Men connected with his business. Sporting gentlemen.

Captain McT: And some that are no gentlemen at all, I'll wager. Was Captain Raff one of them?

Mrs H: The most odious man in the world.

Captain McT: What dealings do you imagine your husband had with Mr Pardew?

Mrs H: I cannot tell. But I have seen Mr Pardew's likeness in the newspaper. I think my husband has had money from him.

Captain McT: Who else has your husband had money from, I wonder? Has he had it from Mr Gresham?

Mrs H: I cannot see that it is any business of yours, but he has lent him money, certainly. Gentlemen very often do lend money to men who have married their daughters, I believe.

Captain McT: And been poisoned by them into the bargain, I don't doubt. Do you know the precise contents of that sleeping draught?

Mrs H: There are no sleeping draughts in my house, I think.

Captain McT: And yet you were seen concocting one. There is no use in denying it. Indeed there is not. How much money has he lent Happerton? Or had taken from him?

Mrs H: It is no business of yours.

Captain McT: Were Mr Gresham to die, it would certainly be my business. And the hangman's too. I am sorry – do I alarm you?

Mrs H: Defenceless women are always there to be frightened, I believe.

Captain McT: Why did you come here, if you did not wish to be frightened?

Mrs H: I came because I thought it my duty.

Captain McT: I have been making a special study of your husband, Mrs Happerton. Why, there is enough evidence to convict him of grand larceny, fraud and several other crimes besides. What if I said it was my duty to arrest him this very afternoon?

Mrs H: You must do as you think fit. It is nothing to me.

Captain McT: I beg your pardon. It is everything. Until you came here I had made various deductions about your husband which I could not corroborate. Now I can. If he is to be taken, it will be your doing.

Mrs H: You must do as you think fit.

Captain McT: What has he done to you that you must betray him?

Mrs H: I cannot say. Truly I cannot.

Captain McT: But you would still be the agent of his doom?

Mrs H: I have told you what I know. Is it not enough?

Captain McT: More than enough.

*

'That's a cool piece,' Captain McTurk said to Mr Masterson, as Mrs Happerton was led away. 'Damns her husband to perdition and never turns a hair. I wonder what is at the bottom of it?'

'That woman in Mount Street, I suppose. It is so very difficult to keep things private.'

'Is that the case? Well, I've no doubt you're right. I knew Mrs H. when she was in petticoats, you know.'

'A charming girl, I dare say,' said Mr Masterston.

'Oh very. But I should not have cared to be the maid who combed her hair the wrong way. Now, the question is: what are we to do with Happerton? He is at the Derby, you say?'

'I believe the race will be run in an hour.'

'Well, we had best go and fetch him I think. If we let him set foot in Belgrave Square again there will be the devil to pay with lawyers. Besides, the sooner he tells us where that man Pardew is the better. And there is nothing like a little drama.'

'No indeed,' said Mr Masterson, who did not look as if he believed it.

'And you had better have Hopkins send to Atterbury at the *Star*. There is nothing like a little publicity either.'

And Mr Masterson supposed that there wasn't.

*

A moralist would be edified by Major Rook's affectionate treatment of his young friend. He is determined to show him the Epsom sights, leads him benevolently among the booths and the sideshows, introduces him to his cronies at the rail, sits him down at their picnic spot and pours him a glass of champagne just as if he had paid for it himself. Champagne doesn't agree with Mr Pigeon's stomach, and neither does the cigar that Major Rook now lights for him with the most tremendous flourish, but he thinks, as his eye drifts over the tribes of people surging up the hill, that he is the most tremendous fellow that ever there was, that Major Rook is his true friend, and Maria the prettiest girl he ever saw, and this the greatest day he ever spent in his life, if only his head would not ache so and his hand not shake so tremulously on the carriage door.

*

Mr Gallentin, walking by the rail with his wife and daughters, spies the butterfly pin before seeing the person who is wearing it: a blue gleam that turns its surround into drabness. For a moment he wonders if he is mistaken, if his mind has led him astray, but no, it is the butterfly pin, right enough, and he stops and gapes at it amid a party of acrobats turning somersaults on the grass and a tipsy woman arguing with a broken-down old man in a nankeen jacket. There is a constable

374

standing thirty yards away, with his back against the rail and a keen eye on the crowd swaying about him, who no doubt ought to be summoned, but Mr Gallentin finds that he can brook no delay in the seeing of the pin and the having of it. 'You sir,' he cries. 'You there.' The Misses Gallentin draw back in astonishment at seeing their papa so provoked. He is a tall man and well built, and his hand is on the wearer of the pin's arm in a moment, but Mr Pardew is the equal of him.

'I think you'll find, sir, that you have made a mistake,' he says, very equably, and Mr Gallentin, whose hand is grasping the arm with all his force, replies that he is not mistaken but knows a d——d thief when he sees one. This is too much for Mr Pardew, who twists easily out of his grasp, jabs upward with his stick and strikes Mr Gallentin in the short ribs, taking the wind out of his lungs and sending him crashing onto the grass, while the acrobats hastily disperse and the Misses Gallentin and their mother set up a cry that would rout out a catacomb. The policeman, summoned from the rail by a dozen voices, finds a fat man collapsed on one knee, with his hat off and his watch chain swinging like a pendulum, being attended to by a circle of outraged ladies. Of Mr Pardew, so thoroughly vanished as if he had never been, there was not the slightest sign.

*

'Which is the horse with the man in crimson and blue?'

'That is Abraxas, Lord Parmenter's.'

Neither Rosa nor Mr Happerton, watching the early races that preceded the Derby, was altogether happy: Rosa because she was bored by the horses and felt that she had been kept purposely from anyone worth the meeting, and was inconveniently hot; Mr Happerton because he had decided that his association with her must come to an end. If Rebecca had been with him, he thought, she would have said sensible things, and not prattled on about the horses' colours. Instead he had brought a simpering, doll-faced idiot whom he could not introduce to his friends. There would be an end to all this, he thought, an end to Rosa, and Mount Street, and irregularity, and perhaps even to horses. He would collect his winnings – they could not be less than fifteen thousand pounds – and retire from sporting life, live modestly in Lincolnshire and cultivate his estate. No, he would follow his wife's counsel – very brilliant counsel it seemed now – and take up politics. Had not old Jack Gully, the bare-knuckle boxer, once sat in the House? Well, surely the proud electors of the Chelsea Districts could find space for a respectable gentleman of independent means such as himself? Thinking these thoughts he became quite virtuous and charitable. An old, white-faced acrobat in a spangled jerkin came stumbling along the path with a small boy turning somersaults in his wake, and he stopped him and put a sixpence in his hand. The great merit of Mrs Rebecca, he told himself again, was that she had his best interests at heart. How many other men could say that of their wives? Wholly absorbed by these imaginings, he strolled along the paddock's edge, not hearing a word that Rosa spoke to him, as the sporting gentlemen clustered around the horses, the crowd stirred and murmured and the white birds spiralled in the azure sky.

*

'You are more of a sporting man than I am,' Captain McTurk said to Mr Masterson as their cab rattled along the Embankment. 'How shall we lay our hands on this Mr Happerton?'

'How indeed?' Mr Masterson wondered. 'There will be a hundred thousand people on the Downs, I dare say. See how empty the city is.'

'I have had Hopkins send a wire to Captain Simms. No doubt he can advise us.'

'What is to be done with Mrs Happerton?'

'What is to be done with her?' Captain McTurk was still frowning at the empty streets, as if he could not quite fathom the urge that had seen them abandoned for a horse race in Surrey. 'Why, we shall see how much of their stories tally. But it would surprise me if she knew everything.'

'And yet it seems to me that she knows a good deal,' Mr Masterson said.

'So did Mrs Macdougall, the wife of that fellow in Brighton who murdered the attorneys in their room,' Captain McTurk said, 'but it was he who went to the block.'

They turned south over Westminster Bridge, where the stink of the river came up and filled the cab, and the pennants on the pleasure-craft drawn up on the southern side glittered in the sun. There were boys out diving for pennies from the ramp beyond Westminster Gardens, and ancient persons, looking as if they had only lately climbed up from the depths, grubbing for flotsam in the mud of the shallows, and Mr Masterson stared at them as he passed. A police launch came into view, moving very slowly, with a man leaning over the side and prodding with a stick at some grey and half-submerged object bobbing under the boat's prow, and Mr Masterson, knowing what the thing was and what would be the outcome of it, turned his gaze elsewhere, out across the church spires, and the factory chimneys, and the mean little streets, and the teeming red-brick villas of South London, and the Epsom Road.

*

'Can't properly see?' Mr Pritchett said to his assistant, as they lounged by the rail. 'I daresay you can't. There are eighty thousand people here can't properly see, but the race will be won just the same. Now take this down: *The paddock, immediately prior to commencement, afforded the most fascinating parade of colour and equine celebrity. I saw Lord Martindale himself, dressed in the very height of sporting fashion* – you might ask, Jones, and see if that old fellow with the whiskers is his lordship – *leading Severus as he took his turn. Mr Grant and Pericles were roundly applauded by an appreciative crowd* ... That Grant is a vulgar man, Jones. Look at him bowing to every navvy that's raising a glass to him. Ugh! ... *Lord Eddington's Avoirdupois was most prettily got up, with Lord*

Eddington walking proudly alongside. There, too, were Baldino and Pericles — such a profusion of horses, each taking their cheer from the crowd, that one despaired of their ever being brought to the start, but somehow Mr Robey's men did their business, and that gentleman, with his handkerchief in his hand, could be seen approaching over the turf, acknowledging the salutations of the crowd, for his is a deserved popularity — It's lies you know, Jones. Dorling would discharge him tomorrow if he weren't Lord Ilchester's son-in-law — *but anxious to bring the business of the day to a swift despatch.*

*

Mr McIvor accepted a final bet on Septuagint from a drunken coster-woman, flung his satchel over his shoulder — how it jingled! — left the twin poles where they stood, caught the eye of his fast friend Mr Jemmy Partridge from the Raven in Shoreditch, laid off a £5 note on Tiberius as Mr Mulligan had counselled him, took the proffered slip and then lowered his head and slipped like an eel through the press of hats and bonnets and nankeen jackets and scarlet frock-coats and varnished boots and shabby highlows to see the fun.

*

As the moment of the race draws near, another change comes upon the crowd. The women grow quieter and less boisterous, conscious that the thing they have come to see will soon be upon them, anxious lest it should lose its savour. The men are seizing their vantage points: a patch on the hill where a pair of field glasses, trained at a certain angle, may engage half a dozen horses as they take the turn around Tattenham Corner. A lick or two of wind stirs up the trampled grass, displaces hats, sets the muslin flounces astir. In the carriages drawn up along the rail the ladies have put away their wineglasses, and had their chicken-bones disposed of by the servants. The Gypsies' stalls and the booths on the hill are quite empty now, for who is there among us who wants his fortune told, or his portrait taken off, or to shy for cocoanuts, or stare at a two-headed baby in its jar, when it wants but five minutes to the running of the Derby?

*

Captain Raff looked at the horses at they ranged out over the grass with benign interest. He could see Septuagint with little Dick Tomkins on his back, taking his place in the line, Dick Tomkins whom he had once given a five-pound note to years ago. How he wished he could have that five pounds back! He knew that should Baldino not win the race he was ruined, that his life would be of no consequence to him any more, but somehow the knowing of it did not seem so very terrible to him, here in the midst of the crowd with the bright sun beating down on his forehead. And so he stared at the horses as they ranged over the grass and tapped his fingers on the breast of his jacket and the thing that lay inside it.

*

'It seems uncommonly quiet,' Captain McTurk said as they came through Epsom, with the hill rising sharply in the distance before them.

'Everyone is at the race, you see. It is quite the event of the year in these parts.'

'Had we better not leave the cab and go on foot?'

'There is a path, I believe, that will take us to the back of the grandstand,' Mr Masterson said.

The track led them through a kind of rural wasteland, defiled and run to seed, composed of cook-tents, horseboxes and discarded lumber, kettles boiling over tenantless fires, rather as if, Captain McTurk thought, a conquering army had passed that way, paused briefly to recruit itself, and then moved on. A clerk at a barred gate hesitated to admit them, but was quelled by Captain McTurk's flashing eye.

'They make a great mess of the place I daresay,' Captain McTurk said.

379

'I believe Dorling keeps the site in very good order,' Mr Masterson said meekly. His own gaze fell upon incidentals: a Gypsy arranging what looked like a skinned rabbit on a spit; a stray horse wandering over the trampled grass; an old lady with a parasol, quite oblivious to the crowds massed a quarter of a mile before her, muttering away on some private errand.

Captain Simms met them at the rear of the stand. He was very much in awe of Captain McTurk.

'They will be off directly,' he said. 'Would you have me stop the race?'

'There is no need for that I think,' Captain McTurk said. 'Where is Happerton?'

'He is in the grandstand. I have a constable directly behind him.'

'He is with a party, I take it?'

'There is a woman with him, I believe.'

There was a sudden roar of enthusiasm from the wooden platforms above their heads, and the sound of a thousand feet drumming in unison.

'There is the race beginning,' Mr Masterson said. 'We had better not waste any time.'

*

A riot of colour. Colour everywhere. The horses are of every imaginable hue: black, bay, chestnut, grey, a multitude of shades in between. The jockeys' silks – scarlet, magenta, carmine, green-and-white, quartered blues and yellows – rustle in the breeze. In the distance a sea of faces, sharp and distinct where the people press up against the rail, fading – as the crowd diffuses up the hill – into a remote generality. Nothing Mr Frith could ever do can convey the enormity of the scene or its infinite particularity, the sway and eddy of fifty thousand shoulders, the women fainting in the heat and being taken out, the flashes of light as the sun catches on the raised opera glasses in the grandstand, the cacophony of individual shouts – 'Baldino!', 'Septuagint!', 'Pendragon!'. The band is still playing 'The British Grenadiers' on the near side of the paddock, but nobody hears it. Nobody hears anything, for there is nothing that can properly be heard. The field is strung out now in a ragged line behind the single restraining rope, and already there is a doubt as to how they shall be got off. Major Hubbins is snug in his saddle, with his whip clutched in his hand, but little Dick Tomkins has turned whey-faced and is having to be put onto his mount by main force, and the crowd groans and cheers according to taste and prejudice, and the rope yields a little and is then dragged back. Here is Mr Robey! Make way for Mr Robey! Mr Robey will take charge!

And Mr Robey looks around him, commands that a horse with no rider nor with anyone seeming to know where he came from shall be taken away, and that the rope be pulled back another yard and that Dick Tomkins' two assistants retire unless they mean to ride the race as a trio. Mr Robey has his flag in his hand, and the crowd stares at it, but no, there is another difficulty, another check, and the line of horses sways backwards and the rope tumbles around their ankles. But then suddenly, and with no obvious help from anyone present, the thing resolves itself. The horses come daintily forward, like dancers in a gavotte, Major Hubbins looks calmly round him, the rope tightens around the first straining chests, Mr Robey drops his flag – that flag that a dozen people will fight over for the luck of it – the rope falls and the race is begun.

*

'Trust Robey to get them away,' Mr Pritchett said to his assistant, 'for all he's Lord Ilchester's son-in-law. Sutherland is supposed to be at Tattenham Corner with his easel ready to take them off as they come round, but it's a precious hard job he'll have of it. Gracious, what a noise these fellows make. Well, there is The Coalman. Heavens! He will run into the rail at this rate. There! What did I tell you? Whose is the grey? Pendragon, you say. No, he has faltered already. There's your shilling gone, Jones. What is old Hubbins doing? Biding his time, I daresay. Here comes Baldino, at any rate. Tomkins on Septuagint looks as if he were ready to fall off. There was talk that he hadn't eaten for a week. There, Pendragon has pulled up, what did I tell you? And Severus does not look much better. Baldino at two lengths. Why, they are nearly half-way now. If Hubbins wants to make ground, now is the time to do it. Still Baldino, but Septuagint nowhere . . . I should think Tomkins will need a week in bed after this . . . Baldino, still, by a length . . .'

*

They took Mr Happerton at the very foot of the grandstand, where he leant on the rail with Rosa beside him. At first, amid the tumult of the crowd – he could hear the voices shouting 'Baldino' and 'Tiberius' in strophe and antistrophe – he could not understand what they wanted of him. Then, when he understood, a kind of terror came into his eye and he made a dart under the rail, only for Mr Masterson to upend him and, with the aid of Captain Simms' constable, take a grip on his collar. Rosa they ignored. Looking up, as they passed back along the rows, Captain McTurk had a sudden glimpse of the line of horses: furious chips of bright colour, black, red and black again, that surged unappeasably over the bright grass, but the spectacle did not interest him and he lowered his head.

*

'Who has won?' Mr Masterson demanded of a steward, as he came out of the back of the grandstand with Mr Happerton's wrist wedged up under his arm.

In the tumult the man did not understand him and tapped at his ear for the question to be repeated.

'Who has won? Who has won the race?' Mr Masterson bellowed again.

'Why, the black 'un. Tiberius! Tiberius has won the Derby!'

*

Captain Raff staggered through the crowd. The people on either side of him surged forward and he looked at them dully. The thing in the inner pocket of his jacket was still quite concealed from view, and from time to time he pressed his hand against it and traced its outline with his finger. The vision of Baldino, faltering and nearly fallen onto her knees as the black horse sped by had now gone, together with the pictures of the grey crags and the distant lake, and all that remained was the people jostling his elbows and the crowd running up the hill. It was no good, he thought, he would have to sit down. There was a restaurant tent just before him, with the canvas flap of its door half open, and putting his head inside he discovered that it was empty, that although urns and plates stood arranged on the trestle at its further end, and there were any number of smaller tables strewn about the enclosed patch of grass, all the people had gone. Swaying a little as he moved across the trampled sward, which was scattered with fragments of bread and other refuse, he seized one of the chairs and sat down heavily, looked around him, put his head in his hands for a moment, sat up sharp, plunged his hand into his pocket and drew out the thing that lay concealed inside it.

*

'You had better keep the people out of that tent,' said Policeman x to Policeman y five minutes later. 'There is a poor fellow just cut his throat in there.'

'What? Dead?'

'Well, perhaps not. But there is blood all over him. Here!'

They bore Captain Raff out of the tent on a rail, with the policeman's cape thrown over his chest and his arm dangling behind him brokenly over the grass.

*

Two hours later a cab rolled up to the little house in Richmond and a number of gentlemen jumped out very anxious to have words with its

383

lessee, whose address Mr Happerton had been prevailed upon to yield up. But there was no sign of Mr Pardew, nor, though a thorough search was conducted of its interior, any trace of his leavings, only Jemima, whom they found, very meek and respectful, cutting out pastry for a pie in the kitchen, a budgerigar singing in its cage and the dining-room table laid for a solitary supper.

*

Slowly the crowds disperse. Epsom High Street is so full of people that there is a danger of being trampled. Singly and severally, joyfully or despondently, resigned or matter-of-fact, the Derby throng ebbs, disperses and makes its way home. Mr Pritchett and his assistant go off to eat whitebait at the White Horse at Dorking. Mr McIvor, who has made twenty pounds, departs in triumph on the back seat of the Bird in Hand's hired drag with a pair of butchers' apprentices blowing cornets in his ear. Mr Mulligan and his companion are sauntering tipsily in the High Street, manifestly out of pocket but in high good humour. Major Rook, Mr Pigeon and their genteel companions roll away in their carriage to a performance at the Drury Lane Theatre, a late supper in the neat house off the Row, and a snug little game of blind hooky in the course of which Major Rook relieves his young friend of exactly £75, reflecting all the while that he will step round and see Mr Trant first thing just in case that gentleman should have decided to take one of his little holidays in Brighton. Mr Glenister hastens – in so far as anyone may hasten in these circumstances – to supper with his clerical friend. Captain Raff is with the coroner. Rosa goes home in tears in a succession of omnibuses.

*

Tall hat tilted back over his forehead, Mr Dorling strides over the wet grass. It is eleven o'clock on a Sunday morning, and the rest of the family is at church, but the clerk of the course knows his duty. For an hour now he has been prowling the area around the grandstand, peering conscientiously into rubbish-wagons, issuing instructions to the men who are taking down the bunting from the grandstand pillars, and generally making himself useful. In truth there is not a great deal to do, and the weather is not satisfactory, but still Mr Dorling prowls and surveys and speculates. There is rain falling over the Surrey Hills and a line of blue-grey clouds over Dorking and Guildford: occasionally he raises his head to inspect them, as if they too could be parcelled up and taken away by the dirt-men and their wagons. Of all the elements, Mr Dorling is most suspicious of rain. It is all very melancholy and bleary.

Up on the hill he can see the Gypsies marshalling their vans and the proprietors of the travelling booths dismantling their stalls. The were-wolf, certified by the rubric beneath his cage to prefer human flesh, will howl no more, or not for another year. The two-headed baby has been returned to its shelf. Mr Dorling likes neither the Gypsies nor the showmen, would have them driven off and the ground given over to respectable folk, but a part of him recognises their suitability to the scene they swell, acknowledges that in their absence a proportion of the spectacle over which he presides would be lost. Besides, who are respectable folk? Mr Happerton's capture, there in the grandstand, for all to see, with a Mayfair whore screaming to wake the dead at his side, is the talk of Epsom. Less noticed, but no less disagreeable to Mr Dorling, is a man who cut his throat in a deserted refreshment tent and was taken out dying with his head covered up in a blanket. By this Mr Dorling is genuinely outraged. The police, he feels, can deal with Mr Happerton, but for a man to destroy himself in a refreshment tent, and then to be dragged out before a thousand onlookers, is a kind of elemental throwing-over of the laws of hospitality, something that, if Mr Dorling had his way, would be prohibited by law.

But there is a great deal, Mr Dorling concedes, that cannot be prohibited by law. Mr Happerton and men who destroy themselves in public places are merely infinitesimal specks among a shoal of doubtful ends and questionable behaviour. Somehow these thoughts remind him of the Derby crowd, which he sees again in his mind, as he has seen it a hundred times before, surging over the hill, the carriages drawn up at the rail, the girls' white dresses gleaming in the sun. But the crowd has gone and will not return for another year. Above Dorking and Guildford the clouds are moving in again. Already the ground beneath Mr Dorling's feet is turning treacherous. From up on the hill, borne on the breeze as the wind gets up, come the melancholy cries of the Gypsies saluting each other. Spread out before him, almost as far as the eye can see, a carpet of abandoned paper, trampled food, every conceivable thing, it seems, that a person could set down and forget, runs away towards the bracken. A yard away, not quite obliterated by the rain, there is a copy of his racecard. Obeying some inner prompting that he cannot wholly explain, he bends down and picks it up, turns it over and scans the list of riders and their mounts. It is quite unmarked, he sees, but that beneath the name of Tiberius, in bright red ink, someone has placed a solitary tick.

XXVIII

Afterwards

How should a story end? For myself, I like the good to triumph and the wicked to be damned. But what about that very substantial number of men and women who belong to neither of these categories, who do a little good here and a little bad there, who are constrained by their situation, pressed into evil ways by force of circumstance, whose sins are venial, whose temperaments are flawed and whose victories, as a consequence, are sadly compromised. How should they be disposed of?

Miss Pilkington's *Lectures on Light Literature* (1867)

It is one thing to arrest a man in plain view of a thousand racegoers and have him taken away by closed cab to a police cell in the West End of London, but it is quite another thing to have him brought to trial. And it is a third thing – the greatest thing of all – to ensure that his trial results in a conviction. All this Captain McTurk knew – it had been dinned into him by long and bitter experience – and even by the end of the day on which Mr Happerton had been plucked from the Epsom grandstand he had taken steps to enable these second and third things to follow unhindered in the wake of the first. He spent the remainder of the weekend in his eyrie above Northumberland Avenue – poor Mr Hopkins was called back from his mama's in Somersetshire – and the Monday morning found him closeted with a great legal eminence at the Home Office, canvassing the various felonies of which Mr Happerton might be found guilty. There were, Captain McTurk deposed, three distinct lines of attack: the matter of the forged bills, which he believed had been used as an instrument to ruin Mr Davenant and hasten his end; the sedative administered to Mr Gresham, which he maintained had been used to enfeeble him and rob him of his money; and the burglary of Mr Gallentin's shop, by Mr Pardew, in which Captain McTurk imagined Mr Happerton to have been confederate. Put them together, and the case against Mr Happerton as one of the most audacious swindlers, poisoners and accessories to grand larceny, could surely be proved beyond doubt.

But the great legal eminence, sitting snugly in his carpeted room, with one young man to bring him in his coffee and another to take his letters off to the post, and a newspaper on his desk offering the most sensational disclosures about Mr Happerton, counselled caution. In the matter of the forged bills, he thought that Captain McTurk might very probably secure a conviction, for the evidence – in particular the sheet of attempts on Mr Davenant's signature – was so very strong, but when it came to the poisoned milk-and-arrowroot he shook his head.

'Plenty of old gentlemen have a sleeping draught put in their milk,' he suggested.

'There is seven thousand pounds gone from Gresham's account at Gurney's,' Captain McTurk declared, not quite liking to say where he had got this information. 'It's as plain as a pikestaff what the man was about.'

'And yet old gentlemen very often give money to their sons-in-law, don't they?' proposed the great legal eminence, who certainly had done so himself. 'If they approve of them, that is. And sometimes even if they don't.'

'There is his wife, who will swear the whole thing is a plot, done with her connivance,' Captain McTurk protested.

'I don't doubt she will. But I think you would have great difficulty in proving it. That is all. Now, what about the robbery at Gallentin's shop?'

And here, too, Captain McTurk found that there was a difficulty. The difficulty was the absence of Mr Pardew, of whom, since the Saturday evening descent upon the house at Richmond, no trace had been found. Captain McTurk had had men watching the Channel ferries; he had an emissary at Paris, and descriptions of Pardew sent by electric telegraph to every capital in Europe; but having engaged in a previous pursuit of Mr Pardew that had taken him (or rather Mr Masterson) across the Atlantic Ocean and back again, he was not sanguine. All he had, in fact, in the absence of Mr Pardew and any evidence of Mr Pardew's involvement in the crime, was a sheet of paper found in the cellar of the premises adjoining Mr Gallentin's shop, consisting of a few sentences that might or might not have been written by Mr Happerton.

'Let us say the letter was Happerton's,' the great legal eminence conceded. 'There are a dozen ways in which it might have got there. Perhaps Pardew committed the crime – and I agree that the chance of his having done so is very strong. But it can't be proved. And neither can it be proved that he has any connection with Happerton.'

'There is his wife, again, who saw him coming out of Happerton's study a day or so before the race.'

'Women very often are mistaken about these things. If you take my tip, you'll be very sparing in the use you make of Mrs Happerton. There is something odd going on there. Some spite or animus – I don't know. Much better to give a jury a forged signature than a woman with a score to settle. If you take my advice, McTurk, you'll give up the burglary and the poisoning and make your pitch on those bills. There's not a jury in the country won't convict him on them.'

At this juncture there was an interruption, caused by the Home Secretary's chief clerk dancing into the room with an urgent summons, and Captain McTurk, rising to his feet, with the headlines about Mr Happerton staring at him from the desktop, said that he would think about it. Then, coming back to Northumberland Avenue, where Mr Masterson had been at work on his behalf, he received a further piece of information that he thought might help to nail Mr Happerton to the slab. This was the discovery, by the Surrey Police, from certain papers found in the deceased's jacket, that the man who had cut his throat in the refreshment tent at Epsom was Captain Raff. Captain McTurk and Mr Masterson were at Ryder Street within the half-hour – very bleak and blear it was, with the Emperor of Prussia ascending the stair in full court regalia – and the door of Captain Raff's chambers broken in with a crowbar (the artists came out of their rooms and stared) but it was surprising how little that gentleman had left behind him. A cabin trunk full of dirty laundry and a stack of bills (unpaid) pinioned by a metal spider seemed to be the Captain's chief legacy to the world, and Captain McTurk, biting his fingers in the shabby room, its plant-tubs quite yellow with neglect and the 'Head of an Officer' staring down at him from the wall, felt that he stood in the midst of a parable, whose moral implications it might be injurious to pursue. There was a letter lying on the desk next to the bill-spider, and he picked it up, read a few lines of it – it was a bastardy suit in which Captain Raff had somehow become involved – and then, disgusted, put it down.

But if Captain Raff, now deceased, was no help to Captain McTurk (they buried him down in Epsom, before a congregation of two persons: Mr Delaney, and a very old lady down from Northumberland, who was thought to be the captain's aunt) then there were other avenues that were worth the exploring. He had Mr Masterson go down to Leather Lane and interview Mr Solomons, to that gentleman's profound alarm. He himself routed out Mr File again in Amwell Street. He would have questioned Mr Gresham, but word came from Belgrave Square that the old man was very ill indeed, so ill as to altogether prohibit any interrogation by the police, or indeed anyone else. Still, Captain McTurk procured a search warrant and, together with Mr Masterson, spent an instructive afternoon in Mr Gresham's study going through his son-in-law's effects. He had the powder which had been put into Mr Gresham's milk-and-arrowroot analysed by a man from a chemical laboratory, who demonstrated that it was a powerful sedative that should certainly not have been given to an elderly gentleman in poor health and had probably come near to killing him. He had Mr Masterson go down to Scroop and see what Mr Happerton had left behind him there. But it was remarkable how comfortless all this was to Captain McTurk. He felt like a digger in the vault of some ancient temple, who has assembled a hundred fragments of some shot mosaic, without having the least

390

idea of the originating pattern. And yet Captain McTurk knew that there was a pattern, and that only the guile of its designer kept it from him.

But all this time Captain McTurk had one trump card up his sleeve, an asset which he thought would enable him to vanquish everything from the caution of the great legal eminence from the Home Office to the evidential desert of Ryder Street. This was Mrs Happerton. A married lady cannot, of course, be compelled to testify against her husband in a court of law. But Captain McTurk fancied that no compulsion would be necessary. At the same time, Captain McTurk had not quite known what to do about Mrs Happerton. He had begun by thinking that he might charge her with old Mr Gresham's poisoning; expedience had then dictated that she might best be used as a witness to her husband's overbearing design. On the other hand, a lady in such circumstances cannot really be allowed out into polite society. So Captain McTurk had conspired with the Honourable Major Stebbings and other interested persons, and for the last two weeks he had had her shut up in a house in Marylebone High Street, with a very discreet woman to care for her and instructions that she should be conciliated and indulged in every way, have friends to visit her, be let out into Marylebone High Street for air and recreation if she wished it, only that – she should not be allowed out of the discreet woman's sight. The discreet woman was called Mrs Martin, and on calling at the house in the week before Midsummer, Captain McTurk made sure that he had a little conversation with that lady in the kitchen. How had Mrs Happerton spent her time? Mrs Martin thought that she had read novels, twenty or thirty novels at least from Mudie's. Had anyone come to see her? It transpired that the Honourable Major Stebbings had called twice. And how did Mrs Martin think her charge was faring? But to this question Mrs Martin had no answer, and Captain McTurk had proceeded to the drawing room, in which Mrs Happerton was accustomed to spend her afternoons, not quite knowing what he would find.

She was sitting in a little high-backed chair by the empty grate – the sun, streaming in through the open window burned off her shoulders

– and there was something about her manner that made him stop in the doorway and look at her. She was simply dressed, in a print frock, with the neatest pair of slippers on her feet, and as immaculate as a fashion plate, but that a strand or two of her hair had escaped from the chignon behind her head and she was chewing at them like an animal that has nothing better to eat. She looked very sandy and dry, as if the heat of the day had quite shrivelled her up, and Captain McTurk thought that he did not envy Mrs Martin her task.

'They are looking after you, I hope?' he said as he came into the room. He could hear Mrs Martin clattering the dishes in the kitchen, and a part of him wished he could be there with her.

'Mrs Martin is very kind,' Mrs Rebecca said, with a little tug of her mouth at a strand of hair that showed signs of escaping. 'Indeed, I think I know every inch of Marylebone High Street and the contents of every shop window in it.'

'You will not credit it perhaps,' Captain McTurk said, 'but I knew you when you were a child. That is – I used to call at your house, when your papa and I had business. Do you recollect it?'

'No, I do not recollect it. Papa knew so many people.'

And Captain McTurk knew that he had made a mistake. He had tried to introduce a personal note into his dealings with Mrs Happerton and it had been thrown back at him. And, thinking this, he remembered the young Miss Gresham, whom he had thought spoiled and captious. That was the end of any sentiment, he thought.

'Tell me about the money your father gave to Mr Happerton,' he proposed. 'The seven thousand pounds from the account at Gurney's bank.'

'The money was lent, I believe,' Mrs Rebecca said, very coolly.

'And what condition was your father in when he lent it, I wonder?' Captain McTurk asked. 'Did he know what was going into his milk?'

'There was nothing went into his milk but arrowroot,' Mrs Rebecca said. Captain McTurk looked at her face, but it was quite without expression. 'Or if there was, I cannot say how it got there. I cannot answer for Mr Happerton.'

Captain McTurk thought that he had never seen anything so disagreeable as the way Mrs Happerton chewed at her hair.

'You realise that this is very serious? Your father is very unwell. There is a man dead in Lincolnshire, and half a dozen bills forged that helped to kill him. It is very probable that you may be charged as an accessory.'

'Everything is very serious,' Mrs Rebecca said. 'I am always being told that. Marriage is very serious, and yet gentlemen don't seem to think it so. Living in a house in Belgrave Square and being driven in a carriage in the park is very serious, or so I was always led to believe, and yet it makes me laugh. So many things make me laugh. Half a dozen gentlemen ruining themselves over a horse, and Captain Raff cutting his throat because his life isn't to his liking. I should like not to be serious. I should like to please myself. I should like to drive my own carriage, and not have anybody to wonder where I go and when I should return. I should like to live my own life, and not to be at anybody's beck and call except my own. And I have been an accessory to nothing, unless it is to my own humiliation. Poor Papa,' she added.

It was that 'Poor Papa' that convinced Captain McTurk that some game was being played with him. Until then he had listened with a sense of something very near wonder – he had never heard a woman speak like that before, and scarcely ever a man. But the mention of Mr Gresham, which Mrs Rebecca could not quite carry off as she had done the earlier part of her speech, made him suspect that she and Mr Happerton had been confederate together – the transfer of the seven thousand pounds could not have taken place without some collusion – but that Mrs Rebecca meant to throw her husband over while saving herself. In these circumstances the 'Poor Papa' struck him as highly duplicitous, but he was anxious above all things – Mr Happerton's lawyers were very pressing – to secure a conviction. And so, going back to the room above the stable yard in Northumberland Avenue, he wrote Mrs Happerton a letter setting out what she might testify to in court, and what she might not, and what the consequences of these admissions, and refusals, might be. To this, a day or so later, Mrs Happerton replied.

'What does she do with herself?' he asked Mrs Martin again at about this time.

'Do with herself?' Mrs Martin repeated. 'Why, nothing now. Nothing at all. Sits in the parlour and twists her hair. That Major Stebbings as is her cousin called again and she wouldn't see him. There was an afternoon the other day when I thought I heard the sound of her crying to herself, so I went in to see her, thinking that she might take a morsel to eat – for she has had nothing this past week, to speak of – and she was sitting in that chair straight as a ramrod, and said to me: "Mrs Martin, ma'am, I'll thank you to come into this room only when a bell is rung for you and not before."'

And Captain McTurk shook his head and thought once again that he did not envy Mrs Martin her task.

There was by this time a Happerton party – not much of one, perhaps but vociferous, and consisting of a few gentlemen from the Blue Riband Club, who maintained that the whole thing was a plot contrived by Mr Happerton's enemies in the sporting world to discredit him. There was also, it goes without saying, a movement for Mrs Rebecca, genteel, and more vociferous still, which held that she had been badly treated, coerced and browbeaten by the man in whom she had placed her trust and was as innocent as the driven snow: driven snow is always thought to be innocent, and yet it takes the dirt like anything else. All this naturally gave Mr Happerton's trial, which began in the first week of September, an unusual piquancy. He was arraigned on two counts – the forging of Mr Davenant's signature on bills, and the administration of poison to old Mr Gresham in pursuit of pecuniary advantage. There was no mention of Mr Pardew, or the robbery at Mr Gallentin's shop, or indeed of Mrs Rebecca, and one or two people thought that Captain McTurk was playing a dangerous game, and that there were weaknesses in the case which Mr Carker, whom Mr Happerton's friends had engaged on his behalf, might very well exploit.

The first two days of the trial were very dull. Serjeant Daniels, the Crown prosecutor, produced the sheet of facsimile signatures from the study at Scroop and handed it round to the jury. Mr Silas was brought to the witness stand to give his account of the despoliation of Mr Davenant's estate. A Sleaford hay chandler testified that a bill in his name with Mr Davenant's signature on it was a forgery. A medical man was brought in to quantify the hurt done to old Mr Gresham by the administration of the sedative powder, and a representative of Messrs Gurney to confirm the transfer of the seven thousand pounds into Mr Happerton's account. Mr Happerton, very soberly dressed in a subfusc suit and with not an equine pin upon him, denied each calumny that was attributed to him, and Mr Carker was judged to have been very clever. He put a question or two to Mr Silas about the legal procedure for collecting a debt that entirely flummoxed him, and the little homily he pronounced on the value of sedative medicines and the possibility of honest confusion by those who administered them was thought to have tied Captain McTurk's medical man up in knots. He interrogated Mr Glenister to such effect that an observer might have thought him entirely motivated by spite against Mr Happerton rather than affection for his dead friend. A sample of the powder which had been used to quieten Mr Gresham was brought onto the stand, and Mr Carker positively snapped his fingers and said it could have been got from anywhere, and never had a solicitous son-in-law been so unfairly stigmatised, and was shushed by the judge for his impertinence. Captain McTurk, watching from the gallery, was almost in despair.

But the arrival of Mrs Rebecca at the witness box on the third day caused a sensation. Quite whether Captain McTurk had had a hand in her costuming was uncertain, but it was noted by the reporters present that she appeared in a dress of the deepest black, as black as widows' weeds, and that this, combined with the pallor of her face, produced a very striking impression. There had been a rumour in the newspapers that old Mr Gresham was very near death, and this created an additional sympathy for her, and the judge ordered that a chair be brought and asked: would she have a glass of water? When she spoke it was in a low voice with her head sunk down upon her breast, and her green eyes were very subdued. Serjeant Daniels was, of course, very gentle with her. She had married Mr Happerton less than a year before, had she not? And Mrs Rebecca nodded her head very meekly and said that

she had. And what had been her impression of the gentleman who –
Serjeant Daniels was a very polite man and made a little bow as he said
the words – won her heart?

And very timorously at first, with frequent shy glances at judge, jury
and a stout woman who sat upon the public benches and was assumed
to be her particular friend, but was later found to have no connection
with her at all, she told the story of her husband's pursuit of Tiberius,
his descent upon Mr Davenant's estate at Scroop to claim his prize, his
desire to obtain his father-in-law's money and the manner in which
this assistance had been procured. Asked by Serjeant Daniels whether
she believed that the powder given to her father – her own father, as
Serjeant Daniels sternly reminded the jury – was injurious, she was
observed to bite her lip, give a sad little twist to a tendril of hair that
had escaped from her chignon and remark that she believed it her duty
as a newly married woman to obey her husband's instructions in all
things. Did she know anything of the forged bills? Mrs Rebecca put
her head on one side and said, with what appeared to be the greatest
reluctance, that she did.

Naturally Mr Carker could do nothing with her. When he hinted –
it was not something he could decently say – that she was determined
to betray her husband because of some personal slight that had no
bearing on the case, there was a cry of 'Shame!' from the public gallery.
When he implied that she was not telling the truth, she stared at him
in such a sorrowful way that even the defence barristers began to look
uneasy and wonder whether Mr Carker had overreached himself. There
was an attempt to prove her an accessory – 'a vixen determined to play
upon a fond parent's partiality' as Mr Carker rather forlornly put it –
but Mr Happerton's defence had by this time collapsed into ruins, and
he was very soon after this found guilty on both counts.

*

Mr Happerton was sentenced to ten years' imprisonment. He is not
much mourned, save by a very few cognoscenti of the Blue Riband

Club. Rosa, now living in Wardour Street, Soho, and perhaps not so well situated as she might be, says he is the most odious man who ever lived.

The election for the Chelsea Districts took place in due course, and despite Mr Dennison's best efforts was lost by Sir Charles Devonish to that hot radical Mr Cartwright, formerly the member for Stepney.

After old Mr Gresham's death, which was attributed by his doctor to pneumonia, six months after the trial, Mrs Happerton retired to Bath, where she lived in a house on the Crescent, attended tea-parties and was fêted by the Bath ladies as the pitiable victim of gross male subterfuge. But somehow Bath and the Bath ladies did not suit her, and within a year she had removed herself to the continent, been seen in Paris, and supposed to have come to rest in Baden-Baden. Certainly a lady answering her description was seen at the tables there, spending a great deal of money, and it is said that a share prospectus issued on behalf of the Baden-Baden Peruvian Mining Company bore the name of Messrs Schickelgrubers' bank acting as her proxy. Mrs D'Aubigny, who wrote to her once, got no reply. Mr Fop, the great dandy, dined at her hotel once on one of his European tours, but he never went there again. It is thought that Mrs Happerton – she still calls herself Mrs Happerton despite her husband's disgrace – may be supported in her new vocations by Miss Nokes, who has certainly not been seen in the Belgrave region or at the Bag o' Nails for many a month.

Mr Pardew was never seen again. A man answering to his appearance was arrested at a lodging house in Vienna, but when questioned was able to supply such convincing proofs of his identity and bona fides that he was released, to the infinite disgust of Captain McTurk, who found out about it a week later.

Jemima is living with her sister in Islington. It is said that this lady, to spite her, produced a Peerage and challenged her to find Lord Fairhurst's name in it.

Major Hubbins, retiring from his profession in glory, accepted an invitation from his friend the Earl of Ilchester to supervise his stud. He lives in Hampshire, has grown stout, and is very comfortable.

There was some doubt as to what might happen to Tiberius. One legal argument held that as he had been fraudulently acquired, he did not now belong to Mr Happerton. In the end, though, he was put up for auction in a sale of Mr Happerton's effects (otherwise inconsiderable) and sold to a sporting syndicate. His subsequent career may be followed in *Ruff*.

Miss Kimble, Mrs Happerton's cousin, married the Captain Powell who always spoke to her so politely in the park – Mrs Venables lent her drawing room for the reception – and is now living, more or less happily, in Bayswater while the captain, having sold out of his regiment, looks for something more suited to his accomplishments and aptitudes.

The Honourable Major Stebbings is still much exercised by the question of army reform.

The house in Belgravia is shut up, with brown paper over the chandeliers and the old housekeeper living on board wages. Mr Happerton's – or rather Mr Gresham's – study is as left, with the portrait of Tiberius still staring from the wall.

Anstruther, RA's 'Head of an Officer' came up for sale at Mr Fitch's auctioneering rooms only the other day, and was knocked down for ten guineas. No one knows who bought it.

Mr Delaney gets by.

The Blue Riband Club is in a very flourishing state.

Mr Glenister went back to Lincolnshire after the trial, where it was thought that he was to be married.

*

It had been a very quiet autumn in Lincolnshire, so quiet that Mr Jorkins arriving in his cart to bring the *Grantham Intelligencer* was a great event and the sound of the Scroop foxhounds out in the lanes beyond Edgard Dyke a Saturnalia that had them talking for a week. And yet Miss Ellington had not been idle, for there had been Evie to tend, and her *Christian Year* to read at, not to mention sheets to turn and restitch – there being no one else to sew them – and a multitude of tasks to perform which would be thought inconvenient for a staff of ten, next to whom Hester, Mrs Castell and she were but the merest makeweights. And so, however precariously, the routines of their existence were preserved. The lamps were still lit, and the stair carpet swept. The windfall apples were gathered up from the orchard floor, and Evie's muslins set to dry on the currant bushes, and they were an example to each other, if not to anyone else, for all that Mrs Castell said she was a fool to stay, and that Hester would be lucky to get her wages paid on December quarter-day.

A visitor who came to Scroop each November to stand on the gravel drive and look at the mullioned windows would no doubt have found it unchanged. The water still dripped out of the eaves; the rooks still flew up at the least interruption; the caryatid still sat in lonely splendour on her fountain-rock; the wild garden still ran down to the wood where Mr Davenant had kept his gibbet. But beyond that all was in flux. There were no horses in the stable, for they had all been taken away; the logs that lay in the stable yard had been sold to the Lincoln timber-merchant; and there was no more milk creamed up in the dairy. Indeed, on the days when Evie and Miss Ellington put on their cloaks and bonnets and went out wandering in the spinneys it was as if they were a pair of ghosts, bred by an age that had passed away and would never come again. There was no money, Mr Glenister said, and would not be until Mr Davenant's affairs were truly gone into and settled by the lawyers, and if Miss Ellington did not turn and restitch the sheets there would be no bed for her to lie on.

And yet if they had been quiet, and secluded, and if the rain had vexed them beyond endurance, they had not lacked diversion. Mr Happerton's trial interested them greatly. The newspapers which reported it were handed about at the breakfast table and discussed among them as they went about their work, and Mr Glenister's account of it, when he returned from London, they listened to as if it were a fresh instalment of the Scriptures brought down that morning from Sinai. Hearing what had taken place in the courtroom, Hester flew into a passion and said that Mr Happerton should hang, but that his wife was worse, because she had not stood by her husband, which was a wife's duty, and she should be put in the stocks to be pelted. For herself, Miss Ellington looked at the portrait of Mr Happerton and, considering what he had done, regretted that she had been so foolish as to esteem him or be flattered by the civility of his address. But as Mrs Macfarlane used to say, Lucifer has many disguises and could be found under the fairest countenance. There was a picture of Mrs Happerton, too, which Miss Ellington looked at and thought that she did not understand the world or the people in it, that she was a country mouse who had best keep to hedgerows and hay-wains where she might be safe from peril.

One day in November the establishment had a visitor. This was Dora, or Mrs Jorkins as they were now to call her, brought over by Mr Jorkins in his cart, and so beribboned that, as Mrs Castell said, it was as if she intended herself as a maypole. She said that Jorkins was the meekest old man in Christendom, and was very happy, and they were very comfortable together. 'And you, too, Annie,' she said, 'I hope you will be happy.' Which embarrassed Miss Ellington very much, not thinking her circumstances widely known, and not liking attention to be drawn to it, which old Mrs Macfarlane said was the sovereignest thing for going to a girl's head and spoiling her chance. But then, when Dora had gone, she repented of her anger, realising that she meant only to compliment her, and wish her well, and gathered up Evie in her arms, to whom she was reading, and made her do as proxy.

Who has a tortoiseshell cat, now, called Arabella, that she torments.

Who sits sometimes in terror beneath the portraits of her ancestors as if they were real people who might jump out of their frames into her lap.

Whom Miss Ellington acknowledged that she did not love, but should do her duty by always.

Evie should be sent away, Mr Glenister said, if Miss Ellington wished it. But she did not wish it, and told him no.

She should be a burden to him, she protested to Mr Glenister, as they walked that afternoon in the meadow, and it was not her place to live at Glenister Court and be its mistress, and Mr Glenister said that she should not, and that it was, that no one knew their places in life until they came upon them and saw that they fitted them. And thinking of this, it was as if Miss Ellington's head was filled with a series of pictures, so sharp and lifelike that she could not comprehend what had driven them there – Tiberius in his stall, Mr Davenant's face upon the rail, the rooks soaring above the elms, Mr Silas's gig grinding up the gravel in the drive – and she took Mr Glenister's arm, who smiled at her, she thought, very winningly, and walked off across the green grass, and was, she thought, so very happy.

*

Nobody quite knew how Mr Synnot had come to Baden. The railway had certainly not brought him there, and the coaching office had no knowledge of him. Despite the enigma of his arrival, there was no mystery about his intentions, for Mr Synnot was plainly in Baden to enjoy himself. He put up at the Imperial Hotel, spent a little money at its gaming tables, loitered among its garden statuary, and could be seen in the establishment's public rooms, reading newspapers, demanding cups of tea and conversing with such English tourists as came his way. Mr Synnot said that he was an Englishman and, like many Englishmen *en route* through Europe, he was certainly very knowledgeable. He knew when the gaming rooms were open and who was likely to frequent them; he knew the dates of the public balls; where *Galignani* could be obtained and the price of hiring a carriage from the livery stable. All this made Mr Synnot an agreeable addition to that part of English society that settles itself in Baden over the summer. He was at all times ready to escort a party to a distant pleasure garden, to play at écarté after dinner or recommend a church worth the visiting, and for this the ladies were disposed to forgive even his red complexion, over-large hands and pronounced Hibernian accent.

Above all things Mr Synnot loved to sit at a table on the terrace. He had cups of coffee brought out to him there, and he read at copies of

The Racing Calendar under an umbrella while the summer rain dripped off his hat-brim. An old lady – one of the old ladies he gallantly escorted to picturesque ruins or to early service – had taught him a patience. But best of all he liked to sit and observe the people as they came and went: the English papas sauntering by with their children and nursemaids; the German bankers lazily recruiting themselves in the sunshine; odd, polyglot women jabbering to each other in languages come from beyond the Rhine. French, German, Italian, Spanish: Mr Synnot could order a meal in any of them, and summon a waiter without using any words at all.

On the first two or three occasions that he amused himself in this way he became aware of an English lady sitting on her own, at the farthermost part of the terrace, somewhat apart from the other coffee-drinkers and newspaper-readers. At first he was not conscious of her singularity: then, almost without registering his interest, he began to remark her. She was a slim, sandy-haired woman with remarkably green eyes, always dressed in the height of fashion, with a pretty little foot that peeped out of her skirts as if it knew it should not be there, yet horribly demure and with her head nearly always bent over a book. When a waiter brought her a message or a note on a tray, or a visitor to the hotel passed by her table – one of the English papas, perhaps, with a Continental Bradshaw under one arm and a child on the other – she spoke to them civilly but seemed anxious that their conversation should not be prolonged. She read a great many books. They were mostly in French, but once Mr Synnot thought that he saw a volume of Mr Thackeray's *Philip*. 'She is one of those d——d bluestockings, I daresay,' Mr Synnot said to himself, but still he continued to watch.

There came a time – it was getting on towards September now, and the English confraternity was breaking up – when this watching was not enough, and he applied to the friends he had made at the hotel for information. 'She is called Mrs Happerton, I believe,' said the old lady who had taught him the patience – the old lady was in the midst of packing her trunks and had not much time for Mr Synnot – 'but there is some mystery about her.' 'She is very disreputable, I daresay,' said a stout mamma whose four daughters he had taken by britzka to a romantic castle in the hills. 'And now, Mr Synnot, will you not join us on our picnic tomorrow, for it is nearly Michaelmas full-term and Mr Davies must be back at chambers within the week?' But Mr Synnot did not want to go on the picnic. He preferred to sit on the terrace and stare. He wondered if the Englishwoman was one of those ladies who frequent the great hotels of Europe in season and out of it and are, perhaps, no better than they should be, but then one night he saw the bow that the maître d'hôtel of the Imperial gave her as he brought her a glass of hock on a salver, and told himself not to be a fool.

Finally there came an evening – it was in the second week in September, and most of the English families were gone – when Mr Synott thought that he could bear it no longer. The terrace was almost empty apart from the English lady and himself, and a breeze had got up to stir the first of the fallen leaves. Emboldened by the solitude, the first faint chill of the autumn and the thought that he should not perhaps be in Baden for very much longer, Mr Synnot seized his coffee cup – the coffee had gone cold an hour ago – and the *Racing Calendar* he had been affecting to study and made his way to the terrace's farther end.

'I hope,' he said, as he drew level with her table, 'that I do not intrude.'

The woman put down her book – it was M. Zola's *Thérèse Raquin* – and looked at him steadily for a moment. 'I do not think,' she said, 'that there is any law that forbids a gentleman to walk over to a lady's table. Will you sit down?'

He sat down, and the wind blew a little storm of leaves against his legs. A number of brilliant observations had occurred to him as he made his way across to her, but now they had all vanished from his mind. 'I always say,' he declared, 'that English people who find themselves in foreign parts should stick together.'

'Certainly,' she said. 'English people. And Irish people, too.'

He began to wonder if he had made a mistake. The evening was setting in fast, he noticed. Soon she would be going inside.

'A wonderful sunset,' he went on, indicating that marvel of nature with an outflung arm. 'They seem to get them uncommonly fine down here. I wonder why that should be?'

'I have often wondered it too,' the lady said. If there was an irony in her tone, he did not notice it. 'Mr . . . ?'

'Synnot,' he said. 'Synnot is the name.' There was something in those green eyes that made him horribly nervous, he discovered. 'You'll be returning to London soon, I take it?'

'Oh no,' she said, 'I never go to London. Or even to Dublin,' she added.

He knew now that he had made a terrible mistake, but still he thought that a little jocularity might carry it off.

'Have you a down against the Irish then, Mrs . . .' he began, with considerably more of a lilt in his voice that he had ever allowed himself in the presence of Mrs Davies the Lincoln's Inn barrister's wife and her four daughters.

'My name is Happerton,' the woman said. 'Do you know who I am?' She saw the *Racing Calendar* under his arm and gestured at it with her hand. 'The wife of the man who owned Tiberius that won the Derby. Does that not mean anything to you?' But Mr Synnot was blinking like a fish hauled out onto the towpath of the River Wensum and awaiting despatch with the end of a hammer. 'I never go to London,' Mrs Happerton said, 'for I find the climate doesn't agree with me. And neither do the people. But the weather in Dublin is very agreeable, I believe.'

But Mr Synnot had not stopped to answer. He had the look on his face of a man who has trampled on a nest of vipers by mistake, and was in piteous retreat across the terrace.

The darkness was welling up across the terrace gardens; from the windows of the hotel dining rooms, lamplight flickered. Somewhere in the distance a band was playing. And Mrs Happerton threw back her head and did something that she had never done in her father's house in Belgrave Square, in Venice on her wedding tour, at Mrs Venables' luncheons in Redcliffe Gardens, or in any other compartment of her adult life – she laughed.

Acknowledgements

I should like to acknowledge the influence of W. P. Frith, *My Autobiography and Reminiscences* (1887), Christopher Wood, *William Powell Frith: A Painter & His World* (2006), Alan Macey, *The Romance of the Derby Stakes* (1930), Sir George Stephen, *The Guide to Service: The Groom* (1840), Gustave Doré and Blanchard Jerrold, 'The Derby' in *London: A Pilgrimage* (1872), Nicholas Foulkes, *Gentlemen and Blackguards* (2010) and Donald Thomas, *The Victorian Underworld* (1997). Much of the detail of the race-day itself is taken from George Moore's novel *Esther Waters* (1894), which is also an invaluable guide to the protocols of off-course betting in late-Victorian London. Certain other fragments have been robbed from A. E. Coppard's short story 'Weep Not My Wanton'.

'Shepherd's Inn' is borrowed from W. M. Thackeray, *The History of Pendennis* (1850). There is a Scroop Hall sixteen miles from Lincoln, but it was built in 1885 and could not have been lived in by Mr Davenant and his ancestors. I am grateful to its current owners, Michael and Jilly Worth, for their kind permission to make use of its name and location. I should like to express my gratitude to Tim Cox of the Cox Library who very kindly read the novel in manuscript and made many valuable suggestions.